PENGUIN BOOKS

BHOWANI JUNCTION

Born in Calcutta in 1914, John Masters is of the fifth generation of his family to have served in India. After being educated in England, he returned to India in 1934 and joined the 4th Prince of Wales's Own Ghurka Rifles, then serving on the North-West Frontier. He saw active service in Waziristan in 1937 and, after the outbreak of war, in Iraq, Syria, and Persia. In 1944 he joined General Wingate's Chindits in Burma. He fought at the Singu Bridgehead, the capture of Mandalay, and at Toungoo, and on the Mawchi Road. John Masters retired from the Army in 1948 as Lieutenant-Colonel with the D.S.O. and O.B.E., and shortly afterwards went to the U.S.A. He turned to writing and soon had articles and short stories published in many well-known American magazines. The first of his novels, *Nightrunners of Bengal*, was published in 1951. It was followed by *The Deceivers* (1952), *The Lotus and the Wind* (1953), *Bhowani Junction* (1954), and *Coromandel!* (1955). His most recent novel is *The Breaking Strain*, and in 1969 he published a biography of Casanova. He has also published two volumes of autobiography.

BHOWANI JUNCTION

BY

JOHN MASTERS

PENGUIN BOOKS
IN ASSOCIATION WITH
MICHAEL JOSEPH

Penguin Books Ltd, Harmondsworth, Middlesex, England
Penguin Books Australia Ltd, Ringwood, Victoria, Australia

—

First published by Michael Joseph 1954
Published in Penguin Books 1960
Reprinted 1962, 1965, 1967, 1971

—

Made and printed in Great Britain
by Richard Clay (The Chaucer Press) Ltd,
Bungay, Suffolk
Set in Monotype Times

CONTENTS

This book is wholly a work of fiction, and no reference is intended in it to any person living or dead, except that a few public figures are mentioned.

In spite of the fact that I have altered, by a few months, the date of the mutinies in the Royal Indian Navy, I hope this book is also a work of history – because I have tried to give the 'feel' of the times and a sense of historical perspective.

This book might have been dedicated to the Anglo-Indian communities of India and Pakistan. But so many thousands of Anglo-Indians, over so many years, have dedicated their lives to the service of the railway that I am happy to follow their example.

This book, therefore, is inscribed with
respect and admiration
to

NUMBER 1 DOWN MAIL

which was to many a prideful train,
to them an obstinate ideal
of service

J. M.

BOOK ONE

Patrick Taylor

male, thirty-six, Eurasian unmarried;
a non-gazetted officer in the Traffic Department of the
Delhi Deccan Railway

1

I HAD a fine Norton that year, in Bhowani. It's got smashed up since, but it was looking good the day I went down to see Victoria after she came back from the Army. I got to the house, cut off the engine, and sat there in the saddle while it coughed, hiccuped once or twice, and died. The truth is I was afraid to go in. She'd been away a long time. She was an officer. She'd have changed.

I left the bike on its stand and walked round toward the side of the house. It was Number 4 Collett Road, it and Number 3 being joined together – what they call a semi-detached bungalow at Home. Then there's about thirty yards of grass between Number 4 and Number 5. Number 5 is semi-detached with Number 6. Collett Road is in the Railway Lines, where we railway people live. There are really three separate Bhowanis – the Railway Lines, the cantonments, where the English live, and the city, where God knows how many thousand Indians are packed in like sardines.

I was still afraid to go in. I stood for a while looking down between Number 4 and Number 5 at an engine on the line beyond. The main railway line runs past the back of all those bungalows on Collett Road.

I like to hear steam engines breathing. That one was an old 2-8-2. It stood there hissing softly, waiting for the signal to change. It was a very hot and quiet afternoon, that, early in May 1946.

I could see the upper part of the engine and tender above the line of straggly bushes at the bottom of the Jones's compound. The crew were all Wogs. They liked to be called Indians, especially nowadays, but I always call them Wogs in my mind still. *We* used to have that run, but it was always Wogs by 1946. It wasn't much of a run, a down goods train, but when they took it over it meant that they were pushing us out of another job. The driver was wiping his hands on a piece of dasooty. When he saw me looking at him he turned his head away. He didn't smile or wave, though I knew him quite well.

I ought to explain here that 'down' means the direction going away from Bombay, and 'up' means going to Bombay. Every railway has its own words, but that's what we use on the Delhi Deccan. Perhaps I ought to say too that 'Wogs' is a word for Indians, and when I say 'we' or 'us' I mean the Anglo-Indians. Sometimes we're called Domiciled Europeans. Most of us have a little Indian blood – not much, of course.

Oh my, it was hot that Saturday. The roofs of those bungalows are flat. It must be like an oven in there, I was thinking; and I made that my excuse not to go in, although it was like an oven everywhere that day. The only thing that made me feel cool was thinking of the footplate. There it must have been – my God, you can't explain how hot the footplate of an engine gets in the hot weather. You have to know.

You must not think there was nothing in me but fright at that time. There was so much love too, and the love kept pushing me toward the front door of Number 4. It was terrible to put the moment off, and it was terrible to face it. The real trouble, I must tell you now, is that, whatever I feel inside me, nothing comes out right when I have to change the feeling into speaking or doing. Not long ago I had a puppy – and, oh my, I was fond of that puppy. One day soon after getting it I bent down to stroke it, but I had a cigarette in my hand and I burned it instead. I tell you that because there were hundreds of things like that, all my life, from the beginning.

But I had to go in sooner or later, so I walked to the front door and rang the bell. Rose Mary, Victoria's sister, opened it so quickly she must have been watching me. I was nervous at seeing her, because I had been going out a bit with her while Victoria was away in the Army, and Rose Mary is a funny girl.

She said quickly, 'Oh, hello, Mr Taylor, do come in. Victoria will be ready in a minute. Won't you sit in the parlour?' Then she walked away, and I went into the parlour but I didn't sit down. I could smell the dinner they'd been having, and Mrs Jones was standing at the end of the passage. She didn't say anything to me. Mrs Jones is – well, difficult. She is very brown, and her stockings always hang in wrinkles round her legs, and she chews betel nut in secret.

10

It was a good parlour, that. Mr Jones had done it up very taste-fully with mahogany furniture he'd bought second-hand. The chairs had embroidered white pieces hanging over the backs to keep your hair oil off them. There was a big mirror, and a beauti-ful fringed green cloth on the table, and on the floor there was the skin of a black bear with its head up. There were pictures of the King Emperor, the Queen Empress, and old Sergeant Duck, and several paintings – a deer in a fog, two dogs with a salmon, and others by famous painters.

I heard Rose Mary stamping about the passage and shouting 'Nathoo!' She has a very shrill voice and she was in a bad temper. Nathoo was the house servant, the bearer, and cook.

It was in the mirror that I saw Victoria first. I tell you, my heart stood still. Victoria is tall, and her eyes are brown, and she has the longest legs and thick black hair. I don't want to talk about her figure, because I love her, but she has a figure like a film star's, only better. I was not even thinking of her figure then, only of how much I loved her, and how she used to laugh at everything and be so happy and smiling, especially with me. It always seemed to me that we'd grown up together, but we hadn't really, because I was several years older than she was.

She moved slowly into the room, leaving the door open behind her. It was dark in there with the blinds drawn. I said, 'Why – why, Vicky, you have grown!' I was nervous, and it was a foolish thing to say, but I have told you about me, so I hope you under-stand.

She said, 'Don't call me Vicky.' She never liked that, but I'd forgotten. She didn't mind me teasing her in the old days, though.

I had my topi in my hand, and she smiled at me and came for-ward. I said, 'You were glaring at me just now as if I was one of your bad Army girls. Should I call you "Ma'am", then, after all? Miss Subaltern Jones?'

She laughed and said, 'No, that's all over, thank heavens. Only please call me Victoria.'

I took a pace toward her, the topi dangling in my left hand, and I put out my right hand to touch her. It was breathless in there, and my voice was hoarse. I said, 'Victoria,' and then I dropped my topi and took her in my arms and kissed her.

It started as a little kiss, a gentle kiss. Then I wanted to put my heart there in that kiss because I did not dare to speak. We kissed a long time. She seemed to be experimenting, like someone tasting a new dish. It was natural, after all, because we had not kissed for four years – but *I* had not forgotten, there was no need for me to taste her lips and kiss harder and softer to see what it was like. I wondered then whether she'd kissed any of the officers up there in Delhi. But I didn't like to think about that. It would only make me miserable to know, and yet I'd love her just the same, which would make me more miserable than ever. So I shook my head, to shake that idea out of it, and stopped thinking about it.

She thought I'd had enough of kissing when I shook my head, so she stood back from me. Then she said, 'It *is* nice to see you again, Patrick.'

'That is exactly what I was going to say, Vicky – Victoria,' I said, and straightened my tie. I was wearing my old school tie from St Thomas's, Gondwara, light-grey flannel trousers, and a sunproof coat. I always like to wear my old St Thomas's tie, and especially in those days, because St Thomas's was in the same kind of trouble as the rest of us – the trouble being that we Anglo-Indians didn't want to sink to the level of the Indians, and the Indians hated us for being superior to them, and St Thomas's was a kind of symbol of the whole thing, because it was only for Anglo-Indians and Domiciled Europeans.

I said, 'Shall we go now? You haven't seen my bike yet, have you? It's a Norton. It makes it much handier for me to get up and down to the station, and I can use it in the yards.'

She said, 'Of course. What a good idea, Patrick. Well, where are we going?'

I told her just for a ride. I thought we would go down to the Karode Bridge to dangle our feet in the water. We might have a swim, I was thinking.

I became nervous again. A lot of people call me cocksure, and that must be the way I sound, but I am not really sure of anything much, except that I love Victoria. This time I got nervous because I was thinking of Victoria in a bathing suit, and that made me think of her getting into her bathing suit. She used to let me touch her there before she went off to the Army, and I got all trembly

12

wondering whether she would again. That was what was on my mind.

She said, 'All right. That sounds fun. I'll get my towel and bathing suit.'

While she was in her room Rose Mary came along and leaned against the passage wall near me. She stuck her bust out and held her shoulders back while she talked with me, and she was looking at me in a funny way. I am afraid she was jealous. I am afraid the truth is that I had – you know, done it several times with her while Victoria was away. I am afraid the truth is that Rose Mary was rather an immoral girl.

When Victoria came back Rose Mary said, 'Good-bye. Don't do anything I wouldn't do. Mind you're back for supper, Vicky. Pater will be home.'

Victoria looked rather crossly at her. Rose Mary was Victoria's elder sister, and I don't think they'd ever exactly loved each other. Victoria said, 'Pater's taking Ninety-Eight Up through to Gondwara, isn't he? So he won't be back here till tomorrow afternoon. What are you talking about?'

Rose Mary flushed angrily and said, 'Oh, yes. I forgot. Well, good-bye then.'

I tried to laugh it off. I said cheerily, 'Abyssinia, Rosie,' but I wasn't feeling happy. Rose Mary was behaving so badly I didn't see how Victoria could help guessing, so I made up my mind to confess as soon as I could.

Victoria was out in the road looking at my Norton. It wasn't new, but I'd only just bought it second-hand. I put my hand on her bare arm. I said, 'Where is your topi? You will get all sunburned.'

'I never wear one,' she told me.

'But the sun!' I cried. 'It is the hottest time of the day! You will get all brown!'

She tossed her head. The heavy dark curls of hair swung round on her shoulders. She looked at me in a funny way and said, 'It isn't sunburn that makes us brown, is it?'

I was bending over the handlebars, turning the twist-grip throttle. It was not a nice thing to say, and I felt frightened that she had said it. If we didn't wear topis people would think we were Wogs – not me, I have pale blue eyes, almost green, and red hair, a sort of dull ginger – but most of us. She knew that, so there was nothing to say.

I felt her taking a good look at me. Her own skin was the same colour as mine, perhaps a little browner, less yellow. We didn't look like English people. We looked like what we were – Anglo-Indians, Eurasians, cheechees, half-castes, eight-annas, blacky-whites. *I've* heard all the names they call us, but I don't think about them unless I'm angry.

I kicked furiously, and the engine turned over. I twisted the throttle so that the engine made the hell of a noise, a real racketing bellow. I didn't dare speak myself, but I could make the Norton say something for me. Victoria seemed to understand about the noise I was making, so I throttled down and told her to hop on.

She stuffed her towel roll down with mine behind my saddle, and picked up her dress a bit to put her leg across the carrier. I watched out of the corners of my eyes and saw quite high up as she got on. She said, laughing, 'Eyes front!' and I laughed too. When she was ready she said into my ear, 'Don't go too fast, now, Patrick.'

Just as the bike began to move Rose Mary ran out of the house, waving her hand and shouting, 'Patrick, wait, stop!' She was breathless and sort of happy, like when you're hurting someone you don't like. I had to stop, though I didn't want to. She said, 'Patrick, you're wanted at the office. They've just telephoned.'

I sat there with my feet spread, holding the Norton upright. I don't think I've ever been so disappointed. I beat the top of the petrol tank with my hands and shouted, 'Oh, it is too bad! Can't that bloody Wog do anything by himself? I've only just left the bloody station.'

'It's a derailment,' Rose Mary told us.

There are accidents sometimes on any railway, but when Rose Mary said 'derailment' the picture that popped up in my mind was of a Wog pulling out a fish-plate, and all mixed up with that was the result of what he'd done – the smash, and the Wog dancing up and down and yelling for joy. That was the awful thing, that anyone should be happy to see a train derailed.

'Who are you talking about?' Victoria asked.

'Mr Ranjit Bloody Singh Kasel, my new assistant,' I said.

Victoria said, 'I'll come to the station with you. Perhaps you won't have to stay long.'

Rose Mary opened her mouth and shut it again. I think Victoria made her suggestion just to annoy Rose Mary, just to show her that I belonged to her, Victoria, as much as I belonged to anybody. But I didn't really care why she'd said it, I was so pleased that she had said it, and especially pleased because it was her idea, not mine.

We roared up the Pike, going past the Little Bazaar and the Silver Guru's tree. The station was about three-quarters of a mile that way, though it was less if you walked down the railway lines.

There were the usual tongas standing in the station yard when we got there, and a couple of buses, and a taxi owned by a smart-aleck Sikh. The station building at Bhowani Junction is made of old red brick with yellow layers and some yellow diamond patterns. It is two storeys high, and there are five wide stone steps leading up to the gate. The gateway is an arch, like an old fortress or something.

I propped the Norton against the outside wall and ran behind Victoria up the steps. The platform was crowded with natives, as usual. She stopped there and looked about her as if she'd never seen it before, as if it was the Taj Mahal or some kind of show-place, like the Tower of London at Home, though it was just the same as it had always been. A row of doorways opened off the platform into the various rooms, and a sign hung out over each door, saying what the room was for: Station Master; Assistant Station Master; Telegraphs; Way Out; Booking Office; No Admittance; Refreshment Room, European; Refreshment Room, Muslim; Refreshment Room, Hindu, Vegetarian; Refreshment Room, Hindu, Non-Vegetarian; First-Class Waiting Room; Second-Class Waiting Room; Third-Class Waiting Room; Ladies' Waiting Room – what we always called the Purdah Room.

I was in a hurry, but Victoria didn't move, and then I calmed down because it was nice to know she still loved the station and the railway enough to stand there sniffing the air as if it had been champagne. The 404 Up Passenger from the Bhanas branch was standing over on Platform 3. Travellers, all natives, were struggling out of it. Number 2 Up Mail was due in any minute on the main-line platform, where we were standing. People out of the branch train were hurrying over the footbridge to catch it. Men and women were shouting, eating, dozing on the stones, rushing up and down, yelling for lost children and lost baggage. The goods train, the one I'd seen with the Indian crew, came clanking down the centre line, and stopped.

An engine whistled angrily to the north. Victoria said, 'Number Two Up Mail.' She knew. She was a railway girl. The driver had got a signal, and he was whistling because they'd left him standing there among the back walls of the city, half a mile out. It is dirty, squalid out there, and the heat always shimmers above the roof-tops like a kind of mirage. That driver was in a bad temper.

At last I took her elbow and said, 'Now let's go up to my office and see what the bloody hell has been happening.'

She followed me as I shoved through the crowd. Several Wogs turned and glared at me, and one or two muttered abuse under their breaths, but they didn't dare speak aloud. Victoria must have heard what they were saying, and that made me angry. They'd all got quite out of hand during the war.

One of the people I pushed out of the way was Surabhai, the local Congress boss. He always wore a collar and tie, a European coat, a white Gandhi cap, and a white dhoti. That day he was wearing green socks and violet sock-suspenders. I heard Victoria, behind me, say, 'I'm sorry.'

Surabhai said, '*You* are sorry? *He* pushed me, the haughty fellow!' but he smiled at her. He had a rubbery round face and huge eyes, rather like Eddie Cantor's. She squeezed past him and came on with me. I wanted to say something – but what?

The crowd on the platform had heard that something was wrong. You can't keep secrets in Bhowani even if you want to, and a derailment isn't a secret. I heard them asking each other, 'What has happened? ... What do you know? ... What do you hear?' A toothless old woman with her lips cracked and reddened from betel chewing reached out a hand like a vulture's claw and grabbed at me as I passed. 'Brother, brother, what's happened?' she whined.

I didn't answer. I could have sworn at her in Hindustani, which I speak very well, but that would have justified her calling me 'brother'. Besides, although she certainly meant to insult me by

16

suggesting that I was an Indian like her, can you really insult anyone by calling him your brother? I feel you can't, and yet I don't want people to think I'm an Indian.

The stairs to the second story went up just beyond the Purdah Room. The platform story all belonged to the stationmaster, but the upper story was a subdivision of the Delhi Deccan Railway. (Don't mix it up with the Bhowani Civil District, which was a subdivision of the province – in other words, a part of the government.)

The railway district had 222¾ running miles of line and thirty-four stations, including Bhowani Junction. Up on the second story there, on either side of a broad middle corridor, were the offices of people like the District Engineer, who looked after the permanent way, and the Assistant Superintendent of Railway Police, and lots of others you don't need to know about. Except you have to know that the District Traffic Superintendent's office was there, at the end of the corridor on the right, facing out over the city. The District Traffic Superintendent was the most important man in the place, and his name at that time was Mr Patrick Taylor – in other words, me.

I pushed into my office. The coolie-messenger was squatting in the doorway, and I kicked him on to his feet as I went by. There were more people crowded inside than I could count. The door was marked clearly: NO ADMITTANCE EXCEPT ON DUTY, but that wouldn't make any difference to an Indian, not even a fellow like my new assistant, Kasel, who was supposed to be so efficient.

The short trip on the motor-bike had dried our clothes on us – Victoria and me – but hadn't cooled us. Now the perspiration broke out again all over me. The electric punkah whirred on the ceiling, its big arms slowly turning round like a windmill. The air was thick as soup, and all the punkah did was turn over the dust and that filthy bitter bidi smoke and the smell of too many Wogs. There were betel-juice stains all over the floorboards, and I noticed how ragged and splintery the boards were. I was imagining how it all would strike Victoria after those luxurious air-conditioned offices in Delhi.

My God, I felt fed up. I stood inside the door and bawled, 'Get out! *Hut jao*, you black bastards!' Some of the people edged out, others edged in. I reached the desk and said, 'My God, Kasel,

17

what the hell is going on here? What are all these people doing in here? What has bloody well happened?' I tell you I was mad, and so ashamed for what Victoria had seen of my office.

Kasel was a slight, tall Indian with a thin face. He was about thirty years old and always wore a turban because he was a Sikh. He had a high-bridged nose and always looked so damned sad I could kick him. He got up quickly when he saw us, and bowed to Victoria. Then he sat down again, twiddling a pencil in his hands, and said, 'The coal train, Number Two-O-Four-Three, ran off the rails at Pathoda. No one was hurt. The District Engineer said – '

I didn't want to know what the D.E. had said or done. I wanted to know what *he* had done. I asked him.

He said, 'I have informed Transportation, Civil, Mechanical, Medical, and Police. I'm holding all branch line traffic, but Four-O-Five is here now and ready to go. I was proposing to send her up to Pathoda on time. She can change passengers there with Four-O-Six. Then I have sent for a light engine from Bhanas to pull the wagons back from the derailment,' and he went on about what he had done.

It sounded all right, so I said to him, 'What the hell are these people doing in here? It is like a bloody circus.' Again I shouted at everyone to get out.

Surabhai, the Congress fellow who looked like Eddie Cantor, had found his way up there. He faced me and joined his palms together and said, 'We are only poor natives, good sir. Forgive us for it. We have come to ask when, by your favour, we may expect to be allowed to entrain on those trains for which we have bought tickets.' He was very excited. He fairly danced around, like a boxer, as he spoke.

I think Victoria wanted to laugh, but I did not see anything to laugh at. It was disgraceful, the whole thing. I said to Surabhai, 'You'll hear in good time. Now get out of here, all of you, *Bahar jao, ek dum!*'

Surabhai danced forward again, his eyes popping at me and his mouth opening, and I was getting ready to be really rude to him. Then Kasel at the desk said, '*Please*, Mr Surabhai,' and the fellow subsided, and after a few mutterings followed the others out of the room.

18

Kasel got out of the chair behind the desk, and I sat down. It was my chair, and I didn't like the way he had butted in with Surabhai. I told him to get a chair for Victoria – 'For Miss Jones,' I said. Then I told him to give me more details. I wanted to know first whether it was an accident or sabotage.

He stood there beside my table, and Victoria smiled at him to thank him for getting the chair. If he heard my question he didn't answer it. He was smiling back at her, almost ogling her. So I said, 'Well?' as sharply as I could. That took the smile off his face.

He said, 'We don't know yet. The District Engineer has gone up on the trolley with the District Mechanical Engineer and one or two others. The breakdown train's gone to Pathoda.'

I stubbed out the cigarette that I'd only just lit. I was getting angrier all the time. 'Well – oh, damn it,' I said. 'I suppose I'd better go up. I bet you it was sabotage, and I bet you the bloody Congress did it.' I said that because I was sure as eggs that Kasel was secretly a Congressman. Railway officers were not allowed to join political parties in those days, but I was sure.

He said – and he spoke quite hotly for him – 'We don't know enough about it yet to say, Mr Taylor.'

'Oh, but I am betting you,' I said. Kasel looked like a boy of about twelve who is hurt over something but trying not to show it.

Then I had an idea that I might still be able to save some fun out of the day. I asked Victoria to come to Pathoda with me. We would go on the Norton. She thought about it a minute. Then she nodded, and I slapped her on the back. I said, 'Good girl! Come on!' I got up right away and went to the door, but she turned to say good-bye to Kasel. There was no need for her to do that.

The ride was hot and dusty. I drove fast because I was in a hurry to get up there, get the work over with, and get on with our picnic. That was a good bike, and I was strong enough to hold it down. We roared past everything – villagers on foot, bullock carts, children playing among the houses, old women, donkeys. The bumping rattled my teeth – and Victoria's too, I suppose. The dust hung in a long spreading cloud behind us. The fields and huts seemed to race toward me, then passed in a flash and disappeared in the dust. The exhaust made a terrific racket against the houses, and I felt a lot better.

We got to Pathoda in twenty-four minutes. I leaned the Norton on its stand, went into the station, and shouted for the station-master, a fat fool called Bhansi Lall. He wasn't there. Victoria and I walked along the platform. Pathoda's a hill village, and the platform is just a levelled gravel standing, faced with brick on the line side and about a foot high. The station is on a curve.

The coal train was standing there, and you couldn't see anything wrong at first because the engine was hidden by the curve of the train. But when we got up past the end of the platform we saw that the engine was standing in the ballast. Twisted rails stuck out like wires from under the tender and the first few wagons. The wood was broken and splintered, and ballast stones had been shot about everywhere. The engine had sunk in a foot or more so that the bottoms of its driving wheels were hidden. A group of railway people stood in a bunch round it, and thirty or forty villagers were squatting on the low embankment opposite, watching. The break-down train had come up from Bhowani and was on the line in front of the derailed engine. Its crane was swinging round as we arrived. They'd lifted the inspection trolley off the rails.

'That was a narrow escape,' Victoria said, and pointed.

I nodded. Twenty yards in front of the derailed engine the line crossed a stream on a girder bridge. There were check rails, of course, but they wouldn't have been enough. The stream ran about forty feet down in a shady gorge. I saw some red flowers down there, and the water was green and cold and noisy, and from thinking about the engine falling down into it I began to think again about Victoria in a bathing suit.

I went over to the District Engineer, but there wasn't much I could do, and soon I went back to Victoria. I found Bhansi Lall, the Pathoda stationmaster, talking to her. He's very fat and he was trembling with fright and excitement. He was saying, 'I say, you know District Engineer is saying this is sabotage? Sabotage, here in my station, Pathoda, my goodness, what next?'

I asked him what he meant, sabotage. His eyes rolled round, and he licked his lips. He said, 'District Engineer is being rude to me! My God, my job! He is asking, how can bloody sabotage-men pull up line in broad daylight without you seeing? He is saying, you must have seen. But Miss Jones, Mr Taylor, I am seeing nothing! Look, station is *there*, and rail was pulled *here*, round curve, under embankment. How can *I* be seeing that villainy? Beside, rascals did not pull up rail but merely loosened fishplates on two rails – there, there, on inside of curve? Oh, goodness me!'

I looked up and down and I had to agree with him although I didn't like him. I wouldn't have been surprised to find out he was another of these secret Congress wallahs.

Then an engine whistled to the east, down the line behind the derailed train. Bhansi Lall unfurled his red and green flags – he had them in his hands and he'd been using them to gesticulate with. He said, 'Oh, goodness me, hark! Relief engine has come to pull back wagons. Good-bye! Excuse please.'

We watched him waddle away along the path beside the line. Victoria put her hand on her head, said, '*Phew!*' and moved in under the trees. She sat down there and looked at the little river below us. I said, 'There's nothing for me to do here. I knew there wouldn't be. Why don't we have our picnic here? A little farther away from the bridge, of course.'

She looked at the water and she hesitated. She never used to hesitate so much, to think so carefully about what she was doing or going to do. Then she said, 'All right.' I hurried back to fetch our bathing togs from the motor bike.

Some way downstream we found a nice pool, about ten feet across, and there was a little waterfall at the top. It was a good place for a cool bathe; Victoria agreed with me.

She went a long way away from me to undress, into some thick bushes. I didn't mind that, of course. People ought not to look at each other naked. But later, when it wasn't so hot and we were back in our clothes, I leaned over and kissed her. I kissed her properly that time and thought I would melt inside.

She kissed me back the same way for a bit, then she turned her head away and looked up at the sky through the leaves. We could hear the clanking and banging from the bridge, but we couldn't see them and they couldn't see us. I stroked her cheek with my hand and said, 'I love you, Victoria.'

She looked at me, and I waited for her to say, 'I love you too, Patrick,' but she didn't say that. She said, 'Do you think I've changed?'

She hadn't changed to look at, except that she was smarter, more English-looking, somehow. But she *had* changed. She spoke la-di-da like the British officers in the regiments, and she didn't smile so much. She looked at you without saying anything, often, and when she was standing up she stood up straight and tall to her full height. It struck me that she was thinking all the time, and noticing us and her home and her people as if she'd never seen us before.

I said, 'I feel as if you've just come out from Home.'

She snapped, 'Don't call England "home". It's not *our* home, is it?' Then she put her hand over mine and said, 'I'm sorry, Patrick dear. I'm tired. Let me go to sleep.'

I didn't know what was the matter with her. She was twenty-eight then, and she couldn't go on being a spinster much longer. I'd known her all her life. Before she went off to the Army we'd been practically engaged. She must have got leave during all those years, but she only came down to Bhowani once, and that one time I was miles away, trying to get a sambhur in the Berar jungles. The war was over, and I loved her, and she wouldn't find anyone with better pay or prospects than me – not to marry her, that is.

I thought, she'll settle down in a few days or a few weeks. After all, she's just come back from the Army and being an officer and mixing with nobody but British officers. I was ready to wait a bit.

2

THE next day was Sunday, and Victoria asked me round to dinner at their house, and afterward we were going to the pictures. It was another hot day, and when I arrived the smell of roasting lamb was all over the place, although the kitchen was separate from the bungalow. They were in the parlour – Mrs Jones, Rose Mary, and Victoria. Mr Jones was on 21 Down. He was a senior driver.

Mrs Jones was sitting in one of the big chairs, her hands folded in her lap, doing nothing. She never did anything, that I saw. Rose Mary smiled at me a lot and called me 'Paddy' and, once, 'darling'. I would have been embarrassed, only I was thinking about the derailment. Things go up and down in your mind like a see-saw, and this time the derailment was up and women were down, even Victoria, because after all I am a railwayman. I was glad when Nathoo came in to say that dinner was ready.

As soon as we sat down, Rose Mary asked me whether anything had been settled about Sir Meredith Sullivan's visit to Bhowani. Sir Meredith Sullivan was the most important Anglo-Indian there was. He had started as a railwayman, of course, but now he was a member of the Legislative Assembly in New Delhi, and the King Emperor had made him a knight, which everyone said was as a compliment to all of us, not just to him. He was like the leader of the Anglo-Indians – the way the chief of a clan is in Scotland.

'Who is he going to stay with?' Rose Mary asked.

'Williams,' I told her.

'Williams!' she cried, putting down her knife and fork and staring at me. 'But, Paddy, there are – oh, many people senior to Williams. There is O'Hara and Fitzpatrick and – my God – Pater – and you.'

I knew all that, and Williams was only the Assistant Superintendent of Railway Police, but what could I do? Sir Meredith had telegraphed that he would like to stay with the Williamses. He had been a great friend of Mrs Williams' father in Howrah or somewhere.

'Oh, it is a disgrace!' Rose Mary cried. 'Mrs Williams will be more stuck-up than ever!'

I noticed that Victoria listened to us in the new way she had, as if she had never heard such talk before. And I thought how clever Rose Mary was to bring up a subject which she and I knew about but Victoria did not. Sir Meredith Sullivan's visit had been arranged before Victoria came back from the Army.

Then Victoria said, 'Does it matter who he stays with? He's a frightful old bore now, isn't he?'

Rose Mary went red in the face and shouted, 'You have no right to speak of Sir Meredith Sullivan like that! Look what he has done for us and is doing all the time!'

Victoria said, 'I know, but that doesn't prevent him being a bore,' and she asked me whether I wanted any more potatoes.

I wished their mother would say something, because it was getting awkward. But Mrs Jones, whom they always called Mater – as their father was Pater – was really only interested in cooking, and in their position they couldn't let her cook, because she was three-quarters Indian and only knew how to cook native food. I particularly wanted her to say something because a feeling was coming up inside me which I knew I would have to push out in words, or in doing something, no matter what happened. Even if Victoria hated me I would have to say it or do it.

It was about us – us Anglo-Indians. If we didn't stand up for ourselves, no one else would. If we weren't interested, no one else was. Victoria looked at us as if we were strangers. Perhaps all this seemed small to her after Delhi, but it was not small to us, and she would have to realize that again.

So when Mrs Jones didn't speak I took some more potatoes and said, 'Sir Meredith Sullivan is going to give us a talk during the whist drive.' I explained that the talk was going to be about St Thomas's, Gondwara – my old school.

When I mentioned St Thomas's, Victoria said thoughtfully, 'I suppose the Presidency Education Trust will have to close it. It's sad, though.'

I stared at her, and this thing that would have to come out got higher in me. I said, 'Close it? Close St Thomas's? They can't! Why, that was my old school.'

'I know, Patrick,' she said. 'You've got the tie on now.' I had. It has blue, yellow, and violet stripes. She said, 'But – things are going to change, aren't they? They *are* changing …'

She spoke quite vehemently all of a sudden. She told us that the past was gone, the present going. She remembered what it had been like living here with us, but now she had seen us from the outside. All the same she was still one of us. I noticed she always said 'we'.

She said, 'We think God fixed everything in India so it can't alter. The English despise us but need us. We despise the Indians, but we need them. So it's all been fixed – the English say where the trains are to go to, we take them there, and the Indians pay for them and travel in them.'

Now she was getting excited, and her eyes sparkled, and she didn't talk la-di-da, she talked the way we do. She said, 'I've been four years among only Englishmen and Indians. Do you realize that they hardly know there *is* such a thing as an Anglo-Indian community? Once I heard an old English colonel talking to an Indian – he was a young fellow, a financial adviser. The colonel said, "What are you going to do about the Anglo-Indians when

24

we leave?" "*We*'re not going to do anything, Colonel," the Indian said. "Their fate is in their own hands. They've just got to look around and see where they are and who they are – after you've gone."'

Now I wasn't going to be sidetracked by that. Victoria talked as if we Anglo-Indians could change, but we couldn't. This business of St Thomas's explained exactly what I felt. The Presidency Education Trust, which was over a hundred years old, was a group of English businessmen who had got up funds to help give a good education to us Anglo-Indians and our children. Mind, we paid too, as much as we could. In 1887 the Trust built St Thomas's, a boarding school for boys, at Gondwara. Besides St Thomas's they ran day-schools in Bombay, Calcutta, and Cawnpore. What the Trust was saying to us now, in 1946, was this: 'St Thomas's doesn't pay its way. It only survives because the Provincial Government gives it more help from provincial funds than it's really entitled to, considering the number of boys it educates. An Indian government will come to power soon. Is it likely that they will continue to give special help to the education of Anglo-Indians? Of course not! So sooner or later you'll have to sell out. But there's a boom on now, and *now* is the time to sell St Thomas's. With the money, you'll be in a position to keep the day-schools open, at least, whatever happens.'

All that made sense, I suppose, but what those Englishmen in Bombay didn't realize was that we *couldn't* sell St Thomas's, because it was in our hearts. It, the idea of it, was part of us. Without it we'd just be Wogs like everybody else. They might just as well have said we couldn't afford trousers or topis, or told us to turn our skins black instead of khaki.

So I lost my temper with Victoria and shouted, 'You want the Trust to sell our school now!'

'It's their school, not ours, Patrick,' she said. 'They bought it.'

'We can buy it back then!' I bawled. 'We have the money. We can run it ourselves. We –'

Then Victoria shouted, 'We only have the money because there is this boom and we've all been employed during the war and pay has gone up. Do you think an Indian government, a Congress government, is going to keep on holding jobs open especially for us on the railways and telegraphs? Colonel McIntyre said –'

25

Then I shouted, 'Oh, to hell with Colonel McIntyre! I am sorry, Mrs Jones–but, Victoria, what does your Colonel McIntyre know about St Thomas's? Was he there? He was at Eton School, I bet!'

Victoria said, 'He knows nothing about St Thomas's! But he thinks the English will leave India very soon,' and I shouted, 'They won't leave, man! How can they leave, with the bloody Mohammedans and the bloody Hindus cutting each other's bloody throats every day?'

Rose Mary screamed at Victoria, 'Of course they won't leave. They can't. You talk as if you *want* the Congress to become our government!'

Then I banged my fist on the table. I shouted, 'My God, if they leave I will go Home with them.'

Victoria sat up with a jerk, very pale, and she screamed, 'Home? Where is your home, man? England? Then you fell into the Black Sea on your way out? I don't want to see the Congress ruling here, but I am only asking you, what else is there that can happen? I am only asking you to think, man!' She pushed back her chair and ran out of the dining-room.

I sat there, feeling a little sick. That last thing I had said, about going Home, was mere foolishness, and I knew it. The whole point that made it impossible to give way, even to argue, was that we *couldn't* go Home. We couldn't become English, because we were half Indian. We couldn't become Indian, because we were half English. We could only stay where we were and be what we were. Her Colonel McIntyre was right too. The English would go any time now and leave us to the Wogs.

Rose Mary said something to me, but I shook my head, and after a time I heard her leave the house. Mrs Jones disappeared, God knows where. The wireless in Number 3 next door was playing music.

I had to get up and go to Victoria. I went to her room and knocked very gently on the door. She did not answer. I knocked again and whispered, 'Victoria – Victoria? I am sorry. Let me come in.'

'Come in then,' she said after a time.

I opened the door cautiously. She was lying on her back on the bed, her hands over her eyes. I stood shuffling my feet and looking at her.

She put her hands down and said, 'Well?'

I tried to tell her what I had been thinking, about how we had no choice and how we must use our hearts, not our brains. She was calm by then. She put her hand on mine and said, 'Do you think I am just trying to run away from you all? My dear, I would be running away from myself, wouldn't I?'

I couldn't speak. She kneaded my hand under hers and said, 'It is my heart that makes me disagree with you, Patrick, as well as my head. There are other ways to live, and I've seen them. You don't realize how fresh and free it is to be English – or Indian. Why must we torture ourselves with ideas that we are better than some people and worse than others? Why don't we put on dhotis or saris if we want to, and marry Indians? I don't despise anyone now, and I don't fear anyone. I'm just me, but I'm not in a cage any more, like I think you are.'

My God, she was beautiful then, with the wet shining in her big eyes and her hair all out over the pillow. She was like a doe in the forest that wants to love the leopard and admire the green grass and do no harm to anyone. But, I thought, she will learn that the leopard can't live unless it eats her, and she can't live unless she eats the green grass, and she can't really love anything except another deer.

Then I realized something very important. To her, now, nothing was inevitable. Being a cheechee wasn't inevitable. *I* wasn't inevitable. I had thought, we are in love, we are practically engaged, now we will get married, there's really nothing else either of us can do. But she didn't think like that any more. I realized I would have to make her want to marry me. The idea, coming suddenly, frightened me so much that the first thing I did was try to make love to her, just then and there.

I pushed the door shut with my foot and knelt down and took her hand where it lay at her side. I whispered, 'Your arms are so smooth.' It sounds as if I was putting it on, but by God it was true, and I loved her. I kissed her arm. She closed her eyes and began to cry. She really did like me, and everything inside her was upset. She did not want to hurt me, I think. All our shouting and thinking and worrying had made her like some girls always are, damp and clinging and loosened up. I kissed her shoulder.

I whispered all the time how beautiful she was. I slipped my hand inside her blouse, and the little ends were standing up. I whispered, 'Do you love me?'

She did not answer and did not move. I think she could not. Suddenly she groaned and put out her arms and held me tightly round the neck. It was too much for me. Oh God, she was lovely.

Then I said, 'Victoria, darling – may I?' I loved her and thought so highly of her that I had to ask. I waited a fraction of a second, and then I knew I had thrown it all away.

She pushed my hand away and said quite gently, 'No, dear.'

I began to argue and plead, but in my heart I knew it was no good, and I knew it was my fault. Here I was, trying to prove that this thing of us loving and marrying had to be, and then I went and asked her! I was her stag all right, and she was my doe. But perhaps she had seen a beautiful leopard. Her heart was running about trying to make the world bigger than it is. She was discontented, but not in a sulky way – just the opposite. I'd have to show her. It would be difficult, because I loved her so much.

And then, thank God, the telephone rang in the hall. We stared at each other for a few seconds, and then I got up slowly and went out to answer it.

3

IT was the Collector on the phone, Govindaswami, the head man of the Bhowani civil district, the Deputy Commissioner and District Magistrate and God knows what else besides, and the first Indian we'd ever had as Deputy Commissioner in Bhowani. It's an old custom to call the D.C. the Collector there, so that's what we always called him – the Collector.

He wanted to see me about the derailment right away. I grumbled that I'd been going to the pictures with Victoria, but that was because I didn't like Govindaswami. I didn't think Victoria would still want to come to the pictures with me. Govindaswami said I could bring Victoria along with me to his bungalow. It turned out that Victoria did want to go to the pictures after all, so we set off to the Collector's.

The Collector's bungalow in Bhowani is an old place, built before the Mutiny. It's on the east side of the Pike in about six acres of gardens. The military cantonments across from it are all fairly new, but the Collector's bungalow is old and low, and it sits squarely on the ground like a sleepy lion. It's built of stone and always kept whitewashed. My Norton sounded funny there, so I went quietly for a bit. Then I thought, Why the hell should I go quietly for Govindaswami? So I revved up and raced the engine before cutting off. There were a couple of cars and a bicycle there in front of the steps under the carriage porch.

On the veranda a chuprassi in a scarlet achkan took our names and went inside. When he came back Govindaswami was with him. Govindaswami held out his hand to Victoria. 'Miss Jones?' he said in his la-di-da Oxford voice. 'Or Miss Victoria Jones?'

I didn't know what the hell he meant. Nor did Victoria. She shook his hand, half smiling but puzzled. He said, 'I mean, are you the eldest sister?'

'No,' she said.

'Miss Victoria Jones, then, for formal introductions. I have to know. So nice of you to spare me some of your time, Mr Taylor. Won't you come in?'

I can't stand people who talk like that when they know perfectly well you've got to do what they ask you to. We followed him in. I'd never been in there before. A District Traffic Superintendent is not important as far as government goes, and the Collector of Bhowani is, even if he's as black as your boot.

Govindaswami stopped at a closed door behind which we heard people talking. Victoria said quickly, 'Where do you want me to wait, Mr Govindaswami?' He told her to come along in, unless she thought she'd be bored.

'Oh, no,' she said.

'Come on then,' he said.

There were two men already in there – Williams of our Railway Police, and Lanson, the Deputy Superintendent of Police – the ordinary civil police, that is. Williams was youngish, tallish, fattish. He was one of us, an Anglo-Indian. He was the fellow Sir Meredith Sullivan was going to stay with, because of his wife. Lanson was a typical square Englishman. He had a moustache and spoke gruffly. He was the Collector's right-hand man.

I'd better describe Govindaswami. He had a bony forehead, the bones sticking out over his eyes, which were black. His cheeks seemed hollow because his cheekbones stuck out. He had thick lips and a thatch of grey hair. He was slightly built, and his hands were thin and his fingers long. He always wore rather narrow white duck trousers and a white coat and a white shirt, all freshly starched and ironed, and a black bow tie. Those white clothes dazzled you, and then, as your eye went up – *bonk*! It was like being hit in the face when you saw that his skin was deep purple-black. He was a Madrassi. Everyone said he was the son of an untouchable down there who'd found a diamond in a village dung-heap and used the money to educate him. I don't know. If he had any religion no one ever found out what it was.

We four men began to talk while Victoria sat and listened, and very interested she was. The Collector first of all asked Williams what he thought about the derailment at Pathoda. Williams thought it was sabotage, but he didn't know who'd done it. The only people who might have seen it done, he said, were some of the women who always hung around the Pathoda well, the same as women hang around every well in India. But everybody in Pathoda said they'd seen nothing.

The Collector said, 'It's probably true then. They are not a revolutionary crowd in Pathoda. And you haven't got a clue, George?'

Lanson shook his head. 'Not a clue. That's the right phrase.'

Then Govindaswami asked Williams whether the stationmaster at Pathoda – Bhansi Lall – was a Congress man.

'He can't be,' Williams said. 'Railway officials are not allowed to take part in politics.'

Govindaswami said he knew that – but *was* he? Neither Lanson nor Williams knew. Bhansi Lall wasn't on any of their lists. And then Lanson said what I'd been waiting for. He said, 'Why do you ask, Collector? Do you think Gandhi's going to pull another nineteen forty-two on us?'

The point is that in 1942 that sanctimonious little bastard Gandhi had decided he'd rather have the Japs than the British. Rather, he said that if the Indians all sat down and were non-violent the British would go away. The Japs might come, he said, but they would only raise their hats, say, 'So sorry,' and go away again. What Gandhi's non-violence turned out to mean was derailing trains all over the country, and pouring petrol over village policemen and setting them on fire, and dragging people out of trains to beat them to death. I'd been through that time, so you can see why I was sitting on the edge of my chair. I didn't want 1942 again.

Govindaswami didn't answer at once. He rubbed his bony black face and turned to me. 'And your new assistant – Mr Kasel – what about him? Is he a secret Congress man?'

I said, 'Oh, I don't know. He might be. He is a cheeky beggar.' I wanted to be fair to Kasel. In fact I was damned positive he was a Congress wallah.

Govindaswami said soapily, 'I see, I *see*.' Then he told us he was going to let us in on some secrets. He flashed his teeth at Victoria (he had a gold tooth in front, upper; all the rest were big and dazzling white, like an advertisement) and told her to be sure not to talk about what she was going to hear.

Then he said, 'I have recently attended a Governor's conference, as some of you know. The Government of India think trouble is brewing – industrial trouble, railway trouble, and perhaps worse. They think the situation will be much the same as in nineteen forty-two. That is, the Congress high command will recommend a campaign of non-violent non-co-operation, with the object of hurrying the British out of the country. The degree of non-violence will depend, as it did in 1942, on the nature of the local Congress men, and on whether they are of the Right or Left wing of the party. The high command will merely say, "Don't co-operate." Mr Surabhai, as the local Congress leader here, might then say, "Don't give the Collector any petrol for his car." But the man at the garage might say, "Better still, why not pour the petrol over the Collector – and throw away my *bidi* at the same time?"'

Govindaswami went on to tell us that these huge campaigns of non-violence were always uncontrollable even when everyone in the lower ranks had exactly the same idea as the leaders. And they hadn't, he said.

He went on. 'Some Congress men genuinely believe a social revolution is the way to get rid of the British. But some people in Congress want revolution for quite another reason – to make it impossible for the Congress itself to rule after the British go.'

31

Victoria was so interested that she interrupted. She said, 'But who do they think is going to rule then? What *do* they want?'

Govindaswami looked solemnly at her. 'They want a complete revolution,' he said. 'Their masters, and their minds, are in Moscow. The thing they must prevent is an orderly hand-over to Congress and an orderly advance under Congress, or under any genuine local rule. Everything must fail so that the people have only one hope, only one friend they can turn to. And these men will make sure they know who that "friend" is.'

I didn't believe a word of this. It was all just making excuses. The truth is that the Wogs wanted to kill us first, and then they'd kill all the other Wogs who didn't think the same way they did.

Govindaswami went on. 'So we have to keep a particularly close watch on Congress, for its own good. *They* don't know who among their own people are really traitors to them. Their intelligence service is not as good as ours.'

'What do you mean, "ours"?' I burst out. I couldn't stand that chap talking about 'our' this and 'our' that, when he meant things that we, the English people and their descendants, had had done and made.

He said, 'Of or pertaining to the constitutional government of *my* country, Mr Taylor.' I was furious, but what could I say? He went on. 'As I was saying, Congress don't always know, and when they do know they often dare not act, for political reasons. For instance, K. P. Roy may be hiding in this district.'

K. P. Roy had been a Congress man. Now he was an out-and-out terrorist, but I could see why the Congress couldn't act openly against him. He was a sort of Frankenstein to them. They'd created him, and made a lot of Indians think he was a hero, so now that he had run off the rails the Congress couldn't openly attack him.

Then Govindaswami asked all of us to keep an eye on any Indians we knew and to tell him of any suspicions we had, however slight. 'By the way,' he said, 'it's possible that the Army is going to send a battalion of troops down here some time this month. I'll feel a little happier if they do.'

We always used to have a battalion of British infantry in Bhowani before the war. But when they went off to Egypt in '39 we had nobody for a time, and then Indian battalions off and on, but now the Lines were empty. I asked if the new battalion would be British. I wanted to know because it was good fun when we had the sergeants and Tommies coming down to our Institute, even though there were always plenty of fights and half our girls got in trouble one way or another.

But Govindaswami thought it was sure to be an Indian battalion, and personally I've never trusted them in this kind of show. After all, they're Wogs themselves, even if they are in uniform; so I was doubly disappointed.

When we got out of there I didn't say anything until we were on the Norton and chugging along the empty cantonment roads toward the cinema. Then I shouted over my shoulder to Victoria, ' "Protect the Congress for its own good," my God! Govinda-swami's a Congress man himself, if you ask me. He is just trying to find out what we know about his murderous friends. If I catch one of those people I will beat him up properly. You watch me!'

Victoria said, 'I thought Mr Govindaswami was very nice.'

You see, I'd done it again. I did not like Govindaswami, but I did not think as badly of him as I'd just said. This thing of saying too much or too little, or being too rude or too polite, is partly just me and partly something that nearly all our people have. Even Victoria had it, you will see.

All through the picture I was thinking of the derailment some of the time and of Victoria the rest of the time. When I thought about derailments and sabotage I thought about K. P. Roy. Everyone knew his name. I thought of him pouring petrol over me in my office and setting light to me. I thought of him derailing Number 1 Down Mail when it was going at full speed down the Lidhganj bank. My hands jerked up to cover my eyes before I knew what I was doing. Victoria looked at me in a funny way in the half-darkness and patted my arm. She understood because, I tell you, after all, she was a railway girl. And then I got to think-ing about her and me, and what had happened to her, and what would happen to us.

4

The noise on Number 1 platform while we were waiting for Sir Meredith Sullivan – that is, me and the reception committee – was perfectly terrible. It reminded me of the monkey house at the Calcutta Zoological Gardens. I checked my watch two or three times against the station clock. I was nervous. I even shouted at the natives to keep quiet, although everyone knows that is quite hopeless.

I was nervous because of Victoria. She stood there with us, but somehow not looking as if she was with us. She watched us, and I couldn't tell whether it was a friendly recognition, like when I meet an old St Thomasian, or something else.

Williams, our railway policeman, was there, and, of course, Mrs Williams. Govindaswami was not there, and we were arguing about that while we waited. Mrs Fitzpatrick, the wife of the Train Controller, said, 'I think he ought to have come. After all, he is the head of the district, officially, and Sir Meredith Sullivan is a knight and a very important gentleman.'

Mrs Williams agreed with her, but I don't think she really cared one way or the other, because while she was speaking she was also putting on more lipstick, violet-coloured stuff. She had made her mouth into an O, and talked indistinctly through it. She dyes her hair, and her topi is always very small and looks funny sitting on top of all that pile of golden curls.

Victoria asked whether her pater was going to bring the train in on time. I said, 'He's six and a half minutes late through Bargaon.' The stationmaster had just told me. Bargaon was the next station down the line toward Delhi, and only three miles away, so the train would be in very soon.

Then I saw two little girls carrying bouquets of zinnias. There was supposed to be only one. I asked Mrs Williams. 'Violet,' I said, 'who is supposed to present the bouquet to Sir Meredith Sullivan? Jane or Mavis? Look.'

Mrs Williams looked at the children and began to shout. Mrs Fitzpatrick began to shout. Williams joined in. So did I. There was a terrible noise, with us shouting, 'Jane, who told you to come here with a bouquet of flowers?' and 'Mavis, what are you doing here, man?' and 'Patrick, you said clearly that Jane –' and 'I never said such a thing! It was left to the committee, clearly, to –' and 'Let go, let go! My mother told me not to give the flowers to anyone but the old sahib who got off the train,' and 'Oh, my God, be quick, here is the express!'

I was ashamed because Victoria stood there with that queer look on her face, and we were making more noise than the Wogs. We always do when we get excited. The English people never do. It put me in a bad temper with myself, deep down.

When I turned to Victoria she was looking down the line. We saw the black smoke above the houses far away. The line curved gently to the left. The smoke we saw was by the old temple beyond cantonments. About there the drivers on the mails and expresses always cut off steam. They'd close the regulator and open the drifting valve and coast in with the smoke trailing low along the carriage roofs. We'd watched them often, Victoria and I, in the evenings. When the sun was low it seemed to paint the carriage sides, which are dull red, with a brighter orange colour. Then a train of dust always whirled along behind the real train of carriages, and that would hang over the rails and for a long time afterward settle slowly on the crops and the patches of jungle and the huts in the fields. Beside the line the leaves on the trees were always grey or dusty red, not green or brown.

The engine whistled. That was for the cantonment level-crossing where the Kishanpur road crossed, where we'd gone yesterday on the way to Pathoda. The train came in sight. The next time she whistled I saw the jet of steam from her whistle, counted, and then heard the whistle. It was for the Street of the Farriers, a narrow dirty crossing in the depths of the city, where there are low mud walls and the backs of filthy tenements on both sides. She wouldn't whistle again until she reached the platform.

The engine came to the points under the signal gantry, and we watched the bogie lurch. It found the points and steadied, then the heavy locomotive frame swung over and steadied. She whistled for the platform. She rolled clanging past.

Victoria waved her hand and shouted, 'Pater!' She left us and squeezed breathlessly away along the platform. It was years since she had seen him on an engine, and I knew it must be a good feeling. When we are on our jobs we are real men, as good as any Englishman, especially the drivers. Mr Jones looked pale and a bit grey and lined and bent in the shoulders, and his eyes were ringed and tired, but, my God, he was the man on the footplate, the driver of the engine, and he had brought 98 Up Express from Muttra and would take it on to Gondwara.

Then I had to turn and watch out for Sir Meredith Sullivan. I had never seen him in the flesh, and now I did, and I was very shocked. He was dying, and he was not really old. He wore a grey suit, collar, tie, and topi. Mrs Williams and Mrs Fitzpatrick and the little girls were tripping over one another to give him posies and introduce themselves and tell his bearer what to do with the suitcases; but Sir Meredith Sullivan was dying. His face was heavy, and the skin on it all slack and greeny white. He moved and smiled and shook hands as if he had already been dead some time.

Victoria came up with her father. It was my job to introduce him, so I said, 'Sir Meredith Sullivan, this is Mr Thomas Jones. He is the driver of your train.'

Sir Meredith Sullivan said, 'How are you, Thomas?' and put his hand out. 'It's a long time since the Allahabad days.'

Mr Jones didn't like to shake hands because he was dirty. He said, 'A long time, yes, sir, it is a long time. Thank you, sir. Thank you. I must be getting back to my engine.'

Sir Meredith Sullivan said, 'Good-bye, Thomas.' I noticed he did not say I hope I'll see you again soon, or anything like that. He was beyond that, and it made me feel cold. Not for him, but for all of us.

Mr Jones and Victoria noticed it too. Mr Jones's face was pitted with dirt and coal dust. His eyes shone out of white circles in the dirt. He was wearing the red and white spotted bandanna handkerchief he always wore on his head when he was driving, tied at the back into a little tail, and he had a mess of cotton waste in his hands. He rolled it nervously, looking at Sir Meredith Sullivan, and rather frightened of what he saw, I think; then he went back to his engine.

I had begun to guide Sir Meredith toward the exit when the stationmaster pushed up to us and whispered in my ear. He said that two English officers on the train wanted to see me. I told him, 'Not now, man! Later!'

The stationmaster said, 'But they say it is urgent, Mr Taylor. They have a telegram.'

Then I saw I'd have to go, so I asked Sir Meredith Sullivan to excuse me.

'Railway business comes first,' he said.

I stood there with the perspiration wet on my forehead until the party had left the platform. Then I noticed Victoria. I mean, I saw her; I'd never forgotten she was there somewhere near. She would be thinking I was just a stooge at the beck and call of every piddling little officer. So I shouted, 'Ah! Now let's see these bloody people. I'll teach them to waste my time. You watch me!' I led the way as fast as I could go toward the back of the train.

The natives in the third-class were caterwauling, and their carriages were packed full, and more people were scrambling in on the top of the ones already there. The sun burned down on the carriage roofs and on the platform canopy. The carriage sides were like radiators sending out waves of heat over the platform. Indians shouted at me because I was pushing, and I shouted back at them. Several men were squatting on the platform edge, as usual, relieving themselves under the train.

The stationmaster said, 'Here, Mr Taylor.'

There were a couple of dusty green valises side by side on the platform, and half a dozen suitcases and three or four gun-cases and a fishing-rod case. Two Gurkha soldiers with slung tommy-guns stood over the kit to prevent anyone from treading on it. An old bearer in white drill livery was waiting on the top step of a first-class compartment. When I came up he turned his head and said in Hindustani to someone inside, 'The railway person has come, sahib.'

'The railway person!' When I heard that, and Victoria there with me, it was the last straw.

The bearer stood aside. A pansy-looking, rather fat young man came out. He wore dark glasses and he had a big fair moustache. He was a lieutenant. He said in a very hoity-toity voice to me, 'I say, are you in charge here? Didn't you get the colonel's telegram? There don't seem to be any arrangements, do there?'

He had full, curved, red lips. I noticed them most particularly because they made me feel funny. Victoria stared at them too. Apart from the lips, which were frightening on a man, I'd seen plenty like him. He was hot and tired, and he was acting superior because I'm an Anglo-Indian.

Well, I was hot and tired, and I'd had enough. I waved my finger at him and shouted, 'Why should there be any arrangements, mister? Did you want the whole staff of the Bhowani district to be lined up here on parade? You people in the military department think that the whole work of the railway department must stop for your benefit, but I tell you the war is over, and I tell you it is high time you knew that!'

The lieutenant blinked as though I'd hit him. He went red and said, 'Here, who do you think you're talking to?' but he wasn't sure of himself. I can always tell, because I'm never sure of myself. When I felt that about him I really felt on top.

I pushed in closer to him and shouted louder. 'I do not care who you are, mister. I tell you I do not know anything about a telegram. You did not send any telegram here!'

Then he said, 'Take your paws off me, you damned cheechee!' I took a pace back and began to swing at him. I would have lost my job, but a job's not everything. I'm six feet two inches, and I weigh fourteen and a half stone. I would have wiped the floor with him.

But someone by my ear said, 'That's enough.' I stopped where I was. The man who spoke was very bitter, and he was as sure of himself as a tiger. I looked at him and saw at once that he wasn't trying to make himself unpleasant, and still his voice hit you like an electric shock.

He wasn't wearing a hat or dark glasses. His eyes were pale blue, bloodshot, and rimmed with dust, and there were crow's-foot wrinkles at the corners of his eyes, and his forehead was lined. His hair was thick and dark. He was thin, about five feet ten inches tall, and clean-shaven. His face was quite long and became narrow below. He wore a single row of medal ribbons on his jungle-green bush shirt. I thought he was ill, of malaria perhaps. I was much bigger than he was, but I never remembered it, not even that first time.

He said to me, 'My name is Savage. I command the First Battalion of the Thirteenth Gurkha Rifles. Have you had a telegram from General Headquarters, Delhi, or from the Railway Board, or from anyone else, warning you that my battalion is on its way here?'

It was like a cold hose being turned on me. I forgot the lieutenant and the crowd, and even Victoria. My mouth opened and shut, and I said, 'Telegram from General Headquarters? Battalion? Here?'

Colonel Savage stared at me. His mouth tightened, and his eyes began to glitter. He said, 'I see you haven't. Nor have you had my telegram from Delhi telling you I was arriving on this train with my adjutant, Mr Macaulay here.'

I stammered, 'Adjutant? Oh, my God, has that bloody man Kasel forgotten to tell me this?' I took off my topi and wiped my forehead.

The colonel said, 'I want to talk to you in your office.'

'But Colonel –' I said. What was the use of talking to me if I knew nothing?

'Don't say "but" to me. Five hundred Gurkha riflemen of my regiment are in the train now – in two trains. It is no joke to be in a troop train in this heat. If the arrangements for their reception are not completed in good time I'll see that you, at least, suffer for it,' he said. He held his Gurkha hat, the wide-brimmed felt hat, tightly in his hand. It was most unfair, what he said.

'But, sir,' I said and beat the top of my topi with my hand, 'I don't understand how – it is impossible –'

Victoria saw what a jam I was in. She said with a little laugh, 'I worked in Transportation Directorate at General Headquarters, Patrick, and I'm afraid it's possible enough. The man who sends those telegrams from Transportation is awfully nice, but he often forgets to send copies to everyone concerned. We've had trouble about that before.'

The colonel's blue eyes came slowly round to her. He looked her up and down. His nostrils were pinched and his lips quite white. She laughed again, trying to make us all less tense, and said, 'I expect you know, Colonel.'

He said, 'You worked in Transportation Directorate? As a WAC (I)? Recently?' He said it the Army way – 'Wack-eye.'

'Yes,' she said.

'Were you an officer or an auxiliary?' he said.

'I was a subaltern. I'm on leave pending release,' she said.

He said, 'You'd better come along to the office with us.'

The stationmaster was still there. He edged forward and said,

'May I let the express go, sahib?' It was impossible to tell whether he had spoken to me or the colonel, because he spoke to the air half-way between us. Only he usually called me Mr Taylor.

I looked at the colonel. The colonel said, 'As far as I'm concerned.' I said, 'Let her go.' The stationmaster waved his hand. The guard blew his whistle. Victoria stepped back a few paces to wave to her father. He was just climbing up on to the footplate with a billy of fresh tea. He saw her and waved, then disappeared into the cab. The first exhaust stroke boomed up, and the express started to move along the platform. The rumbling of the wheels got louder and quicker. Then the lines stood there empty under the sun, and we had to go up to my office.

Kasel stood up behind the desk when he saw us coming in. I said, 'Kasel, there are two military troop specials on the way here. Find out where they are.'

Kasel smiled shyly at Victoria before turning to answer me. He said, 'I know, Mr Taylor. One is at –'

It was too much. I felt myself going pale with anger, and I shouted, 'What the hell do you mean, you know? How do you know? Why didn't you tell me?'

'I was going to,' he said. 'This telegram came from Division Traffic an hour and a half ago. I have been working on it.' He pointed at the papers covering the desk. 'I was going to give you a working time-table for the trains, for your approval, as soon as I had got it ready.'

I grabbed the telegram and read it. To Kasel I said, 'You had no business not to tell me about this at once. At once, do you hear? I am responsible here. Why, there might –'

Savage interrupted me. 'Please finish your squabble some other time,' he said, very cold and grating. He sat down, put his Gurkha hat on the table, and leaned forward. 'Listen,' he said, 'my battalion, less one company, is coming here for Internal Security duties, particularly railway protection. Please take notes, Mr Kasel. I'm leaving one company in Lalkot, and I'm going to use another to provide platoon guards on the three important bridges in this area – the two Cheetah bridges on the main line, at Karode and Dabgaon, and the Kishnan bridge on the Bhanas branch line. I'm keeping the rest of the battalion here in Bhowani. I'm going to patrol every foot of line every day. I want the use of your motor trolleys. My bridge guards can live in those wooden huts I see along the line. There always seems to be one near a big bridge. What do you call them?'

'Gangers' huts, Colonel,' I said. 'But –' I tried to tell him that only the District Engineer and one or two of his assistants could use the motor trolleys, and that the gangers couldn't be turned out of their huts without causing trouble.

'One of you two will have to be in close touch with me all the time,' he said, as if I had not spoken, 'so that my trolley patrols don't run into unscheduled goods trains, specials, and so on.' My God, he was hard, conceited, cocksure, insulting. 'I'll put a field telephone in here for you,' he said. 'Now, the reception of my battalion –'

'Colonel, it –' I tried again to tell him about railway regulations for the use of trolleys.

'Please be quiet. I want you to show Mr Macaulay here where our trains will be put, so that ...'

From the corners of my eye I saw Victoria staring at him. Savage went on, not looking at her, speaking slowly so that Kasel could keep up with his notes. Kasel wrote in shorthand quite well.

When Savage finished I started telling him why all these things couldn't be done. I knew my regulations, and half the things he asked were difficult and the other half impossible. I began to feel much better as I explained. I was getting my own back, because no one can argue with printed regulations. He sat there with his head bent down, saying nothing.

When I finished he looked at me and said, 'Your job is to get these things done, Mr Taylor, not to find reasons why they can't be done.'

It was like the electric shock again, or a spike of ice rammed down my throat. I had begun to stutter – how could I make him understand? – when Kasel put his oar in. He said, 'I think we can meet the colonel's wishes, Mr Taylor.'

Savage glanced at him and said, 'Good. I'll leave it to you.' I turned as red as a beetroot. The sod! Savage swung round in his chair to face Victoria. Victoria's eyes were like stone. He said, 'What is your name?'

'Jones.'

'Initials and Army number?'

'V. WAC-seven-four-six.'

Lieutenant Macaulay wrote it down. Savage said, 'Miss Jones, you obviously know the workings of the railway here, and you know the Army. Mr Taylor and Mr Kasel don't know anything about the Army, and I don't know anything about the railways. I want you to get back into uniform and be a liaison officer between us.'

She said, 'I'm afraid I have other things to do.'

I said, 'But –' because really she didn't have anything to do, and it would be wonderful to have her working with me, to help me with those goddamned bloody stuck-up sods of officers. She frowned at me, and I held my tongue.

Savage looked her in the eye for a while; then he said, 'Very well. That's all for the moment. Please send any new information to me to Kabul Lines, Mr Taylor. I'm going there now.'

'In the cantonments?' I said.

'Are there two Kabul Lines here?' he said. 'We'll be back tomorrow morning.'

He got up. Lieutenant Macaulay handed him his hat and said, 'Your hat, sir.' Macaulay's lips gave me the willies. Savage walked out. Macaulay stopped by Victoria's chair and smiled at her and said, 'Let me know if you change your mind, won't you? He's really not so bad to work with.' He'd taken off his dark glasses, and I saw that his eyes were funny too, wide-set and dull. Then he went out.

I sat there on the edge of my desk for a couple of minutes, then I grabbed my topi, jammed it on my head, and yelled at the top of my voice, 'Oh, damn all the bloody military to *hell*!' Then I asked Victoria to come along with me.

While I was starting up the Norton I asked her why she'd told Savage she couldn't help us as a liaison officer. I told her how disappointed I was.

She said, 'I don't like him, and I'm not going to work with him. I'd have to call him "sir"!'

That was true. I was pleased that she didn't like him. But there was another thing; I felt queer because she had stood up to him and told him flatly she wouldn't do it. I ought to have been proud of her, and I was, but I hadn't stood up to him myself, which made the gap bigger between me and her.

5

I WAS still thinking of Savage and Macaulay when I went down to Number 4 Collett Road that evening. I picked up Victoria and Rose Mary and Mrs Jones and walked with them to the Institute, where Sir Meredith Sullivan was going to speak to us about St Thomas's.

There were two Railway Institutes then, of course, one for Europeans and Anglo-Indians, and one for Indians. The Indians had not made theirs into anything, while ours was a fine big building with a dance floor and card rooms and a bar, just like the Club in cantonments. The Indians seldom used their Institute. They never spent any money on beer, rum, and whisky there, so there was no profit to improve it with. It was the same at the station. We had two running rooms there for the drivers, firemen, and guards who had to stop over an hour or a night between trains. The European running room was twice the size of the Indian one, and had comfortable beds and a room with chairs and magazines and packs of cards.

When we got to the Institute, Victoria went off to play whist. I would have said she got rid of me, almost, so I spent most of the evening in the bar. We used to have good Murree and Solan beer in that bar. I kept an eye on Sir Meredith Sullivan, and about eleven o'clock went to ask him if he was ready to speak to everybody. He was, so I got up on the dais and rang a bell, and everyone crowded on to the dance floor. The younger people sat down on the floor, and the older ones took the chairs that were all round the walls. When they'd all settled down I raised my hand and announced, 'Ladies and gentlemen, Sir Meredith Sullivan will now address us on a subject that is very important for all of us.'

Sir Meredith came forward, and I sat down. He began to talk about St Thomas's. He told us what we already knew – that the Presidency Education Trust had had a good offer for the school buildings and grounds and wanted to accept it. He was on his way to meet with the trustees in Bombay. He wanted to find out what our feelings were so that he could tell them. He said, 'Let anyone speak.'

He stood there, waiting. He looked terribly ill and very tired. Someone spoke up and said, 'I think it would be a damned shame to sell the school, sir. My boy is going next year. Where else can he go?' There was a big murmur of people agreeing. Then they began to clap their hands, and soon everyone was shouting, 'No, no!' 'It is *our* school!' 'They have no right to sell it,' and so on. It made me feel good just to hear them. No one was going to push *us* down the drain without a fight.

Then I saw Victoria standing up, taller than the others. She lifted her arm and said loudly, 'Sir Meredith, I think we ought to ask the Trust to accept the offer and sell the school. What is going to happen in a few years' time, when –'

People interrupted her, and I felt as if I were being pulled in half, because she was so brave but she was so wrong and I loved her. As soon as she had finished, though no one could hear what she said after a bit, everyone shouted that they didn't agree. Sir Meredith Sullivan stood there listening to it all.

Finally he said, 'You seem to be outnumbered, Miss Jones' – he knew who she was. Then he spoke to all of us again and said, 'You wish me, then, to tell the trustees that St Thomas's must be kept going at all costs?'

We all shouted, 'Yes,' and clapped our hands like mad. I watched Victoria as I clapped, and I saw her pushing out of the ballroom through the crowd. Her face was tight and beautiful, but I knew she wanted to cry. I left Sir Meredith – that was a bad thing to do, but I had to – and worked my way round after Victoria.

She had reached the outside doors by the time I caught her up, and Ted Dunphy was talking to her there. They didn't see me, and I stopped short. Dunphy was standing in front of her, twisting his hands with nervousness. I heard him say, stuttering all the time, 'I – I just wanted to tell you that I b-believe you are right, M-Miss Jones. D-Don't think everyone is against you, p-please. I'm not. I think you are absolutely right.'

Victoria smiled at him through her tears. Ted was a young driver, and he was in love with Victoria, I knew that. He worshipped her.

Then a fellow came to tell me Sir Meredith Sullivan wanted to speak to me, and I had to go back with him while Victoria glanced at me and went out through the big doors to the outside.

Sir Meredith kept me for half an hour. I don't remember what it was about, because thinking of Victoria wandering about and crying was like having the fever. As soon as I could I got out of there, leaving them all, and went quickly to Victoria's house. I knocked. No one answered, so I went in. She wasn't there, and I went out of the back door, across the lawn, through the bushes, and on to the line.

The signal light shone red among a lot of floating stars. A little pencil of white light shone straight down from the bottom of the signal lamp, just enough to make a short stretch of rail look like a silver bar. I smelled cigarette smoke and heard an engine puffing slowly a long way off, and the low murmuring, almost growling noise, that Bhowani City makes at night from across the waste land beyond the line.

I knew where to go to find her, because in the old days we had often met to talk under that signal.

I saw the end of her cigarette and then the shape of her, and I whispered, 'Are you there, Victoria? Oh, Victoria, I am glad I found you.'

She didn't say anything, and I could see the wet on her eyes by the signal light. I tried to tell her why I hadn't spoken up to defend her in the Institute. I told her I couldn't, because I didn't agree. She said she understood. She said it was obvious that she and I didn't think the same about a lot of things, important things. I kicked at the ballast with my foot so that the stones crunched together under the toe of my shoe. I said, 'I love you, Victoria. I know what you feel. I understand, honestly I do.' I was trying to find some way of helping her, of persuading her she'd be happier if she closed her eyes and fought alongside the rest of us.

She didn't answer. While I waited for her to speak I moved a little so that some of the red from the signal lamp shone on my face. I must have looked bad, frightening. The engine puffed slowly, like breathing, over there under the Sindhya Hills.

Victoria sighed, and I tried to catch her in my arms. Words were no good. I could smell her hair and her scent all together with the hot steel smell of the railway.

I am very strong, and I was crushing her and couldn't let go because if I did I was afraid she'd leave me for ever. I didn't let go until she said, not angry but tired, 'Let me loose, Patrick. No, I don't hate you. I've just changed, that's all.'

I wanted to cry, because she and I had been so close in everything, and we weren't any more; and because Colonel Savage was able to make me so stuttery and foolish; and because everyone was moving into our places, like the Indian crew on the goods train; and because for me there was no question of thinking what was best, what was right – I had to have Victoria, I had to grovel in front of Savage, I had to fight the Indians for my rights.

The signal wires hissed over their pulleys beside us, the counter-weight of the signal level flopped up, and then I knew that my face shone green and wet instead of red and wet. I tried to apologize to Victoria. I told her again that I loved her. I said, 'What are we going to do?'

She said, 'You and I?'

'No. We, we people,' I said, meaning us Anglo-Indians.

And then she said something which, although she spoke bitterly, made me feel better, because it meant she realized the brick wall she, we, were up against. Savage, for instance. He might have been friendly to both of us, but he'd just been as cruel as he could. He was a leopard, the way I'd been thinking in my mind all the time. So my heart jumped when she said, 'What are we going to do? We? If we stay the way we are we're going to run the bloody railway, of course! Isn't that what we were born for, man?'

6

ON that Monday morning, the day the Gurkhas were due to arrive in the afternoon, Victoria rang me up early. Her voice was trembly with anger, and at first I thought it was me she was angry with, but she said, 'Patrick? Listen to this. This is a telegram for me from the WAC (I) Directorate in Delhi: "Leave cancelled owing to temporary emergency. Report forthwith repeat forthwith to O.C. First Thirteenth Gurkha Rifles Kabul Lines Bhowani Cantt for temporary duty as special liaison officer. Administrative details follow. Acknowledge. All informed." Isn't that the limit?'

She waited for me to say something, but to tell the truth I was delighted. I thought someone up there in Delhi had realized the situation and sent the telegram. I said, 'That's going to help me a lot, Victoria.'

She answered impatiently, 'Don't you see *he*'s done it – Colonel Savage?' She said that he must have sent off a telegram as soon as he left my office on Saturday. She said he must know Mrs Fortescue, who was the head lady of the WAC (I)s.

I asked her what she was going to do about it. She didn't answer for a time. Then she said, 'I could go sick. I could send a telegram saying I wasn't fit enough to report. They'd never find out.'

'Why not?' I asked. 'That Colonel Savage will send his doctor down to look at you as soon as the trains come in, you mark my words.'

She was silent again, and it was funny how clearly I got the impression of what she was doing and thinking at the end of all that telephone wire. She was biting her lip and frowning. She was thinking, I hate him; but she was thinking, I must do my duty. How could any of us know then how serious the emergency might be? She was remembering what Govindaswami had told us. At last she said, 'He's got me. I'll have to do it.'

I said, 'Will I see you here tomorrow, then, do you think?'

She said, 'I suppose so. I've got to find my uniform and get it ironed.' And she hung up.

But Savage didn't waste any time, and I saw her that afternoon. I was busy all morning with my own work and making the arrangements for the reception of the Gurkha troop specials. Mrs Williams rang up to suggest that the ladies from the Railway Lines ought to have hot tea ready for the British officers of the Gurkhas when they arrived, and I agreed. That will make Savage more polite to us, I thought, because he will owe us something. It was going to be impossible to work with him if he always thought we were just useless obstructionists. I had found out that he did know Mrs Fortescue, and it was quite likely that he would be a personal pal of Mr Hindmarsh (H. J. K. Hindmarsh, Esquire, C.I.E.), our General Manager.

I went down to the yards well before the troop specials were due in. The ladies and I gathered at the Yard Foreman's office in the middle of the yards. We were talking together there when Victoria arrived with her father. An engine was shunting over the hump close beside us, and there was a roll of wheels and clanking of buffers all the time.

At the same time Colonel Savage and Lieutenant Macaulay arrived from the opposite direction. Victoria drew herself up and saluted Savage very carefully. He saluted her just as carefully. He looked her up and down as she stood there, and said, 'You can wear mufti whenever you like. Women and uniforms don't go together.'

'Especially when they've got such good figures. Better than Betty Grable,' Lieutenant Macaulay said.

I agreed with Savage about women in uniform. Victoria would look good in a sack, but those WAC (I) clothes were not pretty. She wore a tight, short drill skirt, a khaki shirt, and a fore-and-aft hat perched on the right side of her curls – and khaki stockings and big brown shoes and a blue shoulder cord. I happened to know everything underneath was also plain and khaki, because she'd showed me when she got her first uniform.

Victoria said to Savage very stiffly, 'This is my father, sir. He is an engine driver.'

Macaulay said, 'Oh.' He probably never expected Victoria, who was so beautiful and a subaltern, to have an engine driver as her father. Savage turned to Mr Jones and held out his hand. The wide brim of his Gurkha hat was starched and straight as a board. He wore it almost flat on his head, while Macaulay's was tilted very much to the right and showed a lot of curly fair hair under it on the left. I hung around close by them, waiting to speak to Victoria.

Savage said to Mr Jones, 'I'm sorry we had to take your daughter away from you, sir.'

I started, and Victoria did too, to hear Savage calling Mr Jones 'sir'. Mr Jones wrung Savage's hand very hard and said, 'Oh, don't call me "sir", sir.'

'Well, you're a father,' Savage said and smiled. That was the first time I saw him smile. I couldn't believe it was the same person who had got out of the train on Saturday, this smile was so hot and brilliant, and it crinkled all his face round the eyes. 'We'll look after your daughter,' he said. 'She'll be living at home with you. She's going to help Mr Taylor and me to help you to keep the trains running.' He'd seen me by then and nodded to me when he mentioned my name.

Mr Jones said, 'Good, jolly good! She is a clever girl, Colonel, and works hard. But she is a woman, eh?'

'She looks like one,' Savage said and glanced again at Victoria. Victoria caught my eye, and I think I know what was on her mind. She was wishing her father wouldn't be taken in so easily. These people were snobs really. But Pater said, 'Yes, man! But she works well, for a woman. You should see the reports she got while she was at the General Headquarters.'

'Colonel Savage doesn't want to hear about that,' Victoria said, blushing and angry.

Mr Jones said, 'I expect he knows, girl. You do not become a lieutenant-colonel in the military department while you are such a young man for being a fool. You are not forty, Colonel, I bet?'

'Thirty-four.'

I was surprised. Why, he was two years younger than I was. He looked older.

Mr Jones said, 'Thirty-four! Well, well. My grandfather was a military man, Colonel. Sergeant J. T. Duck. He retired from the Queen's Fusiliers in eighteen sixty-three. He was the first man to take a train from here to Gondwara when the line was built.'

'That's very interesting,' Savage said. He looked interested too, but Macaulay yawned behind his hand.

'Yes, isn't it?' Mr Jones said. He was wearing his topi then, and his bandanna stuck out of his pocket. Macaulay was looking at Victoria and stroking his moustache, and I suddenly thought, My God, that bastard wants to have her in bed with him; and for the first time I realized that though Victoria would see more of me in this work, she would also see more of the young British officers.

Mr Jones chattered on happily. He was so delighted to be talking to a lieutenant-colonel. He even joked with Savage and told him he should leave the military department to join the railway department, and Savage said he'd like to be an engine driver. Then Savage said he'd have to ask to be excused, and Mr Jones wrung his hand again and told him to be sure and come and visit them at Number 4 Collett Road for a bottle of beer and a good talk. Victoria would show him the way, Mr Jones said.

Victoria kept her face stiff until Savage and Macaulay walked away toward Mrs Williams and the other ladies. Then she turned on her father and said, 'Pater! Why did you ask Colonel Savage to come to our house? If he does come it will only be to laugh at us.' But Pater was looking after Savage and smiling in a pleased, happy way, He said to us, just as if Victoria hadn't spoken, 'Now there is a *real* English gentleman for you. No swank, you see, but he will always be treated like a gentleman, because he knows he is one.'

Victoria said again, 'Why did you go asking him to our house? I don't want to see him there. He's very rude. Working with him is going to be bad enough.'

Pater looked at her, and he was surprised and rather hurt. He said, 'Don't speak like that about the colonel, Victoria. It is not right. I must go to the running room. Give me a kiss, girl.'

She bent forward to be kissed. Pater started to go, but he turned back at once and came close to me. He said, 'And I can tell you something, Patrick. The colonel thinks Victoria is a good-looking girl.'

I laughed, because of course Pater hadn't seen how Savage really treated her when a lot of other people weren't around. I thought, if Pater's trying to make me jealous he is talking through his hat.

'Oh, yes, he does,' Pater said. 'I am old, but not as old as that. Besides, she is my girl, and I know. The other young fellow thinks the same. But I don't like him. He is not a real gentleman.'

I agreed with him there. Macaulay gave me the creeps.

Pater stooped slowly under the couplings of a line of goods wagons, looked carefully up and down, and went away. His boots crunched fainter and fainter on the clinkers; then I heard Victoria swearing under her breath close beside me. 'How does Pater claim to know Lieutenant Macaulay isn't a real gentleman?' she said. 'Macaulay hardly spoke a word. As for Colonel Savage –'

We walked over to Mrs Williams. Just then a lot of our servants came up through the yards, carrying the big tea urn from the Institute, and charcoal, milk jugs, water chatties, cups, saucers, everything. To impress on Colonel Savage that we were all anxious to help him, I said, 'The urn is lent by permission of the Institute Committee, of course.' Savage nodded his head thoughtfully. He watched the servants preparing the charcoal fire at the side of the hut. Then he turned to Mrs Williams and said, 'This is really very kind of all of you, Mrs Williams, very kind indeed.' He flashed her another of those brilliant hot smiles.

Violet Williams simpered and put her hand up to her back hair. 'It is nothing, Colonel, a pleasure,' she said.

Savage said, 'I can assure you that our sick – and we're bound to have some – will appreciate it very much.'

I was as astonished as Mrs Williams. She said, 'Oh, but this is for the British officers, Colonel Savage.' Savage knew that perfectly well.

But he said, 'Well, you know, they'll appreciate your kindness, but I don't allow them to have any tea at a time like this unless the men are having some too, and you couldn't possibly cater for five hundred Gurkhas, could you?'

Mrs Williams looked put out, and I don't blame her. I could see she'd been imagining herself surrounded by captains and majors. And I'd been thinking that Savage would owe us something after this. But now, as the tea was only for the sick men, we would have looked like thoughtless people if we hadn't provided it, and Savage owed us nothing. He went on talking to Violet until her face cleared. He had kissed the Blarney Stone somewhere, all right.

Near me I heard Macaulay mutter to Victoria, 'The Sahib's giving her her money's worth, isn't he?'

Macaulay was standing very close to Victoria, touching her, I think, and his hand was somewhere behind her. She muttered, 'Mrs Williams is easily taken in.'

Macaulay cleared his throat, and I was too close to see what really happened next. What I saw – and Savage saw it too – was Victoria, leaning, falling back against Macaulay, and Macaulay's arm tight round her and on her bust. What no one knew, except Macaulay and Victoria, was whether she'd moved away from him and caught her foot in a check rail and stumbled, or whether she'd leaned deliberately against him.

Macaulay said, 'Careful now. You nearly fell.' His eyes were dull and his face pinched. That heavy, foolish moustache helped to hide his upper lip. Perhaps it was not so foolish of him to wear it, after all. He took his hand away, and then it was too late for

51

Victoria to say, Take your hands off me – even if she'd wanted to. I didn't know. I felt very bad then, with the British officers treating my girl that way.

A telegraph peon with a message came through between the wagons and went up to Colonel Savage. Savage took it, said, 'Excuse me,' and moved a little aside to read it. Then he looked up and called us. 'Graham. Miss Jones. Taylor.' We went over to him. 'Graham' was Graham Macaulay.

He said in a low voice, 'A Wimpy spotted some men on the line near Dabgaon – a Wimpy's a Wellington bomber, Miss Jones. Oh, you know that? It got back to base a couple of hours ago, and they checked up and found no railwaymen were working in that area. The RAF have been flying rail patrol since yesterday. Taylor, have a motor trolley ready to go out as soon as the first of our trains come in. There'll have to be a railwayman on board to work it, just this time. Afterwards we'll learn to do it ourselves. It wouldn't do any harm if you came yourself,' he said to me. 'I'm going. Graham, tell the police here. And get a havildar and four from the first rifle company to come in.'

Macaulay said, 'Very good, sir.'

Savage snarled, 'Don't keep saying, "Very good, sir." You're not a bloody butler.' He hated Macaulay, I was sure, and that cheered me up. He'd seen Macaulay pawing Victoria and despised him for that. I said to myself, He thinks it is degrading for a British officer to play around with an Anglo-Indian girl. His thinking that was degrading for *us*, I suppose, but I didn't care. If he thought we and they couldn't mix, he was on my side.

'No, sir,' Macaulay said. He saluted, red in the face, and went away.

Savage watched him go, his face like a wolf's. When he turned to Victoria he seemed to be in as bad a temper as he had been on Saturday when he first arrived. I thought, That's because he doesn't want her fooling around with his officers. He said curtly, 'When the trains are in, go to the Traffic Office, Taylor's, and stay there until we get back from our patrol. If I send a message, sort it out between Macaulay and that depilated Sikh assistant of Taylor's – Kasel – so that what I say is to be done *is* done. Do you understand?'

'Very good, sir,' she said. She said it on purpose, but Savage took no notice. He began to warn me that we might be out most of the night on the motor trolley. I thought he was joking, and anyway I saw the first troop special coming, and I said, 'Here she comes, sir!'

It was a long train, coming slowly up from the north. It passed through the station and swung curving round, carriage after carriage, under the signals and into the yards. All the windows were open and filled with round brown faces, the dust thick on them.

The engine stopped, hissing. The carriages stopped. One man jumped down from each carriage, ran across the tracks, and knelt down, looking outward, his rifle ready in his hands.

Victoria jumped forward, calling, 'Look out!' because one of the Gurkhas had settled in the path of a moving fly-shunted wagon. Savage snapped, 'Mind your own business, Miss Jones. He is supposed to look after himself.' The Gurkha moved aside before the wagon reached him, and Victoria muttered, 'Sorry, sir.'

The other Gurkhas poured out of the carriages, man after man after man in an endless single file from each door. British officers appeared, and Lieutenant Macaulay went over to speak to one of them.

The Gurkhas were dirty and quiet and of course small. They weren't like the sepoys of the Indian garrison battalion that had been here before, nor like the soldiers I'd seen walking about in clean, starched uniforms in Agra. They all formed up close by us, and they smelled of the train and ammonia and the cardamom seeds a lot of them were chewing. A few were thickset older men, but mostly they were young chaps, almost children. Their faces were round and unlined under the dust and the streaky sweat. They moved with a sort of unhurried bad temper, and almost without noise. In less than ten minutes the first batch crunched away, turned on to the Deccan Pike, and marched north toward cantonments. They had come from the war, lots of wars, but it seemed to me that they had brought their wars with them.

Ten or twelve Gurkhas under the old subadar-major came over to the tea urn. It looked to me as if those men had been ordered that minute to be 'sick', but Mrs Williams didn't notice anything. I was drinking some tea myself when Savage came up to me. He had a short rifle in his hand, and he was buckling his equipment on. He said, 'Ready? Miss Jones, we're going now.'

'Very good, sir,' she said again, looking him in the eye.

He was swinging away from her. He stopped, whipped round, and said, 'All right, Miss Jones. Mind you see the chamber pots are clean by the time I come back.'

She was so angry she could not speak, but it was really her fault for goading him. She knew he hated that phrase. He waited a moment, then turned away. A ganger brought the trolley down, and we got on and started off.

On the trolley were Colonel Savage, me, a sergeant (they call them havildars in the Indian Army), and five sepoys – called riflemen in Gurkha regiments. One of the riflemen was Savage's orderly, a thin Gurkha of about eighteen called Birkhe.

It had been still and hot all afternoon, but when we began to move the wind scorched our faces. The trolley seemed to be running all the time through the open door of a furnace, and we had to screw up our eyes against the hot wind and the dust. I soon put on my dark glasses.

The Gurkhas lost their bad temper when we began to move. They pushed each other and joked, and Savage made jokes with them which I couldn't understand because he spoke very quickly in Gurkhali, the Gurkhas' language. We were packed on there like sardines, and I asked him to tell the Gurkhas not to play the fool or someone would fall off.

Dabgaon is twenty-four miles from Bhowani Junction, and we got there in about an hour and a half. Savage got out his map and showed me a pencil mark on it. 'This is the map reference the Wimpy gave,' he said, 'where it spotted those men.' The place he pointed to was near the Cheetah bridge about half-way between Dabgaon and Malra. So we went there and hauled the trolley off the line.

The line curved there and ran in a cutting. At the north end of the cutting it ran out on to an embankment, and then on to the bridge approach. We began to search the line. A gang from Malra was already on the job, and after an hour they reported to us that nothing was wrong with the line and rails. They thought the bridge was all right too, though it would have been much easier to hide something there.

Savage had been standing on the top of the cutting, looking all round through his binoculars. To the west the country was thick, dry jungle; to the east it was mostly fields. He checked against his map the positions of two villages we could see in the fields. Then he pointed into the jungle to the west and said that another village, which his map said was less than a mile away, must be in there. The Gurkhas were searching in the fields and along the edge of the jungle.

The sun went down. The railway gang walked back together, singing, toward Malra. The Gurkhas trotted in, and we all gathered round the trolley. The Gurkhas began to eat chupattis and drink a little out of their water-bottles. I got hungry, and I wanted to go back to Bhowani. We couldn't do anything more out there.

But Savage pointed to his map and said, 'We'll go to these three villages in turn and ask the headmen if any strangers have been seen since midday. It's quite possible that the people the Wimpy saw might be hiding in one of the villages.'

I said, 'But, Colonel – ' and he looked at me, his eyes gleaming in the twilight, and I shut my mouth. What the hell good was it for me, the District Superintendent of Traffic, to go crashing round in the dark through the jungles and across the fields, when my job was in the office in Bhowani?

Savage said, 'Haven't you got anything to eat?'

I said, 'No.'

He said, 'You are a bloody fool. I warned you. Here.' He gave me some of his. He had a tin of bully beef and a few cold chupattis that looked as if they'd been floating round in his haversack for several days, or perhaps in Birkhe's. They were gritty and dusty and tasted of tobacco; he didn't seem to notice but ate them quickly. While we were eating he said, 'I understand the Collector has told you why my battalion has been sent here in such a hurry.'

I said, 'Yes. Because of K. P. Roy.' I had Roy on my mind whenever I thought of the railway.

Savage said, 'Partly him. Would you know him by sight if we happened to see him in one of these villages?'

I said, 'No.'

All of a sudden it came over me what we were really up to. I *had* thought that the men the plane had seen on the line might be K. P. Roy and his followers trying to do something bad. But I had never

55

thought we would go chasing them, and perhaps finish up facing K. P. Roy in a dark corner of a smelly village in the middle of the night. K. P. Roy would fight for his life with everything he had, and he would shoot first.

When it was quite dark we set off. Savage used his compass. There was about half a moon, and the leaves crackled under our feet. It was like some of my shooting expeditions, only we were after a man instead of an animal, and the trees seemed alive and frightening. Dogs began to bark before we got to the first village, and Savage sent two Gurkhas slipping round through the trees to get behind the village before we walked up to it.

We saw the lights, and then, when we went forward, a gun exploded with a tremendous roar. I dropped to my stomach, and slugs of lead and old bits of glass and nails whistled through the branches above us. It was the village watchman, wide awake and very nervous. Savage shouted, 'Don't shoot. We're soldiers.'

We went into the village. No one had gone to sleep there yet, and I could see they were all ill at ease. Savage was suspicious and cross-examined the headman for some time. But if they had seen any strangers they weren't going to tell us, and we hadn't got the time or the authority to search every house.

We left there about ten and marched back through the jungle, across the railway, and across the empty fields to the second village. It was the same procedure, only the watchman didn't shoot at us. I insisted on walking in front that time, because I thought Savage was thinking I was a coward for falling on my face when they fired at us. I had never been fired at before, though I had been in the Auxiliary Force, India, of course, ever since I joined the railway.

I am used to the jungles, but of course I had to trip up two or three times while I was leading the way, just because Savage was expecting me to, and finally he told me to get back and let a Gurkha lead. He was terribly impatient. My shoes were ordinary thin shoes, and my feet hurt, and by then I was hot, thirsty, and tired.

The moon was dull orange when we set out for the last village. It was a clear night, but near the earth in the hot weather there is a layer of hot wavy air packed with dust, and the moon, shining through it, looks orange-coloured. The dogs in that village could hear the dogs barking in the one we were leaving, across a mile and a half of fields. Savage stopped to listen and think, and instead of going the direct way he swung us off to one side. We came up to the last village from the left, where I remembered seeing a low rocky hill.

While we were moving across that hill, going very quietly, I got a tickle in my throat and had to cough. At once something went *pad-pad* a little in front. Savage said in Hindustani, 'Stand still, or I fire!'

The shuffling noise went on among the thin thorn bushes and the rocks, where I suppose the villagers usually grazed their goats. I saw a shape moving. It might have been a man running, it might have been a deer or a jackal or a pig. It looked like nothing but a change of light between the bushes. Beside me Savage pulled his carbine into his shoulder and fired four times very quickly – *bang-bang-bang-bang!*

The shape had gone, or the movement had stopped, I don't know which. I had forgotten how much my feet hurt. The thing might be K. P. Roy with a gun, but what frightened me more was that I was with these people who simply shot at anything that didn't do at once what they told it to. These people had brought the war to Bhowani, as I said.

We spread out and went forward, searching everywhere. There was no sign of anything or anyone. Finally Savage took us to the village. They'd heard the shooting, and again the watchman fired at us. The headman said there had been strangers there early in the day. Some of them had left before dusk, and one had just gone. No one knew who he was, but the headman described him, and Savage made a note.

At last we walked back to the railway line. By then my feet were bleeding, but I didn't complain to Savage. When we reached the trolley he said, 'If you hadn't coughed you could have saved us a lot of trouble – and yourself, I expect.'

I said I was sorry, but that I couldn't help it. He said, 'Imagine a cough will get you a bullet in the liver. You'll find you can help it. Come on, hurry up.' After wasting hours out there in the middle of the night, he was suddenly in a hell of a hurry to get back.

We got on the trolley and headed south. It was two o'clock

before we got to Bhowani, and I realized that Savage had kept Victoria all that time in my office with Kasel. Macaulay had probably been there most of the time too.

We looked a sight as we walked in – Savage, the Gurkha orderly Birkhe, and me. We were covered with dust, my clothes were torn and my shoes cracked. I limped to the chatti in the corner and poured about half of it down my throat. Until I'd done that I couldn't even notice who was in the room.

I saw that there were a couple of empty beer bottles in the waste-paper basket by Victoria's table, and crumbs of bread and a chicken bone on the floor. I thought, Victoria must have had supper in here with Macaulay. There was no one else who would be likely to bring beer up there, except me. Savage saw the bottles and crumbs too and glanced quickly at Victoria, almost nervously. I thought he was going to ask her about them, but he didn't. Macaulay wasn't there – only Kasel and Victoria and us. Victoria was pale, and her eyes looked large and dry. I couldn't be sure, but I thought she was shaking a bit.

'Now can we all go to bed?' I asked Savage.

'Who's on night duty here?' he asked.

'There is no night duty. The Assistant Stationmaster looks after the Traffic Office at night,' I said.

I thought for a minute Savage was going to order Kasel and me to take turns sitting up there all night like military sentries. By God, I would have given him a piece of my mind. But he didn't. He took no notice at all. He stretched his legs comfortably and said to Kasel, 'What's your real name? I can't stand calling you Kasel.'

'Ranjit Singh,' Kasel said.

Savage began to light a cheroot and said, 'Do most of the Kasel clan still live around Amritsar?'

Damn it, it was a quarter past two then. I looked at the clock.

Kasel said, 'Yes, Colonel – there and Jullundur and Hoshiarpur.' He was pleased as punch that Savage knew about his clan, and he could not hide it. He had a very expressive face. I had never heard of the Kasel clan.

Savage picked up a field telephone that was on Victoria's table. The Gurkhas must have put it in during the night. The wires went out through the window. Savage spoke on it to his people in cantonments. When he had finished, Victoria stood up and said, 'May I go now, sir?'

'Yes,' he said. 'The Collector's out of Bhowani and won't be back until lunchtime. I'm going to see him at five o'clock. Meet me then at his bungalow. Taylor, you'd better come too. Bring a pad and pencil, Miss Jones. You know shorthand?'

'Yes, sir. Very good, sir.'

He looked at her with a frown but said nothing and went out, with Birkhe following in his footsteps as he always did.

I got up and sat down again at once, my feet hurt so badly. At last I forced myself to walk because I wanted to take Victoria home. Before we left I told Kasel to close the office.

I followed Victoria very slowly down the stairs, along the platform, and on to the footpath beside the line. I was limping terribly. I said, 'Go slowly, Victoria. If you knew how my feet hurt. It was all a damned waste of time. It was exciting, though. I got shot at!'

Victoria said, 'Oh,' and her voice was sharp. I began to tell her all about it. That made me forget my feet, and soon I was walking faster. Was it K. P. Roy that Savage had shot at? Had he hit him? Or had he fired at a peaceful traveller? What were K. P. Roy and the Congress wallahs going to do, anyway? I talked about all this.

Victoria said nothing all the while, but by the time we came to the signal I felt fine. The last time we had been there was after the Sir Meredith Sullivan evening, when I had felt sad because I wanted to help her and we were drifting apart. Now it was quite different, I don't know why. Perhaps it was seeing the Gurkhas with their rifles and tommy-guns, and even working closely with Savage, who was so beastly sure of himself.

I thought, now's the time to put that right about last Saturday. I said, 'Good night, Victoria.' I caught her in my arms and kissed her properly on the mouth. I wasn't going to say anything or ask for anything that time. I'd learned my lesson about asking permission.

In my arms she was like the signal post, stiff and cold and hard. I stopped kissing her and asked her what was the matter.

She hit me as hard as she could with her fist, right on the nose.

59

The blood spurted out, and my eyes watered. I staggered about for a minute, then I gasped, 'Oh, Vicky, don't do that. What *is* the matter?'

She stood there close to me in the dark, breathing like a train. She said, 'Macaulay tried to rape me. You make me feel like a bitch in heat. All of you. Except Kasel. He's the only gentleman here. Now go away!'

She ran, stumbling, toward her house.

7

I HARDLY slept the rest of that night. Then I got through my morning's work somehow and hung around, smoking cigarettes and drinking tea, until I could go to Victoria's, a little before four. We were supposed to go to the Collector's with Colonel Savage at five. Before we went I meant to find out about this Macaulay business so that I could tell Savage and see that Macaulay was punished. In the night I had thought of beating Macaulay up, but it was too serious for that.

Victoria was sitting reading in the parlour when I got to Number 4 Collett Road. She must have known what I had come for, but all she said was, 'You're an hour early, Patrick. I'm reading.' She spoke quickly.

I said, 'Victoria, what happened last night?'

'It's none of your business,' she said. 'I can look after myself.'

I cried, 'You can't! Tell me, I must know. Then we'll tell Colonel Savage. I'll tell him by myself if you will feel embarrassed. How – how bad was it? What did he do?'

She looked at me for a while, then said, 'You don't really want to know, Patrick, do you? But I'll tell you. But – you've got to promise not to do anything about it. *Anything*, do you understand?'

I grumbled, but I had to promise. She said, 'Kasel was working at the desk when I got up there. Your chuprassi was asleep in the corner, I think. I asked Kasel – I'm going to call him Ranjit; that's what his name is – if he'd seen the Gurkhas come on the trains. I told him we'd never had Gurkhas in Bhowani before.

"Then we shall all be safe now," he said. He was being sarcastic, you understand.'

'I understand,' I said. 'He is a Congress wallah, that's why he doesn't like the military. But what has this got to do with – what happened?'

'A lot,' Victoria said sharply. 'When something important happens to you, you remember all of it or nothing. Don't interrupt. I told you you wouldn't like it. I told Ranjit that even if he didn't like the military he was much better at dealing with them than you were.'

I moved in my chair, but she went on. 'Ranjit said, "We Indians have learned now to bend a little with the wind. Savage is a big wind." Ranjit has a sense of humour, you know, even though his eyes always look so sad.

'Well, we sat there for a bit, talking. Then I began to copy out some of the working time-tables and I didn't really notice anything more until it began to get dark and Lieutenant Macaulay came in. He had a bulging haversack slung on his shoulder. He told me Savage would certainly take you into every village within ten miles. He told me Savage's nickname among the officers was "the Sahib". I knew that already. He didn't take any notice of Ranjit. He behaved almost as if Ranjit didn't exist. After a time Ranjit got up and said he was going off to have his supper.'

Victoria stared straight at me while she was talking, and never blinked. 'Macaulay asked him if he was going to his house, and if he would be gone long. I didn't think anything of it. I was a fool, I suppose. Ranjit told Macaulay he was going to eat in the refreshment room on the platform, and Macaulay told him not to hurry himself.'

Her voice was dry and her eyes hard and angry and fixed on me. I began to feel very uncomfortable.

'Ranjit went out. The chuprassi woke up, saw it was dark, and shuffled off. I heard Macaulay coming close to me. I went on working. He dropped his haversack on top of my papers and said, "Take a look in there." I opened it. There were two bottles of beer, a cold chicken, metal plates, knives, forks, salt, pepper, bread, napkins – everything. He sat down on the table close to me and said, "That's for us. My name's Graham. Do you like beer?"'

I knew Victoria did like beer. She didn't drink it much, but I could imagine how wonderful those two bottles must have looked to her then. My God, what wouldn't I have done for even one of them out on the line?

Victoria said, 'Macaulay opened the bottles and poured out the beer. We ate. It was a good chicken, very tender, but I did not enjoy it. I hardly even tasted it in my mouth. Macaulay was sitting so close that he gave me the creeps. His fly buttons were right under my eyes. But what could I say? How could I get out without making a fool of myself, perhaps? I said to myself, He won't have the nerve to try any tricks. I ate slowly, then more slowly. But I had to finish some time, and Ranjit didn't come back and didn't come back. You see, Macaulay had spoken in such a way that Ranjit thought I would *like* to be left alone with Macaulay, that we had an understanding. Do you see?'

I muttered, 'Kasel had no business to think that. He ought not to have left you.'

She blazed up at me. 'You think so? How the hell could Ranjit know Macaulay's a sex maniac? Tell me that!'

She calmed down and went on. 'I felt trapped in the chair, so I got up and walked to the window. That was a mistake. As soon as I'd done it I knew. Macaulay kept talking, but he came and stood close to me, a little behind me, not touching me. Then he said, "By the way, didn't you know Johnny Tallent?"' Victoria stopped dead.

At last I had to ask her, 'Who's Johnny Tallent?'

She said, 'Johnny Tallent was a captain. Nearly three years ago. He used to say I had bedroom eyes. He ought to know.' She stopped again.

I thought, Why does she have to bring this up? Why doesn't she tell me what Macaulay did or tried to do, and not drag in Kasel's being so nice and her having gone to bed with this Captain Tallent? I thought, She's doing it on purpose because she wants to shake me off, and she's making me miserable and angry and jealous. But I did not say anything, and after a while she continued.

'I used to like Johnny Tallent. I thought he was honest. He never pretended to want anything except to go to bed with me. He used to say I was beautiful, and he meant it, but that's what he said it for. He never pretended he would marry me. He thought that because he was a British officer and I was a cheechee girl I'd

62

do anything. And – Patrick, you're so determined we can't change, you ought to understand this – he was right. Slowly, slowly, I *did* feel I had to do it. Do you understand? Do you?'

I put my head in my hands. I understood, but the tears of rage and sadness were wet on my fingers.

'So I did. Several times. Then he left Delhi. But do you know what he'd done? He'd written to his friend Graham Macaulay in Burma or wherever Macaulay was, and told him about me. I expect he called me a nice bit of homework. Eight-annas, of course. And when Macaulay met me, he remembered. He remembered, and so he said to me, "By the way, didn't you know Johnny Tallent?" I told him I did. I kept my back to him. Macaulay said, "Johnny was a great pal of mine. We were like brothers, almost. Everything he likes, I like – only more so. Much more." He pressed forward and touched me all the way down my back, leaning over me. He talked all the time, but he hardly had any breath. You know what he felt like, pressing against me? Like a mad camel. You've seen camels on musth? He put his arms round me and held my breasts tightly; he was just ready to –'

'Don't!' I shouted suddenly. 'Shut up! I don't want to hear about it! I'm going to go out and kill him!' I jumped up.

She said, 'Sit down. I jabbed back with my elbow – hard. He moaned and bent forward. The sweat was shining on his face; those horrible little eyes were dulled like stones; his moustache was wet where he'd licked it; and his mouth was open. But he pressed on again, saying nothing.'

She looked at me and said very quietly, 'Suddenly I was frightened, worse than I've ever been. I opened my mouth to scream, and at that moment Ranjit knocked and came in. He stopped in the doorway, and I broke free from Macaulay. Macaulay turned round slowly. I ran to my chair and sat down, trembling, shivering. I heard Macaulay say, "Got to go. The lines." Then he went.'

'Did Kasel see – anything?' I asked. I couldn't have borne it if Kasel had seen anything.

Victoria raised her eyebrows a little. She said, 'No, Patrick. He didn't see. But he knew. He got me some water. He was blushing. He wanted to report it to Colonel Savage, but –'

'My God, he'd better not!' I shouted. 'I don't want any bloody Wogs mixed up in this.'

'Oh, you don't?' Victoria said. 'Well, that's too bad, because Ranjit *is* mixed up in it, and he's the only one of all of you men who doesn't make me feel like a bitch.'

She took her eyes off my face for the first time. She looked at the sort of beaded screen that hid the empty fireplace, and spoke quite gently, as if it was all over and we were having a chat, an ordinary talk, about a picnic or something. She said, 'I asked him why Colonel Savage called him a depilated Sikh. He told me he was a Sikh by birth. It was very clever of Savage to know that, he said, since he wasn't wearing a beard. That meant he'd renounced his religion. He's an atheist. His mother made him one. We had to talk about something all that time until you came back. His mother says religion is the opiate of the people, the thing that helps keep people in their chains. He lives with her, here in the city. She is a wonderful woman, he says – a widow, of course. Ranjit's a B.A. from Punjab University, you know, and –'

I shouted, 'Do not keep talking about Kasel! Come on. It is time for us to go to the Collector's.'

'All right,' she said. 'But remember, you're not to do anything about Macaulay.'

'We'll see about that,' I said.

She said, 'I've told you, Patrick. I've warned you. Don't say you haven't been warned. No, I'm not coming on your Norton. I have an Army bicycle. I will need it after we're finished there.'

'I'll give you a tow.' She was so worked up about me and Macaulay that I decided I had better not tell anyone after all. It wouldn't be worth it. She got on the push bike. It was a heavy ugly thing, painted dark green and weighing about two maunds – what the Army calls a G.S. bicycle. There was a lever on one handlebar to work the front brake, but the rear brakes worked by back-pedalling. So when Victoria put her hand on my shoulder and I towed her slowly up the Pike she had to lift her feet on to one of the frame members so that the pedals could go round. It was a man's bike, of course. I couldn't help thinking that anyone in front would be able to see half-way up her skirt, and that got me to wondering – had she spoken the truth, the whole truth? Had she led Macaulay on? But it was only because I loved her that I felt so confused and helpless.

So it was just unlucky that as we turned into the Collector's driveway I saw Colonel Savage and Birkhe right under my wheel. I jammed on my brakes, and Savage jumped aside, but Victoria wobbled forward and her bike keeled over and she had to slip off quickly and very awkwardly in that tight skirt.

Savage said, 'That's why they give WAC (I)s khaki safety-first knickers.' He smiled at her, that smile I knew, and it was too much for me.

I jerked the Norton on to its stand and I shouted, 'We have had enough of those kind of jokes, sir! Victoria is under your orders because you were unfair and sent telegrams to your friends in Delhi, but she does not have to be insulted. Even Mrs Fortescue can't order her to stay here and be insulted.'

Savage had stopped smiling and looked at me, his blue eyes going flat and calm.

I said, 'I am going to report something else that happened too. Last night.'

Victoria sighed, and I noticed the Gurkha, Birkhe, standing there. I didn't want any natives mixed up in this, so I asked Savage to send him away. Then I said, 'I am going to make a complaint about last night. It is what happened to Miss Jones. I –'

Savage interrupted very quickly. He said, 'I know. I'm sorry I ever left Miss Jones alone with Ranjit in the office at night. I shouldn't have done it. I'm not used to having women working under me. Was it serious enough for me to take up further, or –?'

I could not believe my ears, and Victoria was staring at him too. My God, I thought, was it really Kasel? What if everything happened just as Victoria said – only the other way round? Macaulay must have reported something to Savage already. If that was true, did it mean that Victoria had been egging Kasel on?

I was dumbfounded, and I know my mouth was hanging open. Savage said, 'But do think seriously before you make an official complaint, Miss Jones. It would not be a small matter – a year or two in prison, at least. If it had been a soldier it would be worse. And as for an officer! My God, an officer would get about ten years and cashiering. So – here, let me wheel your bike.' He took her bicycle, and I began to push the Norton alongside, feeling in a daze. Now he was talking as if it might have been Macaulay after

65

all. 'So,' he said, 'unless it was really serious, please don't tell me any more about it. I'll see that your conditions of work are made safe for you. I'm afraid part of the trouble is that you are such a very beautiful girl – no, please, I'm not trying to insult you – and that's a rare and rather wonderful thing to meet, even for men who haven't just come back from Burma and Malaya and Indonesia. You're five foot eight, aren't you? Five eight and a half? I'll get you a lady's bicycle as soon as I can. And forgive me about the telegram. Mr Taylor says I was unfair, and I expect you feel the same, but please remember I've got a job to do, and five hundred men to look after. It is my duty to them to get the best help I can. Here we are. The Collector wants us to go straight in. After you, Miss Jones. Go ahead, Taylor.'

And then we were inside the Collector's study.

8

FOR a few minutes I couldn't concentrate. I didn't know what to believe about the Kasel business. I tried to catch Victoria's eye, but she did not look at me once, and there was no expression on her face. When she got her note-pad and pencil out I shook my head to try to forget and think of why we'd come here.

Govindaswami and Savage had introduced themselves by then, and Govindaswami was beginning to go over the same story he'd told Lanson, Williams, me, and Victoria the week before. Savage listened without speaking.

Then Savage explained how and why he had positioned his men, and about our patrol in the night. Savage finished by saying, 'So I can keep the line well patrolled. I can destroy any attack in force. But it doesn't look to me as if that's the principal danger. I can't prevent one or two men pulling a rail or loosening a fish-plate in the middle of the night. And it's going to be difficult for me to keep proper military secrecy about the movements of my patrols and other activities. Too many railway people have to know about them.'

'You fear saboteurs, or their collaborators, within the railway organization?' Govindaswami asked.

'Yes. But your police are supposed to keep me informed, aren't they? Meantime I'm going to treat all the railway people with suspicion – except the Anglo-Indians.' It was funny to hear myself talked about like that, especially to an Indian.

The Collector said, 'The present danger is that men whose aims are constitutional may be used by men whose aims are anti-constitutional – the danger that Congress man A gets information and passes it on to Congress men B, C, and D, in order that they may organize a legitimate protest of some kind. Whereupon Congress man D – or Congress-hanger-on D – uses that information to blow up a train.'

'Your innocent Congress man A being secret Congress man Ranjit Singh Kasel, for instance? Or do you think he's D, the wrecker?' Savage said.

'I don't know about him for certain,' Govindaswami said. 'But I do know that the Congress high command has just passed us word, most secretly, that K. P. Roy is certainly somewhere in this province. It might easily have been him you shot at last night.'

Savage said, 'That's the same Roy who went to Japan with Bose in nineteen forty, isn't it?'

Govindaswami said, 'Yes. After that, though, he went to Russia. He left Russia last year.'

Savage said, 'I'll recognize him again if I meet him in the same circumstances. That is, if it was Roy I shot at last night.'

I opened my mouth, ready to say, How could you? It was nothing but a shape, a change of light, that we had seen on the hill outside that village. I was ready to protest that no one could recognize it again. But I held my tongue because Savage's words reminded me of something I had felt out there – that Savage used the darkness the way other people use tools or pens. It wasn't exactly that he could see very well at night, though he could. It was the *using* as an instrument, like a good shikari or a cat burglar or a photographer in a dark room – or a leopard.

Govindaswami said, 'Good. But there's other trouble brewing – a U.R.W.I. strike.'

The Union of Railway Workers of India was an Indian trade union. None of *us* belonged to it, though they kept trying to get us to join. We had our own federation, which covered us, whatever job we were in. Sir Meredith Sullivan was the head of it.

Govindaswami said, 'The union's central committee is meeting in Calcutta now. They've got some genuine grievances. The main one they're concentrating on is that European and Anglo-Indian train crews are excused from duty on shunting and van trains where there is no separate running room for them. That is the case, isn't it, Mr Taylor?'

'We always have been,' I said. 'How can they expect our train crews to pass the night in an Indian running room, among –'

Govindaswami said, 'Well, the U.R.W.I. think you shouldn't be excused any more. You understand, Savage, a problem like that can't be settled out of hand. At least, it can be, but only in one way – by making all running rooms common to all communities. That is a big step, which the Railway Board is not willing to take yet. So this strike is brewing, and I'm trying to find out what is known about it here. The chairman of the union's Bhowani branch is a fellow called Kartar Singh – another Sikh. He's a – what is he, Mr Taylor?'

'A signals fitter,' I said. Kartar Singh was a Bolshie bastard, always making trouble. I knew him.

Savage waited, and Govindaswami said, 'I'd like Miss Jones to talk to Kartar Singh.' His gold tooth glittered when he talked.

'What good's that? He must know she's with the Army,' Savage said.

'Yes. But he also knows that she's a sensible and sympathetic young woman. He's a sensible fellow himself, though he can't often afford to show it, or he'd lose his union position. Do you mind, Miss Jones?'

'I will do my best,' Victoria said, but not very enthusiastically. We all looked at her. I wondered whether she was still thinking of the Kasel business.

Govindaswami stood up. He said to Savage, almost as though he wanted to change the subject, 'I'm afraid we're in for a thin time, Savage.'

Savage stood up. He said, 'In fact, Collector, you suspect there will be dastardly outrages?' He spoke in a funny, precise way.

Govindaswami stroked his chin and said, 'I am sure of it.'

Savage said, 'Govindaswami, you are marvellous.'

Govindaswami said, 'Elementary, my dear Savage. I rely on you, old fellow. The scoundrels will stop at nothing.'

Savage was smiling by then. He said, 'Cheltenham and Balliol?'

Govindaswami said, 'Correct. Wellington and Sandhurst?'

Savage said, 'Correct – but that's not a guess, that's a bloody certainty. I've got to go. You'd better see Kartar Singh right away, Miss Jones.'

'Very good, sir,' she said, and we went out.

As soon as we were outside I said to Victoria, 'What were they talking about at the end there? Why were they speaking in that funny way?'

She looked at me and said, 'It is a joke. An English joke.'

I can see a joke as well as the next man, I hope – in fact I have a jolly good sense of humour – but I didn't see anything funny about it, although I thought for a few moments.

Then I went ahead on the Norton to the station. I wanted to find Kartar Singh before Victoria arrived on her bicycle. Govindaswami hadn't asked me, a railway officer, to speak to the fellow, which was just like his damned nerve, but I was going to be there all the same.

By the time I'd found that Kartar Singh was somewhere round the North Box, Victoria had arrived. I met her on the platform. It was a little after six o'clock; the sun was low and the rails empty and shining. Ninety-Seven Down Express was the next passenger train due, in about twenty minutes. Number 2 platform was already crowded.

I told Victoria where Kartar Singh would be, and I also said, because I was fed up with everything, 'The U.R.W.I. people are always talking of strikes. The Collector has got the wind up, that's all, I think.'

She said, 'Oh?' and stepped down to the footpath to walk along to the North Box. I stepped down after her. She said, 'There's no need for you to come.'

I said, 'He may refuse to answer you. He'll talk to me. He is just a stuck-up coolie.'

She must have seen that I had made up my mind, so we started out. She did not talk at all as we walked up there alongside the batteries of point bars and the sheafs of signal wires and the lamps and the low ground shunt signals. Soon we came to the foot of the tall north gantry and, a few yards after that, to the signal box.

I have been on or near railways all my life, but I hope the time

69

will never come that I will be bored in a signal box. From the windows of Bhowani North Box you can see all the lines and over the platform canopy into the yards. The row of big shiny steel levers stretches along under the front windows, and the block instruments are just above the windows. The lights move on the track-circuiting diagram whenever a train moves about within the station limits, and the telegraph bells ring, *ding-ding*, and you can hear the clank of buffers and smell the engine smoke.

One of the telegraphs was ringing the call-attention beat when I spotted Kartar Singh. He was under the far windows, and I beckoned to him. The signalman took no notice of us. He was busy.

Kartar Singh is stocky and strong and has a thick black beard. He always wears a dark-blue turban, and his legs are short and thick and hairy. His face is broad and usually expressionless.

I told him that the miss-sahiba wanted to speak to him. He looked at Victoria and said, 'What does the lieutenant miss-sahiba want to speak to me about? I am only a coolie.'

He was actually smiling at her – like his damned cheek – and Victoria smiled too and said, 'I'm not really a lieutenant, Kartar. I'm Driver Jones's daughter. You know me, surely?'

'Jones-sahib is a good man and a good driver,' Kartar Singh said.

Victoria said, 'Well, it's about him. About the railway. I'd like to speak to you. Can you come outside a minute? It's very busy in here.'

The telegraph bells kept ringing, and the lights were moving on the diagram. The signalman put his bare foot up against the lever frame and hauled back with all his might with both hands on a lever, and it slammed back.

Kartar Singh said, 'Very well, miss-sahiba,' and followed us down the steep steps to the ground. When we got down Victoria said, 'There's no need for you to stay, Patrick.'

I know what she was thinking – that Kartar Singh didn't like me, and she'd get more out of him if I wasn't there. That's what Govindaswami had thought too, when he didn't ask me to investigate the strike. But they were wrong. Natives like Kartar Singh don't respect you unless you keep them in their place. I wasn't going to leave Victoria alone with that fellow to be insulted.

I said, 'I will stay, Victoria. I have nothing else to do.'

'Very well,' she said. She turned to Kartar Singh. We were standing close together under the north wall of the box. Victoria made a couple of false starts – she didn't know what was the best way to begin – and then she thought, I suppose, that she'd better get straight down to brass tacks. She said, 'Kartar, is there going to be a U.R.W.I. strike here?'

It was twilight then, and the sky was turning grey-blue. The electric lights came on in the station and in the box above us. Kartar looked at her without moving a muscle of his face, and without speaking.

I said, 'Answer the lady!'

Victoria said, 'Patrick, will you please shut up?'

Kartar said to her, 'Why do you want to know particularly? Your father will get paid whether there's a strike or not. They will not lay off the sahib drivers and firemen and guards.'

She said, 'It's not that. You know I'm working for the Army. They're worried in case a strike might lead to violence. They have to be ready to help the police, and you know how unsettled people are everywhere.'

'We in the union will not be violent,' Kartar Singh said. 'But we will not be forced to work, either. That has happened in the past.'

'Yes,' she said, 'but, Kartar, there *may* be violence if there is a strike. You want to help prevent any possibility of that, don't you?'

'Not a bit of it,' I said then. 'Kartar Singh would like to cut everybody's throat, wouldn't you?' I said it with a laugh to show that I was making a joke.

Kartar Singh looked at me and said, 'Some people's throats, yes. Everybody's, no.'

Victoria said, 'Can you tell us about the strike, then? Surely it's not secret.'

'I can't tell you, miss-sahiba.' He looked at her, and she looked at him. Then he looked at me, and then she looked at me. He said, 'We have cause to strike.'

This was too jolly much. I said, 'No, you don't, no cause at all! You are just getting jolly well too big for your boots, that's all.'

Victoria turned to Kartar Singh and said very politely, 'Would you mind waiting here a minute? I'll be right back.'

Kartar Singh nodded. Victoria took my arm and led me a little apart. It was obvious that she had a plan to make him talk. I thought, She will suggest that we take him up the line and then I beat him up until he tells the truth. That was the way to deal with him.

When we got fifty yards or so away from the North Box she said, 'Patrick, I came back from Delhi ready to love you. And I found you were everything I didn't want to be. When I'm in trouble, you don't notice. When I'm happy, you spoil it. When I'm depressed, you are more depressed. When I ask you to do something, you don't do it. When I ask you not to do something, you do it. You allow Colonel Savage to make a fool of me. You think I was necking with Ranjit last night – oh, I know you do, don't try to deny it. And now you're preventing me from doing my work.'

I stammered, 'B-but, Victoria –'

She whispered angrily, 'Don't "but" me, you *fool*! You're a bully, and you're self-satisfied, and – and, oh, you're a bloody chee-chee! Now go away. I don't want to see you again except on duty.'

'But, Victoria –' I said.

She was gone, walking quickly back toward the North Box.

I sat for a long time in the refreshment room, drinking beer. At first I was crying and trying to hide my face by turning my back to the room. It was empty, I think. There may have been someone in there; I can't remember. Victoria and I were going off on separate lines, and we used to have such fun together. I had tried to bring her back to our line, the only main line possible for Anglo-Indians, but she wouldn't come. And I couldn't go where she seemed to want to go.

I drank more beer. With the beer, I began to get angry. She would not come back to me because she had become a fast, loose girl in the Army, that was the truth. She had slept with this Captain Tallent, and she was necking with Macaulay and making eyes at Kasel – a Wog, my God – and she thought *we* were finished. She hated me and did not care what happened to me. I said to myself, My God, I will show her she can't push me around!

That was a time of the evening when, before Victoria came back, I often used to take Rose Mary out for a ride. I left the refreshment room and drove the Norton like hell to Number 4 Collett Road. Rose Mary was in. She was reading, which she never did. It was just as though she'd been waiting for me.

72

BOOK TWO

Victoria Jones

female, twenty-eight, Eurasian, unmarried;
daughter of Thomas Jones, driver,
Delhi Deccan Railway

9

BEFORE going back to Kartar Singh I dried my eyes and blew my nose, but I was not sad. There was nothing to be sad about. I had honestly tried to find in Patrick all the qualities I used to love, and none of them were there. In the old days he was always making jokes, and I was always laughing at them. We would dance together and drink a little and hold hands. I had seen nothing but the good things about him – his bravery, and the way he stuck to things, and the soft heart he was always trying to make out he hadn't got. Then somehow being in the WAC (I) changed everything. I ought to have come back to Bhowani more often, but there'd always been something new and exciting to do instead. Now I had to come back, and all I could see in Patrick were the worst trade-marks of our people – inferiority feelings, resentment, perpetual readiness to be insulted, all the things I was determined to get rid of in myself.

So when I had forced myself to be rude enough to get through his thick skin, I thought, That is over.

There was the job Savage had given me. I pushed Patrick down to the bottom of my mind. The harder I worked, the sooner he would stop being an uncomfortable lump, a small pain, in me.

When I got back Kartar moved a little away from the wall of the signal box. The Indian signalman was leaning out of the end windows above us. The inside lights silhouetted him sharply, for it was dark then. Kartar said in a low voice, 'I have warned all our people to be ready to strike. Those are the orders I have received, and they are secret. Tell the Collector and the colonel-sahib.'

He spoke with some agitation, and I whispered, 'What's the matter? Are you afraid there will be real trouble?'

'Yes. In the yards. It is very bad and difficult,' he said. 'We have a right to strike. We ought to strike. But there are men in this union, and outside it, who will use the strike to do things that are no good for any of us. If I am not their leader someone else will be. Let no word leak out that it was I who warned you. But you understand that it is not certain yet?'

I jerked my head up and back at the signalman, and Kartar said, 'He may suspect I have talked to you about the strike, but he won't *know*. Besides, he does not belong to the union. He will be a dirty blackleg.' He raised his voice and said aggressively, 'No, miss-sahiba, it's no use trying to bribe me. I don't know, and I would not tell you if I did. Tell the military that.'

I took him up quickly and answered as angrily, 'Very well then! You will be responsible for any trouble.' And I walked away from him.

Near the station I slowed down. I found myself thinking of Patrick, and I was crying again. He was *such* a fool, and I understood him so well. I thought of going to find him. He would be in the refreshment room, drinking beer, or perhaps in the Institute.

But I would not go. I had finished that, for the good of both of us.

The news that Kartar had given me ought to be taken to Colonel Savage at once. I couldn't use the telephone, because there would be other people in the Traffic Office. I bicycled up the Pike to the cantonments.

Kabul Lines consists of scattered stone bungalow-barracks and offices, each surrounded by a veranda, the roofs held up by pillars round the outer edges of the verandas. In the battalion office building a Gurkha orderly with a tommy-gun was standing at ease outside the door marked COMMANDING OFFICER. He glanced at my rank badges, told me that the colonel-sahib was in, and stood aside.

I went in, closed the door behind me, and stopped quickly. My heart missed a beat. It was a bare room with a desk and three or four chairs. A naked bulb hung low over the desk on a long flex from the ceiling. There were maps on the walls, and the man looking at one of them was not Colonel Savage but his adjutant, Graham Macaulay.

He turned round, and I moved back half a step. He said in a low voice, 'Sorry about last night. Don't hold it against me.'

I said, 'Where's Colonel Savage?'

'He'll be back in a minute,' he said. 'My office is through there.' There was a door in a partition to his right. 'Yours is there.' He nodded at the opposite wall; there was another door, open, and through it I saw a corner of a small dark room.

He said, 'Am I forgiven? You're so – damn it, you're beautiful. I just forgot myself.'

I said, 'I haven't forgiven you, and I won't forget.'

I looked at him, and he still gave me the creeps, but I didn't hate him. In a kind of unpleasant way I was grateful to him, because he'd set me free. I have always admired the English and, like the rest of us, pretended to be more English than I am. When Macaulay tried to rape me he broke that chain. I was free. If I wanted to like Ranjit, I could. If I wanted to turn toward India, my home, I could.

He said, '*Shhh!* Well, you must expect some male admiration, with those eyes. I just can't help liking you, you know –'

Colonel Savage came in through Macaulay's office. He glanced from Macaulay to me. Macaulay had come quite close to me while he talked. Honestly, I think he was sure that I would have let him do what he wanted to the night before, if only Ranjit had not interrupted him.

Colonel Savage said, 'All right, Macaulay.' Macaulay went back to his office. Colonel Savage said coldly to me, '*That*'s your office, Miss Jones. What did you find out?'

He thought that I had been encouraging Macaulay again. His nostrils were pinched with anger, but I didn't care by then. I told him what Kartar Singh had said. When I had finished he said in the same hard voice, 'Good. I'll talk to the Collector. I'll let you know if we decide to move any troops. We probably won't just yet. Your father has been kind enough to ask me down to your house tomorrow evening. He is also going to invite Mr Taylor. I am telling you in case you decide to be out at that time.'

He was making me angry in spite of myself. I said, 'When did you see Pater – my father – sir? He's not in today.' It was a foolish thing to ask.

'He takes Ninety-Eight Up through, doesn't he?' Colonel Savage said sarcastically. 'I saw him on the platform – at sixteen-forty-four hours, if you want to know the exact time. And if you want to know what I was doing, I was just hanging idly around. And when I left the station I went straight to the Collector's bungalow, where Taylor nearly ran over me, and you fell into my arms. You may go now. There is a lady's bicycle waiting for you outside, complete with lamp, pump, and tool-bag.'

I saluted and went out, feeling that my face had been drained of blood and was sallow and pale brown and ugly. But there was still the undercurrent of thankfulness, of release. Macaulay had freed me; now Savage was pushing me farther away – from the English, from Patrick, from all the stagnation of the past.

At home, exasperated and tired and a little lightheaded, I was pleased to see that Rose Mary was not in. At that time of the evening Mater would usually be sitting in the back of a certain shop in the Little Bazaar, chewing betel nut and gossiping with the shopkeeper's wife. She only went there when Pater was on a train. It was an open secret that she did go, though, and Pater was probably the only person in the Old Lines who didn't know it. (The Railway Lines, where the bungalows of the railway people are, are called the Old Lines because they are built on the site of a military cantonment that was destroyed in the Mutiny.)

I ate a cold supper quickly and went into the parlour to read. But I could not read. On the page I saw faces instead of words. Inside myself I felt the lump that represented Patrick, and that made me think of all the people who seemed determined to drag me down. I brought their faces up, one by one, into my mind, and tried to see a single expression that was not set against me. I got up, switched off the light, sat down again, and closed my eyes.

Colonel Savage. He was hard, cruel, rude, self-willed. I did not really understand why he made himself so unpleasant to me. But he did, and it helped. I had noticed three small round patches, near the neck, in the bush shirt he'd been wearing that evening. The ugly white light in his office showed them up on the faded green of the material. And he had a puckered dead-white scar in his neck a little higher up, on the left – bullet wounds from a machine-gun, I supposed. He was lucky to be alive.

Macaulay. It is difficult to describe how 'bad' he felt. Not that I do not like to be admired by men, but he was like a rubber lizard that came crawling through slime to get at me.

Rose Mary. We were sisters, but no more. She had always been man-crazy, and from the way she spoke to Patrick, and Patrick's embarrassment, I was sure she'd slept with him while I was away. I didn't blame Patrick, somehow, but it made everything Rose Mary did aggravate me even more than it used to. For instance, when the telegram came from G.H.Q. that Monday morning, we were both still in bed. Our rooms were next to each other, and we shared the same bathroom. As soon as Nathoo had given me the telegram, Rose Mary came into my room. Her hair was in curl papers, and her face was wet with perspiration. When she'd read the telegram she was very anxious that I should somehow get out of the job. I knew she wanted to keep me away from working with Patrick. That was probably the main reason, foolish though it was, that I did not pretend to be sick.

I wondered where Rose Mary was. I think I knew, but to myself I pretended to be wondering.

Patrick. I tried not to think about him, but he came up. He had a loud voice. Sometimes he acted like a bully, sometimes like a soft-hearted old woman. He thought he was a good driver, but he just held that precious Norton on the road by sheer strength, which I know is not right. He wore his topi all day and most of the night, to show he was not an Indian.

And then I thought, he loves me, and I've known him since I was a little girl. I know him best of anyone in the world.

Quickly I thought of Ranjit – Ranjit Singh Kasel. Ranjit was sure the Congress had had nothing to do with the derailment at Pathoda. Why was he sure? Was he secretly a Congress man himself? I was beginning to sympathize with anyone who was against the British, and Congress was certainly against the British. Ranjit wasn't angry with Savage or the soldiers. He had said, that night after Macaulay had gone, that Colonel Savage was only a representative of the system – imperialistic capitalism. He talked earnestly, and all the time he quoted his mother. He knew about our troubles over St Thomas's School. He looked at me with his large solemn eyes, and I thought he was weighing me up. Would I snap at him if he gave his honest opinions? Was I interested enough to listen? He must have taken confidence, because what he said then about our situation, the position of the Anglo-Indians, was exactly what I'd come to believe myself since my return to Bhowani.

He was upset when I asked him why he didn't wear the Sikh bangle, why he'd cut his hair, why he was an atheist. Atheists are very rare in India. He didn't really explain; he only defended his mother's point of view. He was a very sweet-tempered, kind man. If he kissed a girl, I thought, the girl would feel sweet and dedicated, but I did not think she would be excited. I wondered.

Sitting in the darkened parlour, I tried to imagine that the light was on and Ranjit was sitting there with me. What would we talk about? Dancing? He couldn't dance, not our way. Music? His music was so different that it sounded to us like cats fighting. Food? Houses? Clothes? Drinks? There would be nothing for us to talk about, at that time, except serious things like politics and strikes and the future of mankind.

But now I couldn't talk to the English or to my own people about anything except clothes and drinks and dancing.

I opened my eyes slowly. The front-door latch clicked with a tiny noise. Through the wall I heard fast, light breathing in the passage. I sat still, my hands gripping the arms of the chair. I heard Rose Mary's whisper. 'She's not in. I've looked.'

But hadn't they seen my bicycle? No. I'd put it away at the back, and they hadn't enough sense left to look for it there. They were thinking of other things. Patrick gasped 'Quick, oh, quick!'

The words and the gasping were like a trigger. Johnny Tallent had said that to me, the same way, the same voice, in another dark passage as we struggled to another dark bedroom. I had had even less excuse. I had not been drinking, while Rose Mary and Patrick had. But the trigger clicked in me, and I stood up, my legs stiff and trembling, my eyes dry, and my hands like claws, the nails piercing into the palms.

I heard them shuffling along the passage and thought, Why do I care? I heard Rose Mary's door squeak, and I thought, Why won't Patrick disappear from inside me? I heard the bed creak to welcome them on to it.

I stood, shaking, in the middle of the room and searched round in the darkness for something – a knife, a club. There was nothing. And yet I could still reason. I thought, I can make this another break, another horror like Macaulay's, which will free me from another set of chains. And yet truly I was helpless. What I did I had to do.

I slipped out into the passage, making no sound, and went silently to Rose Mary's door. They wouldn't have heard me then if I'd fired a pistol. I waited, listening, shaking, writhing, until the worst moment, the best; then I smashed the door open and switched on the light and ran in, screaming at them.

IN that moment I had gone back where we came from, which was the Indian loose women of a hundred years ago, and I had taken Rose Mary and Patrick with me. I heard the words pouring out of my mouth, out of my heart – a flood of Hindustani and our cheechee English, thick with language that I have tried all my life to believe I never knew. I saw those two locked together like animals, going red and white by turns, and I knew that I, no less than they and the whole incident, was disgusting and degraded. It was the worst side, not of our blood but of our circumstances, and I knew I had not reached any freedom or broken any chains by wallowing in that filth.

The next evening I saw their half-naked bodies still in my mind, though actually they were fully dressed and sitting together on the sofa opposite Colonel Savage. Mater was to my right, perched on the edge of the small hard chair. Pater stood in front of the firescreen. They were all, except me, dressed in their best. I had deliberately not changed out of uniform. Pater's blue serge suit shone because it was old, and his face shone because the night was hot. It was eight o'clock, and a couple of heavy showers had cooled the air but made it more humid.

Colonel Savage had just arrived. I saw with annoyance that he had changed into his pre-war khaki drill trousers and tunic, with which he wore a shirt, collar, and tie. I had expected him to think that any old clothes were good enough for an engine-driver's house.

Pater gave him a foaming glass of warm beer and at once began to ask him about his medals. The first one was the M.C. with two bars. I know you can get the M.C. only for bravery in actual fighting against the enemy. It is not like the D.S.O., which your soldiers can win for you. Colonel Savage told Pater what the medals were, but when Pater asked how he had got them he said, 'Fighting, Mr Jones. Look, I don't know about you, but I'm hot as hell. Would you and your wife mind if I took off my coat and tie?' He mopped his brow with a big khaki handkerchief and smiled at Mater. She smiled back, like a wooden image, but said nothing.

Pater said, 'My, of course not, Colonel. Take off your coat. I think I will join you.'

Colonel Savage praised the beer. Then he raised his glass and pointed at the big picture of my great-grandfather and said to Pater, 'Is that your grandfather?' So Pater talked happily about the Sergeant, as we usually called the man in the picture.

Mater sat quiet, apparently seeing nothing, but after a few minutes she said, 'Father, you are sweating through your best shirt.' Pater interrupted himself and looked at her with disgust, and then tried to continue what he had been saying about the Sergeant. But he could not. I could see very clearly then that really he was disgusted with himself for marrying her and sleeping with her. He was three-quarters English; she was one-quarter.

Colonel Savage said, 'Do you mind if I smoke one of these?' He pulled out his cigar-case. 'Perhaps you don't care for the smell, Miss Jones. They are rather strong.' He glanced at Rose Mary, but not at me.

Rose Mary said, 'Oh, no, Colonel Savage, I *love* the smell of cigars. It is so rich.'

'Trichinopolies. About eight annas each, Miss Jones, that's all, I'm afraid.' He offered the case to Patrick and Pater, who both accepted. When his cheroot was drawing well he nodded at the picture of the Sergeant again and said, 'He must have been a fine man. You know, I wouldn't be surprised if he and my great-grandfather hadn't met in these very parts.'

'What a surprise!' Pater said. 'When could that have been?'

'The Mutiny,' Colonel Savage said. I could not honestly make out whether he was being nice to them as a sort of joke, something he could describe and laugh at when he got back to the mess, or whether he was really pleased to be there with them. He made no attempt to be nice to me.

Pater said, 'Ah, the Mutiny was a bad time. We learned our lesson then, Colonel, didn't we? You can never trust the niggers.' Pater shook his head and puffed deeply at the cigar. He was very happy.

Some words are like goads. In the old days it hurt me to hear such words as 'cheechee' or 'blacky-white'. In the last year, and particularly in the last week, it had become increasingly painful to me to hear 'Wog' or 'nigger' or even 'native'.

Colonel Savage said, 'In some ways the present situation is rather like eighteen fifty-seven.'

Pater said, 'You mean there is going to be another mutiny, Colonel? Don't say it – my God, no, don't say that!'

'There won't be another mutiny,' Colonel Savage said confidently. 'But change is in the air. People are restive.'

Here was another goad – for Patrick this time. Even before Savage had finished speaking I turned toward Patrick, hoping he wouldn't make a fool of himself, but knowing he would burst out with something.

Patrick said, 'Everyone is always saying that. But nothing happens. Nothing will ever happen.' I think that he had already drunk a lot of beer to give himself the courage to face me.

Colonel Savage said politely, 'In many ways I hope you're right. I'm not sure that I want any change, and I certainly don't want it to be the cause of fighting, or to be caused by fighting. I don't want to fight any more just yet.'

The light shone full on his long row of medal ribbons. Rose Mary asked him whether he liked fighting. Rose Mary had a trick, which she thought attracted men, of sometimes speaking very hesitantly and coyly, as though she was a little girl of eight.

Colonel Savage laughed quite naturally. He said, 'On the whole I do like fighting. But not this week.'

'Oooh, you *like* it!' Rose Mary squealed. 'You like killing people? I think you must be a very dangerous man, Colonel.'

Pater smiled fondly at her and at me, to see us both here talking freely with an English lieutenant-colonel. Patrick poured himself more beer, spilling some on the bearskin. Colonel Savage said, 'It's too difficult to explain unless you've been to the wars, and heaven knows I –'

Patrick said loudly, 'Everybody couldn't go to the wars.'

Colonel Savage said, 'Of course not. I was only –'

'The railways had to be run!' Patrick said. I think it had been a long time since anyone had interrupted Colonel Savage like that while he was speaking. Patrick got louder and more excited. He said, 'It was essential work. Four times I tried to enlist, but they would not take me. They said –'

Then Pater interrupted him by saying, 'They would not make

you a captain like you deserve, you mean!' Pater meant to be unpleasant. He did not really like Patrick.

'That's not the point, Mr Jones,' Patrick shouted. 'They said I was essential! I had to stay and run the railway. There were no medals for that, though there was danger too. There were strikes and derailments sometimes, and men burned alive on the footplate in forty-two. There was plenty of danger on the railways, Colonel Savage, I tell you, but there were no medals.'

Colonel Savage kept calm, but Patrick's shouting and excitement had infected Pater, so that now he was yelling. 'Did they derail your desk, then, man!' he yelled. '*I* was on the bloody footplate in forty-two, not you. You were making out your bloody graphs!'

I couldn't stand it. I said, 'There is no need to shout, Pater.' I tried hard to speak softly, but I know that I was shouting.

Patrick took no notice of my warning. I had tried to tell him, to tell all of them, that we were behaving just the way Anglo-Indians are supposed to behave in the worst stories against us; but he blundered on. He shouted, 'There was danger everywhere. I say the colonel does not know what it is like to be in danger *all* the time from people all round you, not knowing whether the police even would come in and cut our throats in bed, and having no guns to look after ourselves with. Nothing! I bet the Gurkhas would not like that, eh, Colonel?'

It was strange, since I understood Colonel Savage so little, and cared less, that I knew immediately that he would retaliate when Patrick mentioned the Gurkhas. His mouth relaxed, he leaned back more comfortably in his chair, and he said lazily, 'Oh, the Army had that kind of danger too, you know. I hear that a good many chaps were evacuated with shellshock after three weeks in Calcutta – taxis backfiring on Chowringhee, Dakotas buzzing the Great Eastern, military policemen with dirty great guns in their holsters – *loaded* guns – American Pfcs with ten-ton lorries and six rows of gongs. I tell you, it was really terrifying.'

The telephone began to ring. I had not spoken to Patrick since the night before, but now I saw a chance to stop this unpleasant argument, and I said quickly, 'Go and answer it, Patrick.'

He stood up, swaying a little and glowering at Colonel Savage. He muttered something under his breath, but he went out. He came back in a minute and said, 'Mr Jones. For you. Someone wants to know where that fellow Wayali is.'

'The cleaner?' Pater said, shuffling to the door. '*I* don't know.' Soon he came back, shaking his head.

Colonel Savage said cheerfully, 'Mr Jones, I'd very much like to have a ride with you on the footplate one day. Do you think that would be difficult to arrange?'

'You would really like that, Colonel?' Pater said, so pleased and surprised, though why he should have been I don't know. I've never met a man who didn't want to ride on the footplate. Pater said, 'It is very dirty. On the branch line, now, it would be easy to arrange. The traffic officers never go to see what is happening there.'

'Oh, yes, we do,' Patrick muttered sullenly.

Pater said, 'But on the main line it is more strict. It has to be, you understand. And I only run on the main line. I am a mail and express driver. I am on Bhowani Number One Roster.'

'What does that mean?' Colonel Savage asked. He got it in before Patrick had time to open his mouth to start the old argument.

Rose Mary said eagerly, 'It means that he is one of the very senior drivers, Colonel. A roster is what we call, on the Delhi Deccan Railway, four or five drivers who drive certain trains. Bhowani Number One Roster takes the top trains – one man today, another tomorrow, the third the next day, and then the day after that the first man again. It is quite simple.'

Pater said, 'She has made it as clear as mud, eh, Colonel?' He pinched Rose Mary happily on the cheek. He went on. 'It is like this, Colonel ...'

If Colonel Savage understood what Pater then told him, he was a very clever man. Pater rattled off numbers and figures and mileages and times like a machine gun. He was just beginning to give Colonel Savage a *viva voce* examination – 'What time did I get in today, then, Colonel, and where from and on what train?' – when the telephone bell began to ring again.

Pater said crossly, 'I don't know what is the matter with that thing tonight!' He went out. We sat in silence until he came back. He said, 'This time it is the sheds, looking for my fireman. He is probably drunk in the bazaar. You see, Colonel, he is a Number-

85

One-Roster fireman and does all my trains with me. My trains –
the mails and expresses – are taken by XB or XC locomotives.
They are –'

Rose Mary was getting impatient. She never liked to stick to
one thing for long. Besides, Pater had taken the limelight away
from her. She interrupted. 'Pater, I have just thought of a *wonderful* idea! All-India Radio is broadcasting a concert of hot jazz
music. Why can't we dance? I *love* to dance. Do you like to dance,
Colonel?'

'I'm very fond of dancing,' Colonel Savage said.

'In here?' Pater said. He wasn't sure about it, but he was
pleased that Rose Mary should be so modern and go-ahead.

Rose Mary said, 'Of course, Pater. We can push the chairs
back. Patrick, help me with the rug.'

She turned up the wireless and pirouetted once or twice in the
middle of the floor. Colonel Savage put his cigar carefully in the
ashtray on the mantelpiece and bowed in front of her. He said,
'May I have the honour of this dance, Miss Jones?'

I got up quickly to go out. Colonel Savage was making fools of
us because he was that kind of man. We were making fools of
ourselves because we had to. Before I reached the door Pater
called to me, 'Hey, Victoria, where are you going?'

'The bathroom,' I said, and went out.

I didn't go to the bathroom. I sat in the chair in front of my
dressing-table, feeling unhappy. The loud, jerky music shook the
whole house. Patrick and Rose Mary had been on her bed just
through the wall I was staring at. And who was to blame for that?
Not Rose Mary. She was only a silly, scheming, promiscuous
cheechee. Not Patrick – no, not him. That left only myself.

BLAH blah blah, I said angrily to myself, like the trumpet on
the radio. It was the American, Louis Prima – a wild, hiccupping,
screaming noise. Johnny Tallent used to play that record to me.
But how could anyone dance to it? I went back to the parlour
before Pater could send Mater to come and fetch me.

Rose Mary and Colonel Savage were still dancing together.
They jigged like mad people on the little square of clear floor.
How foolish, how ridiculous Colonel Savage looked! Rose Mary's
behind bounced, her thin legs jerked, her breasts bounced, her high
heels tapped. It was nice to think how unattractive they looked.

Pater shouted to me, 'You dance with Patrick, Victoria.'

'I don't feel like dancing,' I said, and Patrick said the same thing at the same time.

'What is the matter with you tonight, girl?' Pater asked me crossly. I saw that Colonel Savage and Rose Mary had heard what I said. Rose Mary was smiling. Pater said to me, 'You have been behaving very badly.'

The telephone bell began to ring. I said quickly, 'I'll go.'

Macaulay was on the line. He said, 'Miss Jones? Miss Victoria Jones? Could I speak to the colonel, please? He's with you, isn't he?'

'Yes. I'll get him,' I said.

'Is he behaving himself? Don't get taken in by that crown and pip, Victoria, he's –'

I put the phone down on the table, went back to the parlour, and told Colonel Savage. He excused himself and went out. When he had gone, Pater whispered irritably, 'Turn that thing down, Rose Mary. How can the colonel hear himself speak?' Rose Mary shrugged and turned it down. We all sat for a few minutes. Pater stared from Rose Mary to me and back again, and then at Patrick. He muttered, 'What is the matter with all of you tonight? Please behave better in front of my guest.' No one answered him. We could hear the murmur of Colonel Savage's voice.

Colonel Savage came in. He said, 'I think that explains the mystery of the disappearing cleaners and firemen, Mr Jones.'

'Why, what is it, Colonel?' Pater asked.

'A strike,' Colonel Savage said. 'It began at eight o'clock. All U.R.W.I. members. I'm afraid I'll have to go back to the Lines. Miss Victoria had better come along with me.'

Pater banged his glass down on the mantelpiece. He cried, 'Oh, that is too bad of them to strike just when we were having such a good time.' The wireless squeaked rhythmically. I went and fetched my handbag. When I came back Colonel Savage gathered up his tunic and tie and said, 'I've got the jeep here; you needn't worry about your bicycle.'

He thanked Pater and Mater nicely, as though he meant it, and in a couple of minutes we were driving fast up the Pike. It is less than half a mile to the turning where the road to the station leads off on the right, but in that half-mile Patrick overtook us. His headlight bored up behind us, he hooted noisily, and the Norton leaped past us, making a loud shattering noise from its exhaust. As soon as he had passed, he had to swing wildly to take the corner.

Colonel Savage muttered, 'Bloody fool,' and drove straight on up the Pike. At the battalion offices he told me to keep in close touch with Patrick and the Railway Traffic Office. He ordered me to find out particularly what trains were likely to be held up in the district, where they would be held, and what they contained.

I picked up the field telephone as soon as I had sat down, called Patrick, and gave him the message. I thought of calling him 'Mr Taylor', but it sounded silly. I could be just as cold with 'Patrick'.

Patrick knew nothing yet. The district staff were all busy trying to find exactly who had walked off their jobs. There would be a conference of non-striking traffic personnel – all the Anglo-Indians and about half the Indians – later in the night. 'Don't pester me,' he shouted at last, and hung up.

The battalion offices had come alive. They throbbed quietly, like an aeroplane waiting to taxi out on to the runway. People came and went in Savage's office next door. Twice he called me in to hear and note down orders to troops. A platoon had already gone to the yards and was in bivouac there. A night patrol had gone out. The battle radio sets were in operation. I had felt sleepy, but I began to wake up. Colonel Savage's little personal orderly, Birkhe, brought me tea – sweet milky tea with pepper in it. He was a boy of about eighteen, slender above the waist, sturdy below, and his skin was no browner than mine. The telephones buzzed and rang all the time in the adjutant's office. The *peep-peep* whistling of the radio, like birds, sounded in every corner of the offices.

Colonel Savage called me. I went in with my notebook and pencil ready. Major Dickson, the second-in-command, was there, and Macaulay. Major Dickson was a heavy, stolid man. I had known his wife in Delhi, but I did not see any reason to tell him that. Colonel Savage had lit a cheroot. I thought he was less tense than usual.

He said, '*Le ballon, il ascend*. This has just been deciphered.' He took up a message from his desk. 'This is from Army through Kishanpur Sub-Area. Most immediate and top secret. Some Royal Indian Navy ships at Bombay and Karachi in state of

88

mutiny. Ratings have ordered all officers, both Indian and British, overside. No violence reported yet ... Now we know what K. P. Roy has been rehearsing for. And what the people behind the strike were waiting for.'

He put the message down and looked round at the three of us. Dickson's forehead puckered like a bloodhound's. He said, 'H'm. Er. That's serious, sir.'

'Yes. We've got to make sure the Collector knows,' Colonel Savage said. 'I'll bet he doesn't. You go and tell him, Henry. Take the message – here – and tell him I'll be coming round as soon as I'm free. That oughtn't to be long.'

'H'm. All right, sir. You don't want to change any of the orders to the companies?' Dickson said.

Colonel Savage shook his head. Dickson saluted and went out. For a minute we were silent, thinking our thoughts. For Colonel Savage this would be another Mutiny. He would be thinking how to destroy it before it turned into something as bad as 1857. He would have read all about that in school – I certainly had. A few weeks before, I would have been thinking the same way, from my point of view as a woman and an Anglo-Indian. Now the news, for all its horror and all its implications, was more of a bitter disappointment than anything else to me. It refastened the chains that had been breaking and falling all round me. If the Indians rose against the English I could not be free, because they would count us Anglo-Indians as we counted ourselves – among the English.

Then the tension and seriousness was broken by a brief incident that was really ridiculously funny, and very typical of the Army. After it, I understood better how soldiers don't go mad in wars.

Major Dickson came back, almost hurrying, and said, 'The brigadier's here, sir. At least, I think that's who it must be.'

'Kishanpur Sub-Area?' Colonel Savage said quickly. 'Old People-Psmythe?'

'Yes, sir.'

Colonel Savage said, 'Okay. You go out that way. I'll make my obeisances.' Major Dickson went out.

The orderly-of-the-day marched in, saluted, and said, '*Briga-dier-sahib ayo.*' Over his head I saw the top of an immensely tall thin man. The man came forward, and I saw that he was wearing polo boots, breeches, and a pinkish shirt. We saluted. He wore no medal ribbons and no rank badges. He was swinging a short cane in his hand. His hair was silver-grey, curled, and very long. First he bowed to me, then he shook the others' hands. He did it like those courtiers in knee-breeches in old pictures.

'Savage?' he said. 'I'm Nigel ffoulkes-Jones. I hate bein' called "sir". Been away from Kishanpur, buyin' carpets. Rodney, isn't it? Everything all right, Rodney? I don't believe in worryin' people. I have a great deal to do, and I'm sure you have. We're all grown up, aren't we, even though we do have to keep it a secret from the Army, eh?'

Colonel Savage said, 'All quiet here, Nigel. Well, there's a little railway strike and a small naval mutiny, but everything's in hand. Do you want us to carry on, or do you have an Internal Security scheme you'd prefer us to join?'

The brigadier said, 'Carry on, Rodney, carry on by all means. I've got that big record office to look after, and they take up all my time. Very intelligent young men they are, really. You must come over and spend a week-end with us. I've started an art class.'

'Life studies?' Colonel Savage said.

The brigadier shook his finger and said, 'Ah, Rodney, I see you have a coarse mind. No, just an introduction to modernism. And we have a Gourmets' Society, and I've lured an Alsatian chef into the club. As a matter of fact I manoeuvred him out of an internees' camp. Do bring the young lady when you come. What is your name, my dear?' He bowed to me again.

I tried to find the nerve to answer, Call me Victoria, Nigel; because I was enjoying myself. But if I shared a joke with Colonel Savage I would be going back where I had come from. I said, 'WAC-seven-four-six, Subaltern Victoria Jones, sir.'

The brigadier put his hands to his thin, fine-boned head. 'Oh, this Army!' he cried. 'Well, you must come too, Victoria. Now, Rodney, I must be going. No, no, I've had a meal, thank you so much all the same.'

Colonel Savage said, 'I'll keep you informed, Nigel.'

The brigadier said, 'That would be nice, Rodney. Tell it all to Reggie. He's my staff captain. Ask Reggie for anything you want.

A most charming young man. No, please don't bother to come out, I can see you're busy. Good night, good night, Victoria.'

He wandered out. Colonel Savage sat down slowly and began to laugh without making a sound. I was angry with myself for standing there like a dummy. Colonel Savage would think I had as little sense of humour as poor Patrick. It took an effort to remind myself that I didn't care what Colonel Savage thought.

Colonel Savage said, 'Brigadier N. F. Q. St D. ffoulkes-Jones, M.B.E. – and that's the most unkindest cut of all.'

'What was his regiment, sir?' Macaulay asked politely.

'Need you ask?' Colonel Savage said. 'Probyn's. Ah well, it's a relief really. He hasn't got any other troops in the sub-area, just that record office and an Army school or two, and Kishanpur's nearly fifty miles away. I'd much rather have him than one of those keen G.S. type of armchair brigadiers who'd hang round my neck and try to command my battalion for me. Show some of those people a real soldier, and they think they're Napoleon. We'll go over to the Collector's as soon as Major Dickson comes back, Miss Jones.'

Now the mutiny and the strike were on us again, but the brigadier had done something useful. He had helped me, at any rate, to keep fairly calm from then on. If he could go on worrying about his Alsatian chef and his art classes, surely I need not get into a panic over my own problems.

An orderly came in with a message. Colonel Savage stood up, reaching for his hat. He said, 'We're in action on the Karode bridge. An attempt to blow it up, apparently. Kulbahadur reports that he opened fire – too soon, of course, so he didn't get any-body. He's an impatient little devil. No damage to the bridge as far as he knows. Karode's to the south. Miss Jones, ring up Tay-lor and find out what trains are held up north of here, and what's in them. Goods trains.'

I saluted, hurried out, and called Patrick on the field telephone. Patrick shouted that at Lidhganj there was a coal train over-lapping the short stretch of double track there, and so blocking movement in either direction. A relief driver was going out to it. Lidhganj was two stations south of Karode, where the troops were at the bridge. Then to the north there was a goods train at

Malra on the main line. Malra had a long siding, so the train did not block the line.

'What's in that one?' I asked Patrick.

'How the hell should I know?' he shouted. 'It will take me hours to find out what is in every wagon. I am too busy.'

Savage was beside me again. He could hear what Patrick said. He said, 'Are there any arms, ammunition, or explosives on that train? That's what I want to know.'

I repeated the question to Patrick. He shouted, 'I tell you I don't know.'

Colonel Savage said, 'Tell him to find out.'

I said, 'It will take time, sir. He will have to telegraph the main offices, and they will have to ask perhaps fifteen stations.'

Colonel Savage said, 'Tell him to get started. Macaulay!' Macaulay came running. Colonel Savage said, 'Get on to the Malra bridge guard and tell them to send a section at once to guard a goods train which is now in Malra station, until further orders. Report to me when they've acknowledged the orders. To-morrow, send an officer out at first light to see what's in the train.'

Macaulay said, 'Yes, sir,' and hurried out.

Colonel Savage and I went to the signal office. The clerks were deciphering a message, and we waited till it was ready. It said:

MOST IMMEDIATE AND TOP SECRET. NEWS OF THE NAVAL MUTINIES IS ALREADY KNOWN ALL OVER BOMBAY. PRESUMABLY ALSO IN OTHER MAIN CENTRES OF POPULATION. BOMBAY CITY TENSE. ALL LEAVE CANCELLED IN SOUTHERN ARMY. ALL LEAVE TO BOMBAY CANCELLED FOR OTHER ARMIES AND COMMANDS.

Colonel Savage took the message, and we got into his jeep. Birkhe hopped into the back seat. The Collector's bungalow was only a couple of hundred yards away across the Pike, but we drove to it, and a second jeep followed us. That one contained a big radio set and two signallers, as well as the driver.

In the Collector's study I was astonished to see Ranjit Singh Kasel. I wondered whether he was being bullied about his supposed Congress membership. I smiled at him because I did not want him to think I was against him.

The Collector said, 'Thank you for sending Major Dickson

round, Savage. I haven't heard anything from my own people yet.'

Colonel Savage said, 'Is the news on the wireless, the ordinary news service?'

The Collector said, 'No. They must be censoring it for the time being. Your adjutant has just told me about the attempt on the Karode bridge. This is it, I imagine, the big trouble the government have been waiting for.'

Colonel Savage said, 'Yes. Who do you think's responsible for the bridge business?'

The Collector said, 'George Lanson will be on his way to investigate in ten minutes. You remember him – the Deputy Superintendent of Police.' He turned to Ranjit. 'You haven't heard of any violent revolutionaries or nihilists hiding in these parts, have you, Ranjit?'

Ranjit muttered, 'No. I have not.'

The Collector said to Colonel Savage, 'I had asked Ranjit to come and talk to me about the strike situation, but now I think we can deal with both things at once. What do you imagine the Railway Board will do to keep the trains running, Ranjit?'

I could tell from his face that Ranjit inwardly seethed with excitement. His eyes were large, and he had difficulty in standing still in one place. He said, 'If it was just the strike, I think they would not do anything special, Mr Govindaswami. There are enough non-strikers to keep a skeleton service going. But now, with the R.I.N. mutiny, I do not know. We ought to run pilot engines in front of the trains. There are also armoured wagons with machine-guns manned by the Europeans and Anglo-Indians of the Auxiliary Force. But there will hardly be enough non-strikers to do any of that. Will the government be wanting to send many troop trains through?'

'I don't think so,' Colonel Savage said. 'They can fly troops into Bombay and Karachi if they want to. There's plenty of armour in Southern Army that can get to Bombay by road. There's armour near Karachi. There must be a Royal Navy cruiser in Trincomalee that can come up and blow those R.I.N. sloops out of the water if it becomes necessary.'

Ranjit's eyes grew bigger and sadder while Colonel Savage was speaking.

'I don't think the government will ask help from the Royal Navy,' the Collector said. 'I think, as far as possible, they will use only Indian troops.'

'There may be some troop trains, though,' Colonel Savage said. 'But I don't suppose they'll be anything to do with the mutiny. There are battalions and service units being disbanded every day, and British troops are being sent back to England by the shipload.'

The Collector said, 'Our main problem here is going to be the reaction of the civil population – and of the Indian Army. You realize that there are people about who want this to develop into a blood bath, another Great Mutiny? Another eighteen fifty-seven?'

Colonel Savage said, 'God help us all if they succeed.'

I got an idea that they were speaking like that for Ranjit's benefit. It was not quite the way they had talked to each other before.

'God help us all, especially the Indian National Congress,' the Collector said slowly. 'I don't think there's much else we can do tonight. Ranjit, do you know if the news of the R.I.N. mutinies has got up here yet?'

Ranjit hesitated so that we all noticed it, and then answered, 'Yes. I heard it before I came here.'

'From whom?' the Collector snapped quickly.

'A shopkeeper,' Ranjit said unhappily, 'someone in the street. I did not know him.'

'I see,' the Collector said. After a while he spread his hand in a very Indian gesture and added, 'Lanson has a few extra police out, and my personal spy ring is in operation.' He smiled a queer smile. 'I'll see you in the morning, Savage. I'll come to your office.'

When we were outside, Colonel Savage said, 'Macaulay hasn't rung up yet about the goods train at Malra. I've got to go and find out. I'll walk across.' He told Birkhe to drive Ranjit and me wherever we wanted to go, and then left us.

'I have to go to the station, please,' Ranjit said, and we went there first. He said nothing on the way; he sat in the back seat, and I could hear him shuffling his feet on the floor and tapping his fingers on the side of the jeep. Before leaving him at the station I felt I must say something to him, because he was obviously very upset. I said, 'It's bad news, isn't it? What do you think's going to happen?'

'I don't know, Miss Jones,' he answered, while Birkhe sat quietly in the driver's seat beside me. I wondered whether Birkhe understood any English, but I didn't care. Ranjit said, 'I can tell you, if the British murder those sailors, who are only protesting, there will be trouble everywhere – bad, serious trouble. There are people who will not put up with it any more. There are leaders who know how to make our protests effective.'

We drove away then and left him standing there, looking thin and unhappy under the lights in the station yard.

In bed I lay awake a long time, listening, wondering whether I would hear the growl of crowds, or shots, or the awful clanging of a derailed train. Pater might be driving the first train to reach the break. I saw a great engine rolling, plunging down the embankment. I heard the splintering and grinding and breaking and tinkling, and a scream from a hundred men and women, but all that was only a background to the roar of superheated steam filling the overturned cab where Pater was. Or was it Patrick? I could not see; he was huddled there with his arms across his face. It was one of us, though, in a topi.

In fact I heard none of those things, only the ordinary sounds of the night; yet I imagined there was something different, something urgent, about those sounds on that night. Anxiety prevented me from sleeping except in fits and starts.

At four o'clock in the morning I awoke with a jump. I heard a steady rumbling noise and soon made out what it was. It was the faint thunder of aircraft high in the sky. I lay awake for half an hour, listening, as they passed up there from north to south. They were going to Bombay.

At five o'clock I remembered Colonel Savage saying confidently, earlier that very night, 'There will be no mutiny.' That made me feel better. I would remember that. I would use it one day, when he was so cocksure that I could not stand it any longer. Then at last I went to sleep.

11

THE Royal Indian Navy mutiny began on Wednesday evening. The next Sunday I was working in the battalion offices, as I had done every day of the week. I found that work slowly accumulated on me. I liaised with the railway, and while I was doing that I became responsible for operational maps, which were sprouting like big green cabbage leaves on the walls of my office. More and more Colonel Savage gave me Intelligence Summaries to read, collate, and pass on. I knew WAC (I)s were not meant to do this kind of work at the headquarters of a battalion. A battalion is a fighting unit.

I wondered sometimes what I would do if Colonel Savage ordered me out on operations or manoeuvres in this role I had somehow got of Battalion Intelligence Officer. I had only to send a telegram or a letter to G.H.Q., and half a dozen senior WAC (I) officers would be down there like a ton of bricks. But against that, Colonel Savage had his infuriating knack of making everybody do what he wanted. And I stayed there because I had a nice feeling, which I think most women will understand, of being the only woman who'd ever been allowed so close to the real soldiers, as one of them. There are nurses, of course, but they are different and even they don't go as far down as a battalion. I felt like one of those Russian women you see in pictures, carrying tommy-guns. Besides, I told myself, he is short of officers, and I am doing a useful job in a real emergency.

Colonel Savage had ordered me always to leave the connecting door open between his office and mine – 'So that you can hear me without my having to yell,' he had said with a cold smile. He still thought I was looking for opportunities to flirt with Macaulay. I didn't care what he thought. The order prevented Macaulay from making himself much of a nuisance, although he often had to come into my office. When he did he always spoke to me in the same way, a mixture of joking and slyness that was uncomfortable but not sufficiently bad to let me be really rude to him in return. And sometimes, unfortunately, he made me laugh. He had a gift for turning a sentence, especially about Colonel Savage, whom he always called 'the Sahib', so that I could not always keep my face straight.

The trouble is that I am an ordinary woman and I could not keep my anger at boiling-point all the time, against Macaulay or Colonel Savage or any of them. I thought, too, that Macaulay must realize by now that I did not want him to make love to me. Even the next thing that happened that Sunday did not warn me as it should have.

About eleven o'clock Colonel Savage left his office to go to the Lines on some business. Macaulay came in to me a few minutes later and began to copy some details off one of the maps into his notebook. Half-way through he turned and said, 'Why did you want to go telling the Sahib about – about our misunderstanding? Can't we keep the old man out of this? I apologized, didn't I?'

I looked up, surprised, and said, 'I haven't told him anything.' That sounded too friendly, so I added quickly, 'But I will if you make me.'

Macaulay looked absolutely dumbfounded. He said, 'You didn't? You're joking, Victoria – you *must* have. Well, I'm *damned*! The cunning sod! He took me to his bungalow the other day and sat down, looking like a hungry wolf, and asked me *why* I'd done it. Of course I confessed. Extenuating circumstances got me off a court-martial.' Macaulay made motions in the air outlining a woman's breasts. 'The Sahib tore into me as if I was a little boy he'd caught making a mess on the carpet. He's stopped all my leave for six months.'

'You deserve it,' I said as curtly as I could. I began to puzzle out what Colonel Savage's various actions and innuendos could mean. Macaulay said, 'I say, the Sahib isn't turning sweet on you himself, is he?' He had come close to my chair and was looking at me suspiciously.

'No,' I snapped. 'Don't be ridiculous. I wouldn't have anything to do with Colonel Savage if he was the last man in the world. He's a – he's a *swine*.' I know my face was flushed, and I found myself standing up.

Macaulay said, 'Well, that's good. But oh, honey, don't be angry with me. I admit I was a fool and I do apologize. Please forgive me. Please let's start all over again, properly this time.'

I have sometimes seen myself in the mirror when I am getting into a bad temper, and I can't deny that it makes me look better than usual. My chest was heaving, and I suddenly noticed Macaulay's eyes fixed on it. They had gone dull again, and the end of his tongue was just out, moving from side to side and licking his moustache. His eyes wandered down over me, to my stomach, to the middle of my skirt.

It is impossible to think of less attractive, less woman-like clothes than WAC (I) uniform, and yet he licked me with his eyes as though I had no clothes on at all. I sat down quickly and said, 'Go away. At once.'

He said, 'Not until you forgive me.'

To get rid of him I said, 'All right. I forgive you. But that's all.'

He said, 'You must be in love with somebody else – that railway pal of yours, Taylor.'

I said, 'Yes. No. But I'm not going to start anything with you. *Please* go away.'

'Why not?' he said. 'You're beautiful; I'm young and healthy; I love you.' He kept on talking, but the spasm had passed, and his eyes looked normal again. He asked me to go to the flicks with him, and I had just refused when a Gurkha orderly marched in with a signal form.

I interrupted Macaulay by saying, 'Ah, this is the final reckoning of what's missing from that goods train at Malra. I've got these figures already. Do you want to keep the message?'

'Yes, please,' he said and stuffed it in his pocket. He sat down on the near corner of my table and said, 'My God, I thought the Sahib was going to chew the inkstand to pieces that morning, didn't you?'

'Haven't you got any work to do?' I said.

Sulkily he said, 'Oh, all right,' and left me.

As soon as he had gone I sat back with a phew of relief. I rummaged in the table drawers and found a list: 3,000 pounds of PEK; 96 detonators; 6,000 feet of cordtex; 1,000 feet of slow-burning fuse; 12,000 rounds of SAA ·303 Mark VIII Z; 96 grenades – a lot of oddments. Then at the end was a note we'd had from the ordnance depot: 'All the above explosives and ammunition are DEFECTIVE AND DANGEROUS to use though safe under storage conditions. All stores on this train were en route for drowning under Operation Neptune. See G.H.Q. No. ....' and then the usual long reference number.

I lit a cigarette. The goods train stopped by the strike at Malra that night had been looted, and it had contained a few wagon loads of explosives and ammunition. They were scrapings from an ordnance depot in northern India, which were being sent to the coast to be loaded into ships, taken out to sea, and dumped overboard in deep water. The same thing was going on all over India as the ordnance depots cleared up after the war.

Whoever looted the train had known beforehand that it contained ammunition. They can't have known that it was going to be held up exactly at Malra, but they probably had a general idea of where it would be when the strike began.

The train had been in Malra about three hours, in darkness, before Colonel Savage found out it was there. Then he had ordered soldiers from the Malra bridge to guard it, but when the Gurkhas reached the train they found it already looted. Hardly two tons had been taken, but the thieves had come and gone and got clean away. There were the marks of bullock-cart wheels beside the train, but Colonel Savage thought the ammunition had very soon been transferred to a car or a lorry. Anyway, it had vanished.

No one was to blame. Colonel Savage had been very quick to get a guard on the train at all, considering it might have been full of nothing but ballast or gravel. Patrick had done nothing wrong. Nor had Ranjit. Only I couldn't help wondering in the bottom of my mind whether Ranjit might not know something. When he said, 'There are leaders who know how to make our protests effective,' did he mean 'by arming us'? I said nothing of this, which was much smaller than a suspicion, to Colonel Savage.

Colonel Savage returned just as I finished my cigarette. He said, 'I'm going round the city with the Collector. Do you want to come?'

I said, 'Very good, sir,' got my cap and bag, and followed him. The Collector's little black Austin Seven saloon was waiting in front of the steps. I squeezed into the narrow back seat. Colonel Savage sat in front, his knees hunched up under the dashboard. The Collector was wearing his usual white duck suit and bow tie. On his head he had a panama hat with a faded black and red ribbon. The little car buzzed down the Pike and into the city.

The narrow streets of the ramshackle old city were crowded, as usual, but the atmosphere of the place was peculiar. People stood in groups, talking noisily, or squatted in rows under the house walls and shouted to one another, or were gathered in the dark back parts of the open-fronted shops. The rain earlier in the week had brought out millions of flies. The air was still a little moist, though it had become very hot again.

The Collector drove slowly, hooting all the time on his bulb-horn. People moved out of the way slowly, often frowning and sometimes turning to shout or mutter at us as we squeezed past. The men against the walls stared at the car and at us cooped inside it like monkeys in a cage. It was a bad feeling, and I was glad that Colonel Savage had his carbine. He always carried it now. 'The citizens are not in a good temper,' he said.

The Collector said, 'No. There's too much noise for it to be serious yet, though. When the city becomes quiet, and no one's in the streets, then you have to be ready.'

We drove on, and after going slowly all round the city we went to the station. Patrick was there, getting on to his Norton. He stopped kicking the starter when he saw us, and came over. He said to the Collector, 'I was just going to look for you. I have been trying and trying to reach you on the telephone, but the servant said you were out.'

'As you see,' the Collector replied, smiling. We were all out of the little box now.

'Well, it is jolly serious,' Patrick said. 'Just now someone shot at Dennis. He is guard on an up goods train. A bullet went through his brake van while it was passing the level-crossing at the Street of the Farriers. I want to know what you are going to do about it.'

'Try and catch the man who did it,' the Collector said. 'You've told the police, of course?'

Patrick said, 'The police? Oh, no. I was trying to tell you.'

The Collector turned to me. 'Quick, Miss Jones,' he said, 'ring Mr Lanson, and see that Mr Williams is told too. Tell Dennis to wait here until the police come.'

I hurried off, thinking, Really, Patrick is a fool; he needs looking after every minute of the day.

When I came back Patrick was arguing loudly with the Collector. He was saying, 'We have the rifles in the Auxiliary Force kote here. *Why* can't we give them to our guards and drivers? The strikers throw stones at us – from hiding, of course. Now we are being shot at. You must do something.'

Mr Govindaswami kept calm. He said, 'I will, Taylor, but not that. Such a step would merely exacerbate an already touchy situation. You agree, Colonel?'

'Oh, yes, Collector,' Colonel Savage said. 'Disloyal rascals would certainly distort your motives.' He spoke in that odd voice again, and I saw with anger that he was laughing behind a straight, stern face.

'Precisely, Savage,' the Collector said. He was laughing too.

'Well, it is your responsibility,' Patrick shouted. 'Do not come and blame me if the drivers and guards refuse to take the trains! Do not blame me, that is all.' He stalked away.

We squeezed back into the Austin and rattled off toward the Collector's bungalow. Savage said, 'That fellow Taylor's got ten thumbs and a soul like a boiled ham. I'll put a couple of my men on each train if you like, one with the driver and one with the guard.'

'Can you spare the men?' the Collector asked.

Colonel Savage said, 'Not really. Don't forget I'm responsible for security over the whole of your civil district as well as on the railway. And People-Psmythe might ring me up any moment and demand a guard for his art class.'

The Collector stopped the car with a jerk and held out his hand. The Deputy Superintendent of Police, Lanson, was coming the other way in his old Chevrolet station wagon. The Collector talked to him for a few seconds about the shooting, across the gap between the two cars, then Lanson said, 'A couple of houses are on fire at the other end of the city. Near the Benares Gate. Did you pass there?'

'Not right by it,' the Collector said.

'The fires must have started just afterwards, or you would have seen them,' Lanson said. 'The police report that the crowds are moving together now. I've got all my chaps out on duty.'

The Collector nodded, the cars separated, and in a moment we reached the big bungalow. Colonel Savage walked quickly to the telephone and began giving orders. Five minutes later three jeeps arrived – his own, his command radio jeep, and a third with a trailer, both jeep and trailer full of armed Gurkhas.

I sat near the telephone in the hall. Messages kept coming in. The first soldiers had been put on the first train. The platoon standing by in the yards reported by walkie-talkie that all was quiet there. Colonel Savage came out and spoke in Gurkhali on the set, ordering the jemadar to leave a section guarding the yards and to take the rest at once to the station. Lanson rang for the Collector. The Collector said, 'Yes ... No ... Yes ... No ... Soon.' I found my hands were not quite steady.

The Collector put down the telephone. 'Mr Surabhai is leading a large crowd toward the station,' he said.

Colonel Savage said, 'The chairman of the local Congress committee?'

The Collector said, 'Yes. They've got banners – "Long live the mutineers!" "A blow for freedom!" and of course "Quit India!" They're quite calm except that they're shouting slogans and won't disperse.' His hands behind his back, he walked up and down the big stone-flagged hall under the portraits of British governors and collectors who had ruled from that house before him.

He stopped suddenly, turned, and said, 'I wonder – Miss Jones, ring your traffic people and find out if any specials are on the line in the district, or coming into it.'

I got Patrick at once. He said, 'My God, what do you want to know for? I'm busy.'

I said, 'Please tell me quickly. The Collector's waiting.'

Patrick said, 'Oh, all *right*! There is an up troop special at Sithri. It will be here in about forty minutes. All the trains are going very slowly because of signalling difficulties and –'

I said, 'Thank you,' hung up, and told the Collector.

He turned to Colonel Savage and said, 'I won't say that Surabhai knew this troop special was coming, but I suspect that somebody did. I'd like to find out what kind of troops they are. I am positive that Surabhai will try to stop that train.'

'How?' Colonel Savage asked.

The Collector said, 'Non-violence. He and a lot of his volunteers will lie down on the line. It's been done before, and it's very difficult to deal with. I'm going to the station right away.'

Colonel Savage said, 'Okay. I'll go with the jeeps and stop the train at the level-crossing here.' He jerked his head toward the back of the bungalow. The railway ran at the far end of the gardens there, and the level-crossing where the Bhowani–Kishanpur road crossed it was not far from the corner of the Collector's wall.

The Collector said, 'Good. After that you'll come to the station?'

Colonel Savage said, 'Yes,' and ran down the broad steps. I followed him. He turned, one foot in the jeep and one on the ground. He said, 'Are you coming? We might get some bricks thrown at us this time.'

I told him I wanted to come because Pater might be driving that special. I was a little frightened.

He said, 'Hop in.' As we drove off, the other jeeps trailing close behind us, he said, 'All those rosters your father explained to me have gone to pot since the strike, then?'

I said, 'Yes, sir. Pater's been on goods trains, shunting, everything. They've cut out practically all the passenger service.'

'I know,' he said.

We were there. He stopped the jeep, jumped out, and walked forward to the gatekeeper's shanty. A minute later he came out with the gatekeeper and a red flag, and called three or four Gurkhas to join him. A row of trees grows along the road there, and I sat in the jeep in the shade, waiting.

At last the gatekeeper closed the gates, and in a few minutes the train came slowly up from the north. As soon as it came in sight it began to whistle. The driver had seen the party on the crossing. Colonel Savage stood on top of one of the gates, waving the red flag. The Gurkhas stood in a row across the lines, all grinning and jumping up and down in excitement.

I thought for a moment that the train would not stop. Then, about two hundred yards away, it began to slow down quickly, and I heard the grinding of its brakes. I looked hard and recognized Pater. There was only one fireman, a man in a topi, who was standing on top of the coal in the tender, a big lump in his right hand ready to throw. I got out of the jeep and hurried forward.

The engine stopped on the crossing, and Pater swung down to the right of way. I arrived in time to hear him say, 'Well, Colonel, this is a surprise! Do you want a ride *now*?'

Colonel Savage laughed and said, 'No, Mr Jones. I want to know who's in this train.' He looked up and back at the carriages. Hundreds of dark heads were sticking out, mostly wearing green tam-o'-shanters.

He ran back and called up to the faces in the windows. After a minute he came forward to the engine again. He said to me, 'R.I.A.S.C. drivers and supply personnel, going back to their depots for disbandment. Madrassis. Mr Jones, there's a chance some people in Bhowani are going to try to stop your train. You'll know as soon as you get round that corner. Give me ten minutes to reach the station ahead of you, and then start up. All right?'

Pater said, 'I will do that, Colonel. My fireman here has plenty of good Bengal coal to throw at the bastards. Good for throwing, too!' He waved at me and said, 'Hullo, Victoria. You are looking well. Is she helping you properly, Colonel?'

Colonel Savage said impatiently, 'She's wonderful. We've got to hurry.' He waved his hand, and I shouted, 'Keep your head down, Pater.' Pater grinned and made the thumbs-up sign with one hand as he clambered up into the cab. As we drove away I saw him pull out his big railway watch.

We raced down the Pike with the klaxons blaring, swung into the station yard, and pulled up. Colonel Savage jumped out and walked quickly over to the Collector, who was standing beside his Austin talking to Mr Surabhai. The yard was full of people, all very quiet. The banners swayed as the people moved about and shuffled their feet – 'Quit India!' 'A blow for freedom!'

I noticed some men filing quietly into the station while the Collector was talking. I didn't say anything. If it had not been Pater's train I would have been happy to see the Indians make a fool out of Colonel Savage. Colonel Savage saw the men too and asked the Collector whether he wanted the station gates shut.

The Collector said, 'No, let them go in. There is no law against it. Besides, there are about a dozen lying on the line already.'

Mr Surabhai joined his palms in greeting when he saw me, and smiled very sweetly at me. 'Good afternoon, Miss Jones,' he said. 'So nice to meet you here.' Then his face fell back like rubber into the expression it had had just before, excited and determined. He raised his voice and said, 'As I was saying, Mr Collector, we will make our protest against the slaughtering of our naval brothers, whether it is lawful or no. They are your naval brothers as well as mine, Mr Collector, even though you glory in your post as lackey of the British imperialists. We will make protest, I assure you – peaceable, non-violent protest, but we will make it.'

The Collector said, 'No one's been slaughtered yet, Mr Surabhai.'

'The brave Indian sailors!' Mr Surabhai shouted, his eyes popping. 'The naval seamen are being shot and shelled and bombed! What for? For the simple act of raising high the flag of our country, Mr Collector.'

The Collector said, 'None of the mutineers has been hurt yet. There's been no violence anywhere except in the streets of Bombay. There all the rascals of the city have come out – to take advantage of protests like this of yours – and started looting and rioting.'

A stone whizzed through the air, missing Colonel Savage by inches, and broke the windscreen of one of the jeeps. The Gurkhas in it jumped out, frowning, and unslung their rifles and tommy-guns.

The Collector said, 'A non-violent missile, Mr Surabhai?'

Mr Surabhai faced his shuffling, silent crowd. He cried, 'No violence, I beseech you, my friends. Do not let your natural feelings get on top of you.' He turned back to the Collector and said, 'Enough of this confabulation. It is to no purpose. I am going now to join my comrades.' He walked into the station. An engine whistled down the line, a long continuous whistling.

I had been watching the crowd. I didn't see exactly where the stone had come from. Most of the men seemed determined but quite calm. They were well dressed on the whole, a few in European trousers and shirts, the majority in white dhotis. Practically everyone wore a Gandhi cap. There were several women among them.

'We'd better get into the station,' the Collector said.

Colonel Savage said, 'I'll bring Singbir's platoon up.'

The Collector agreed, but told him to keep them back. He added, 'There's practically nothing anyone can do until the volunteers get tired and go home. If it was really vital we could turn the hoses on them, or even run over them – though I don't suppose we'd have to run over more than one. But it's not vital. Who's in the train?' Savage told him, and he said, 'That might be useful to know.'

A file of twenty Gurkhas followed us on to the platform. Colonel Savage told Jemadar Singbir to take them up to the far end and to allow no one within twenty paces of them. He also said, 'Drink three full glasses of water each. That's an order.'

Lanson arrived with ten policemen.

The southern part of the station was crowded with Mr Surabhai's volunteers. A few of them stood about on the platform, but the majority were lying down comfortably across the tracks, their heads pillowed on the rail and their hands folded on their stomachs. They shouted slogans as they lay. Pater's troop train had arrived and was stopped in the middle of the station, its cow-catcher a few feet from Mr Surabhai's side. Pater had climbed down and was standing on Number 1 platform, looking at the people on the rails. I heard him shout, 'Get up, you bloody fools! You will get hurt. I have to take this train to Gondwara.'

Mr Surabhai said, 'Never!' and closed his eyes.

Then the Collector walked to the edge of the platform and spoke down to him. He said, 'Mr Surabhai, do you realize that this train you are holding in the heat here is full of Indian soldiers who are returning to Madras for disbandment?'

Mr Surabhai opened his eyes, and I saw tears in them. He was very soft-hearted, and he was crying because he had to hold up the Madrassis in the heat. But he had to. He said, 'It is immaterial. They are lackeys of the British, like you.'

Suddenly I saw that there were a lot more people on the platform than there had been. I did not know where they had come from. They pushed and eddied close around. They were not well dressed. A policeman shouted, 'Keep back!' and swung his brass-bound lathi with the full weight of his arm behind it. The crack as it hit a man's head, just beside me, echoed up and down the station. The man fell forward without a sound and lay there, blood trickling from his ear on to the stone. He was badly hurt, I saw by his face. The crowd growled and edged back. Stones and bricks hurtled out of it, but I could never see the throwers.

The Collector said, 'Get on to the engine, quick.' I scrambled up, with Pater right on my heels, and ducked behind the steel cab side. Stones clattered against it, and one broke the glass. The fireman began to throw lumps of coal. The police were all swinging their lathis now. I peeped round the corner of the cab and saw Colonel Savage and Mr Govindaswami, together, standing in the same place. I saw a half-brick strike Mr Govindaswami's shoulder in that instant, and he staggered back. Colonel Savage held him until he found his balance again.

I was on the edge of nervous tears and had to gulp and swallow to control myself. They were all so horrible and brutal. I had never seen anything like it before – the police, mouths twisted, lathis flailing; the men in the crowd; the people with the brutal faces, full of lust to hurt. I saw a woman stumble, and screamed, 'Oh, no!' but the policeman hit her again, and she fell. I could not stay under cover. I stood up and watched everything.

Colonel Savage pointed his carbine upward and pulled the trigger. At the shot a sudden silence fell. Mr Govindaswami cried in Hindu, 'I order you all to disperse. In one minute the military will open fire to clear the platform.'

The Gurkhas had come up silently. A few stood or knelt near the side of the tender. The rest were farther back, standing at ease. The Collector got out his watch.

From the tracks Mr Surabhai shouted, 'Murderers!' but the crowd on the platform ebbed sullenly and quickly away. In less than a half minute the platform was empty. They had carried their injured away with them.

I climbed down from the cab and stood beside it, holding the handrail because my knees were weak and the front of my skirt was shaking with my trembling. I prayed for it all to be over, for us all to go home and try to forget what we had done, what we had seen. The people lying on the rails meant no harm. They looked silly but somehow dignified. Let them lie there. Perhaps they were right after all. It would be their country soon.

Colonel Savage said, 'What about these people?' and pointed to the volunteers on the line.

The Collector took off his panama and scratched his thick grey hair. He said, 'I don't honestly know. I don't want them hurt.'

Colonel Savage said, 'Okay. I'll fix them. Get your engine all ready to start, Mr Jones.'

'Yes, Colonel, I'm ready now,' Pater said. He opened the cylinder drain cocks, and steam hissed out below the cylinders.

He touched the regulator, and the huge driving wheels inched round. Mr Surabhai stiffened convulsively and clasped his hands tighter together.

I couldn't stand it. I cried desperately, 'No! They won't get up. Mr Surabhai won't.' Pater closed the regulator, and the wheels stopped moving. The cow-catcher was now touching Mr Surabhai.

I caught the Collector's sleeve. I was ready to get down on my kness. I said, 'Please don't let him, sir. Mr Surabhai won't get up. It'll be murder!' I was thinking of the wheels going slowly over Mr Surabhai, who had cried because the Madrassis were being kept out in the heat.

'Why do you think he won't get up?' the Collector asked me. He was hurt in his mind as well as his body, where the brick had hit him. His lips were tight and his eyes dull and tired.

I said, 'Because he believes he is right, sir. And because he is brave.'

The Collector said, 'I think she's right, Savage. Surabhai has always wanted to be a martyr.'

'I am not trying to frighten them off the rails, Miss Jones,' Colonel Savage said unpleasantly. 'I expect I am as good as judge of Mr Surabhai's character as you are. If you would mind not interfering, I will show you that I know quite well what I am doing.'

I stepped back unwillingly, and he spoke in a low voice with Jemadar Singbir. The jemadar chuckled and spoke to the Gurkhas. They all grinned. Colonel Savage motioned with his hand, and the Gurkhas lined up on the edge of the platform.

Colonel Savage leaned over and said politely, 'Mr Surabhai, are you a high-caste Hindu?'

Mr Surabhai said, 'Yes. But all castes are like one in the fight for freedom.'

Colonel Savage said, 'Good. Because you are about to be used as a urinal by Rifleman Tilokbir Ale. He is hard pressed. He is a Hindu of a sort, but his caste is medium low. You have five seconds to get up and let these Madrassis go on home.'

Mr Surabhai sat up with a jerk. 'Wh-what did you say?' he stammered. 'What are you going to do?' He stared up at the platform. The Gurkhas stood with their backs to me, but I could tell they were opening their buttons.

Mr Surabhai said, 'Oh, you beastly –'

'Three ... two ... one ... fire!' Colonel Savage counted and dropped his hand. Pater opened the regulator. The Gurkhas all began to urinate. Pater pulled down the whistle, and the station was full of its shrieking. The volunteers scrambled up, shouting, on to the platform or crawled over to the other line, urine staining their clothes and dripping from their faces. The troop train gathered speed and quickly rolled through and out up the line, southward.

I turned away and walked to the Purdah Room and was sick. On the platform there were blood and broken glass and torn clothes and a few teeth. The banners and flags lay abandoned on the line, with some caps and a woman's slipper. They'd done that to the women too. I saw every detail while my stomach contracted and my throat swelled and my eyes bulged. When the vomiting and retching passed, and I had washed and sat down to rest and bathed my eyes again, I came out.

'You don't look well, Miss Jones,' Colonel Savage said.

I whispered, 'You are a cruel bully.'

He said, 'The path of Duty is the way to Glory.' His voice was still hard when he said, 'You've got guts. I'll drive you home now.'

Anything but that. I couldn't bear to be near him another minute.

Then I saw Patrick there – he must have just come – and because at least I knew him through and through, and was not afraid of him, I said quickly, 'Mr Taylor will take me home.'

Colonel Savage glanced at Patrick. Just before I spoke, Patrick had looked away to avoid meeting my eye. When I spoke he could not believe what he heard. Then he slowly gathered his wits, and at last said, 'Yes, certainly. Yes, I will take Miss Jones home, Colonel. Kasel, you stay in the office until I come back.'

Ranjit's voice said, 'Yes, Mr Taylor.' I saw then that he was there too, standing at the foot of the stairs. His face was pinched and his eyes very sad. I wanted to tell him it wasn't my fault, that I didn't have any say in these brutalities and indignities. But I couldn't; he was too far away.

As Patrick and I walked along the line-side path, he seemed to be feeling round in his mind for something to say. I knew he wanted to tell me he was sorry for what he had done with Rose Mary, but he didn't know how to begin. He is always tongue-tied when it is important not to be. Those seconds were important to both of us, because I was feeling weak and afraid and suddenly very female.

I wanted him to say, Don't worry, don't think, I'll look after you. If he would say the right words, do the right action, I would go to him and submit.

He needed looking after. I would look after him, and yet I would serve him, because I was surrendering. There was plenty of hatred and fear inside our little world, but they were of kinds that I knew and could face. The hatred and fear outside had proved too much for me. Patrick could face them because he was brave and stupid and never really felt what other people were feeling. Those were his qualities, and they would shelter me, and for that shelter – and his love – I would honestly give him everything I had to give. Even love, I could find to give.

Patrick said, 'What happened about the troop special, Victoria? How did those people get off the line?'

I suppose he thought that was a safer subject to talk to me about than any other – certainly safer than Rose Mary.

I said, 'I don't want to think about any of it. It was all horrible.'

He said aggrievedly, 'But I want to know. I did not see. I was up in the office.'

I told him.

He stopped and doubled up, and slapped his thigh and shouted with a loud bellowing laugh, 'My God, that is good! That was Colonel Savage's idea, was it? Well, I will never think so badly of him again. Oh, my God, that is priceless!'

Still laughing, he looked at me. He saw I was not laughing. He said, 'Don't you think it is funny? That will make them feel foolish, I bet.'

I screamed, 'Can't you understand anything? Can't you see what they feel like? Or me? Stay here, don't come another step with me.'

I left him there and ran all the way home in the heat, so that when I fell on to my bed every stitch of my clothes was soaked dark with perspiration.

12

THE headlines in the paper said: PARATROOPS ENGAGE MUTINEERS; and then, on the line underneath: WITH MORTARS, MACHINE-GUNS.

The date-line was Karachi. I read the story as if it were happening on a far-off island. The man who wrote the editorials was not angry with the R.I.N. mutineers. He was sad and hurt that they should have done it. It was an English paper published in the Punjab. He – or another man – was angry about the strike, though, and so were the people who wrote letters to the editor. 'Pro Bono Publico' and 'Paterfamilias' were very angry. Paterfamilias used sentences and thoughts that made me sure he was an Anglo-Indian.

I was reading the paper in Mr Govindaswami's study. He and Colonel Savage were talking quietly at the far end of the room about nothing in particular. It was four o'clock in the afternoon of Tuesday, 21 May 1946. The men had had a short discussion on military matters when I first got there, but since then they had just been sitting and chatting. When I saw that they didn't want me for any more note-taking I got up and walked over to read this newspaper, which was spread out on a table in the window.

They didn't waste their time like this for nothing in those days. I knew we were all waiting for something.

I looked at the garden sleeping in the afternoon sun. There was an empty bench in the shade of a big dark-leafed tree. Mr Govindaswami was a bachelor. There should have been children and an ayah, and his wife perhaps, sitting on that bench. The railway ran behind that garden, and Bhowani city lay on the other side of the railway. I had seen and heard too much of the city these last few days. It murmured day and night like a kettle simmering on a sigri. There were little sandbagged posts at three or four of the main street crossings, and the police always moved in pairs.

The night before, the city had flared up into a senseless shouting and throwing of bricks. Even more senselessly, it was the Mohammedans who had thrown the bricks at the Hindus. There were very few Mohammedans in Bhowani, and there were very many Hindus, and the Hindus had done the Mohammedans no harm. The Collector had had to call out the troops at 11 p.m. As soon as they arrived the police were able to break up the riot with a couple of lathi charges.

I heard the familiar, distinctive sound of jeep engines, and the two men got up. Colonel Savage said, 'Time to go now, Miss Jones.' I knew better than to ask where to, but I knew this was not an ordinary ride.

The Collector led the way in his Austin. We passed a small fleet of military vehicles, all their engines running, drawn up on the dusty edge of the Pike. As soon as the radio jeep swung out on to the Pike behind us, the lorry drivers engaged gear and followed. I folded my hands in my lap. I had seen that all the lorries were full of Gurkhas, but still I would not ask him.

But I asked myself, What on earth were they going to do? Colonel Savage must have had great difficulties producing all those men. I knew exactly how many of the battalion were on duty – in the yards, on the detachments along the line, finding the mobile patrols and the quarter guard and barrack guards. These men must be everyone else – all the signallers and mortar men and anti-tank gunners and pioneers and what Colonel Savage called the 'odds and sods'.

The trouble must be in the city, I knew, so I was not surprised when the Collector's Austin, immediately ahead of us, turned into Station Road. It was a strange time of day to be there. The city reminded me of a bad-tempered bear, sprawled out all round us, dozingly asleep. Why should they want to disturb it?

The lorries stopped in the station yard. The Gurkhas streamed out and fell in in thick ranks. Colonel Savage said, 'Keep close to me, Miss Jones.'

The Collector went a pace ahead of us all, walking by himself, uncannily clean in his white suit as he picked his way carefully down a dusty lane beside the railway line. The Gurkhas pressed close on our heels.

We came to a place where the houses edged back from the railway, and a street coming in from the right became a sort of barren square. I saw perhaps a hundred Indians gathered there, and for a moment faltered in my pace. Colonel Savage said – rather, he snarled – 'Keep close!' I tossed my head – it is an automatic gesture I cannot help – and went forward again.

A section of Gurkhas moved round under the buildings and blocked off the street. The Collector forced gently through the crowd, pushing with his hands and calling out, 'Make way there, please. Do not leave the square.' Then I noticed for the first time that there were no police in that place. That was strange.

We reached the far buildings. There was a kind of empty shop toward the end of the row nearest the railway. In front hung a faded blue sign with red lettering: UNION OF RLWY WORKERS OF INDIA. A table blocked off entrance to the shop, and behind the table sat Kartar Singh, the signals fitter. He was squatting on top of a bench, his feet on it. Two other Indians, seemingly coolies, stood in the shop behind him. There was a lot of money on the table and on the floor.

Kartar straightened slowly until he was standing upright on the bench, and so stood much higher than the Collector. The Collector gazed up at him and said, '*Jai ram*, my friend.'

Kartar said loudly, '*Jai Hind* to you. What brings you here?' They both spoke Hindustani with an accent, the Collector's guttural and throaty, Kartar's tripping and tonguey. Mr Govindaswami's native language would have been Tamil if he hadn't made it English, and Kartar Singh's was Punjabi.

The Collector said, 'A state of emergency has been declared by the Government of India, and you must all return to work. Your complaints have not been rejected. They have only been put aside. You can take them up again as soon as the emergency is over.'

'I hear what you say,' Kartar Singh said, and raised his voice. 'Do you hear what the Collector says?' The crowd murmured, 'No,' and Kartar Singh then repeated the message word for word.

The Collector said, 'Please instruct them to go back to work. Otherwise I shall arrest you, and then use my best efforts to see that they do go back to work. I have authority.'

Kartar Singh shouted to the crowd, 'He says he has authority from government. What answer am I to give him?' To the Collector he added, 'I am their servant, not their master.'

The men in the crowd said many things, some loudly, some doubtfully. They said, 'Why should we go back?' and, 'I don't mind,' and, 'Let our grievances be put right. Then we will go back.' There was one persistent loud voice somewhere back in the crowd, which shouted, 'Don't go back to work, brothers, whatever Kartar Singh says. He is a lackey of the Railway Board and the British. Don't go. Fight for your rights!'

The voice stopped with a scream, and I looked round quickly. I saw three Gurkhas dragging a man through the crowd by his arms. Colonel Savage said, 'He's not really hurt. They hit him on the foot with a rifle butt.'

The Collector said impassively, 'What answer, Kartar Singh?'

Kartar's face reddened, and he became angry. He bawled at the Collector so that everyone could hear. 'Go to hell, that's our answer. We're not going to work for you or the Railway Board or the British or anyone. We know our rights, and we won't be bullied out of them.'

'That is your last word?' the Collector asked quietly.

'Yes. Go to hell!' Kartar Singh shouted.

The Collector turned to Colonel Savage. He said, 'Carry on then, please, Colonel.'

Colonel Savage saluted, pulled out the whistle on the end of the black lanyard round his neck, and blew two short blasts. Some of the Gurkhas spread out in pairs among the crowd, others stayed in line across the street and the lane and along the low railway embankment. They had all unslung their arms. All the men who carried rifles now fixed their bayonets.

The Collector said sharply, 'Get down,' pushed Kartar off the bench, and himself hopped up on to the table. The crowd began to panic, surging to and fro, separating, scrabbling on the ground for stones and sticks. The Collector raised his black hand. It was almost invisible against the dark shadows inside the shop, so that his white sleeve seemed to end in nothing, an amputated stump.

He called out, 'Do not move about. Do not attempt to throw anything or molest the soldiers. See, your leader is a prisoner. He is going to jail. The rest of you are going to work. No one need be hurt.' A pair of Gurkhas held Kartar Singh firmly and pushed him back on to the bench so that all could see. He struggled and kicked and swore, but he could not escape.

The Collector said, 'The rest of you, file past here. The station coolies first. Hurry up, now. You – you're a station coolie. Come here.'

114

The man he pointed at came slowly forward, looking from right to left, letting the brick fall from his hand as a Gurkha raised his bayonet.

From the centre of the crowd another voice yelled, 'Don't go! They can't make us work!' The coolie stopped and bent quickly for the brick he had just dropped. A bottle whirled out of the crowd and smashed against the house-front above the Collector's head.

Again I heard the shouting voice choke off in a scream. 'Keep still, everybody,' Colonel Savage said. He jumped up on the table beside the Collector and stood with legs braced and carbine pushed down at the crowd. 'Keep still, keep quiet.' Two Gurkhas dragged forward the man who had shouted and thrown the bottle – at least, I supposed that was the man. His eyes were closed, and blood trickled from a long gash in his bare stomach. Colonel Savage motioned with his hand, and the subadar-major scrambled up on to the table. Savage and the Collector got down.

Subadar-Major Manbir was small and fat. His moustache was like an old Chinese mandarin's, his nose was flat, and his nostrils were wide. He had no eyebrows, and his eyes were set at a ferocious Mongolian angle in his old, round, wrinkled face. The sun shone on the three bright rows of medal ribbons on his chest. He had a paunch, and he was carrying a tommy-gun loosely in his hand.

He said softly, 'Look at me.'

Everyone looked at him. I looked at him. He was terrifying. He was a Tartar. He was everything the Tartars had done, all their sacking and killing and destruction, all that we had heard of mountains of skulls. The crowd sighed and fell quiet.

He licked his lips slowly, frowned, and suddenly pushed forward the muzzle of the tommy-gun. He said, 'Do what you're told. *I* don't mind killing the whole lot of you. I've killed more men than there are in this square.'

His Hindustani was atrociously bad, but everyone understood every word he said. He went on, 'But I've been ordered not to kill you unless you disobey the government. Come on, someone throw a brick. That would be a joke, wouldn't it? Throw a brick, a bottle, anything!'

He waited. No one moved. No one breathed.

He suddenly raised his voice and roared, 'Well, you –' and he

ripped out a single Hindustani word that made everyone jump –
'step forward then and do what you're told.'

The dam broke. The Collector mopped his forehead; the strikers hurried forward. As they came up, in twos and threes, pairs of Gurkhas stepped up beside them and escorted them forward. The Collector checked off names against a list lying on the table and gave them their strike pay. Then the Gurkhas took them off to their work.

In half an hour the square was empty. The few remaining Gurkhas fell in, and the whole party marched back to the station yard. Kartar Singh, his face impassive and stern, walked with us, his hands tied and his legs hobbled. They put him in one of the empty lorries, and as the convoy returned up the Pike I saw that lorry turn into the Kutcherry. The Kutcherry is the enclosure where the jail, the treasury, the Collector's court, and the civil district offices are.

Our jeeps followed the Austin into the Collector's compound. As soon as we were inside the building Colonel Savage took off his hat and sat down with a long 'Pheeew! That was a tight corner, Govindaswami.'

The Collector laid his hands on Colonel Savage's shoulders and said in that precise voice, 'My boy, you were a credit to your regiment.'

Colonel Savage stood up, clasped the Collector's right hand in his own, and stood a moment there with his jaw set and his chin up. For days on end those two men would be hard, impersonal, and grown up, and then suddenly this joke would make them act like schoolboys.

Colonel Savage relaxed and said, 'My upper lip needs unstiffening. It's got set. I suppose you drink toddy?'

Mr Govindaswami spread out his hands and said, '*Beshak, huzoor*, but I keep whisky for the sahibs who visit me. Miss Jones, you look as if you need a drink too.' He called for his bearer.

I took a whisky. I did need one. It had not been anything like as bad as the affair over the troop train, but it had been bad enough. I resented the highhanded way Colonel Savage had dealt with the strikers, who were all Indians. He wouldn't have done it if they had been English, or even Anglo-Indian, I thought.

We all sat down with our drinks. Colonel Savage looked at me

116

and said, 'Let your hair down. Swallow your pride. What do you want to know?'

It must have shown in my face. I wanted to know how they thought they were going to get away with it. Colonel Savage said, 'What you've just seen, or something like it, was done in three or four key railway towns all over India today.'

I asked how that would prevent trouble. The Gurkhas couldn't make the men work.

'Oh, can't they!' Colonel Savage said. 'They're carrying three days' rations. They'll sleep when and where the men sleep, right with them.'

I said, 'The union will get the Congress to protest in the Assembly, sir.' I thought not only that they would, but that they should.

The Collector said, 'Some Congress members of the Assembly will protest. They will protest vigorously, and quite rightly, against peaceful Indians being driven to work at bayonet point. On the other hand, and not in public, they will advise the union to bow to *force majeure* and return to work. Then the union can start the strike again whenever they want to, after the mutiny's over. That's the arrangement.'

'The arrangement?' I said incredulously.

The Collector said, 'Yes, the arrangement. The Congress high command are worried about their extremists. They've sent a posse of Congress luminaries down to Bombay simply to keep some of their own firebrands away from the sailors. Congress don't want this kind of revolution.'

'Then everything that happened in the square was pretence?' I said. 'And was Kartar Singh in on it?'

The Collector said, 'He was. None of the others. Though you heard the agitators shouting, giving hints. *They* knew. We've got a couple of them safe, but they're only little ones. This has been a perfect example of what I told you about the first day you came here, Miss Jones. K. P. Roy and his Communists help to foment a perfectly legitimate strike. Congress approve of it – they have to or they'd lose their influence. But secretly the Communists are also fomenting a mutiny, which Congress do not approve of, having just realized that it's soon going to be *their* Navy. But Congress mustn't disapprove too loudly, or the sailors too will go

117

elsewhere for encouragement. So Congress have been searching wildly for a way to get the strike ended and take the R.I.N. mutinies out of the Communists' hands into their own, and at the same time to seem to support both the mutiny and the strike.'

Colonel Savage said, 'Gandhi ought to give me a bloody medal when he gets in the saddle up there – the Order of the Radiant Dhoti.'

I sat there thinking. It was all very clear now. All of us were puppets of the people on top, and it didn't make any difference whether the people on top were British or Indian. They argued and manoeuvred among themselves, decided which way to pull the lever, then pulled it – or had it pulled – and all of us below jumped and grimaced on our strings. There were no Anglo-Indians on top. Even Sir Meredith Sullivan was a puppet.

I said slowly, 'Does Mr Surabhai know all this?' Though he was the local Congress boss, I hoped he didn't. If he didn't, Ranjit certainly didn't. As long as they were not in the know my sympathies were entirely with them. If they were puppets I could understand them and feel with them and be one of them.

The Collector said, 'Almost certainly not. He's the sort of person with whom, if the Congress high command seemed to be co-operating with the government, they would lose influence.'

'And that's the kind of sentence up with which a sensitive Old Wellingtonian should not on any occasion be asked to put,' Colonel Savage said. 'But I presume you dislike Churchill.'

'Talking about language,' the Collector said, 'that subadar-major of yours is really rather a wonderful man.'

'Manbir's a good egg,' Colonel Savage said shortly. 'Also he's a good actor, like all Gurkhas. His grandfather was my grand-father's orderly.'

'Same regiment?' the Collector asked.

Colonel Savage said, 'Yes. No imagination, that's our trouble.' He fell silent. I knew he didn't like talking about the Gurkhas with outsiders. Once he'd said to me, 'Now, Miss Jones, if you ask me any questions about the wonderful little Gurkhas and their wonderful little boomerang-knives and their wonderful bravery and loyalty and good humour, I'll tell one of them to cut your wonderful little throat.' I knew that he always called the subadar-major 'Father', except on parade.

The liveried doorman passed in with a small visiting card in the middle of a huge silver salver. The Collector glanced at it and said, 'Ask him if it's private.'

The doorman salaamed and retired. Mr Govindaswami said, 'Mr Surabhai.'

Colonel Savage said, 'Then perhaps he does know about our little subterfuge?'

The Collector said, 'I don't know. He wouldn't come here unless he thought it was serious.'

The doorman came back and whispered something. The Collector raised his eyebrows. 'Show them all in,' he said and stood up.

Mr Surabhai entered the room and stood stiffly at ease a little inside the doorway. Two Indian gentlemen followed him, bowing to the Collector, and stood one on each side of Mr Surabhai. All three wore dhotis. Mr Surabhai's sock-suspenders were maroon and his socks yellow, and he was wearing tan and white co-respondent shoes. On his arm he had a loosely-furled umbrella with a long ferrule.

The Collector held out his hand, but Mr Surabhai ignored it. He said, 'I have come, Mr Govindaswami, to lodge a complaint. These gentlemen are my two witnesses.'

The Collector dropped his hand and said, 'But shouldn't you come to the Kutcherry during the proper hours, Mr Surabhai?'

'I have only just this very minute thought of my idea,' Mr Surabhai said excitedly. 'Besides, you have no right to order the hours when the people may come and lay their complaints in front of you. You are a servant of the people.'

The Collector said, 'I see. Can you give me some idea of the subject of your complaint?'

Mr Surabhai rummaged in his coat pocket and brought out a sheet of paper. He looked at it, then glared at the Collector with large, excited eyes. He said, 'This is not in correctly legal form yet, you understand that? I just dashed it off: "I, V. K. Surabhai, pleader, of such and such an address" – you know quite well where my house is situated, mister – "do hereby depose that at or about one p.m. Indian Standard Time, on Sunday, May the nineteenth, nineteen forty-six, parenthesis, being Vaisakha Vadya 3 Saka 1868, Vikrama 2003 of the true calendars, end of parenthesis, on platform Number One of the Bhowani Junction railway station of the Delhi Deccan Railway Company Limited –" '

Colonel Savage put down his whisky and began to light a cheroot.

Mr Surabhai continued to declaim: ' "– did see and observe a Gurkha soldier, name unknown, commit the following hereunder described misdemeanours, that is to say, first, indecent exposure of the person by opening his buttons and exhibiting in full view of the public of all sexes there assembled his –" '

Mr Surabhai had been reading angrily and banging the ferrule of his umbrella on the floor and glaring at the Collector to emphasize his points. The other two gentlemen stood solemnly beside him. Suddenly Mr Surabhai caught sight of me. He stopped short and said aggrievedly, 'Why did you not inform me there was a lady present? How do you do, Miss Jones, so nice to see you here.'

The Collector said, 'I thought you'd seen her, Mr Surabhai.'

Mr Surabhai said, 'I had not, of course not, why should I? Well, "a disgusting object," I shall say here, mister, but you know very well what I mean. And – oh, yes – "secondly, a public nuisance in that he passed his water otherwise than in the authorized and plainly marked public convenience. The following undersigned gentlemen also witnessed the above facts and" – you know who these gentlemen are also, mister. Now, what are you going to do about *that*?'

He put away the paper and stood with his arms folded, the umbrella hanging from his left forearm.

The Collector said, 'That's a serious charge, Mr Surabhai.'

Mr Surabhai said, 'I know very well it is a serious charge! That is why I made it, you see. There are two charges actually, obviously. I demand that the man be punished most severely. But there were several soldiers engaged in the same disgusting way, mister. In my home I will write a complaint against each and every one – name unknown in each case, naturally – but I have not found the leisure to do all that yet.'

'I think I can help you to find the culprits, Collector,' Colonel Savage said.

'I should say you can,' Mr Surabhai said warmly. 'They were soldiers of your command. You know very well who they were!'

'One was Rifleman Tilokbir Ale,' Colonel Savage said slowly. 'I'll have to ask the subadar-major to find out the names of the others. But I'll get them. When do you want them in court, Collector?'

'Tomorrow morning, eleven o'clock,' the Collector said.

Mr Surabhai seemed to deflate. He said, 'But – but –' His eyes shrank, and he looked depressed. He said, 'But do you mean that the soldiers will come and confess guilty to their crime, and accept punishment?'

'Certainly they will!' Colonel Savage got up and spoke energetically. 'Certainly they will. They are subjects first, and soldiers second. Wearing uniform doesn't put a man above the civil law. Military discipline doesn't protect a soldier from the legal consequences of an illegal action. You'll see them tomorrow.'

The Collector escorted Mr Surabhai and his party out. I looked at my fingernails. I didn't want to catch Colonel Savage's eye. He really had something to laugh about now. He had been like a lazy well-fed cat playing with foolish little mice. By nature and by blood I was one of the mice.

Mr Govindaswami came back and sat down. After a time Colonel Savage said, 'Is that the best the poor little blighter could think of?'

The Collector said moodily, 'I suppose so. He might have charged the Gurkhas with assault – it was, technically – but then he'd have made himself and Congress a laughing-stock. He hoped I'd refuse to bring the Gurkhas to trial. Then he could have said that we were protecting criminals, without having to go into too much detail. Now I doubt if he'll go on with it.'

The Collector got up and paced angrily up and down, talking as if to himself. He said, 'Poor Surabhai. He only wanted one thing – to get into armoured cavalry. He'd have preferred a horse, but a tank would have been better than nothing – a tank with the top open and him standing up in it. He hated Hitler and Mussolini and Hirohito. He's a liberal, a romantic of the romantics.'

Colonel Savage said, 'Why didn't he enlist, then? He would have been young enough, and he'd certainly have got a commission.'

The Collector said, 'Because of you and your damned grip on this country. I hate the lot of you sometimes.' He picked up his glass and refilled it from the decanter. He said, 'Surabhai's the stuff heroes are made of. Heroes never have any sense of proportion.'

Colonel Savage said, 'Well, I'll take my white face out of here. It'll be gone for good soon enough.'

The Collector said, 'Yes. Run away. Mr Surabhai makes me very bad-tempered. Look here, don't go wandering round the city tonight on one of those prowls of yours. There'll be a mass meeting of protest about our strike-breaking.'

'You've heard already?' Colonel Savage asked.

The Collector said, 'No. But I'm an Indian. Tonight there'll be protests. Tomorrow morning the union chiefs will telegraph all their branches to get the men back to work – under protest and without prejudice to their right to start the strike again. By God, I wish I could catch K. P. Roy.'

I went out with Colonel Savage, leaving the Collector hunched in his big chair. The short time of twilight had come while we were in there, and from the steps I could see the lighted ends of the Gurkhas' cigarettes glowing in the jeeps.

'How are you getting home?' Colonel Savage asked me.

'I came on my bicycle, sir,' I said.

He said, 'Okay. You heard what the Collector said. You'd better keep out of the city too, unless you go in a sari.' He stood there a moment, drawing on his cheroot. Then he said, 'In a few days now I intend to tell G.H.Q. I have no further work for you. It's getting less, isn't it?'

I said, 'The railway work is, sir. That's nearly all routine now. The battalion Intelligence work is increasing.'

He said, 'I know. But I can't keep a female Intelligence officer as a pet, even if I wanted to. Been having any more trouble? Sex trouble?' He looked hard at me, frowning and biting the end of the cheroot.

I said, 'No, sir,' and couldn't help blushing, though I don't suppose he noticed it in the gloom.

He said, 'Have you made up your mind about Taylor?'

For a moment I was too surprised to speak; then I said, 'That is none of your business, sir.'

He said, 'Up to a point. But Taylor's behaving like an angry water buffalo, and God knows he's inefficient enough when he's

122

not angry. I expect the other men in your life would also feel much more at ease if you made it plain who *was* going to get it. If you pretend no one's going to get it, men just don't believe you – neither black, white, nor khaki men.'

I stood, still and angry, on the top step while he got into the jeep and switched on the engine. I could see his teeth flash as he smiled suddenly and said, 'But if I were you I'd give Mr Taylor to Rose Mary, and throw in a pound of tea.'

13

I SALUTED as the jeep swept away. He hated to have me salute him. When he was out of sight I got on my bicycle and pedalled slowly toward our house. I wondered why Colonel Savage took a delight in using the full force of his personality, all its hard and unpleasant side, against me. He was quite different with the Collector and with the Gurkhas. He didn't seem to like his own British officers very much. A few of them liked him; the rest managed to hide whatever feelings they had. To them, he was 'the Sahib'. He liked to live that way and to be that way, and they were under his command – so be it. He was the only Regular Army officer among them.

I felt very lonely pedalling down the Pike among the straggling houses and gardens that cover the strip of land between the railway and the Cheetah. There was no one else on the road. But the cause of my loneliness was what I had seen and heard this day. The Collector and Colonel Savage made a strange pair, but the ties between them were very close. I had no ties – except to the railway line over there on my left, and to the ladders of unwinking green and red lights on the north gantry.

That ride was like a time of slack water in my life. I was not English or Indian or Anglo-Indian. I was Victoria Jones and sat alone in a boat with everybody equally far away from me. There were two things which, so to speak, pointed my boat in a certain direction. One was the obvious truth that the English and the Anglo-Indians were sinking. I don't say I would not have gone down with them, and very happily, if I had felt any real affection

123

for even one of them; but I hated all of them. Colonel Savage and Patrick Taylor were their representatives.

The second thing was that I really knew nothing about Indians. As I didn't know, I could imagine. I was imagining – all the good and nice things the others hadn't got.

Then I remembered that a Gurkha office orderly, who could hardly read, had taken down and accidentally burned a rather complicated graph Colonel Savage had told me to make in the beginning. The graph was to help him see when the line was clear for his trolley patrols. If normal rail service was going to begin tomorrow or the next day, I'd better be ready with a new graph. I turned down Station Road.

The sight of the city ahead of me reminded me of the Collector's warning and Colonel Savage's repetition of it. I pedalled more slowly and thought of turning back.

But the station was only just inside the limits of the city. I free-wheeled down the ramp into the tunnel that passes under the tracks beyond the north end of the platforms. When I came out of the tunnel I had a quick view of a long, narrow street with many people in it. I heard the noise they were making, and again I stopped pedalling. Then I thought how Colonel Savage would sneer if he did happen to ask for the graph and I hadn't got it. I turned right and pedalled quickly into the station yard.

It was deserted. The tonga wallahs had gone, with their ponies and their tongas and their little piles of chopped grass. The hawkers had gone. The beggars had gone, even the man with his leg twisted around his neck, even the legless armless body in a basket. Two policemen were talking in the shadows of the arch. They stood aside for me, and I hurried past them and along the platform. The coolies were there, waiting for trains that would not come. The Gurkha soldiers stood a little way from their prisoners. The bright lights in the refreshment rooms and in the ticket office shone out over the bare platforms and the steel rails.

I ran up the stairs, along the upper passage, and into the Traffic Office. I sighed with relief as I closed the door behind me.

Ranjit Singh was there, and so was Macaulay. Macaulay's carbine lay on my desk. Though I did not like Macaulay, I was glad at that moment to see the carbine.

Macaulay looked at me and said, 'You're done in, Victoria.'

124

I was out of breath from running and from the foolish inde-scribable fear of the crowd in that narrow street. I said, 'It's so quiet outside, but it's noisy a little farther off in the city. I – I got the wind up, I suppose.' I laughed nervously and smoothed down my skirt and lit a cigarette.

Ranjit said, 'May I get you a drink of water, Miss Jones?' He spoke politely, so politely as to be almost cold. I refused, thanking him, and he sat down at his desk and bent his head over his work. I wanted to ask him what was the matter – but what could I say?

I went to my table and sat down. 'What are you doing here?' I asked Macaulay.

He said, 'Working. What else can you do when the Sahib's got you in his sights? He sent me out on a trolley patrol as a matter of fact. When I got back just now I thought I might as well re-do that graph that got burned.'

I said, 'That's what I came here to do! It's my job. You shouldn't have bothered.'

He said, 'I thought I'd save you a little trouble. But I hardly got started.'

I said, 'I'll finish it. Thank you, though.' I had to thank him, and he was standing well away from me. Ranjit Singh's pen scratched unobtrusively in the background.

Macaulay said, 'Look, I'll do the branch line graph and you do the main line. Then we can get finished quicker. And the sooner the better, if you ask me.' He glanced out of the window and mut-tered, 'Not a bloody soul in sight anywhere now.' He got some sheets of graph paper, sat down opposite me, and began to work.

I tried to concentrate on the work, but sounds outside kept in-truding, and then there would come silence more pressing than the silence in the room. Once there was a tremendous distant shout that rumbled and boomed toward us from the farthest parts of the city. I dropped my pencil and started up, to see Macaulay looking at me. He shrugged, and I picked up my pencil, smiling at him – smiling from nerves.

Once a woman on a nearby housetop screamed for three min-utes to another woman down in the street; it was a message, but I could not understand it. They shouted in some dialect. I only knew that both women were terrified – the one crying from the roof and the one hiding in the street. Then silence again, a big flat silence that crept up and caught hold of my pencil hand until it slowed and slowed and stopped. Ranjit Singh noisily got out a typewriter and furiously banged the keys. The silence was like the sea, and drowned even that.

I finished at last. It could not have been more than three-quarters of an hour. As I put down my pencil the noise boomed up again, a steady drumbeat and a rhythmical chanting from the centre of the city, perhaps six hundred yards to the east of us. I said, 'I'm going home now. Please take this to the office with yours and leave them in my room.'

Macaulay pushed his chair back and picked up his carbine. 'I'll go with you,' he said.

Automatically I said, 'No, there's no need for that.'

He was hurt and answered me very stiffly. 'Allow me to ring for a jeep. The telephone line's still through.'

'No,' I said quickly, 'thank you. It's too close.' I didn't say, besides, Colonel Savage warned me. I said, 'I'll walk down the line.'

He went to the door and held it open for me. He said, 'I'm coming. My God, Victoria, the Sahib would tear my guts out with his bare hands if I let you go back alone now. Listen to them!'

I heard the booming drum, and the tramp of feet that held no discipline, and the rhythmical high chant. I shivered, and said, 'All right. Thank you.'

Macaulay said, 'Are you sure you're all right here, Ranjit?'

Ranjit looked up at the two of us, his eyes meeting mine for a second and at once dropping. He said, 'I'm all right, thank you, Mr Macaulay.'

Macaulay shrugged and followed me along the corridor and down the stairs. On the platform he spoke to a Gurkha standing in the beam of light from the first-class waiting-room, then led on. At the end of the platform he said to me, 'The password tonight is *shikar* and the countersign, *Kabul*. That mob's coming this way.'

He stepped down on to the line-side path and walked carefully along. I wondered whether there were any police with the crowd, and what the people meant to do when they got to the station. I felt cowardly, and as if I had somehow betrayed Ranjit by showing this fear of Indians, even though they were a mob.

Macaulay didn't have Colonel Savage's extraordinary ability to see in the dark. He picked his way so slowly over the slots where the point rods and signal wires crossed under the line that I whispered, 'Let me get in front. I know the way.'

He muttered, 'Okay,' and stood aside. As I brushed past him he said, 'For God's sake, stop at once if anyone says, "Halt!" Stop and answer, "Shikar." '

I whispered, 'All right,' and moved forward quickly. The lights of the yards came up on our right, and almost immediately a soft voice challenged me from close by – 'Halt-who-go-da?'

I stopped at once and whispered, 'Shikar.' Macaulay bumped into me and stood close.

The man answered, 'Kabul.' He and another Gurkha appeared from the shadow of a wagon and came close to us, their rifles carried like shotguns in the crooks of their arms. Macaulay said, 'It's me, the adjutant. I'm seeing the lieutenant-lady home.' He spoke Gurkhali slowly and with many Hindustani words.

The Gurkhas drifted back into the shadow.

A little farther on I said, 'Let's cross the line here. There's more light in the yards.' I led on at once, crossed the main line, ducked under one row of wagons, then another, and came to a third. The yard lights shone brilliantly from their tall standards. A few big moths were up there round every light, circling and beating their wings and crashing into the reflectors so hard that we could hear them from down below. The shadows were thick along the sides of the empty, standing trains. The heat they had been gathering all day poured out from their iron sides.

Just ahead there, at the end of the yards, I'd be in the Old Lines and nearly opposite the Institute. I stopped with a sigh of relief and leaned back against the frame of a wagon. I said, 'There's no need for you to come any farther now, Mr Macaulay.'

He was close behind me. He said, 'Yes, I think you're out of the wood now.' He whispered, but I could swear it was not from fear. It was the kind of whisper men use to a girl at night, when there is really no need, to say those things they always say in whispers.

I said quickly, 'I'm sure it's all right now. Well, thank you. I must go.'

He said, 'Aren't you going to thank me properly?' The whisper

127

was light and dry. Again I said, 'Thank you.' I said it quickly, wanting to run. But I couldn't get away from him even if I did run. I knew suddenly I must turn to face him.

He had his carbine in his right hand, and his left hand was reaching out for me. It went round my waist. He said, 'Thank me – like this.' He bent forward and pressed close, and his hot face clamped against mine, moving round like an animal's to find my lips. For a second I stood stiff and still, thinking, The fool, the damned bloody fool, he will get into trouble. Colonel Savage will kill him. Then I couldn't stand the dribble on his moustache any longer. I began to struggle.

When I writhed in his arm it might have been a signal, a trigger. He dropped the carbine and leaped on me with both arms out. The carbine fell with a small sound on to the clinkers. He tore at my shirt and skirt and pressed me back and mewed, 'I can't stand it – please, Victoria. Please let me, let me. It's no use, I can make you, you did with Johnny – you've got to!'

I fell back and slipped on the rail under the wagon. He scrambled silently after me. I swung my arm round and hit him. There was a heavy sharp-edged steel thing in my hand. He fell sideways and lay across the rail, his head out in the open. I stood up, aimed carefully, and hit him again as hard as I could, swinging the piece of broken fishplate up in both hands and bringing it down, edge on, against the side of his head.

I had not heard any other sound, but swung round, the fishplate raised, when a darker shadow fell across me. I saw it was Ranjit Singh. He came forward slowly, stopped, and whispered, 'Oh my God, oh my God.' He knelt slowly, fluttered round with his hands looking for some place to touch, to feel, to assure himself. He whispered, 'Put that down, Miss Jones. Come with me, quickly.'

I put the bar down and watched Ranjit Singh pull at Macaulay's body until it was all under the wagon, lying between the rails. He beckoned with his hand, palm toward me in the Indian way. I followed him for fifty yards between the empty trains, then he crawled under the one to our left, under the next, and the next, until we stood beside the main line. He looked both ways and crouched low, and we hurried across. His teeth were chattering all the time. There is a low wire fence there. I climbed it after him, awkwardly in my tight skirt, and we passed into the city. I followed down a dark lane; left, another lane; right, a short street with lights in the shops but no one about and the windows shuttered; left again, the thick stink of a tannery; on for a hundred yards.

Ranjit opened a door and beckoned me in. His face showed pale and strained in the dim light from a curtained window across the street. The pupils of his eyes were huge. We stood at the foot of a narrow stair. He scurried up. There were two doors at the top. He hesitated a moment there, standing irresolute, looking across the hall, and at the doors in turn, and back at me. Then he opened the door on the left and held it for me. I walked into a room of light colours, whitewashed walls, light from oil lamps, very little furniture.

A woman got up slowly from the floor and slowly came toward me. She was brown and square, and her hair was iron grey. Her sari was white with a blue border. She set her feet wide apart as she walked. She said in Hindustani, 'Who is this, my son? And whom has she killed?'

'I didn't kill him!' I gasped.

The woman said, 'Look, girl.'

I looked down. The blood lay in spots and streaks and whorls over the breast of my khaki shirt. The horrible night came down on me, all together, reflected in the woman's hard brown eyes. Even in that room I heard the boom of the drum and the faint chanting of the crowd. Fear and hate and heat and lust were all round me. I stood helpless. I felt my face twisting and an icy cold creeping up in me in jerks and spasms. I opened my mouth to scream.

14

THE woman rocked back on her feet, which were so strongly set against the floor, and her square hands swung round – left, right, *bang-bang* on my face. My cheeks stung, and the teeth rattled in my head. She took hold of my arms at the elbows and said quietly to Ranjit, 'Whom did she kill, son?'

'A British officer of the Gurkhas. Lieutenant Macaulay. In the yards. He was a beastly swine.'

She said, 'Is he still there? Do you think he will have been discovered yet?'

He said, 'I don't know. I don't think so.'

I could not cry now. My hysteria had gone. I stood in the woman's grip, so tired that I couldn't tremble. I said, 'He tried to rape me.'

She said, 'Ah. Son, call our friend.'

Ranjit wiped his forehead with his hand and shuffled his feet. He said. 'Do you think it would be wise, Mother? I mean, to tell anyone else? The fewer people –'

Tell? Tell! Of course. I knew there was something I had to do. I said, 'I must go and tell the Collector. And Mr Lanson. At once.'

She said, 'Why did you come here if you want to go and tell the Collector? What will he think when he knows you came straight here? Eh?' Her voice was strong, not harsh but full and deep and firm. She said, 'Now hurry and fetch our friend, son.'

Ranjit still hesitated, but his mother turned to look at him, and he went out with a little movement of defeat. The door closed behind him.

The woman led me through a side door into a small bare room. A lamp, a newar charpoy, and a tin trunk were its only furniture. She said, 'Now get those clothes off, girl. Be quick.'

I took off my skirt and shirt and stood shivering in the hot, close room. There was no window. Faint sounds and a little starlight filtered in through a high skylight. The woman said, 'Take everything off. Was he trying to undress you? Some of your things may be torn or bloodstained.'

I took off the rest of my clothes and stood naked. The woman gave me a pair of bloomers, an Indian-style bodice, and a sari, and helped me to get into them. As I dressed I heard the creak of footsteps in the other room, and the mutter of men's voices. The woman opened the door an inch and called through, 'Water. Basin. Soap. Sigri. That stain remover.' She came back and fingered over my discarded clothes. Her hands moved quickly, and her eyes darted from side to side. She left some on the floor and carried the rest back into the big room, pushing me in front of her.

Ranjit was there with a short pale Indian in a loincloth. Ranjit stared at me as if I was a ghost. The woman said to the other man, 'You know what's happened?'

The Indian said, 'Yes. I'll go at once. I ought to be back in half an hour at the most.'

He walked quickly to the door. I said, 'What are you going to do? I must tell the Collector. I must –'

The woman said, 'You must not tell the Collector. Who do you think they will put the guilt on? My son. It won't matter what you say. Do you want to go through examination in court, cross-examination? Are you a virgin? If they don't fix it on my son, they'll say you led the Englishman on and then asked him for money. They'll say anything to protect his reputation. Our friend will arrange it so that they will never find out who did it.'

The Indian went out. I listened but could not hear his feet on the long stairs. The invisible charcoal fumes from the sigri tingled in my nostrils.

The woman squatted in the middle of the floor and began to rub the marks of blood out of my clothes. As she worked she said, 'Sit down, girl. I am this one's mother. I am a widow – the Sirdarni Amrita Kasel. Mrs Kasel, you would probably say. You should call me Beji when you speak to me.'

I hardly heard her. I sank slowly on to a cheap rickety chair. I said, 'You don't seem to realize. I've killed somebody. I've *got* to go and tell the Collector.' I tried to speak firmly, but it came out in a hoarse whisper.

She said, 'You've killed an Englishman, an Army officer. That is not a person. That is an animal. Give her a drink, son. Our friend keeps several bottles in his place.'

Obediently Ranjit hurried out and soon came back with a half-full bottle of Solan whisky and two glasses. Shakily he poured out half a glass for me and as much for himself. I gulped it down and watched him drink in slow shuddering sips.

The Sirdarni said, 'Why should you support the British law? You're half Indian, aren't you?' She held up the front of my skirt in front of the sigri. 'Get the iron,' she ordered Ranjit, and when he brought it she put it on the sigri to heat.

The whisky began to smoke in my head. I felt loose and large and on the edge of something enormous. I had to tell them about it. I said, 'He tried before. He was awful.'

The Sirdarni said, 'Quiet!'

My voice had been trembling, edging up the scale in little high shivers. The Sirdarni looked at me and said, 'My child, you have done a great thing. Now you are a heroine of the new India. I seldom drink, but I will drink to you now. Fill her glass again, son.' She carefully propped the clothes on a bench and a box so that they faced the sigri, and took the whisky bottle from Ranjit. She said, '*Jai Hind!*' and poured a lot of whisky down her throat. I watched her throat muscles moving up and down as she swallowed. She handed the bottle back. I drank again and shook my head and shivered.

'We'll have to check our stories,' the Sirdarni said.

I said, 'I must –'

She cut in. '*You must!*' She stood, feet apart, by the sigri and fixed her eyes on me. She said, 'Have you ever met an Englishman who didn't insult you? Haven't your people worked for them for a hundred years? And now how are they going to reward you? You know. They're going to leave you here to us. And what do you think *we're* going to do? We're going to make you realize that you are Indians – inferior Indians, possibly disloyal Indians, because you've spent a hundred years licking England's boots and kicking us with your own boots that you're so proud of wearing. *I* saw the soldiers pissing on our people at the station. I saw you. You didn't look happy. Why don't you see that you're an Indian, and act like one? We're strong now. We'll look after you.'

My teeth chattered on the rim of the glass. Ranjit stood there fidgeting in front of me but as silent as a dummy. Why didn't he say something?

The Sirdarni said, 'These clothes are nearly dry. We're all moving together, moving forward. Soon the British will go, and we are hurrying them up. We don't all agree among ourselves – some are conservatives and reactionaries – but we're on the move, we are marching. That fool Surabhai, and me, and our friend – millions of us, all moving. Come with us. Here. Look!'

She picked up a mirror from the gimcrack table behind her and held it in front of my eyes. I gasped and stared. I saw an oval pale brown face and large eyes framed in the gold and green curve of the sari. I knew why Ranjit had been staring at me. I moved my head and opened my lips and spread my fingers. It was me, but this person in the mirror was more beautiful than me. She was a beautiful Indian girl in her own clothes. I could appraise her as honestly as if she had been any other woman I might see in the street, because she was not 'me', Victoria Jones, the Anglo-Indian.

The Sirdarni took the mirror away, and I was looking at the sigri and the foolish, short, hard-edged skirt, the masculine shirt. I have always hated short skirts. I had to wear them and I had got used to them, but now I *saw* them for the first time. The Sirdarni said softly, 'India is your home, my child. The dawn is breaking now – our dawn, our sun, our freedom. We will stand by you always, whatever you do, once you find that you are an Indian. Trust us.'

I met her eyes, and I did trust her. My roots had been in bitter soil, and then for a time I had been without roots. Searching for home, I had not found home – only Home and a house.

Home was where the English came from and went back to, though I never could. Home was where they did not have a city and a cantonment in every big town, so that the officers could laugh themselves sick at an Anglo-Indian who talked about how he was going 'Home to Southampton Cantonment'. Our house was Number 4 Collett Road, a bungalow sitting on a tired piece of land belonging to a country which Pater and everyone who lived in the house repudiated.

The presence of Macaulay was very strongly on me. He was typical of the British. He was pleasant when it suited him, cold when it suited him, and all the time selfish, cunning, lord of all he wanted to take. I know he was unbalanced, but I didn't take that into account then. Colonel Savage was a cruel bully. Johnny Tallent pretended to love me and then told all his friends I was free for the taking. Patrick was as bad as any of them, and a bigger fool besides. Rose Mary. Mrs Williams. Sir Meredith Sullivan.

An overpowering nervous excitement filled me, coming up like a high fear that choked me in my throat. All those people I had been thinking of stood on one side, and on the other – the dawn. I realized that it was not fear that I felt, but triumph, which is so often the same as fear.

My boat was moving fast to shore then.

The strange Indian came back. His face was pale and smooth

and without expression. His eyes were calm. He had large ears, set low, and he wore a big shapeless moustache. Both his moustache and the untidy hair showing below his turban were pepper-and-salt, black and grey. The Sirdarni said, 'This is our friend, Ghanshyam. And you are Victoria Jones. My son has spoken of you.'

I glanced at Ranjit and smiled proudly. He did not smile back. He was silent and troubled and could not stand still for more than a few seconds at a time.

Ghanshyam, the pale Indian, said, 'I have brought the body into the city and hidden it in a dungheap, where it should not be found for several days. The Gurkhas did not see me. I have buried the piece of fishplate, first washing it clean. No one saw me.' He spoke in a soft, careful, polite voice.

The Sirdarni said, 'Good. Now we must get our stories straight. Do not worry at all, my child, there is nothing to worry about. You are an Indian, and because you have struck a blow for us – for yourself – we will see that you come to no harm. What happened?'

I told her. The excitement was dying away in me; the effect of the whisky had passed; but my boat was moving on a new clear course. All this was nothing but sensible people sensibly planning.

The Sirdarni said, 'Then only my son knew that this Macaulay was going to see you to your house? And those who saw you leave the station with Macaulay would be – several Gurkhas and coolies on the platform, the two sentries who challenged you. Those sentries would also know that you got as far as the beginning of the yards together. Then the same sentries saw my son following you very shortly afterwards. Yes?'

Ranjit said, 'I didn't see any sentries in the yards.'

His mother said, 'They may have seen you though, and remained hidden, recognizing you?'

'No, they would have challenged,' I said.

The Sirdarni said, 'I do not think it matters.' She walked once up and down the room and stopped in front of Ghanshyam. She asked him, 'What do you think?'

Ghanshyam said, 'It is not difficult, Beji. Lieutenant Macaulay and Miss Jones went on along the line, just inside the yards, without being challenged again. Ranjit went after them because his work was finished and Miss Jones had left her bag behind. He caught them up near the Loco Shed junction and gave Miss Jones her handbag. Then he came home here, there being no reason for him to return to the station. Lieutenant Macaulay left Miss Jones by the signal outside her home. She at once went into her garden, and that was the last she saw of him.'

'But after that why didn't I go into the house?' I asked quickly.

Ghanshyam looked at me with a little nod of approval. He said, 'Because you decided you could not face your sister – or your mother. Because you had personal problems you wanted to think over in peace. About your position as an Anglo-Indian, for instance. About Mr Taylor, perhaps.'

I said slowly, 'Yes. I had things to think about, and I wanted peace and quiet.'

'Very well,' Ghanshyam continued. 'Now where did you go for, say, two and a half hours? It is not late even now – a quarter to nine.'

I would have said it was nearer midnight.

Where on earth could I have been hiding for two and a half hours at this time of the evening? I wouldn't have crept into the bushes like a jackal; that didn't make sense. It had to be some quiet but ordinary place. It had to be the reading-room of the Institute. I said it aloud, and Ghanshyam asked, 'Did you do any reading?'

I said, 'I had a magazine in my hand. I hardly remember what it was. I was just sitting there thinking of Patrick, thinking that I couldn't marry him. I was thinking of Colonel Savage. I was deciding the Anglo-Indians were wrong not to throw in their lot with the Indians.'

Ghanshyam said, 'The lights would be on all the time? There is a place you could be, where a person glancing in from the door *might* not see you?'

I said, 'Yes, but –' I had no regrets, no qualms, and I was glad I had killed Macaulay, but it was becoming risky, of a sudden.

Ghanshyam said, 'You must remember that it is almost impossible to get anyone to swear that a person was *not* in a particular place at a particular time. Witnesses will only swear that someone *was* somewhere. You walked round a bit. You went to the ladies' room – there is no ayah permanently on duty there?'

I said, 'Only on week-ends. For dances and whist drives.'

He said, 'Good. You will go to the Institute now, and use the bathroom in case the sweeper should later recall that no one did. It is very important that you should be able to prove that you were not in the reading-room all the time. All this is merely precautionary. Lieutenant Macaulay will be seen at about this hour, now, in a house of ill fame at the other end of the city. He will leave it at eleven o'clock – that is, in two hours from now, more or less.'

'The doctors will be able to tell better from the body,' the Sirdarni said sharply.

'I think not, Beji,' Ghanshyam said. 'The corpse is in a dung-heap, you will recall, and with ordinary luck it will not be discovered for several days. The dung emits strong gases and powerful chemicals.' Ranjit was swaying on his feet, and his eyes were half closed as he listened to this. Ghanshyam said, 'But I think Miss Jones should now leave, with all cautious speed.'

I stood up. My legs were strong and my head clear. The Sirdarni said, 'Tomorrow my son will invite you to come here for a visit. You must come. Some interesting people may call. I wish to see you again. And please remember that no one except us here, and our two servants, knows that our friend Ghanshyam is staying with us. Now go quickly and put on all those underclothes you were wearing. Better still, put on all your clothes, and then I will drape the sari over everything. Hurry.'

She pushed me into the little room. I undressed and redressed as quickly as I could. When I came out the Sirdarni adjusted the sari again so that it hid all the other clothes. She stepped back, and for a moment her hard face softened and she smiled. She muttered, 'You are a very beautiful woman, my child. Take her along now, Ranjit.'

Without another word I followed Ranjit down the stairs and out of the house. There was no one about, and we walked quickly along empty streets. I found that I swung my hips naturally, as Indian women do, holding my head up and my chest out. If I didn't walk like that the sari did not move properly.

Ranjit did not speak until we were on the wasteland nearly opposite our house, and I could see the tall signal against the stars and the white glow of light escaping from the side of the signal lamp. Then Ranjit muttered, 'My mother is a wonderful woman, isn't she?'

I said, 'Yes. Why mustn't I mention Ghanshyam? Who is he?'

He said, 'A gentleman from Western India. The British want him for printing seditious pamphlets, in Karachi or Multan, I think it was.'

We were at the line then. Ranjit whispered, 'Will you take off the sari now?' I unwrapped it and untied it and gave it to him. 'Your bag,' he said. 'Don't forget that again. Don't take too much notice of what my mother says always, Miss Jones. She is a great patriot, but – well, I cannot always agree with her.'

I understood. She was of a much more ruthless character than he was. I whispered, 'Good night, Ranjit, and – thank you. I'll see you tomorrow.' I crossed the line.

Lights were glowing behind the curtains in the Institute. The sweeper would be in his quarters. I walked round to the back of the building, opened the outer door of the ladies' bathroom, and slipped in. When I had finished I opened the inner door an inch and looked down the hall. No one was about. I walked slowly over to the reading-room. It was empty. I sat on a sofa with my back to the door and picked a magazine off the table, riffled over the pages, and noted one or two pictures.

I found myself thinking about Patrick. I resented everything about him and wondered for a moment if it could be jealousy. But that was ridiculous. I thought about Rose Mary, and about Ranjit. Macaulay never crossed my mind.

The Institute was as silent as an empty church. No. Some men were playing billiards at the other end of the hall. They wouldn't have come in here. Cigarettes – I looked at the ashtray. There were a couple of old stubs, both stained with lipstick. I couldn't tell how old they were. Anyway, I had been to the bathroom, out on the steps getting some air, walking about. And I had not smoked tonight. Not in here.

Where was my bicycle? At the station. Why had I left it there? Because Macaulay had offered to escort me down the line. I must go and get the bicycle in the morning – if it hadn't been smashed or stolen.

I got up, glanced carelessly around for the last time, and walked

137

out of the front door, down the three steps, and turned on to Collett Road. I stopped to light a cigarette.

The lights were on in the parlour of our house, and I stood a moment on the path, carefully considering them. Who was it? Patrick's motor-cycle was there at the edge of the road to my right. I went closer, walking softly on the grass, and listened at the window. No one was talking. Pater was out. Mater would be out. Rose Mary might be in there with Patrick, but I didn't think so.

I opened the door and walked in. Patrick was in the parlour. He had left the door open so that no one could pass down the little hall without his seeing. He was sitting in a chair by the fireplace, a book in his hands. He looked at me, his big face suddenly anxious, and stood up. I walked slowly into the room. I saw myself in the mirror over the fireplace and stared carefully – no blood, no mark, my skin smooth, my eyes dark.

Patrick said, 'Where have you been? I have been waiting.'

I said, 'For Rose Mary?'

He said, 'Oh, Victoria, don't talk like that. Rose Mary is – you know Rose Mary is nothing to me. I was waiting for you. I want to explain about why that happened the other night. I want to ask you to forgive me. I –' His voice trailed away. His pale eyes were hurt and shiny, and I felt the tears coming up in mine. But I was a new girl. I was not his Victoria Jones.

I said, 'I have been in the Institute – reading. I have nothing to say to you, and I don't want to hear your excuses. Now please go.'

He put out his hand for me, and I backed a step away. He muttered, 'Oh, Vicky, this is an awful way for us to be. What have I done to you that you should treat me so very badly? If you would only marry me I would not get drunk from being so miserable, and then I wouldn't see Rose Mary any more, and –'

I said, 'Marry you! You, with ten thumbs and a soul like a boiled ham! Do you think I'm going to marry you and have children like you and sit in a house like this all my life wondering whether anyone will mistake me for an Indian? I'm not going to marry you.'

I had become breathless with seeing him standing there so dumb and miserable. In a minute I would cry openly, and then where would I be? I ran out of the room.

I heard Patrick try five times to kick the Norton into starting. He did not succeed; it only wheezed and coughed, and at last he wheeled it away. I heard the wheels clicking over, then the silence, like rubber.

Now someone would ring up from the Gurkhas, about midnight, and ask whether I'd seen Macaulay.

The Sirdarni might have killed several men. I wondered why I was not thinking of Macaulay's battered head, and why there was no slipperiness of blood between my fingers. When I looked in the mirror I saw myself as I had been in the sari. Eventually I went to sleep and did not dream.

15

Two days later I was sitting in my usual place in the Collector's study, the notebook on my knees and my pencil ready. There had been a big streak of blood on the front of my skirt directly under where the notebook lay. But that was – that had been – on the other skirt. I owned three sets of uniforms. *The* set had gone to the dhobi yesterday morning, the morning after the Sirdarni washed the blood away from my skirt and all the conscience of blood from my mind. Macaulay's body hadn't been discovered yet.

Govindaswami said, 'What did you make of the Sirdarni-sahiba?'

I dropped my pencil, picked it up, and had time to consider the question. Savage and Govindaswami knew I had visited Ranjit Singh's house yesterday. I hadn't attempted to keep that second visit secret. Ranjit had openly invited me in the Traffic Office – while Patrick glared sullenly at us – and openly I had accepted.

I said, 'I think the Sirdarni is a wonderful woman, sir.'

Govindaswami said, 'Yes. Very politically minded. Who else was there?'

They were a little like an examination in court, these questions, but Govindaswami was rocking easily back on the legs of his chair, his fingers locked together, and smiling comfortably at me. I thought suddenly that he already knew very well who had been there. It had not been a party, just a visit, but there were tea and sweet cakes, and people kept dropping in. I thought the Sirdarni had asked those people to drop in, to have a look at me perhaps – or for me to have a look at them.

I said, 'There was Ranjit, of course. Mr Surabhai. Those two gentlemen who came here with Mr Surabhai the other day. One or two others. Practically everybody's wife.'

The pale and calm stranger, Ghanshyam, had not been there. During my visit no one mentioned him. No one gave a hint that they knew of his existence. Nor did I. His loincloth would not have gone well with the others' neat white khaddar, but he was just as well educated as any of them, perhaps better – that I was sure of.

'Quite a Congress gathering,' Govindaswami said easily.

I didn't answer. It was on the tip of my tongue to be sharp, to ask whether I didn't have the right to meet anyone I liked anywhere I liked. But I decided not to say it.

'What did they talk about?' It was Colonel Savage who asked the question, looking at me through the thin blue smoke of his cheroot.

'Politics, mostly,' I answered truthfully.

But it had not been pure politics all the time. Someone had mentioned Govindaswami, and that had reminded me to ask Ranjit what the Collector meant when he talked of his 'personal spy ring'. Ranjit had told me. 'Mr Govindaswami's father was an untouchable. So of course he is an untouchable too. Every sweeper in Bhowani knows it. They will do anything for him, because they are secretly proud of him. They'll tell him anything they find out which they think he'd like to know.' I nodded. Every household has a sweeper, and the sweepers are untouchables. The sweepers are everywhere. They squat silently outside latrines and urinals and private bathrooms and wherever there is filth for them to clean up, and no one notices they are there until they die or are too drunk to do their job. I was glad I had really used the ghuslkhana at the Institute. It was Ghanshyam who had insisted that I must.

'Did you hear anything of interest to us?' Govindaswami asked. He was affable and offhand. I couldn't make up my mind what exactly he did know about last night. The Kasels had a sweeper, of course, but he would be as politically minded as the

140

Sirdarni-sahiba, and so perhaps would not help Govindaswami. I thought I could afford to be rather vague.

I answered, 'Oh, the Cabinet Committee. Jinnah and the Moslem League. The Mahatma. The usual things.'

'There were no Moslems present?' Govindaswami asked.

I said, 'I don't think so. None of the women were in purdah.' Govindaswami nodded.

Actually, Mr Surabhai had been planning to organize another procession of sympathy with the naval mutineers. Someone there had agreed to letter a lot of posters for him. Someone else had wanted to know whether Mr Surabhai was going to get the Collector's permission for the procession, as he was supposed to do under the city by-laws. Mr Surabhai said he was not going to ask for permission, as an act of defiance. Mr Govind Dass, the pleader, thought he should. While I was there, it had not been settled what they were going to do.

Govindaswami said, 'Did they discuss the stolen ammunition at all?'

'I didn't hear them,' I said.

That was a direct lie. Mr Surabhai had in fact got very excited about the missing ammunition. His theory was that the British had deliberately allowed the train to be looted – by extremist members of the local Moslem community, he insisted. 'Of course that is what occurred,' he had said, waving a teacup wildly in one hand and a small green cake in the other. 'It is Jinnah's fault. He has stirred up his people until they believe we are merely preparing to assassinate them on their charpoys the very first hour after freedom is sounded. The British have helped Jinnah with all their might and main. The British would be highly pleased with themselves, indeed, if the Moslems could feel enough strongly armed to assault *us*! Poor misled people! It is a scandalous state of affairs.' Mr Surabhai spoke in English mostly, especially when the subject was political.

I had told him I didn't think he was right there. After all, I knew what had really happened – I thought. I told him about how Colonel Savage had tried to get a guard to the train, and how he had failed through no fault of his own. Ranjit backed me up, but we couldn't persuade Mr Surabhai. He said, 'My dear young lady, your Colonel Savage was merely pulling wool over the eyes of the record. He was keeping his tongue in his cheek throughout that flim-flammery!'

During the night, last night, I'd thought carefully about what Mr Surabhai had said. It was possible. Savage and Govindaswami *did* have secret schemes which they told no one about – the way they had dealt with the strike, for instance. What Mr Surabhai asserted was certainly possible.

But it had worried me that all those men and women at the Sirdarni's house, except Ranjit, believed Mr Surabhai's theory implicitly, and I didn't see how they could be so sure. They might suspect – as I was beginning to suspect – but how could they know? They had inside information on the R.I.N. mutiny too, which I had never seen in Intelligence reports. They knew that seven sailors had been tortured in Bombay. Govind Dass had the sailors' names and ranks on a little list in his pocket. Three more sailors had been shot out of hand. The battle at Karachi was a great deal bloodier than the newspapers or the Intelligence reports had said.

I had told them what I knew, and doubted whether their sources were accurate. They became excited and a little scornful. They told me I was a dupe. Did I think the British would tell the truth, even in Intelligence reports? Those reports were printed documents, available years later as permanent records. Would the British be likely to print their infamy in them? They were read by thousands of Indian officers and officials, weren't they? Only a few real traitors, men who had sold their souls to the British – such men as Govindaswami – would continue to work for the British if they knew the real truth.

Again I had had to admit it was possible. I knew things *had* been suppressed in Intelligence reports. The real truth about the Malayan campaign, for instance, had not yet come out. I'd met a lot of British officers in Delhi who knew bits of the truth and were convinced that the government was hiding something, but no one could find out.

The Collector said, 'I hope Mr Surabhai didn't hold it against you that you were at the railway station on the day of the troop-train business.'

I said quickly, 'No, not a bit, sir. He knows I didn't have anything to do with that. I like him.'

'So do I,' Govindaswami said at once. 'So do I. I like him very much. You know, there is nothing against your seeing as much of Ranjit and Mr Surabhai and their Congress friends as you wish. Don't think I am censuring you or warning you off by asking these questions.'

'Oh, no, sir,' I agreed. I thought Govindaswami was hinting that I would be a good spy, a useful part of his intelligence net, if I wormed my way into the confidence of the Congress group. But he must know they would not say anything secret in front of me unless I actively joined them.

Govindaswami said, 'Congress is not an illegal organization. One is not allowed to join it while in the Indian Civil Service or the Army, of course, just as Ranjit is not supposed to join it – or any other political party – while he is a railway officer.'

I nodded. Ranjit had talked about that too. He didn't say outright that he belonged to the Congress party. He said, 'I'm not supposed to join any political parties. But the railways are owned by the government and run by the government. Government is English and, though they won't admit it, they are of course a party, the party in power. Congress is the party in opposition. So, as a railway officer, I have made myself an official of the English government. That is, I am a member of the English party. I don't think they have the right to force me into this position.' Mr Surabhai had overheard and joined in. 'Ah, but they are very clever fellows,' he said. 'Very clever fellows indeed! What *they* want is peace and order, so they are above the political party. What *I* want is blood-stained revolution, and so I am a dirty dog and should feel ashamed of myself from end to end.'

'What do you think's happened to Macaulay?' Govindaswami said.

I looked up slowly, but he was speaking to Savage.

Savage knocked the ash off his cheroot and said, 'I have no idea. He leaves Miss Jones at the signal and disappears. No one sees him. If you want my opinion, you should have the proprietors of the local brothels thoroughly cross-questioned. Lanson and his police should give them all the third degree.'

Govindaswami said, 'Oh. Macaulay is that kind of man, is he? I'm so bad at telling about these things.' He dusted off his white suit, seeming rather embarrassed.

'He is,' Savage said. 'He came within an inch of a court-martial in 'forty-four. He raped an Assamese coolie woman – or just about. I saved him by sending him out on a long patrol while the subadar-major persuaded the woman, with a good chunk of the Battalion Fund at his disposal, that she had a bad memory for faces.'

I sat stiffly in my position. I must relax, but I must not move about and draw their attention to me. I must be prepared at any moment to say something about Macaulay. If they spoke to me this instant I would whisper triumphantly that I had killed him and I was glad of it.

Govindaswami said, 'H'm. Have you checked your funds? People like Macaulay often need money.'

Savage said, 'I know. Yes, I have. Dickson did it this morning. He's a thorough old boffin. All the money's where it ought to be. But Macaulay's carbine is missing.'

'With him, of course?' Govindaswami said. 'He had it?'

'Yes,' Savage said. 'It makes me wonder whether someone hasn't hit him on the head to get it. Particularly after the looting of the ammunition train.'

Govindaswami said, 'It's possible. But we're not sure yet that he hasn't just deserted, are we?'

Savage said, 'He might have. I've been pretty rough on him lately. But how the hell did he get away, and where has he gone?'

They discussed the case unconcernedly. They didn't seem to care very much whether Macaulay was found or was not found, whether he was alive or dead. It had been like that since the telephone call I had expected that midnight, which duly came. The voice had said, 'Victoria? Duty Officer, First Thirteenth Gurkhas. George Howland. Wotcher! Say, have you seen Graham Macaulay? He's not back in his quarters. The Sahib's going off his rocker. Oh, did he? Yes. 'Arf a mo'. I'll write that down. Sure. Thanks a lot. Cor stone the crows, this is a rum go, i'n'it? Good night, Vic.' Howland was an awful young man, always imitating Cockney to be funny.

In the morning Savage had asked me a few more questions, and after lunch I'd heard him discussing with Major Dickson whether they should invite the police to share the Thirteenth Gurkhas' little mystery. Later they decided it might be as well, and then they

144

told Lanson. The D.S.P. had not asked to see me yet, and I was beginning to doubt whether he would.

The conference drifted to a conclusion. Govindaswami thought there would be a procession or two the next day. Savage thought that would be fun. I got on my bicycle and wondered again how much Govindaswami knew and how much he guessed – about the stolen ammunition, about K. P. Roy, about Lieutenant Macaulay.

But I went home thinking more about my visit at the Sirdarni's than about Macaulay. There had been much political talk, but that was not the chief memory I had carried away with me. I remembered their playing an old gramophone with a huge horn, scraping and squeaking. The music was not music to me, but it mixed cheerfully with someone singing in the bazaar and the men's thin voices conversing. I remembered the smell – what was it? Curry, incense, clean linen? I absorbed some of the Sirdarni's bitterness. It was not a conscious single thought; it was a gradual seep, drop by drop. I said to myself, looking around me, this I could have loved; this the English have spoiled for me; sneering at me, they have brought me up to sneer at myself.

Perhaps no one but a Jew would understand what it was like to be my sort of Anglo-Indian, and not even a Jew could really know, because the Jews are there in the history books before the English. A Jew would see, though. There was a clerk in Transportation, a Jew from Stepney in London. I used to avoid him even before I was commissioned, because of his furious self-mockery – the more painful the funnier, the jokes curling up and round like the tail of a scorpion that wants to kill itself.

I cheered up. That was over, for me. I was going to meet Ranjit and go to the pictures with him just as if he had not been an Indian.

16

I MET Ranjit in the Sudder Savoy. It was the big ground-floor room of a dirty house outside the northern corner of the city. There was a long signboard over the door: SUDDER SAVOY RESTAURANT, A. COWASJEE MILKMAN, PROP. IN BOUNDS FOR B.T.

I'd seen the place, on Friday nights particularly, when there'd been a hundred Tommies in there, eating greasy fried eggs and drinking beer and shouting. They were real old sweats with tattooed arms and hollow cheeks and no sunburn. Rose Mary used to come here often then. In those days she'd had a boy friend who was a corporal. When the last British battalion left Bhowani in 1939 the Sudder Savoy began to decay. Now Rose Mary never came, and Mr Milkman had returned to Bombay, leaving an old Mohammedan cook in charge.

I arrived a quarter of an hour late. I couldn't afford, even in 1946, to be seen sitting alone in there. In the old days the regimental police would have asked me who I was waiting for and then tried to make a date with me themselves and made trouble if I had refused. Rose Mary said that happened to her once.

Ranjit was sitting at a table in the far corner under a 1944 calendar that had a picture of a blonde girl in a white bathing suit. He was watching the door and he had a glass and a bottle of fizzy lemonade in front of him. There was no one else in the place. In 1939 he wouldn't have been allowed there. The glass front was half screened with brown paper. Tins of beans and pineapples and peaches, all flecked with rust, filled the dusty shelves up the wall behind the counter. After all those years the place still smelled of stale beer.

Ranjit got up with a quick shy smile as I sat down. 'You know,' he said, 'I have never been in this place.'

I knew that, but I said only that he hadn't been in Bhowani long.

He said, 'No, not long.'

The old cook was standing beside me, and Ranjit asked what I wanted. I ordered lemonade, the same as his, though I did not like the stuff. It was too sweet. When I got my drink Ranjit said a little nervously, 'I have some bad news, Miss Jones. The projector at the Mahal has broken down. They are not showing any picture tonight.'

I said, 'Oh, dear!' and smiled at him. He seemed really worried, so I said, 'It's bad luck, I know, but it won't kill us. I did want to see those two dancers, though.'

He began to talk about the dancers. He said, 'They are the best classical dancers working in India today, but I do not think they are as good as they used to be. This is a rather recent film of theirs.

146

They have been to London and New York – before the war, of course – and their dancing is not so good, not really classical. There is more posturing, if you know what I mean. They have become too obvious.'

I didn't know what he meant, because I've never been to London or New York. But I knew what he thought I thought he meant – that the dancers had westernized themselves; in other words, betrayed his India.

He said, 'I am so sorry. I suppose I had better take you to your house.'

I was sure it had been in his mind to ask me to his own home. But I had been there only yesterday, and obviously he was too shy to force himself on me. I would have liked to go there again.

But if my mind was made up, and my boat was moving, why did I have this feeling, almost of guilt, to be sitting there with Ranjit? Why were we meeting in a deserted restaurant and going to an Indian cinema where I knew no one would recognize me? It had got to stop. The time for feeling guilty and 'different' had passed. I said, 'Let's go to the cantonment cinema, then. They're still showing *Hell's Angels*. Have you seen it?'

He said, 'No, I've never seen it, but –'

I said, 'But what?' I lit a cigarette slowly. I felt responsible for him, in this half-English place. It was extraordinary how that feeling made me like him more.

He said in a low voice, 'Do you think it would be wise, Miss Jones? I am an Indian, and you are not. I mean, you do not look like one. See, you are smoking, and your dress is European. My mother is a wonderful woman, but she does not always understand how difficult it is for people to change from things they are used to.'

'You think I've always got to be half and half?' I said. 'You think I've always got to wear a short skirt?'

He said, 'No, no, Miss Jones. Please!'

Looking at him, with my cigarette in my hand, I was suddenly sure that he thought I might have led Macaulay on. He couldn't make up his mind whether I had or not. He had seen me smile at Macaulay. He had seen me accept Macaulay's offer to escort me home. All that, after he had saved me the time before. He couldn't understand. I began to feel cross with him. This was something that must be settled. I said, 'You think I was flirting with Macaulay, don't you?'

It was foolish of me to say it, even to think it. Why should he meet me to take me to the cinema if he thought that about me? But in truth I am sure he was afraid of me then. I attracted him, yet I terrified him.

He said, 'Sssh!' and glanced nervously around. He would have made a very bad conspirator. He was agitated, and his large soft eyes were fixed on mine, terribly anxious that I should not misunderstand him. He said, 'It is of you I am thinking. What will your father say, your sister, Mr Taylor? They are not sophisticated people like some, who do not mind.'

I said, 'I certainly don't care what Patrick Taylor thinks,' and felt myself tossing my head. 'I'm finished with him. I told him so the other day. As for the rest –' I played with the empty glass, turning it over and over in my hand. What did I think about the rest? I said slowly, 'I will be sorry to hurt Pater, but I cannot stand still because of him. It is like being in prison, I tell you.'

I stood up quickly and said, 'Come along, Ranjit. I want to see *Hell's Angels*. Jean Harlow is terrific in it.' Of course I had seen it years before.

So we went to the cantonment cinema, going slowly side by side up the Pike on our bicycles, then through the dark cantonment roads between the low square-cut shapes of the barracks. A few Gurkhas were sitting on one of the verandas with a little drum, beating it and singing together. They sounded sad, and I had learned to become very fond of them even in this short time, so I said, 'It is a shame they can't have their families down here. They are nice little men, you know.'

Ranjit said, 'They don't have to join the Army, Miss Jones. They have come of their own free will from Nepal to oppress us. I cannot feel sorry for them.'

A breath of exasperation stirred me. I wanted to ask him whether he would say the same thing if it was the Indian Government of the future, instead of the Government of India of the present, that found it necessary to station the Gurkhas in barracks where there was no accommodation for their families. But I held my tongue because I was willing to believe that all my ideas and my thoughts needed looking at with a new eye – my new eye.

Ranjit bought the tickets, and we went in. The cinema was already dark, and when I got used to the darkness I saw that it was less than a quarter full. A few Gurkhas sat down in front, in the cheapest seats, the foul smoke from their cigarettes curling up like a shaky curtain in front of the screen. I wondered what they thought of Jean Harlow and the long kisses and the huggings. When I turned to look back, peering up along the smoky, flickering beam of the projection lamp, I saw the silhouettes of a few people scattered in the more expensive seats behind. I settled down to enjoy the film. The fans in the ceiling whirred noisily, blowing hot air down on my head.

At the interval, when the lights went up, I sat blinking for a moment and then said, 'Let's go and have a lemonade. I'm thirsty, aren't you?'

Ranjit said, 'Well, yes. Certainly, Miss Jones.' He stood up very correctly, glancing round him as though he was afraid to be recognized. He said in a low voice, 'Mr Taylor will be there.'

I said, 'Where?'

I looked round and saw Patrick's back as he walked, head bent and shoulders swinging, up the side aisle toward the bar at the back of the cinema. I knew from his walk that he had been drinking – not a great deal, perhaps, but probably enough to make him difficult. It might be more sensible not to force a meeting with him now. But I was not doing anything wrong. If I hid now I might as well give up altogether.

I went up the aisle behind Patrick, Ranjit not too close on my heels. Patrick was leaning over the bar when I went in. The big double doors to the road were open on both sides, and a little wind blew through to stir up the dust on the checkered imitation marble floor. Colonel Savage was standing at the opposite end of the bar, leaning against the wall with a big glass of whisky in his hand. He saw me come in with Ranjit. Patrick did not. Savage's eyes did not flicker, and he said nothing.

Patrick said, 'Good evening, Colonel.'

Savage said, 'Good evening. Enjoying the picture?'

'Oh yes,' Patrick said listlessly. 'It is jolly good.'

The barman asked me what I wanted. I said, 'Lemonade. The same for you, Ranjit?'

Patrick swung round on his toes at the first sound of my voice.

I saw that his eyes were bloodshot. Then Savage said, 'Good evening, Miss Jones. Good evening, Ranjit.'

Patrick said, 'What are you doing here?' He stood upright, one hand on the bar, swaying a very little.

'Seeing the picture,' I said as lightly as I could. 'With Ranjit.'

He said, 'You are seeing the picture with Kasel? You have come here with Kasel to see the picture?'

I said, 'Yes, Patrick, I've just told you – Look out for the lemonade bottles! Oh, Patrick you are the most –' The lemonade bottles smashed on the floor as Patrick jerked his elbow back.

Now he was cornered by his own clumsiness. He was drunk and nearly crazy with jealousy and hurt pride – because Ranjit was an Indian. Patrick turned to Savage and said in a low voice, 'That was a jolly good idea of yours at the station the other day, Colonel. You know, what you told the Gurkhas to do on those bloody Congress wallahs.'

Savage said coldly, 'Do you mind not trying to drag me into your mating squabbles?' He swallowed his whisky and went into the cinema. A bell above the outside doors rang continuously for half a minute. The audience began to drift back from walking up and down in the road or on the weedy grass.

Patrick was swaying more noticeably. His pale blue-green eyes were dull and blinking and watery, as though Savage had hit him on the nose. He said, 'You are just a bitch, Victoria. You can't go out with this fellow. I'll show you!'

He wandered toward us, his fists doubled. Ranjit said, 'We ought to go, Miss Jones.'

I shook my head. I shouted at Patrick, 'You call me a bitch, you – you fornicating swine!' I stood right in front of him, glaring at him, and my voice had gone shrill and all cheechee. It was such a little, easy step to be with Patrick again.

Patrick said, 'I am not going to hit you, Vicky. It's not your fault. It is that fellow.'

I stared at him until his eyes fell. Then I said, 'I am going to see the picture with Ranjit and do whatever else I bloody well like, see? Now go home and get sober and learn to behave yourself!'

I walked back into the cinema with my head up. The light began to dim as I went in, but I had time to see Colonel Savage sprawled back in the double fauteuil nearest the aisle, nearest the door to the bar. His feet were up on the back of the seat in front. He must have heard.

Ranjit sat silent through the rest of the picture and did not talk on the ride to my house. Patrick passed us in a tonga. The Norton must still be out of action. I shook hands with Ranjit in the road outside Number 4, pressing his fingers because he had been hurt and I liked him. On an impulse I said, 'Do you know what I think I'm going to do?'

'No, Miss Jones,' he said.

I said, 'For heaven's sake, call me Victoria. I think I'm going to wear a sari. That ought to show them!'

Ranjit was still worried. He said, 'It will cause you a lot of trouble.' Then he cheered up a bit and said, 'But it will be worth it. You don't know how suitable a sari is for you, Miss – Victoria.'

I said, laughing, 'Oh, yes, I do! Why else do you think I'm going to wear one?'

The smile was wiped off his face, and he said, 'Good night, Victoria,' stiffly and suddenly.

I said, 'I was only joking, of course, Ranjit. You didn't think I was insulting people who wear saris, did you?'

He said, 'I didn't know. You see, it is difficult, as I told you. That is what my mother does not understand. Everything is plain and easy to her.'

Once more he said good night, and left me. I stared after him, watching his slight body on the bicycle moving from light to dark and dark to light, each time fainter and smaller under the lamp, until he turned out of Collett Road. I thought over what I had said that had upset him – 'Why else do you think I'm going to wear one?' How could he have thought I meant to be insulting?

I gave up. It would be difficult for a time. They were so touchy. *We* were so touchy – whoever I meant by 'we'. I opened the front door of the house.

Patrick was there, standing in the middle of the hall, and with him Pater, and, in the door of the parlour, Rose Mary. Patrick pointed his finger at me, his arm stretched straight out. He said thickly, 'There she is!'

'Where's Mater?' I said, putting my hand up into my back hair and pushing out my curls and walking slowly forward to meet them until our faces were only an inch apart, my voice rising and hardening and my back tingling.

17

THE battalion offices were hushed when I got there the next morning. A couple of orderlies sitting on the bench in the corridor leaped to attention as I came up, but there was no one else. I went to the window of my office and looked out. The parade ground was several hundred yards away, but a corner of it showed between two barrack blocks. I saw the twinkle of movement there, and then the pipe band struck up and the drums thudded and the Union Jack fluttered to the masthead, and I remembered. Today was 24 May, Empire Day.

I sat down and began to look at the reports and summaries piled up in my In tray. I felt extraordinarily fresh and clearheaded. It had been a good fight last night. The others were at a disadvantage because Patrick was drunk and needlessly abusive, so Pater had spent as much energy in trying to control him as in arguing with me. There would be more to come, but for the moment I felt strong and confident.

I heard a car arrive at the offices, then voices, then footsteps. Someone went into Colonel Savage's office, and a Gurkha said, 'In there, sahib.' Mr Lanson, the Deputy Superintendent of Police, stood in my doorway, his topi in his hand. He was in uniform and looked pale and grumpy, as though he had not been long enough out of bed. Normally he was quite stolid and even-tempered. Slowly I folded away the Intelligence summary I had been reading and stood up.

'Morning, Miss Jones,' Lanson said. 'Sorry to disturb you at this ungodly hour.'

'Not at all, Mr Lanson. Won't you sit down?' I said, trying not to sound wary.

'Thanks,' he said. He lowered himself carefully into a chair and looked around for a place to hang his topi. Finally he put it on the floor beside him. He said, 'It's about Macaulay.'

I held myself, waiting, and Lanson said, 'The fact is that when he left you he seems to have gone direct to a – well, a brothel.'

He pulled a notebook from his tunic pocket and slowly turned over the pages. He was a slow-moving man. He said, 'He got there, the man who owns the place says, at about a quarter past eight. He doesn't remember exactly. They never do. I've talked to Colonel Savage, and he says Macaulay might easily have gone to such a place. In fact it was Colonel Savage who advised me to pay particular attention to them. I hope I'm not embarrassing you, Miss Jones.'

'No. But how can I help?' I said. Today I was wearing *the* skirt and shirt.

He said, 'Of course Macaulay wouldn't have told you he was going to such a place, but I wondered if he had said anything that would show he intended to go somewhere else – back to his quarters, for instance, or to the station, or the offices here, or the cinema. The man, the owner of this place, is no more and no less reliable than any other witness in a murder case. Somebody might have murdered Macaulay and bribed the brothel man to fake an alibi.'

'He'd have to bribe the girl too,' I said. Ghanshyam must have done all this.

'The woman was – ah – the proprietor's – ah – wife,' Lanson said disgustedly. 'What I mean is that Macaulay had about a hundred rupees on him, apparently – so his orderly thinks – and of course he had the carbine. Either of those would be quite enough to get him murdered. Besides, it seems so damned silly of him to go into the city when those processions were under way, and he'd been specially warned not to go near the place. And he must have known that he'd be missed here if he didn't get back at a reasonable hour. Yet he is supposed to have stayed in the brothel for about three hours, till some time past eleven o'clock. So I wondered –'

'No,' I said, shaking my head. 'He didn't say anything to me. He just said good night, and then I left him. I didn't even see him start back from the signal.'

153

Lanson wrote carefully in his notebook. When he had finished he said, 'Did he try to kiss you, Miss Jones, or did you kiss him, or – ah – anything? I really am sorry about this, but I have a reason for asking. It seems that Macaulay had been telling some of his friends here that he was very fond of you. He even indicated that you returned this feeling. What I am getting at is that if you did in fact like him –'

I heard the tramp of boots, the squeak of hobnails on stone, a door opening and shutting. Colonel Savage was in his office next door.

Lanson lowered his voice. He said, 'If you did return this – passion, Macaulay is supposed to have called it – it is less likely that he would have gone direct from you to such a place. You see what I mean?'

I said, 'I did not like Lieutenant Macaulay, Mr Lanson. He did make advances to me once, very unpleasantly. I gave him no encouragement then or at any other time.'

'But you did let him accompany you home that evening,' Lanson said gruffly. 'I don't like this any more than you do, Miss Jones. But you did, and the Gurkha sentry in the yards says you were very close together when he challenged you. He thought Macaulay –'

The inner door jerked open, and Colonel Savage was standing there, his Gurkha hat on his head and his jungle-green uniform clean and newly pressed. He said brusquely, 'If you want to interview one of my officers, Lanson, you will ask my permission.'

Lanson stood up slowly and turned to face Savage. He said, 'You weren't here, Savage, or I would have.'

Savage said, 'These are my offices, and you may not use them as a police court. I heard the last part of what you were saying. The partitions are thin. Miss Jones never encouraged Macaulay. In fact, she so obviously disliked him that I ordered Macaulay never to be anywhere alone with her.'

'Then why –?' Lanson said, and Savage overrode him, saying, 'If she'd gone home on her bicycle she would have had to pass through a bad corner of the city. The railway was safer, and she didn't want to go alone. There was no one else except Macaulay to go with her.'

'There was Ranjit Singh,' Lanson said.

Savage said, 'He didn't offer to go. Miss Jones has got work to do.'

Lanson stooped for his topi. When he straightened up his face was red. He said, 'All right, Savage. I haven't got any more to ask her now. But when I have, you want me to subpoena her officially and make her come down to the Kutcherry, is that right?'

'That's right,' Savage said, 'and she will come, provided she isn't on urgent military duty. Or you can ask me if you want to see her here.'

Lanson nodded stiffly and went out. When his footsteps had died away Savage said curtly, 'Bring the map of the city into my office,' and left me.

I sat a moment in my chair, forcing myself to be calm and cold. It looked as if I was going to be saved by the quarrelling of the British among themselves as much as by Ghanshyam's schemings. The fools.

When I went in with the map Henry Dickson was there, and Savage was asking him when he expected his wife.

Dickson said, 'Early in June, sir. Probably on the fourth.'

I stood at the side of the desk, the rolled map in my hand, while the two men talked. I ought to have been thinking of Lanson, but I wasn't. I was remembering Molly Dickson. She used to ask me quite often to her bungalow in New Delhi. She was a faded blonde woman, youngish, full of nerves. She laughed loudly and suddenly, and moved jerkily, but she was nice. She had a couple of children and used to be an 'abandoned wife' in a little house off Lodi Road.

Savage said, 'The bungalow in good shape for them?'

Dickson said, 'Yes, sir.'

Savage said, 'Good. Let's have that map, Miss Jones.'

I unrolled it for him and stood looking over his left shoulder. He said, 'This is the form: The local Congress committee, headed by Surabhai, have got the Collector's permission to stage a procession in sympathy with the R.I.N. mutineers. The local branch of the Moslem League, not to be outdone, have done the same. Govindaswami believes in safety valves. He's allotted this as the route for Congress –' He ran his finger along a zigzag course in the eastern half of the city – 'and this for the Mohammedans.' He traced a route in the western half of the city and went on,

155

'Govindaswami thinks the two processions will try to meet. Rather, he thinks that Surabhai will take his procession through to join the Moslems if he can. And he doesn't want that, of course.'

Why not? I thought; why on earth not? There could be no reason, except that Govindaswami did not want to give the Hindus and Moslems an opportunity to show in public a unity which the British told the world they did not have.

Savage went on, 'There are too many places where Surabhai can leave his authorized route and go barging through to the other route. Lanson's police can't guard them all in strength, especially as half of them are out in the back blocks dealing with a local messiah in Aslakheri, who's persuaded the villagers that the landowner's wife is a witch. I haven't got enough men to do the job properly either. What I'm going to do is this ...'

He began to explain. All the battalion trucks would be out, with their canvas covers on and fastened down. In every truck there would be at least two men, but some trucks would be full of men. The plan was to station trucks near every likely corner and junction on both routes. Surabhai would not know which were full and which were, for practical purposes, empty. He would not know that the Gurkhas had orders not to shoot except to protect their own lives.

Colonel Savage rolled up the map and said, 'I'll keep this until tomorrow.' He was in a good humour and seemed to have forgotten all about Lanson and the investigation into Macaulay's disappearance. He said, 'I'm going to be hanging round with my advanced headquarters radio. Have you got anything else to do?'

'Yes, sir,' I said. 'I'm going to work in the railway traffic office this afternoon. I have to get some information about several coal trains they're going to run through now that the strike's over.'

He said, 'Good.' He looked at me and added, 'You ought to have an enjoyable time whether it's Taylor or Ranjit on duty – Miss Starkie.' He went out.

Major Dickson said, 'What did he call you Miss Starkie for? You haven't changed your name, have you?'

Wearily I said, 'No.'

Dickson shook his head. He said, 'I don't understand the C.O. half the time either.' As he moved to the door I turned to speak to him, to tell him that I knew his wife. But by the time Mrs Dick-

156

son came down I might be out of uniform again. And what would I have to talk about with Molly here in Bhowani, even if she did take the trouble to find out where I lived and invite me up for coffee? So I said nothing. Dickson saluted me – he always did that, and it always made me simper – and ambled out.

I had lunch at home and afterwards bicycled slowly up the Pike toward the station. It was the first hot, still hour of the afternoon, when the Europeans were going to their beds to lie down after tiffin, or sitting at the table and smoking, and the Indians were dozing in the backs of their stores, and everyone was putting off the time when he would have to get back to work. There were few people about. I recited bitterly to myself:

> There was a young lady called Starkie
> Who had an affair with a darkie,
> The result of her sins
> Was an eightsome of twins –
> Two black and two white and four khaki.

Savage, Savage, savage. Why? It *must* be his nature. And for whose sake had he really ordered that door kept open – mine or Macaulay's? Savage, cruel and mysterious.

I free-wheeled down the slope into the tunnel under the tracks. It was dark there and not as burning hot as in the sun. I saw a dim face, a man walking my way on the raised pedestrian footpath on the left of the road, looking back at me over his shoulder. When I came nearly abreast of him he turned, and I thought it was Ghanshyam. He said distinctly, 'Stop. Your chain is off.'

I stopped and slid my feet to the ground. It was Ghanshyam. He said aloud, 'I will fix it, miss sahiba, I know all about bicycles.' He stepped down to the roadway beside me. He squatted on his heels by the back wheel, while I held the bike upright and leaned over the saddle to see what he was doing. He jerked with his finger, and the chain came off. He said, 'Ah, I thought so. Are the soldiers going to be out this afternoon?'

I muttered, 'Yes. Can you fix it?'

He said, 'In time, in time. Will they be at the corner where Blue Lane meets the Streets of Suttees, near the station yard there?'

I saw the map of the city in my mind, and Colonel Savage's finger on it. 'This one will be full, this one empty. Empty. Empty.

157

Full. Empty.' I said, 'No. The truck will have only two soldiers in it. Won't the chain go back on?'

He said, 'Don't you bother, miss sahiba. You'll get your hands dirty. There's a lot of oil here. Two soldiers with rifles can stop a crowd without any.'

I said, 'They have orders not to fire. It's no distance to the station here. I can wheel it.'

He said, 'There, it's done,' and stood up, his round face twisted into what ought to have been a beggar's smile. He held his palm out. I fumbled in my bag, thinking that perhaps he could not really smile. The lips split his round, calm face and were shaped into the thing called a smile, but he was not smiling. I gave him a four-anna piece and got on to the bicycle. Colonel Savage would look a fine fool this evening for all his jokes about Miss Starkie.

Patrick was on duty in the Traffic Office. He glanced up when I came in but quickly turned his head down, clearing his throat, and said nothing to me. I sat down at my table, collected my papers, and began to work. It was awkward trying to forget that Patrick was there. I felt a fool pretending he did not exist, and there were a couple of things about the work which I wanted to ask him.

But there was work to do, and continual distraction outside. Jeeps and trucks came and went in the station yard below the windows, and the Collector's Austin and the D.S.P.'s Chevrolet – I could tell them by the sound of their engines. I tried to guess what each coming and going meant. Then I heard Gurkhali, and the subadar-major's unmistakable voice, and others I didn't recognize.

I hoped at first that I would be finished and gone before four o'clock. That was the time both processions were due to begin. I completed my work at a quarter to, but by then the time was so close that I wanted to see what happened, so I stayed in the office. I got up, walked over to the window, and stood there, looking down at the square. The Street of Suttees led out from it at the north-east corner. About fifty yards up, Blue Lane turned off to the left. I half expected to see Ghanshyam squatting in the yard pretending to be a beggar, or driving a tonga, but there was no sign of him.

Patrick said, 'I bet you wish you could join in your friends' bloody procession, don't you?'

I did not answer him. The same old angry impatience rose in me again, but I forced it down and tried to think of Patrick as pathetic and unimportant.

One by one the tongas clattered out of the yard. A young Sikh who ran a taxi service cranked up his old Buick tourer and drove away. The beggars shuffled and hopped and rolled themselves out of sight. A band struck up in the distance, and I heard the shrieking of Indian music. I wondered who had got the processions started on time. Certainly not Mr Surabhai. Savage might have sent the jemadar adjutant to see that there was no hitch. It was the kind of thing he would be capable of.

Patrick said, 'You think that is the most wonderful music in the world now, don't you?'

An Army six-by-six Dodge rolled into the yard, its canvas battened down. It backed up to the station arch and stopped. Ten Gurkhas scrambled out through the narrow opening in the back of the canvas and slipped into the station. When they had gone I saw a face, an eye, and the muzzle of a Sten gun at the crack. I remembered – that truck was to unload a detachment at the station and then stay here, its armed driver beside it and the threatening face at the back slit. Not many people would know whether it was empty or full. Another six-by-six passed across the yard, drove up the Street of Suttees as far as Blue Lane, drew in, and stopped there.

Savage arrived in his jeep, the radio jeep close behind him. The two jeeps backed up to the wall. Savage and Birkhe got out and stood looking up the Street of Suttees. The music wailed a little louder. It must have been unbearably hot inside the trucks with the canvas covers closed down and the sun pouring its heat on to them. It served them right.

Govindaswami returned in his Austin. I leaned out of the window, expecting to see the D.S.P.'s Chevrolet. It wasn't there. Perhaps he'd been hurriedly called to Aslakheri on the witch case. I felt sure suddenly that Ghanshyam had had a hand in that. Standing up there and looking down on them all, I got a fine comfortable feeling that Savage and Govindaswami and Lanson were the puppets now, dancing on strings that I recognized while they did not. They were fools. India was too strong for them.

Savage, Birkhe, Govindaswami, and a head constable of police

159

walked together up the Street of Suttees. I saw them turn into a house on the right, a little beyond Blue Lane. It was a tall house, six storys high, built of old brick, with crumbling balconies, peeling yellow paint, and iron grilles. It had a flat roof. In a couple of minutes the party appeared up there.

The music went *boom-boom-bom-boomty-bomty-bom*. If there was a tune, I did not recognize it, and the rhythm was jumpy and eccentric.

'Music!' Patrick said. 'It is more like cats caterwauling.'

The head of the procession swung out of a side street a long way off, turned left into the Street of Suttees, and came directly on toward the station yard, its flags and banners swaying triumphantly. It was too far away yet for me to be sure of any faces except Mr Surabhai's. I wished I had binoculars. Savage on the roof there had just lent his to Govindaswami. They were staring down. Govindaswami turned to peer along Blue Lane. *Tee-*BOOM. *Boom. Bo-*BO*-bo-bomty.* TEE*-boom.*

Patrick said, 'I bet that black boy friend of yours is down there beating a big drum.'

I gathered up my bag, stuffed some papers into the pocket of my shirt, and walked out of the office. In the corridor I began to hurry. Down the stairs I ran, faster and faster, and out through the arch and across the yard. A policeman shouted after me, but I did not stop. I knew they'd be looking at me with the binoculars from up there on the roof.

The head of the procession was close. Mr Surabhai carried a huge Congress flag. Today his suspenders were blue and his socks yellow. His eyes flashed, and he marched like a soldier, sticking out his chest and throwing his feet forward so that the brown and white co-respondent shoes twinkled. As he marched he shouted, '*Jai Hind!*' and, 'Long live our brothers the sailors!' Two policemen marched on each side of him, their brass buttons flashing and the brass tips of their lathis swinging steadily on their shoulders. There were other policemen down the sides of the procession, eight or ten in all. There were a couple of hundred people in the procession itself, with a forest of placards and flags. The people watching it all were crowded in the gutters and in the shops, clapping their hands.

As I passed the Blue Lane turning I saw down there the head of the other procession. That one too had music and banners, but its banners were dark green and lettered in white in the Arabic script that looks so beautifully curved and graceful, and they had only forty or fifty marchers with five police. Just about there they were due to turn left up a street parallel to Suttees. Two policemen were standing in Blue Lane near them, ready to direct the turn. The six-by-six, its armed driver, the Sten gun and the face at the canvas, they were here by my left side.

I ran into the door of the house where Savage and Govinda-swami stood on the roof six storys up. It was too late for them to move trucks or troops now. I was among a thick crowd of Indians. I found the Sirdarni-sahiba at my side and smiled at her. She said, 'The two processions are going to unite, to show that all Indians are united in this struggle.'

At the corner of Blue Lane Mr Surabhai suddenly swung his flag, like an officer with the Colours on parade, and shrieked, 'Follow me!' The policemen struggled with him, holding their lathis across to prevent him from turning, but he dodged them, hopping about like a dancer, while his followers surged round and past. The policemen could not stop them and were swept along like driftwood in a river. I saw a fist come up and box a police-man's ear, a hand tear off another's turban, but that was all. The Congress men chanted and shouted, but they were not in a violent mood. The Gurkha face peered at them out of the back canvas of the Dodge, and they shouted insults and jeered at it, but no more. The Moslem procession had stopped where it was supposed to turn. Its band was playing and its leader haranguing it, his back to Mr Surabhai and the Congress men as they dashed on toward him.

I was roaring with excited laughter – it was really very funny. The crowd was laughing. It was coming off exactly right – not with any beastly violence, but just making the British and the police look foolish.

'Now!' the Sirdarni said in my ear.

I scrambled up on a table and stood on tiptoe to see over the crowd. The two processions met.

Mr Surabhai flung his arms round the leader of the Moslems. The big Congress flag hovered and swept down and round, Mr Surabhai made such large generous movements. The top of the pole hit the Moslem banner, which a man with spectacles was

161

carrying immediately behind the Moslem leader. The Congress flag knocked the Moslem League flag down. Both flags fell into the dirt. The other man's spectacles were knocked off.

Mr Surabhai stood back and flung out his arms. I heard him cry, his voice cracked with emotion, 'We are brothers for freedom!'

A terrific shouting began. A lemonade bottle flashed in the sun and hit Mr Surabhai on the side of the head. Somebody shouted, 'They are trampling on our flag!' Mr Surabhai and the Moslem stooped to pick up the flags. They fell or were pushed. They disappeared, and the shouting suddenly changed pitch. Green flags mingled with striped flags, Arabic with English; sticks and stones flew, and an awful roaring filled the lane.

I said aloud, 'Oh, no! Oh, no!' I found my hands up and my cheeks dry and burning. 'Oh, no!' I whispered.

Boots clattered down the steps behind me, and a hard hand pushed me to one side. 'Out of the way!' Colonel Savage snarled in Hindustani and ran into the street, followed by Govindaswami, Birkhe, and the head constable. Simultaneously the ten Gurkhas arrived at the double from the station. He must have signalled to them from the housetop.

I was in front of the crowd by then, and I heard Savage say, 'I'll get them lined up here, facing down Blue Lane.'

Govindaswami said, 'Good. Keep a tight hold.' He and the head constable moved forward, but the Congress men had their backs to him and could hear nothing of his orders. Savage signalled with his hand, and the useless six-by-six backed out of the way and went to the station yard. Savage nodded his head, and two buglers, side by side, blew a short loud call. The ten Gurkhas stood in a row, at ease.

In the part of the crowd nearest Govindaswami and the Gurkhas, the people turned round, saw, and began to run away. But they had nowhere to run to. The struggling mass of Congress men and Moslem Leaguers was in front of them, filling the street from side to side. The Gurkhas were behind them. Govindaswami shouted, beckoned, and pointed to one side, showing them that they could get out past the end of the row of Gurkhas.

At my side the Sirdarni shouted in a deep clear voice, in Hindi, 'Charge them! They are few!'

Before I could think, let alone speak, Savage whipped round

and threw his carbine into my hands and snarled, 'You, shoot that woman the next time she opens her mouth!' He turned back to watch Govindaswami and the crowd.

'Please!' I whispered to the Sirdarni. 'Don't tell them to charge, Beji. Not now. The Collector's trying to get them out without a panic.'

The carbine wavered in my hands. I would only have to pull the trigger. Savage always kept it loaded. The queer uneasy thing was that I wouldn't have minded. If the people did what the Sirdarni was inciting them to, there'd be another massacre like the Jallianwala Bagh. And – I didn't like her. She was like Savage.

I do not know what I would have done, but the Sirdarni said, 'He's cunning, that colonel. I wouldn't stop for him. Or for you – or for *that* – if it was really important.' She wrapped her sari round the lower part of her face and struggled out and away through the back of the shop.

Gradually Govindaswami began to make an impression on the crowd in front of him. Gradually the people heard him, turned, saw the line of Gurkhas, began to panic, were calmed down and waved at, and filed away along the sides of the street. When Govindaswami reached the Moslems it was easier for him because they were already facing him. They saw the Gurkhas at once, and they only had to turn round to get away down Blue Lane. At last there were only three groaning men, a pale woman being sick, and Mr Surabhai lying flat in the filth, face up.

Govindaswami knelt down beside Mr Surabhai and shook him gently. A woman came out of a house with water. Mr Surabhai sat up, held his head in his hands, looked at the Collector, looked around, and climbed slowly to his feet. Govindaswami, immaculately black and white, tried to help him, but Mr Surabhai shook him off and picked up his big Congress flag and limped slowly away up the Street of Suttees. I saw tears glistening in the corners of his big eyes and a puckering round his mouth as he passed me. He had a big bruise between his right ear and eye.

Savage and Govindaswami were talking together. The carbine was burning my hands. Oh, he was a quick, cunning swine to give me that, then. I gave it back to him and crept away from them in the crowd, walked to the station yard, got on my bicycle, and went slowly back to Number 4 Collett Road.

18

THAT was a Friday, and, as the normal duty rosters were working again, Pater was not in. He had left early in the afternoon to take 98 Up to Gondwara.

At supper I noticed that Mater was wearing her purple satin evening dress embroidered with large white flowers. I thought she must be going over to drink tea with Mr Williams' mother. That was an occasional invitation for which Mater always put on her best dress. But after supper Rose Mary knocked on the wall between our rooms and called, 'Victoria! Hooks, please!'

I said, 'Do it yourself.' Rose Mary had a nerve, after the things she'd said to me last night. But then I thought, Oh well, we're always quarrelling but we have to be hooked into tight dresses just the same, so I went through and found Rose Mary standing ready by the mirror, her white organdie gaping at the back.

I fastened the hooks and couldn't resist telling Rose Mary she ought to wear a brassière with that dress. She hadn't any panties on either. I was disgusted, but I wondered whether she was hoping Patrick would do something. Then I got angry and for a moment wished I had a man. Savage's face, and the way his wrists looked as they lay on his office table, came suddenly into my mind and then I had to admit to myself for the first time that, simply as a man, he was terrifyingly attractive. I was furious with myself and with him.

I watched Rose Mary shrug and wriggle and tug, and, to get the thoughts out of my mind, I said, 'Where are you going?'

Rose Mary sat down and began to put on a thick coat of pale cream powder. 'To the Empire Day social and dance at the Institute, of course,' she said. 'You wouldn't be coming to *that*, of course. You will be chewing betel nut with Kasel.'

The family expected me to keep away from the Institute because I'd had tea at Ranjit's house and gone to the cinema with him. I said, 'Of course. I almost forgot. I'm coming.'

Rose Mary looked at me in the mirror, sniffed, and said, 'You won't have a good time.'

I went to my own room and began to change. I had a pale green long dress and two short ones, a white dress and a dotted red and white one. And there was the old white organdie, the twin of Rose Mary's. Mater had bought the two together many years ago, thinking we would look nice dressed as sisters. I put that one on. Soon I was able to call out, 'Rose Mary! Hooks, please.'

Rose Mary came in and stopped in the door, crying shrilly, 'You're not going to wear *that*?'

I said, 'Why not? I've got it on.'

She cried, 'I won't hook you into that! Oh, you are a beast!' She stormed out, slamming the door behind her. I went to Mater and got myself hooked up. Mater said, 'That is good. Rose Mary and you, you will look like sisters.'

We walked together to the Institute, Mater in the middle, Rose Mary tripping sulkily on five-inch heels.

The big hall was hung with red, white, and blue bunting and dozens of Union Jacks. I saw at once that we girls would be in our usual majority of at least two to one – more when it came to dancing. Many of the men were on duty, and others would not leave the bar or the billiard room the whole evening.

Two groups of older ladies had already settled down to whist with their glasses of port-and-lemon beside them. There was no band. Bill Fitzpatrick and his girl friend stood beside the big gramophone on the dais and fed it with records. The Institute had no loudspeakers, so the music sounded faint and tinny in the far corners. Two girls were dancing together, giggling. Mr and Mrs Williams walked on to the floor to dance as we arrived. Mr Williams' old mother was sitting on a chair against the opposite wall, her gloved hands folded in her lap.

Mater said, 'We will sit there, near Mrs Williams,' and shuffled flatfooted across the dance floor, and we followed her obediently. We sat down in a row. Mrs Williams said, 'Good evening, Mrs Jones,' and Mater answered, 'Good evening, Mrs Williams.' Rose Mary flipped open her fan and began to fan herself, glancing to right and left. I sat with my hands in my lap, feeling that I must look exactly like old Mrs Williams.

Patrick appeared from the direction of the Gents' and stood on the edge of the floor opposite us, fingering the knot of his Old St Thomasian's tie. I met his eyes as he looked about, and quickly turned away. Rose Mary waved her fan, and then Patrick walked over to us. He asked Rose Mary to dance with him, and she accepted.

Mater talked comfortably with old Mrs Williams. I watched Patrick and Rose Mary but turned away whenever either of them might see me. At the gramophone Fitzpatrick mixed polkas, fox-trots, waltzes, two-steps, and rumbas with no pauses between. Many people were dancing by then, about half of them girls with girls. Rose Mary and Patrick left the floor but did not come back to our chairs. I forced myself not to watch them to see where they were going.

After three-quarters of an hour I went to the Ladies' and stayed there for nearly twenty minutes. A girl I knew well came in to mend a broken shoulder strap with a safety-pin. She glanced at me but did not say anything and quickly went out again.

I set my face to look calm and confident, and lifted my shoulders and walked slowly back to the dance floor. The first person I saw was Colonel Savage sitting at a little table where two old drivers were plying him with whisky. He saw me but gave no sign that he knew who I was. Nearly next to him the Dunphys were sitting together – Ted, the young driver who had always been fond of me, and Mary, his sister. When Mary was a child I often used to look after her, sometimes taking her out in the pram. She was seven years younger than I. I had taught her to dance.

I walked over to them. Ted Dunphy got up quickly, blushing hard. I think he was really in love with me. I smiled at him and said, 'I know you don't like dancing, Ted, but I do. Mary, let's dance.'

Mary Dunphy said, 'I don't feel like dancing.' She went red as she spoke. I had seen her dancing earlier in the evening. She had even made Ted dance with her, she wanted so much to dance. I stared at her. Obviously she didn't want to dance with *me*. Obviously the proper thing for me to do was to take the hint and not press her any more. If Savage had asked me to dance then – he was sitting there behind me – I would have accepted. But Savage said nothing.

I said to Mary, 'You do feel like dancing. I've been watching you.'

'No, I don't, a bit,' she said breathlessly.

At my shoulder Patrick said, 'She does not want to dance with you, that's the God's truth.' He'd had several beers, and his voice was hoarse. Rose Mary was with him. Everyone at that end of the hall must have heard us.

I did not turn round. I said to Mary Dunphy, 'Well? Are you going to dance with me?'

'No. I don't want to dance with you,' Mary said with a sneer. She was braver then, because of Patrick's being close and on her side.

'*No*body wants to,' Patrick said triumphantly.

'Yes, they do. I do,' Ted Dunphy said. He was on his feet still; he'd been standing there all the time since I came up. His face was scarlet, and he was rubbing his hands against his trousers.

Patrick said, 'No you don't, Ted. You stop him, Mary. Don't let him. Why doesn't she go over to the Indian Institute? They have jolly good dances there, I must say.'

Colonel Savage laughed.

Ted Dunphy turned to me and said, 'Will you please dance with me, Victoria?'

I put my hand on his arm and said, 'Thank you, Ted. Thank you very much. But it is time I went. Let me know if you want to see Doctor Faiz Ali again, Mary.'

Mary jumped up, her fists clenched. I turned my back and walked out, across the middle of the floor and out through the middle of the wide centre doors into the hot close night. I walked down Limit Road, watching the moths that were so thick round the bright yard lamps. I came to the line, turned left, and walked along it.

Mary Dunphy was a little bitch! She had lost her virginity when she was sixteen, to a Scottish private in the Royal Engineers – right here, under a wagon, during an Institute dance like this. And got pregnant, and tried to kill herself by leaving a sigri on all night in a closed bedroom. For her sake I had gone to an Indian doctor and begged him to help. He had thought it was me at first.

And Colonel Savage laughed, when I was standing there without a friend among my own people, when I was an officer serving with his regiment, when he could have done so much for me at so little cost. Oh God, however much I thought I hated him, God knows what I would not have done for him if he had used his rank and his being English to freeze those cheechees the way he could, and in front of all of them asked me to dance with him. He must have known all that, and he laughed. My inside knotted together, I hated him so much.

I stopped, holding up my wide skirts that crackled as I walked. I found I was more than half-way to the station. They'd driven me out as if I'd already had an illegitimate brown baby, and I was walking aimlessly, thinking black angry thoughts. They couldn't beat me down like that.

I turned right, passed behind the Loco Sheds, crossed the branch line, and waited in the street until a tonga came. I told the driver to take me to the Sirdarni-sahiba Kasel's house.

The moon had not come up yet, so it was very dark, and when the tonga stopped in front of the door I hesitated about paying the driver off. But I could not stand there for long in my white organdie in the dim alley, so I paid him and knocked on the door as the horse clopped away. I waited for two minutes; then the door opened.

'Miss Jones! Victoria!' Ranjit said, his large eyes wide and anxious. 'What is the matter, what has happened?'

'I haven't –' I began to say, I haven't killed anyone this time, but I stopped in time. I said, 'I would like your mother to help me choose a sari, several saris.'

'Now?' Ranjit said. We were still standing in the doorway, and I asked if I could come in for a minute.

He said, 'Oh, yes, please. I am sorry.' He followed me up the stairs. On the way he said, 'My mother is out. That is why I hesitated just now. There is only Mr Surabhai and myself here.' He opened the door of the big room for me and stood aside.

Mr Surabhai got up hurriedly, holding a small cake in his hand. Plaster in the shape of a big X on the side of his forehead made him look like a cartoon of a man who has been in a fight.

Ranjit said, 'Miss Jones wanted my mother to help her buy some saris.'

Mr Surabhai, whose expression had been dejected and hang-dog, came to me with both his arms outstretched. He cried, 'Miss Jones! That is quite wonderful. You have genuinely decided to don the national garb? Oh, I say, this is grand!' He clasped my hands in his, popping the cake into his mouth just in time, and squeezed my fingers hard. He said, with his mouth full, 'We must order my wife to be present here at once, and she will choose the most suitable saris that exist in Bhowani.'

'Isn't she rather ill?' Ranjit said doubtfully.

'You mustn't disturb her for my sake,' I said. 'I can wait till tomorrow. Only I thought the Sirdarni-sahiba would probably be up, and I really would rather like to have them tonight.'

'Don't think of waiting for one minute!' Mr Surabhai cried. He licked the cake crumbs off his fingers. 'Strike when the iron is hot, that's it. Eh? Well, perhaps it will be more thoughtful on my part not to upset my good lady at this time. She has been upset already on her bed by the events of the day. I was wounded! See?' He leaned forward, showing me the plaster cross.

'I saw it all, Mr Surabhai,' I said.

'You did?' he said. He deflated as he remembered what a disastrous misunderstanding it had really been. As suddenly he cheered up, and said, 'The police put it up to the Moslems, that's what. They had their agents provocateurs in the crowd and were just awaiting their chance. A fine chance they had too, my word! It was a jolly disgraceful shame after all the Sirdarni-sahiba's good efforts.' He shook his head.

I sat down. Ranjit poured me some lemonade, and I drank thirstily. It was wonderful the way neither of them asked any questions. Because of that I felt at home in spite of the white organdie evening dress. Perhaps Mr Surabhai was talking so continuously, and with such forced animation, in order to give me time to settle down. I must have looked very upset. Now Mr Surabhai was describing the procession in minute detail.

When he came to the end of the story he said, 'You must cease to be a member of the Women's Auxiliary Corps (India), Miss Jones. It is your patriotic duty. Oh, I dare not blame you for joining the corps when the war was in full swing. Hitler and Hirohito and many tyrants undoubtedly needed conquering. I will tell you secretly that I myself felt it my duty to join the Army then. Eh, what do you think of that? But they rejected me, like the stone which turned into the head of the corner, eh? I am somewhat colour blind in my left eye – this one.' He took another cake and ate it quickly between sentences. 'You must resign from the corps, because now the military are fighting nobody but us. Why, what would you think if you were compelled to shoot *me*?'

'WACs don't usually carry arms, Mr Surabhai,' I said. 'And anyway, I wouldn't shoot you.'

Mr Surabhai's eyes popped, and he leaned over me, showering cake crumbs into my lap. He said, 'Ah, but what if I was in the act of exploding a train? Blowing a bridge to fragments? What then, eh?'

I said, 'You wouldn't blow up a train, Mr Surabhai, would you?' Even the thought of it made me serious, and I said, 'That isn't going to get rid of the British any quicker. All it will do is kill people like my father and lots of Indian passengers.'

Mr Surabhai said, 'Ah, but what if it was a *troop* train full of British soldiers and no one else besides? What then, eh? There will be a driver, two firemen, and a guard, naturally, but you can't make omelets without breaking the eggs, eh? You saw today what *they* are doing. You know their cunning aims and habits. Divide, divide! Set brother against his brother! Rule, rule! I tell you we are perfectly well justified in blowing up a train – a troop train, that is. Today I have been only slightly wounded – walking wounded, they would call it in the war, you know – but I am fully willing and able to die for the same cause, so why should not others? Even your father? Though of course I would not think for one second of blowing up Mr Jones. Absolutely not for one fraction of a second! But the principle is just. There is no help for it. It is the truth, so help us God.'

Ranjit said, 'Victoria, I think if you want a sari tonight you had better come out now. Har Singh usually goes to bed at about this time.'

Mr Surabhai looked at his wrist-watch, shook it, and looked again. 'My goodness me, do you know it is seven minutes past eleven p.m.?' he cried.

'Yes,' Ranjit said, dropping into Hindi, 'I know. You would talk till five in the morning if I let you, wouldn't you? You'd better get on home now or you'll be in trouble. I can help Miss Jones with the saris.'

'I am afraid you are quite correct,' Mr Surabhai answered in English. 'I must hurry to my home or Mrs Surabhai will give me six bells and all kinds of assorted hades.' He went out, gesturing with joined palms toward each of us, and we heard his light shoes hop-hopping down the long staircase.

A minute later I followed with Ranjit. This time I felt very conspicuous and was glad the little shop was near. Har Singh lay comfortably stretched out there on several bolts of cloth, fast asleep, but the lamp was still burning above him, and the door was not locked.

I bought two khaki saris for uniform, three white ones for daytime, and two beautiful evening saris, one black and one of patterned pale blue silk. I bought plain borders for the white saris, a gold bordered for the black sari, and a silver border for the blue one. Har Singh stitched a border on to one of the plain white saris right away. The others I would do the next day, at home.

I put on the sari and waited while Har Singh fastened the rest and my organdie into a big bundle. When we got outside, Ranjit looked anxiously up and down, and we waited for some time in the street, but no tonga came. It was about midnight.

It was a lovely night, and a little cooler by then. There was a breeze. I asked Ranjit if he would mind walking home with me.

He smiled at me then, really smiled, and said, 'I was hoping you would suggest that. Are those shoes all right for walking?'

I said, 'They're comfortable, but I can't walk fast. Which way shall we go?'

'The quickest way is down here,' he said, pointing. I remembered that street. I had walked along there with him once before, at night, in a sari. I didn't want to go that way ever again.

I said, 'Let's walk down the line from the Loco Sheds.'

He agreed, and we set off. We walked slowly, I because of my shoes, Ranjit because of me. We didn't say much until we had climbed the low embankment by the Loco Sheds and turned up the main line. It was late by then, but someone in the sheds had a wireless set and must have been squatting in the dark listening to music among the big quiet engines.

'Patna, I think,' Ranjit said. 'That is a Bihar love song. It is quite well known.'

'Let's stop and listen a minute,' I said. 'We can sit on the fence. I want to rest my feet. I have an awful lot to learn.'

'About the music?' he said.

I said, 'Yes. That, and everything. I am ready to like the music, if you know what I mean, but it doesn't make sense to me. I have heard it all my life and I've never really listened to it or tried to understand it.'

Ranjit lowered my bundle carefully to the ground. He said softly, 'I cannot explain to you how glad I am about the sari, Victoria.'

I said, 'You didn't look very pleased when I came tonight. You looked more frightened.' I examined him carefully. I could not see his face well, but I thought he was pleased and also nervous. I wondered if he was nervous because he was screwing up his courage to kiss me. What would I do then?

But he wouldn't, he wasn't going to, I was absolutely certain of it.

He said, 'I am so pleased, but I am worried too. You know what happened at the cantonment cinema. I think something else like it must have happened tonight?'

I said, 'Something happened – but I don't want to talk about that. Let's get on.'

Ranjit picked up the parcel. We walked side by side between the rails. He said, 'You will never regret this. India will open up like a flower when she is free, Victoria. We will all share in her beauty and happiness. India will sing like a bird out of its cage when she is free.'

I pressed his arm. It was strange to know I could do it and not be misunderstood – never with any other man in my life. I said, 'I know. It'll be wonderful for you personally too, won't it?'

I meant he would feel that the railway was truly India's, that he would be working at his own job for his own country, without despising himself half the time as a servant of the British.

He said, 'It will be wonderful. I will go into politics. There is need of a new outlook. Congress has been very good in many ways, but it is too much controlled by the Bombay capitalists and the steel millionaires. I want to work on the educational programmes.'

I said, 'Don't you want to stay on the railway?' I was surprised and perhaps a little shocked to hear what he said.

He was becoming less constrained with me. He swung the parcel on its strings as he walked, and waved his other hand in the air to emphasize what he said. 'The railway is merely a mechanical thing. It takes our bodies from one place to another, that is all.

It is material. But the mind, the soul, is what is important to India. There are so many bars here that it is like a prison for many people. India is like a giant chained, and not all the chains are ones that the British have tied on. I say, I am using almost as many beautiful metaphors as V. K. – Mr Surabhai.' He smiled at me, boyish for that moment, and yet not quite carefree.

He said, 'The future will excuse our metaphors. It will justify them.'

I said, 'I suppose your mother approves of your plans?'

The parcel stopped swinging in his hand. He held it then carefully in both hands. I could not miss the change in his voice as he said, 'She approves. Oh yes.'

I didn't believe him, but I didn't want to corner him. He was too defenceless. I wanted to pat his hand and say, 'There, there, it doesn't matter.' We were at the signal, and it was off, for Number 599 Down Passenger, nearly an hour late. I stopped there because that was where we would have to say good night.

Ranjit's hand came out slowly, as though someone invisible behind him was forcing his elbow forward. He took my hand and squeezed it. He said, stammering and more nervous than I had ever seen a man with me, 'Miss Jones -- Victoria, I am getting – I admire you more than – I think you are the bravest girl in the world. Please don't think I'm pushing you.' He was perspiring freely, and his hand was clammy. He looked the same as he had the night Macaulay was killed.

He burst out, 'I don't want to hurry you, Victoria.'

'Then why do you?' I said as gently as I could. I held his hand, instead of his holding mine, and said, 'I like you too, Ranjit, very much. I think you are the nicest man I've ever met. I think – I think this may be too valuable to hurry. Don't forget how strange everything is to me – even the music.' I finished with a laugh and let his hand go, and stood back from him. Far away I saw the bright little eye of the train as it came on down.

My words seemed to have opened a gate for Ranjit. Still keeping well apart from me, he cried, 'I am honourably in love with you, Victoria. I didn't want to say it yet. I wanted you to have time to know me. And I am afraid of you. I am afraid for your sake as well. But –'

I waited, knowing what must be coming.

He said miserably, 'But you have said you are going to think of yourself as an Indian. My mother –' I sighed. Here it was. 'My mother told me to hurry up or you would marry someone else. She told me that if I didn't make up your mind for you, she would.'

I was wearing a sari, and I did understand. Girls who wore saris had their marriages arranged for them. Everything should have been settled for me long ago, before I knew what it was about, years before I was twenty-eight. The light of the train was bright in my eyes, and the earth shook under it as it came on.

I said, 'I don't want to hurry, even for your mother, Ranjit. I'd rather you asked me.' I was ready to cry of vexation. Here I was, so proud of my new sari, and this was what happened the first time I wore it. I felt as if I were insisting on wearing a topi on top of it.

He muttered, 'I will not know how to ask you.'

I said, 'Well, I will ask you – when I want to!'

I had to put out my arm and pull him away from the line as 599 Down Passenger rocked past us behind an ancient 4-6-0, the brakes grinding and the sparks flying from the brake shoes as the driver slowed for his stop at Bhowani Junction.

Dear Ranjit was not really a railwayman at heart, or he would have felt that train in his bones even though he had his back to it – even though I had been promising to marry him.

19

I STRUGGLED out of sleep, miles down. My sister was knocking on the wall between our rooms. There was another noise – the telephone ringing, standing silent, ringing again. Rose Mary's muffled, sleepy voice called, 'For God's sake go and answer it, Vicky. It's always for you.'

I scrambled out of the sheet and the mosquito net and found the light. I stood by the telephone, one hand on the wall and my eyes closed against the light, and lifted the receiver. I thought dazedly it would be something to do with the mutiny. But the mutiny was over at last, and the sailors had gone back peacefully to their duty.

The man said, 'Duty Officer, First Thirteenth Gurkhas. The C.O. wants you to get into uniform at once. A jeep will come and pick you up in ten minutes. There's been a crash.'

'Oh, a crash,' I said, still dazed. 'On the road? I haven't had any nursing training, you know.'

The young man at the other end was excited and exasperated. He said, 'A rail crash, a troop train derailed near Pathoda, Miss Jones!'

I woke up properly and said, 'What does he want me for?'

The duty officer said, 'Good God, I don't know, but you'd better hurry up. I've got a hundred things to do. Good-bye.' He hung up.

I went back to my room and began to dress. When I was stepping into my skirt I remembered that I had been wearing a sari since yesterday. This was Sunday. I muttered crossly to myself, took off the skirt, and found my uniform sari.

'What's happened?' Rose Mary called.

I told her. She said, 'Near Pathoda again! I bet I know who's done that. Your Congress friends!'

'Oh, shut up!' I said.

I wrestled with the sari and my hair, and with powder and lipstick and sari brooch. The jeep arrived before I was quite ready. The driver did not toot his horn or come running up the path to knock on the door, so I knew Colonel Savage wasn't in it. I found my watch, saw it was two o'clock, and hurried out. Birkhe was waiting, and I scrambled in beside him. The sari took some managing. I had always wondered how the Indian girls in the WAC (I) managed to ride bicycles and get in and out of jeeps and do their parade-ground drills so efficiently.

Birkhe smiled shyly at me, his beautiful white teeth gleaming in the faint starlight, but he did not speak then or on the short drive up the Pike. The battalion offices were alive with lights and men and the sound of talking and the throb of engines. Savage called me at once and said, 'Ranjit's at the Traffic Office now, and Taylor's on his way there. Find out at once what they're doing. Tell them Chaney's already gone up with our Regimental Aid Post, and that I'm going in fifteen minutes with Howland and B

Company. Tell them Lanson wants me to cordon off the roads round the crash, and I'm doing that.'

I picked up my telephone and began to find out what was happening. I knew from the tone of Ranjit's flat, non-committal voice that Patrick had arrived in the Traffic Office. Then, in the background, I heard Patrick booming on another telephone. Ranjit told me that the Divisional Traffic Superintendent was taking the necessary steps. They wanted all the help Colonel Savage could give at the scene of the accident. Ranjit gave me details of the movements of breakdown trains, of extra engines, of medical rescue parties. I listened, my chest beginning to feel empty as the urgent instructions and messages piled up. I made notes and with the other ear overheard snatches of Savage's orders next door. I heard him phoning to the D.S.P., and it sounded as if Lanson would be on his way to the accident at once. I heard Savage tell someone to get Kishanpur 6, priority. From the signal office down the passage I heard the duty officer on the R/T: 'Dogfish Six speaking ... Hello, Able Zebra Uncle, Able Zebra Uncle calling ... Christ, I want your Number Nine. *Timi ko ho?* ... Roger, over.'

Savage got his connexion and began to speak in his special 'languid' tone. He managed to suppress all the force he'd just been using and somehow blunt the edge of his voice. He must have been bursting with the effort. He drawled, 'I'm sorry to disturb you at this ungodly hour, Nigel ... Yes, of course. There's been a derailment near Pathoda ... Yes. It's a troop train with about half a British battalion on board ... Well, yes – you see, Pathoda's almost as close to you as it is to here, and I was going to suggest that if you hadn't made any other plans you might consider sending a few men to help dig in the wreckage. I expect some doctors and ambulances would be well received too ... Oh, yes, I think so, Nigel, really quite serious ... Well, thank you ... Yes, I'll take care of it if I may have your authority to pass on your suggestion ... It *is* a beautiful night. Quite wonderful ... It is extraordinary, I agree ... Yes, I can see it from here ... Yes. Beautiful. Good night, Nigel.'

I heard him put down the receiver and lift it up. In a voice with an edge like a saw he said, 'Kishanpur three-one-one, priority.' There was a short wait. Then Savage snarled, 'Say who you are!

... I don't care a purple — if your name's Reginald or Ramfurley. Are you the staff captain of Kishanpur Sub-Area? ... For Christ's sake, wake up, you chairborne bastard. This is Savage, C.O. of the First Thirteenth Gurkhas. Take these orders, they are from the brigadier ...' He began giving orders in an emphatic monotone.

When he had finished I went in to him and told him what I had learned. He was dressed in fighting order. He picked up his hat and carbine and shoved me out to the jeep ahead of him as I struggled to put my information into short concise phrases. Birkhe had already moved into the back seat. The radio jeep and the escort jeep were waiting. A line of lorries and six-by-sixes, with lights blazing and engines running, stood along the side of the approach road. Dickson was waiting on the office steps, his brow deeply furrowed and a paper in his hand. Young Chris Glass, the new adjutant replacing Macaulay, was gabbling excitedly with Howland, the commander of B Company.

To Dickson, Savage said, 'Deal with it, Henry. You're a major, aren't you? Christ, tell them to stuff it up, then!' He jumped into the driver's seat, engaged gear, and we shot off.

After a mile I looked round and said, 'The trucks can't keep up, sir.'

He said, 'Do you think I'm running a kindergarten? My God, I nearly broke a blood vessel when I was talking to People-Psmythe. He didn't understand how the engine driver could run off the rails on a beautiful night like this, with the Great Bear so clean and sparkling. Jesus! Pathoda again. The goods train must have been just a rehearsal.'

He was in one of his strange ferocious good tempers, and I could not understand why. A deer stood peering into the lights at a corner and did not move till Savage swung the jeep six inches clear of its nose. I saw its little white tail flashing among the trees at the edge of the jungle as it bounded away. Farther on a pair of eyes reflected back like headlamps from a thicket beside the road. 'Leopard, sahib,' Birkhe said. Savage answered in Gurkhali, and Birkhe chuckled.

I said, 'Do you know if many people have been killed, sir?'

Savage said, 'The Stationmaster thinks so. His first telegram was practically incoherent, Ranjit told me.'

I was listening for the sound of the breakdown train. The road was not far from the railway here. I asked which way the troop train had been going, and Savage said, 'West. From Allahabad.'

He meant up. I said, 'It must have been going downhill, then.'

Savage hooted at a jackal standing bewildered in the lights, and said, 'Yes, it will be a thoroughly unpleasant scene. That sari suits you, as I forgot to tell you yesterday, but it's an impractical garment for this kind of life.'

The two remarks were not altogether unconnected, I was sure. 'It will be a thoroughly unpleasant scene,' he said, and he meant, That's why I'm taking you to it, so that you can see with your own eyes what happens when Mr Surabhai's kind of patriotism runs wild. I remembered Mr Surabhai's justification of train wrecking and started suddenly in my seat.

Savage said, 'Thought of something?' He didn't give me time to reply but went on, 'or just got ants in your pants?'

He had nearly forced me to say something then. My start had been so obviously connected with the wreck and the carnage and nationalism and my sari. Then he'd saved me from having to answer.

'Something is on fire,' he said. I recognized Pathoda station, the lights burning in it, just ahead on the right. The road ran straight for some distance there, and Savage slowed down and ran without lights. Then I saw a jumpy glow in the dark jungle-covered hills to the east. It was perhaps a mile or two away. I sniffed but could smell nothing. 'West wind,' Savage said curtly.

He stopped the jeep at the Pathoda station, jumped out, and talked hurriedly to two men there. The jeeps and the rest soon caught up, and at once we started off again. After a bit the jungle thinned on the right, and I saw the dim gleam of steel rails. The rails swung away from the road, and almost immediately the jungle in there was aglow with red and yellow light, the trees standing in thick ranks against it, all silhouetted and motionless on a gentle slope.

The convoy halted, and the Gurkhas jumped down. I hurried into the jungle at Savage's heels, thorns plucking at my sari, and twigs whipping across my face. As we came near to the railway I saw the long hard line of a carriage standing on one end, the other end high among the branches. The carriage was dark and still, and

178

the trees creaked under its weight, and there was a smell of newly broken wood. I saw other carriages, and men moving about. I had thought the men would be running, with the flames crackling so loudly in front of them, but they were moving slowly, or standing or sitting. The track ran in a shallow cutting there, and some of the grass on the banks had caught fire. British troops in every stage of uniform and undress were moving about like sleep-walkers and padding at the fire with coats and rolled trousers.

I tripped over something and cried out, seeing it was a man sprawled on his side in the undergrowth. His head lay anyhow on his arms, and he was wearing a pair of wrinkled drawers, a white vest, ammunition boots, and nothing else. He rolled over when I trod on him, and mumbled, 'Go 'way.'

Savage laughed suddenly. 'Asleep!' he muttered. 'Good old Mr Atkins. Now, let's see.'

He stood on top of the side of the cutting, while the Gurkhas gathered behind him and to right and left. The battalion doctor's jeep was a little farther up, and I wondered how he could possibly have got it there. An Englishman in blue and white striped pyjamas came up to Savage and began to point and explain. I could see seven carriages now – one on the rails, one burning, one up-ended in the jungle, one half into the jungle, and three welded into a single Z-shaped heap across the cutting. There must be more carriages behind there, out of sight and probably un-damaged.

I hadn't seen the engine and began desperately to look for it. An engine and tender couldn't disappear. They weighed a hundred and fifty tons together, and carried three men. I saw them at last, recognizing the engine's funnel and then the battered curve of its boiler among the wreckage of the three tangled carriages.

Now I was alone with Savage. All the Gurkhas were at work. The breakdown train had arrived without my noticing it, and now its searchlight flashed on so that the dying red flames of the burning carriage flickered and jerked against a background of even white light. Savage said, 'Go and help Chaney in the R.A.P.'

I hadn't then seen any dead or injured men, not close to. The soldiers were pulling lumps out of the wreck, and some of the lumps were strangely shaped. They might have been bedding rolls, or frame members, or men. I didn't want to go to the Regimental Aid Post. There I would have to see those strange shapes close to, and look at them. The men would have raw wounds, and some of them would be bent and blind and dead. In truth I felt that I had somehow done all this by wearing a sari.

'Go on,' Savage said.

I said, 'I won't! I'm not a nurse. I *didn't* do this.'

Savage put out his arm and caught my shoulder. His fingers tightened into my flesh, and his eyes glittered. He said, 'Go and help Chaney to help the poor sods who've been hurt. They didn't do it either.'

'Don't use filthy language to me!' I said. 'I won't have it. I'll report you to Mrs Fortescue. I'll –' I was struggling back as though Savage were pushing me, but he wasn't.

He said, 'Go on.'

I gasped. 'They did it. It's their fault for –'

Savage stepped away from me and said, 'You mustn't let the old school sari down – you little slut.'

To get away from him I turned and stumbled along the top of the cutting. After twenty steps I got hold of myself. In trying to hurt me, Savage had only cleared my mind. Everyone must help now. If Mr Surabhai had been there he would be killing himself trying to help – even if he'd done it. But he couldn't have done it. He wouldn't. What he had said was just talk, principle, theory – surely?

I came to the R.A.P., swallowed, and went down to report to Captain Chaney. There was a strong smell of cooking meat and burned sugar there, downwind from the burning carriage.

I began to bandage and patch, inject and splint and bathe, blindly doing whatever Captain Chaney told me to. The soldiers were mostly young men, obviously conscripts because they were very polite, especially when they were badly hurt. They lay in a quiet row at the edge of the jungle and called me 'miss'. Some of the injured were excited, and then often, later, they'd relapse as the shock hit them. While they were 'high' they talked to me in tense bursts of soldier-Urdu. I was puzzled at that until I remembered the sari.

The pieces and the strange shapes were there in the corners of the R.A.P., but Chaney did not ask me to help with them.

Suddenly as I worked it was light, and I started up, thinking there must be another fire, but it was the dawn, and then I saw two breakdown trains and two big mobile cranes working, and there was a locomotive under steam at the back of the wreck, and there were scores of railway coolies and gangers and men in topis. Chaney told me to go and have a cup of tea.

The Gurkhas had brought degchies with them, and lit cooking fires among the trees and made lakes of stewed tea. I walked to the nearest fire and sat down slowly on the dry leaves. A Gurkha came, gave me tea in half of a mess-tin, and begged me to drink it. I saw it was Birkhe, Savage's orderly, and watched him fill the other half of his mess-tin and carry it carefully away between the trees.

I drank thirstily, my head bent over the mess-tin. After a time I saw a pair of shoes in front of me, and above them blue uniform railway trousers. A man's voice said in quick nervous Hindi, 'Oh, daughter, can you tell me if it is lawful for me to drink this tea? My caste is –'

I looked up and saw Bhansi Lall, the Stationmaster of Pathoda. He was shaking and stammering, his fat cheeks aquiver. When my face came up he stopped, began again, and at last got out in English, 'Miss Victoria Jones, my word! My sainted aunt! Miss Jones, you were in train? You have lost all clothing in horrible accident?'

I shook my head and said wearily, 'No. I'm wearing a sari, that's all. I'm sure it's all right for you to drink the tea.' Really I had no patience with the point then. If he wanted tea, why didn't he drink it? That was another time my sari was difficult to fit into.

I beckoned to a Gurkha, and he brought Bhansi Lall a mess-tin of tea. Bhansi Lall sipped noisily, staring at me, his small eyes darting from my face to the sari, to the Gurkhas, to the ugly black and red wreck not far off. He said, 'You are wearing sari always now? Very good show. Accident took place outside station limits of Pathoda, Miss Jones. Outside by *miles* – by two miles and three furlongs, approximately. Oh, I would like to catch bloody rapscallions responsible for all this to-do. Twenty-seven officers and soldiers of all ranks killed in Koyli Light Infantry, besides two soldiers missing in burned carriage, that is meaning colonel-sahib is

181

not saying whether horrible objects in carriage are one soldier or how many soldiers.'

'Was the driver killed?' I asked. 'Who was it?' I thought suddenly that it might have been Ted Dunphy. He did an occasional turn on the branch, usually on specials.

Bhansi Lall said, 'Driver was killed, both the two firemen were killed. Guard was not killed. My God, Miss Jones, why are every derailments and sabotages performed in vicinity of *my* station? When nothing but calamities are occurring here, who will get the bloody sack but me? It is no dashed tommyrot!'

Savage cut in. 'You look as if you want a drink, Stationmaster!' He was standing over Bhansi Lall. I hadn't seen him come. An uncorked bottle of Army-issue rum swung in his right hand. Bhansi Lall scrambled to his feet, burbling thank-yous, took the bottle, and poured a lot down his throat, holding the bottle high up and away from his mouth.

Savage said, 'Now, Mr Lanson wants you. At the back of the train. Down there.'

Bhansi Lall tugged at his coat and set his cap straight on his large hairless head. He said, 'I shall conceal nothing, Colonel-sahib. This persecution must be halted in military fashion – that is, with back to wall. Light of day is needed.' He crashed off through the bushes.

Savage said, 'We're going back to Bhowani.'

I walked behind him to the road. There were many well-beaten paths now. Police and Gurkhas were keeping watch over a small knot of spectators. The jungle was dishevelled, with pieces of equipment lying everywhere, and heaps of salvage, and soldiers sleeping, and a couple of tents, and Gurkhas making tea, and splintered glass glittering high in the branches. The sun rose out of the crest line of the Sindhya Hills to the east, and we turned our backs to it and got into the jeep.

Savage drove slowly on the way down. I'd forgotten all about the terrible things he'd said to me earlier. When I remembered them, I was almost grateful to him. He had made me do what I ought to do.

His eyes were rimmed with dust and ashes, his uniform was filthy and the black hair on his forearms matted with perspiration and grey soot. He said, 'We've got all the injured away now, to

Bhowani and Kishanpur. Chaney told me you'd done a good job of work.'

I said, 'I didn't do anything.'

He said wearily, 'Please don't be modest. It doesn't go with that heroic sari. Well, I suppose someone else thinks he's done a good job, in killing those fellows and stopping all traffic on the branch line for two or three days.'

I said, 'Do they know for certain yet that it was sabotage?'

He said, 'Yes. The District Engineer found two fishplates missing. Later someone picked them up in the jungle the other side of the line. Do you think Surabhai did it?'

I said quickly, 'I'm sure he didn't. The police can find out where he was last night. I'm sure he will have been in Bhowani and will be able to prove it. He's always talking to people.'

Savage said, 'Surabhai doesn't have to unscrew the fishplates himself to be responsible. I asked whether you thought he did it – ordered it done, knew about it.'

I answered angrily, being a little frightened. 'And I said I'm sure he didn't do it. He wouldn't murder people like that. He's a very nice, kindhearted man.'

Savage said, 'Yes, but he has a blind spot just the same as I have and you have. I'll do a lot of queer things for this regiment and not care a damn who else suffers. He'll do the same for what he calls India. Still, if he had to wreck a train, a troop train – especially one full of British troops – was about the fairest he could have picked.'

'Mr Surabhai had nothing to do with it, sir,' I repeated.

He said then, 'We'll see,' and said nothing more until he stopped the jeep in front of our house. There he said, 'It's nine-fifteen. The Collector wants to see you at five in his bungalow.' He engaged gear and drove away. I saluted his back and went inside.

Why did Govindaswami want to see me? Why hadn't Savage told me so earlier? How and when had the appointment been fixed between them? Was it about the train wreck? If so, Savage and Govindaswami must have talked on the radio-telephone during the night. Why were they asking me about poor Mr Surabhai when it was obvious that K. P. Roy had done it? I felt suddenly very tired and very dirty and very small. I had a tepid bath and climbed into bed. As I was dropping asleep I thought that Govindaswami might want to see me about Macaulay – but by then I didn't care. Nothing could stop me from trying to find rest and some peace in sleep.

20

GOVINDASWAMI kept me waiting in his study for ten minutes, and then I heard him talking with another man in the hall and recognized Ranjit's voice. I had had no time to think what this might mean when Ranjit came in. He looked drawn, tired, and handsome. He must have been working all night and all day. He was so sweet-tempered that it hurt me to see him looking worried. I wanted to tell him not to worry, that I did like him, that I was sure I would marry him if he would give me time; but that wasn't the cause of his worry now, I knew.

The Collector was wearing a dark red carnation in his buttonhole. He looked as tired as Ranjit, but as soon as he began to speak I knew he was going to come to grips with us. He began at once, 'We are three Indians. We have different backgrounds and we believe in different approaches to the goal. But our goal is the same, as far as patriotism is concerned. I want a free, strong, democratic India, and I want it as soon as possible. Do you, Ranjit?'

Ranjit nodded. Govindaswami glanced at me, raising his eyebrows, and I nodded. It was like a breath of fresh air to have it publicly acknowledged and said aloud that I was trying to be a good Indian.

Govindaswami said, 'But this train wreck is the work of men who want violent revolution. Specifically, it is the work of K. P. Roy.'

'Roy?' Ranjit said. 'You weren't even sure that he was in the province.'

Govindaswami said, 'Yes, but now we are just about positive that he's actually in Bhowani City. The looting of the ammunition train was certainly his work. We do not know what he intends to do with the explosives that he stole, except that he will certainly use them to increase dissension. He might arm the Moslems against the Hindus, or the peasants against the landlords, or the lawless against the police. Or he may blow up more bridges, wreck more trains. He doesn't care who's in the train. It might be me or Colonel Savage – but it might be Mr Surabhai, and it might be a thousand pilgrims. Who do you think engineered that fiasco when the two processions met the other day? We have got to remove Roy and everyone like him.

'Now, we are working on two lines of approach. One is that someone may know where the stolen explosives are hidden – someone outside Roy's own small circle of faithful Communists, that is. The "someone", if he exists, is not telling. The "someone" may think it is none of his business, or he may think that the explosive is being kept for some justifiable cause. A Moslem might know, for instance, but might have been told that it is intended for the defence of the Moslem community here when the Hindus rise up to massacre them. You can think of other "justifications".'

'Why do you ask us?' Ranjit cried distractedly. 'I do not know. I'm sure Miss Jones does not know.'

Govindaswami said sharply, 'I think your mother knows.'

Ranjit started, and his mouth worked. Govindaswami went on. 'Wait a minute. The other line of approach I mentioned is that we do have a picture of Roy. Here.' He stepped behind his desk, lifted the blotter, and came forward with a glossy eight-by-ten print. He handed it to us where we sat together on the sofa, and said, 'That's K. P. Roy in nineteen thirty-seven.'

It was an enlargement from a poor negative. A man in European clothes – trousers, shirt, tie, collar, coat – was standing by an ancient taxi, with a big turreted building in the background. The man had short hair and was clean-shaven and smiling. I had seen Ghanshyam 'smile', and I was almost sure this man in the picture was Ghanshyam. But I wasn't *quite* sure. Nine years is a long time, and a moustache makes such a difference.

'Have either of you ever seen this man recently, here in Bhowani?' Govindaswami asked carelessly.

'No, I've never seen this man,' Ranjit said and handed back the print. He carefully kept his eyes on the Collector, so as not to look at me.

185

'And you, Miss Jones?' Govindaswami said.

I was ready and did not hesitate, but answered at once. 'No, I've never seen him either.'

Govindaswami put the print away. He said, 'Well, he's about, and he is a real danger to what we have agreed that we want. Perhaps you think he's just one nihilist with a few crazy followers, and what difference can it make to the future of India if he does blow up a train – or ten trains, for that matter. Have you been thinking that, Ranjit?'

'I don't think it is right to kill people and do damage, of course,' Ranjit said. 'But yes, I don't see how Roy can really do great harm – great political harm, and that is all that is important now.'

Govindaswami returned to his blotter and got out a plain outline map of India. On it several large areas had been shaded with red pencil strokes, and in a few places there were red circles and the names of cities or towns. He said, 'Those are the areas and the cities where revolutionary groups that stand far to the left of the Socialists, for instance, are waiting to see whether what K. P. Roy told them is true or not – whether they can do on a large scale what Roy is doing on a small scale and almost by himself. Whether it is feasible and practicable to disrupt government and communication by terrorism – all government, any government. The R.I.N. mutiny, coinciding with the railway strike, was to be the first big bang, leading to a wider, ever-spreading train of explosions. But the mutiny failed. The derailment of this troop train is, I think, Roy's first effort to show that the rest of the plan need not be abandoned. By this act he is saying, "Look, it can still be done." '

Ranjit looked at the map, shook his head, and said, 'It is very interesting.'

Govindaswami said, 'Your mother was associated during the nineteen twenties with men and women who we know are now in K. P. Roy's group. That's all I wanted to tell you, Ranjit. Think it over. You, Miss Jones – I wanted you to be here because you have made it clear that you are changing worlds, as I did when I went to Cheltenham. You will be seeing your new world with new eyes. I want you to use those eyes and help me, for India's sake and your own. Try and persuade Mr Surabhai to help me. I don't want him to stop being a Congress man. I want him and others like him to examine their friends carefully at this time, and sniff the air, and make sure there isn't a rat i' the arras. What do you think Mr Surabhai would do if he knew another Congress man, or a friend of Congress, was going to derail a troop train?'

He shot the question at me suddenly. I started and looked at him with surprise and said, 'What?' He repeated his question.

I said, 'I think he'd try first to persuade the man not to do it.'

'And if he failed to persuade the man?' Govindaswami said.

I said, 'I'm sure he'd give you or the police all the information he had.'

'Do you agree with that, Ranjit?' Govindaswami asked.

Ranjit was unhappy. He mumbled, 'Yes, I think so. I don't know. Mr Surabhai is not a murderer.'

Govindaswami said, 'No. But it would hurt him just as much to send a patriot, even a misguided one, to jail or to the gallows – wouldn't it?'

His tone insisted on an answer, and we had to give it. We had to agree. He said no more then, but apologized for keeping us so long – it had not been long – and showed us out and stood on his veranda while we bicycled side by side down his long drive.

As soon as as bank of azalea bushes hid him Ranjit said, 'We must talk.'

I asked him where we should go.

He said, 'Down to the river. This way.' He turned to the right off the Pike, and we pedalled along a rutted causeway that soon brought us to the bank of the Cheetah. The grass was long and patchy and broken up by outcropping stones and a few thorn bushes. The river was running, at that time of year, in several shallow streams scattered over its wide, almost empty bed. We heard a bugle call quite close. Kabul Lines were not far off, beyond a row of big dark trees.

We laid our bicycles on the grass and slowly walked forward to the bank. I sat down on a low boulder, and Ranjit sat at my feet.

I said, 'I thought that picture was Ghanshyam.'

Ranjit had found a stick and was busy scratching in the earth as he answered, 'It was quite like him.'

I looked down on the top of his puggaree and wondered what

to say. I was sure – almost sure. I thought Ranjit didn't want to be sure, didn't even want to talk about it. But I couldn't get close to him if I hid my thoughts from him, or he his from me. I said, 'Ranjit, you know it was Ghanshyam. Why didn't you tell the Collector?'

He muttered, 'I don't *know*. It was very like.'

I said, 'You do know. Why didn't you say so?'

He threw away his stick and looked up into my face. He said, 'If they catch him – Ghanshyam – he will tell the truth about Lieutenant Macaulay.'

I said, 'That will be unpleasant, Ranjit, but it's not serious enough to make us hide K. P. Roy. They won't hang me, you know.'

Ranjit said slowly, 'They will arrest my mother.'

I was silent. I had got to the bottom of Ranjit's thought then. I wanted to say something like, What does that matter? or, What does she have to fear if she's innocent? – but obviously Ranjit thought she wasn't innocent. I didn't see how she could be innocent.

Ranjit began to speak in a tense, low voice. He said, 'My mother has fought the British for twenty-six years. She's been to jail five times – nineteen twenty-one, nineteen twenty-five, nineteen thirty, nineteen thirty-one, nineteen thirty-seven. She's not a revolutionary, she's a patriot – but they'd put her in jail again. I don't agree with everything she says, but I can't blame her. She's seen too much, fought too hard. Besides, she may not know that Ghanshyam is K. P. Roy.'

'You can tell her,' I said.

Ranjit lifted his shoulders and dropped them in a sudden gesture of hopelessness. He said, 'I was trying to deceive myself. If he is K. P. Roy, she knows it very well. But that doesn't mean Mr Govindaswami is right. *He* says Roy is doing all this, but how do we know he is telling the truth? How do we know someone else, some other group, isn't responsible and the British are only trying to put the blame on Roy so that they can hang him, because they know he is a man who could unify India against them? How do we know? I'd rather trust my mother than Mr Govindaswami. Why should we believe any Indian who joins the Indian Civil Service and serves the British so faithfully they make him a Commander of the Order of the Indian Empire and an Officer of the Order of the British Empire? Two empires! You can't be more imperialist than that.'

Neither of us had mentioned Mr Surabhai and what he had said that night about derailing a troop train. He had said it was justifiable. But he would be in a terrible quandary – of the spirit – if someone he admired and respected had determined to do it. I thought of asking Ranjit what, if anything, we ought to say to Mr Surabhai, but I decided not to. The problem was really much bigger. What were we going to do?

I opened my bag, got out my cigarette case, and lit a cigarette. Ranjit was looking at me with his face sad and strained and his eyes puckered at the corners as though he was on the edge of tears. I dragged the smoke into my lungs and said, 'What are we going to do, then?'

He broke into a smile that lit his face, and lay back on his side, propping himself up on one elbow. He said, 'I shall never get over seeing you pull out a cigarette and just smoke it, Victoria.'

'In a sari, you mean?' I said, smiling at him.

He said, 'Yes. All the ordinary Indian ladies will have a fit when they see you. Mrs Surabhai will give you a severe lecture.'

'What about your mother?' I asked.

Ranjit became serious at once and said, 'My mother won't mind. She is not ordinary.'

I wanted to catch again the butterfly lightness that had linked us just then. I flipped open the case, offered it to him, and said, 'Have a coffin nail yourself.'

He shook his head and said, 'I don't smoke.'

I asked him if he didn't like the taste. He said he'd never tried.

I said, 'But you're not a Sikh – I mean by religion? Didn't you tell me your mother persuaded you to give it up?'

He said, 'In nineteen thirty-five. But I've never wanted to smoke, and –' He stood up quickly, dusting off his clothes. 'I think I'm going back. Back to my religion. I tell myself it is ridiculous, but I can't help it. I am feeling more lost every day. I think I will go to see the guru here soon and ask if I can go back. Will you mind?'

I said slowly, thinking as I spoke, 'I don't mind, Ranjit. You

189

won't want me to become a Sikh if – if we get married, not at once, will you? Not till I understand more about it?'

There, I'd said right out that I was thinking of marrying him. It was what I'd agreed to do, take the lead, when we talked by the signal that night. But I didn't like it. Why couldn't he take some of the weight of responsibility off me, some of this perpetual having to think and decide?

He said, 'I would like you to become a Sikh, of course, Victoria – if you marry me. You would have another name then. Victoria is not a good name for an Indian.'

I laughed and shook my head and said, 'No,' but I was thinking, Victoria is my name, and I will always call myself Victoria; I don't see how I can help it.

Ranjit took my hand and brushed his lips across it. He said, 'It is not as important as marrying you, though. Do you think you will marry me, Victoria?' He was so docile and spoke as though he were asking me whether I meant to have a permanent wave soon.

I held his hand tight and said, 'I don't know, Ranjit. I wish it could all be arranged for us. Whenever I think about it I get afraid that I will make you unhappy. I get afraid that I will be unhappy myself, for a time. Then I wonder – for how long a time?'

Ranjit said, 'I will wait.'

He stood beside me, and our hands were joined, his left with my right. Even holding my hand made him nervous because Indians don't do it in public, but he had forced himself to come that far toward me. We faced west where the sun was low over the hills of the State of Lalkot. It was a quiet sun sinking in a quiet evening, a warm red sun settling into long sheets of pink and green silk.

An engine whistled long and shrill from the city behind us. I knew without looking at my watch that it was 97 Down Express whistling for the Kishanpur road crossing. A bugle blew a short call, like an order in brass, from the barracks. I knew the call was the 'Orderly Havildars' of the First Thirteenth Gurkha Rifles. I knew Ghanshyam was K. P. Roy. I knew K. P. Roy was a murderer and a train-wrecker. But he was an Indian. For me there would be no floating in a boat, on a calm tide, to a sheltered shore.

I said, 'We'd better get back.'

21

I WORE the saris from then onward. Pater had seen me in them
once or twice, but he had said nothing. He didn't show astonishment, not even the first time, so Rose Mary must have warned
him. He didn't show anger either, which probably meant he was
taking thought about what he should do.

It wasn't many days, though, before he called me to the parlour
one evening after supper. Rose Mary was in there, talking sweet
to him, obviously intending to join in the attack on me. When
Pater asked her to leave the room she grumbled but flounced out
and left the house as well. Mater was in somewhere, but she didn't
come near the parlour. She never did normally, unless Pater told
her to, and this time I thought Pater had definitely told her to
keep away.

Pater was sitting in the big armchair on the right of the grate.
He was having trouble lighting his pipe, and I sank into the chair
opposite, watching him and loving him but prepared to fight him,
while he lit a dozen matches and at last got the pipe going. Then
he said, 'I want to talk with you, Victoria.'

I said, 'Yes, Pater?'

He said, 'You know what it is about. That!' He pointed the
stem of his pipe at my sari. 'Why are you wearing those clothes
now? Aren't the clothes your mother and sister wear good enough
for you? What is the matter? Please tell me, girl.'

I took a deep slow breath. I said, 'I don't mean to hurt you,
Pater. I don't think it's any of your business, actually, but I will
tell you. We are half Indian.' Pater moved uncomfortably in his
chair. I went on, 'Well, we are, aren't we? But there's not going
to be any place for half-Indians soon. I can't make myself a whole
Indian, but I can show that I don't think of myself as whole-
English. I can show that I think India is my home.'

Pater shook his head obstinately. He said, 'Of course I believe
there is some Indian blood in our family. Very good blood, too.
There is a rumour that my grandmother, Mrs Duck, was a princess. But even if the rumour is true – and of course it is nothing
like as much as *half* Indian that we are – it is stepping down to

pretend to be an Indian. Indians are dirty and lazy, Victoria. They will run around like chickens with their heads cut off if the English Government ever leave them to their own devices. God forbid! I hear you are great friends with Kasel. Now, he is not a bad fellow at all – mind you, I like lots of Indians very much – but have you thought that Kasel wipes his bottom with his hand, with nothing but water on it? That is the hand you shake, man!'

I said, 'No, it isn't. They use their left hands.' I was short with him because I had thought of just that, more than once. What Pater chose to ignore was that Mater did the same thing when she thought she wouldn't be caught out. And I said so.

Pater banged his open palm down on the arm of his chair and cried, 'I won't have you saying such a horrible thing, Victoria! That is your own mother you are speaking of! What is the matter with you, girl? Do you hate us, all of a sudden? What would *he* think of you? He was a fine man.' Pater pointed at the Sergeant's empty, silly face.

'You've just said he married an Indian,' I answered.

Pater said, 'Yes, but he didn't take off his trousers and put on a dhoti, my God! He raised her to *his* level, he did not sink down into all the Indian ways and use water instead of Bromo, and pick his nose and eat it, and belch after his meal, and go crawling on his stomach in front of the idols in the temples, and keep filthy statues in his room and worship them.' He ran out of breath, then frowned at me as an idea came to him. He said, much more sharply, '*You* are not thinking of marrying an Indian, are you?'

I said, 'I'm twenty-eight, Pater. Surely I can marry whoever I want to. And how does a sergeant *raise* a princess to his level?'

I had got him sidetracked for the moment. He said, 'How, you ask me? By being an English gentleman, that's how. Well, my grandfather was not a real English gentleman, as a matter of fact, like Colonel Savage. He was only a sergeant, but he was a fine and upright man, and he raised my grandmother to behave decently. Oh, Victoria, for God's sake tell me you are not thinking of marrying Kasel!'

I said, 'Why shouldn't I, if he asks me and I want to?'

There it was again. Now Pater was pushing me along. Why didn't he ask, instead, whether Ranjit was thinking of marrying me? Why were all the decisions left to me? The more he pushed one way, the more I would go the other.

He said, 'You are a beautiful girl, Victoria. You can do better for yourself than that. Oh, I know some of our girls have married Indians – just one or two that I have heard of – but it has always been unhappy, a terrible mistake. You are not getting any younger, but you could marry anyone. If you don't put it off too long you could even marry one of the officers of the Gurkhas.'

'Like Lieutenant Macaulay?' I snapped.

Pater shook his head and said, 'That man would not have asked you to marry him, Victoria. He would only have taken your affection and then cast you away like an old shoe. He was not a gentleman. He was not as much of a gentleman as my grandfather, who was only a sergeant. But I don't like to speak badly of the dead. I hear he is missing. They think he has been murdered?'

I said, 'Yes.'

Pater shook his head and relit his pipe. When he next looked at me I saw that his eyes were damp, and immediately my own eyes began to water. When he spoke, his voice was low and trembly. He said, 'I am not really a fool, Victoria, like you think. I know I am only a cheechee engine driver, and my grandmother was not a princess at all; she was nobody – she may have been a loose woman, even. I know as well as you do that a high-caste Indian girl would not marry a sergeant, not in those days. But that is exactly why we have to fight so hard, that is why we must pretend and keep our self-respect, even if we shut our eyes like ostriches to do it. Because that is what we will go back to if we don't. You don't realize that if the English had not helped us and given us jobs, and if we had not held on to our self-respect, we would have been worse than outcasts. We would be lower than our grandmothers. And now you talk of going back, stepping down. You are throwing away what we have taken a very long time to build. I shall never go Home, but you could. You say there will be changes in India, and I am afraid it is true – but *you* don't have to see them.'

He pulled out a big handkerchief and dabbed his eyes. He said, 'I think I know how badly you feel sometimes about this. But don't you realize you could see yourself to marry a British officer, and then you could go Home and never see us or think of us again? You could live at Home in a big cantonment all your life and have an English butler. No one will know what you are. You can say you are partly Spanish. That is what Jimmy D'Souza's girl did. She wrote secretly once and said it was fine. In England no one cares, she said; no one even suspects, unless they have been to India. You could have all that instead of this.' He waved his arm round the pokey little parlour – at my sari, at Sergeant Duck, at the glaring road and the barren barrack-like little houses.

I muttered, 'Perhaps. But how much self-respect could I keep then, Pater? I'd be not much better than a loose woman myself if I did that. It is now, doing what I am doing, that I am beginning to be able to respect myself.'

He didn't answer. We sat for a little longer; then I got up and ran over to kiss the top of his head and put my arms round him. He caught my waist and muttered, 'Don't think I am against you, Victoria. I am only thinking of your own good, nothing else.'

I said, 'I know, Pater. I'll always trust you.'

I did not sleep well that night. In my thoughts I saw myself always in one or another of my saris. Sometimes I saw things of the past, things that had happened; sometimes I imagined things to come. Like – in the past: On Saturday morning Colonel Savage had looked me up and down and said, 'Please remember that caste marks may not be worn when in uniform.' George Howland, the awful young man, had come into my office and started back with his hand across his eyes, crying, 'What's the fancy dress in aid of, Vicky?' Major Dickson had looked at me, opened his mouth, and said, 'Good morning, Miss Jones – er – good morning.' Rifleman Birkhe had smiled at me and said nothing.

But the subadar-major had marched in to return a map, saluted, frowned, and said brusquely in his painful Hindustani, 'You have got oil mark on sari, miss-sahiba. Sari is not good clothes for running or bicycling.'

And – in the future: I was a bride, being prepared for marriage. I stood in a light and airy room with my arms outstretched while Indian girls ministered to me, I and they in flowing diaphanous saris. There was no bridegroom in that room, of course. Then I was in a big hall of parliament, and again I had my arms lifted up and stretched out, but that time I was exhorting the men in there, and the sari made me like one of those pictures of Romans in the school history books.

22

THE next morning Lanson's Chevrolet was standing outside the offices when I got there. The orderly told me the colonel-sahib wanted to see me. I went in at once, saluted, and waited.

Savage and Lanson were standing beside the big desk. Savage said, 'Mr Lanson wants to talk to you in his office at the Kutcherry. They have found Macaulay's body. I have just identified it. You have the right to have a legal adviser present with you during the D.S.P.'s questioning.'

'I haven't accused her of anything, Savage,' Lanson protested indignantly. 'What do you want to frighten her like that for?'

'I'm telling her her rights, in case you forget to,' Savage said. 'Well, Miss Jones? I can get anybody you want.'

'No, thank you, sir,' I said. 'There's no need.'

He said, 'All right. Will you send her back afterward, Lanson?'

'Of course I will,' Lanson said stiffly. Savage sat down at his desk, and I followed Lanson out into the passage.

His office in the Kutcherry was three doors from the Collector's. It was a small book-littered place with a table, three or four chairs, shelves, an almirah or two, and a typewriter. It was very hot in there. Lanson brought me a chair and began to light his pipe. He took longer over it even than Pater did. I noticed his eyes wandering over my sari and thought he did not like it. When he began to speak his tone was noticeably harder than at our last interview. He said, 'Macaulay's body was found this morning in a dungheap in the city. It had a notice hung round the neck – "Quit India", which is the current Congress slogan. His head had been battered in, his stomach ripped open, and other mutilations carried out.'

I kept my mouth tight closed. Too tight, for he was watching me sharply, and he said, 'You're surprised? Why?'

I shook my head. I said, 'I was thinking, how horrible. A dungheap, and – all those horrible things.'

Lanson looked at me for a minute, the pipe rattling as he sucked on it. He said, 'I expect you've read a good many detective stories, so you'll know that the police always have to ask a lot of questions of the last person who saw the victim alive.'

I nodded. I didn't feel a bit sick. I wanted to know why Ghanshyam had done those things to Macaulay's dead body.

Lanson said, 'I have to find out what you were doing during all the hours in which Macaulay might have been killed. I have to have proof of everything you say.'

'When was he killed?' I asked automatically. About eight o'clock, it had been, but I would be supposed to ask.

'We know when he was killed, Miss Jones,' Lanson said shortly. 'To the hour, and nearly to the minute.'

I didn't know what to do with my eyes. If I looked out of the window at the pleaders and their clients in front of the court opposite, I'd be avoiding Lanson's eyes. If I stared at him, I'd be over-anxious. But he couldn't know the exact time, Ghanshyam had said, because of the dungheap. But suppose Macaulay's watch had been broken in the struggle? They might be bluffing, though. Ghanshyam was quite as clever as they were.

Lanson said, 'Well? Can you give me these proofs?'

I said, 'I can't prove I was in bed, Mr Lanson.'

He said, 'No, but tell me everything you can.'

I said, 'You've got it all already. I've told you.'

He said, 'I want to check it again.'

I told my story again. If they did know the exact time of Macaulay's death, it would sound thin. Why had Ghanshyam put the 'Quit India' sign on his body? That threw suspicion on Congress.

I interrupted myself to say, 'But why do you think I did it, Mr Lanson? It must have been some Congress extremist, or someone who wanted to put the blame on Congress.'

He said, 'Perhaps, Miss Jones. You know the Congress crowd here pretty well by now, though, don't you? And I haven't said you did it. But I have my duty, you know, just as much as Colonel Savage has his. Now, who saw you in the reading-room at the Institute?'

The interrogation went on.

At the end Lanson relaxed a little. He said, 'Thank you, Miss Jones. Have you ever heard anyone threaten – or promise, or talk – about derailing a troop train?'

I held my hands close in my lap and shook my head. I answered, 'No,' but my voice was very small.

'Are you sure?' he said.

'Yes,' I said.

He said, 'I asked because about twenty people *have* heard such talk. From Mr Surabhai. He's made no secret of his belief that an Indian patriot would be justified in derailing a troop train, regardless of the fact that the R.I.N. mutiny is over. It's funny you haven't heard him, because nearly everybody else who knows him has.'

'Well, I haven't,' I snapped, getting angry.

He said, 'Very good. Have you seen this man recently?' He pushed the photograph of K. P. Roy into my hands.

I gave it back at once and flared up because anger and fear were pressing together in me. I said, 'No, I haven't, and the Collector's asked me all this already, and you know he has. Why do you keep on at me? Just because I wear a sari now, I haven't become a murderess, a train-wrecker!'

Lanson said calmly, 'I'm asking you because we think this man' – he tapped the photograph – 'has been seen in the district around the Sirdarni-sahiba's house. You've been there quite a lot, naturally, since you are engaged to Ranjit Singh.'

'I'm not engaged to him,' I gasped. 'Who told you that?'

He said, 'No one told me directly. But the Sirdarni is telling other people. About this man, though – I heard that someone rather like him was talking to you in the tunnel where Station Road crosses under the railway lines, the day the two processions clashed ...' He gave details.

I thought of two things at once. How dare the Sirdarni announce my engagement before I had consented, before Ranjit had even asked me properly? Someone must have passed by while Ghanshyam was putting my bicycle chain back on. Or someone might just have been able to see into the tunnel from the lower windows of one of the houses beyond.

I said, 'I remember that a man helped me to put my bicycle

chain on when it fell off. I don't remember him at all. I gave him a few annas.'

Lanson stood up, his chair squeaking back on the stone floor. His pipe was rattling again. He said, 'Then that will be all for now, Miss Jones.'

I had been thinking. I said, 'If this man hangs about near the Sirdarni-sahiba's house, why don't you search it or surround it or something?'

The telephone rang. Lanson spoke into it stolidly and slowly in Hindustani. When he put it down he said, 'That was a message from the tehsildar in Pathoda. A fire started in the jungle just west of a little village called Maslan at about six o'clock this morning. There was a pretty strong west wind up there then, he says. The fire has completely destroyed Maslan. There were only about twelve houses, but they've all gone.'

I said, 'Oh,' wondering what was coming next.

Lanson nodded and said, 'It's interesting, and I'll tell you why. We've been able to get a little information bearing, perhaps, on accident to the troop train. Nothing much – only that, the evening before, a villager crossing the line on his way back from an errand in Pathoda saw three men moving through the jungle near the place where the train was later derailed. They weren't local people, he said. They didn't see him. When we began our inquiries up there, this villager came forward at once and told us what he had seen – told us publicly.'

'Oh,' I said again.

Lanson went on. 'He was from Maslan. He gave us help. Now his home is burned and his cattle dead. He's penniless. So is everybody else in Maslan. It is very unlikely that the fire was accidental. You were asking why we don't search or watch the Kasel house for K. P. Roy. The answer, Miss Jones, is that we have, several times, and we are. But I think the bird has flown. Not far, but he's not in the house, if he ever was – unless he can turn himself into a rat and hide under the floor. That's what he is, Miss Jones, as a matter of fact – a murdering rat, a red rat.'

Hearing this was far more terrible than killing Macaulay. Ranjit and his mother were sheltering K. P. Roy, and I was helping them. But for the moment I'd have to control my doubt and fear.

Lanson walked round the table and held out his hand. He said,

198

'Good-bye for the moment. I think I can tell you that we have a pretty good idea about Macaulay's murder. We won't be able to clear it up – dispose of it tidily, you know – until we find this fellow K. P. Roy and stop the derailments and everything else that has been going on in the district, such as this fire at Maslan.' He walked beside me to the door. Then he said, and looked straight at me, 'The murder's bad, of course, if it was a real murder and not, say, self-defence – but it's not important compared with Roy. If the murderer would get all the people who know something about Roy and the stolen explosives and the derailments to talk – we'd be very pleased with him. My driver will take you back, and I think you'd better not leave Bhowani without my permission until all this has been cleared up.'

23

I ARRIVED at the Sirdarni's house that evening determined to settle two things – K. P. Roy and my engagement. The Sirdarni and Ranjit were in the big room. I waited for a few minutes of general conversation to pass by, meaning then to say what I wanted to say. But when I was ready the Sirdarni said to Ranjit, 'Our guests will be here in half an hour, and I have forgotten to make pakhoras. Please go and buy some. Don't hurry. I have things to talk over with Miss Jones.'

When Ranjit had left the room the Sirdarni said, 'You looked as if you wanted to say something to me, my child. What is it?'

We were talking in Hindustani. I said, 'Beji, I heard from Mr Lanson this morning that you have been telling people that Ranjit and I are betrothed.'

The Sirdarni nodded and said firmly, 'I have. You are the girl for him.'

'But – but –' I said, suddenly feeling helpless, 'I don't know that he's the man for me.'

'Any man will do for you,' she said. 'Now don't be angry. I mean that you need a man – why, you are quite old – but you are the sort of woman who will remain herself whatever the man is like. Ranjit needs such a woman. You are stronger than he is, and you will be able to make him into whatever you wish.'

'I don't wish to make him into anything,' I said. I tried to explain to her that I had always thought the man I married would make me into something.

'That is a Western idea,' the Sirdarni said impatiently. 'In India we women make our men, whether we act from behind the screen or whether we come out into the open, as I have. You have become an Indian – by what you did in the yards that night, by the sari you are wearing – yet you have no Indian father and mother with whom I can make arrangements. So I am making them myself. It is all settled.'

I said, 'I don't know whether I –'

She interrupted me, poking her hard finger into my knee. 'Didn't you tell Ranjit the other day that you wanted the decision taken out of your hands? I've done it.'

I thought, Ranjit must tell her everything. He must have told her all that we did and said there by the river. Now the Sirdarni had made the decision for me, as she had said she would, and it still didn't feel right. But I ought not to think or feel. I ought just to accept.

The Sirdarni said, 'The marriage will take place one month from now.'

'In what religion?' I heard myself asking.

'I am an atheist,' she said. 'Religion is the opiate of the people. Ranjit talks lately of returning to Sikhism. I think he is a fool, but I will not force him one way or the other. It will not matter soon. Someone as clever and as well educated as you cannot believe all that nonsense, and *you* are all that will matter. I want him to rely on you, not on the stupid gurus and their pious hocus-pocus out of the Granth Sahib. You have got a hundred years of wrongs to avenge. You can put some fire into Ranjit. Don't think all will be well when the British go. It won't. I'll show you things, tell you things I've seen, that prove you cannot trust any of them – Gandhi, Jinnah, Nehru, Patel, Rajagopalachari – none of them. But we will have plenty of time to talk after the marriage, when Ranjit is out at work.'

It took me a long time to realize what she had said. Then I said, 'You don't want us to live here, Beji?'

She smiled grimly and said, 'Oh, yes, I do. Certainly. It is the Indian custom. You will get used to it.'

I said, 'But I think I must have a home of my own.'

She said, 'Don't talk about it now, my child. Remember that Ranjit is my only son.' She dropped her strong hand from my elbow, which she had been holding.

I wanted to press the point. Many Anglo-Indians lived with their mothers-in-law, but I didn't want to. Then I remembered I had something else even more important to say.

I said, speaking carefully, 'Beji, the British keep asking me now whether I know K. P. Roy. They showed me a picture of him. It was very like Ghanshyam, your guest who was there.'

She said, 'The man who hid the traces of the murder you committed? What did you tell them?' She was looking at me calmly, as though she had heard all about this before. She probably had. Ranjit would have told her.

I said, 'I said I hadn't seen him. But Beji, is Ghanshyam really K. P. Roy? I must know.'

She said, 'Why?'

I said, 'It's worrying me. Lanson and Govindaswami say he's a Communist agitator and a murderer. They say he wrecked the troop train the other day, and stole the explosives, and burned down Maslan, and caused the riot of the processions. If he's as bad as that, ought we to hide him? Oughtn't we to tell the police everything we know or suspect?'

'Ghanshyam is K. P. Roy's brother,' the Sirdarni said calmly, 'and he's not doing anything except help hurry the British out of the country, as the necessary first step to further progress. We have been searched. Ghanshyam was not in, and now he has left. About those things that K. P. Roy is supposed to have done – you must use your brain, child. Why should that black baboon Govindaswami tell you the truth? Why should Lanson? They're just trying to drive a wedge between us – between the Moslems and the Hindus, between different wings of the freedom movement. Tell them nothing!'

I heard voices on the stairs, and a moment later two middle-aged Indian couples entered the room. There were many questions I still wanted to ask, but for the moment my time had run out. Soon everyone was talking Hindi, and Ranjit had returned

201

with the pakhoras, and a sweet shy girl was congratulating me on my betrothal and in the same breath asking me to describe what European girls wore as underclothes. For the moment I had to give in. The Sirdarni had won – for the moment. But I knew I could never allow matters to rest as they were. Ghanshyam *might* be K. P. Roy's brother; I still thought he was Roy himself. Ranjit was a clean, fine man, but he was standing neck deep in foul water. I felt the stench of it in my nostrils as I tried to get closer to him. I was becoming obsessed, nervous, and torn by knowledge or guilt. I began to pray for something to happen that would force me to act.

24

ON the following Sunday, which was 2 June, I went to the Sirdarni's house again. Ranjit came down to the Old Lines for me on his bicycle at about ten o'clock in the morning. I wondered at first why he had not telephoned, as he usually did to avoid the unpleasantness at Number 4 Collett Road. When he came in person they never asked him into the house but left him standing outside. I'd often told him to come in, but he wouldn't.

On the way up the Pike I asked, 'What's on? Surely your mother's not having a political meeting at half past ten today?'

'She just wanted to see you,' Ranjit said. 'So did I.'

The Sirdarni's pressure on me was increasing. She was trying to make me realize my place as an Indian daughter-in-law, and I began to feel obstinate. Perhaps this would be a good time to take up where I had had to leave off the other evening.

The Sirdarni was sitting, European style, in a wobbly chair and staring out of the window. She greeted me and then did not move or say anything for fifteen minutes. At last she looked up at us where we were standing a little to one side and talking quietly. Without apology she interrupted us, 'Victoria, what is the latest about the mutinies? Is there really no spark left in either Karachi or Bombay?'

Her strong hands were folded in her lap, the white sari lay across her shoulder. She looked grim and untidy that morning, but very powerful, as usual. I told her, The mutinies were over; the government were picking up the pieces. They were holding courts of inquiry and taking summaries of evidence, forming judicial commissions and rounding up deserters. The warships lay peacefully at anchor in their ports. About fifteen ringleaders were under arrest; the other sailors were doing duty.

The Sirdarni said angrily, 'There is a great opportunity wasted! The German revolution of nineteen eighteen began in their navy. The sailors played a big part in the glorious Russian revolution. And now we've wasted ours, let the fire go out, because of the treachery of Indian lickspittles. Look at that street!' She jerked her head in an extraordinarily male gesture. 'Look at it. The fools walk up and down as though they hadn't just thrown away their best chance. The policeman's on his platform at the corner. He ought to be ten feet above it, hanging from Mir Khan's second-floor balcony.'

Ranjit said, 'Mother, can we please not talk about politics this morning? I want to –'

She said, 'Not talk politics, son? How often have I to tell you that politics isn't something you talk? It's not even something you do. It's something you live. That's the trouble with the Nehrus and Gandhis you admire so much. If they'd had one ounce of real fire in their livers, this street would be running in blood, and Govindaswami would have died where he was born – on a dung-heap.'

Ranjit said, 'You really ought not to speak of the Mahatma like that, Mother. You will –'

She said, 'The Mahatma! He's a tool of the millowners, a cunning, ambitious little lawyer. He's going to sell the country to the millionaires when the British go – *if* they go – and then you had better look out for real trouble. The people must rise then, and blood must flow in rivers.'

I steadied myself and said, 'I think you are talking nonsense, Beji.' I waited quietly, looking the Sirdarni in the eye.

She blinked as though I had hit her. I felt Ranjit staring at me in fearful astonishment.

At last the Sirdarni said, 'Nonsense? That is a very rude thing to say to your mother.'

'I do not mean to be rude,' I said obstinately. 'But I had to tell you that I don't agree with you, in case you thought I did. Can't we talk about something else?'

'Such as what?' the Sirdarni said, again folding her hands in her lap. I did not think she was really angry, just astonished and perhaps a little pleased. She had no use for weaklings, and now perhaps she was thinking I would be even more useful than she had thought. She obviously never doubted that she would master me in the end.

I said, 'Let's talk about something nice and unimportant, like – well, have you seen the new picture at the cantonment cinema, *The Road* to somewhere or other with Bing Crosby, Bob Hope, and Dorothy Lamour?'

It was a silly thing to say, perhaps, but it was the first that came into my head. When I had said it I thought, That does sound as if I'm fed up with Indian politics; it sounds insulting. Perhaps I meant to be insulting.

'I have not seen the picture you mention,' the Sirdarni said. 'I never go to the cantonment cinema, as you know, and even here in the city I never see any film made in England or America. It is wrong to put money into the pockets of the capitalists. They use it to make guns and hire mercenaries like Govindaswami and your Colonel Savage and his Gurkhas to suppress freedom everywhere.'

'Have you ever been to Paris?' I said. 'I'd love to go.'

She said, 'I have not. I have never left India. The French are just as bad as the British, if not worse. They –'

It was like a rather bad-tempered game – I trying to change the subject, she trying to show that politics could not be avoided.

I said, 'Wouldn't you like to go to Paris, Ranjit? I've heard it's so gay and free there, and there are beautiful flowers everywhere in the spring. Wouldn't it be wonderful if someone gave us a lakh of rupees as a wedding present so that we could fly to Paris for a week?'

'It would be wonderful,' Ranjit said, smiling nervously. 'But I do not think anyone will give us a lakh of rupees.'

The Sirdarni said, 'If they did, you should use it to increase political awareness among –' and at the same time I said, 'I would love to see the clothes they really wear in Paris. I've often wondered if the women are as smart as they're supposed to be.'

The Sirdarni said, 'Fashions in saris do not change. The money those people spend on one dress – what they call a cheap dress – would feed a whole Indian family for ten years – *ten years*!'

I stood up, feeling hot behind the eyes. I would burst into tears or lose my temper or do both at once if I did not go away. I said, 'I think I must go home now, Beji.'

She got up quickly and came over to me. She put her arm round my shoulder and said, 'Don't go. Don't be angry, Victoria. It is my fault. I am a headstrong, rude old woman. You can teach me something while I teach you something. I have arranged the marriage for July the first.'

Ranjit said, 'But Mother, I told you I had to see the guru.'

She said, 'I've seen the old fool. I've told him everything he wanted to know. He pretended he wasn't keen on marrying you when he knew that neither of you were practising Sikhs, but he agreed in the end. I stayed in there arguing until he did. Now come to your room, Victoria, and tell me what I should do to it to have it all ready for you.' She began to guide me across the room.

I felt weak from the continuous effort of forcing myself to contradict and fight her. In her mind, probably, she had made a great concession by allowing me to have the room the way I wanted it. I didn't really feel strong enough to keep on with this struggle now, but I had to.

I stopped moving and said, 'Beji, I can't live here. It isn't that I don't want to live with you, but I do want a house of my own, and I must have one.'

She still held her arm round my shoulder. She said slowly, 'You refuse to live here with me? People will say Ranjit has thrown me out, you know that?'

I wished Ranjit would say something; but perhaps that was too much to ask. He would feel quite as horrified as his mother did – perhaps more so, because he was more conventional. I didn't think the Sirdarni really cared what people might say. She was using that as a weapon against me. She wanted to be with Ranjit always and keep her hands on him, who could always be moulded and on me, who would be the easiest instrument for her to mould with.

I said, 'I'm sorry, but I know I must have my own home.'

The Sirdarni said, 'You and Ranjit go out and have a nice walk. Talk about it. You will eat here?'

I agreed thankfully. I would have agreed to anything that got me out of there quickly.

Ranjit went with me, and we bicycled off through the city. I was thinking of the Sirdarni and what on earth I was to do, so I did not notice until we were nearly out of the city that everything had been very quiet. The people walked up and down, as the Sirdarni had pointed out, but there were few of them, and those few walked as though they had some definite job. They did not stroll. I knew the 'feel' of Bhowani and looked round for other signs. Soon I saw a shopkeeper barring his store against the street. 'What's happening this time?' I asked Ranjit.

He hadn't noticed anything, and I had to explain what I meant. He said, 'I don't know. I think you may be imagining it, Victoria. The shopkeeper is probably going away for a few days. Surabhai hasn't told me about any plans.'

'What about the Moslem League?' I asked.

He said, 'They're not big enough to cause any trouble. Where are we going?'

I had been leading the way toward the same place on the river bank where we had gone before. I said, 'To the river. I want to talk again, Ranjit. Only this time we must get things settled.'

We went to the same place, but now the sun was high and the ground yellow, dry, and glaring hot. We wheeled our bicycles a little back over the grass and sat under one of the big dark trees. From there we could see the river on one side and the parade ground of Kabul Lines on the other.

I put my hand on Ranjit's and said, 'Ranjit, do you love me?'

He said slowly, 'I worship you, I think, Victoria.'

I squeezed his hand hard, demanding, 'Yes, but do you *love* me?'

However close I got to Ranjit there was always a thing like a very delicate gauze screen or curtain hanging down between us. I had asked him if he loved me. I had never asked any man that question before, because it hadn't been necessary. Men had breathed hard on me and tried to get close to press against me. They wanted only one thing, but at that moment they wanted it from me, and I had it. The point was, I knew them, I saw them,

206

I felt them. There was no gauze screen. There were other men who liked the look of me but didn't want me – perhaps they had other girls, girls of their own. And I always knew that, because there was no gauze screen. There were men like Ted Dunphy, who loved me but had made up their minds they were not good enough or clever enough for me, or couldn't offer me enough. I wouldn't have cared if I had loved them. But there was no gauze screen. Then there were men who just weren't interested, and to them I was a thing in a skirt, sometimes a nuisance, sometimes a bore, sometimes quite pleasant, sometimes just a thing. But I knew, because there was no gauze screen.

All those men had been white, or thought they were white, or said they were white. Savage had been all those men to me – even the lover, even like Macaulay. The meaning of a look I'd caught in his eye, of a brutal word, of a roughness that might have been a tiger's caress, burst on me in a sudden flash. Usually he was the last sort and treated me like a mere thing.

Patrick didn't fit anywhere. He had been none of those men. There was only one sort of man left that he could be, the one sort I didn't know about – the husband. It was a frightening idea, because it was what Patrick himself thought – logical and inevitable.

But – Ranjit? What was the sign in an Indian, what was the language? It might be nothing to do with Indians in general; it might just be Ranjit, which made it even more difficult.

I said, 'Kiss me, Ranjit.'

I closed my eyes and dropped my head against his shoulder. I suppose I turned my face up to him, but I don't remember. Ranjit said agitatedly, 'Oh, dear Victoria, I can't! We don't do it like that. We think it is shameful, insulting. Not here. Look!'

I opened my eyes and saw a man walking along a footpath a hundred yards away. I said, 'I don't care about him. *We* think it's insulting for a man not to kiss a girl who asks him to, especially if he's engaged to her.'

Ranjit dabbed his face down, and his dry lips touched my cheek.

I said, 'On my lips.' It was like the game with his mother, only much more important.

He said, 'I *can't*. It is – indecent. It is not done until we are married, Victoria. When we are married and alone in our room.'

I sat up slowly. I still didn't know anything, and still the gauze screen hung there between us. It was shaking now, because we were wrought up, but still it hid more than it showed. Ranjit said, 'I do love you.'

'How do I know what you mean?' I asked.

He said, 'Love is more than this kissing. That is something animal —'

I said tiredly, 'I know, Ranjit. I don't want a lecture.'

So at last I had to think about sex. I knew all about respect and affection and devotion. I *didn't* know whether I would ever get that far with Ranjit. I wasn't Rose Mary, to plot and plan and go to bed with a man and be unchanged, untouched through it all. I didn't dare think about, to treat, the idea lightly, because the God's truth is that when it happened I was flooded and over-whelmed. I loved it and myself and the man, and was filled with hot thoughts and love and respect and affection all mixed up to-gether, so that I couldn't separate them. I suppose Johnny Tallent told Macaulay what I was like, without understanding at all, and that is partly why Macaulay couldn't control himself. In that way I had led Macaulay on. And in that way I had murdered him. There never had been a man who understood what I was trying to give him. They called me 'a piece of hot stuff', and still I had to go on wrapping my heart and soul and body round them, and dying to make them happy, until it was over.

Ranjit had my respect and affection and devotion. If only he would start on the other thing, to show at least that he cared about it, that he knew it was important, I'd have everything, and so would he.

I said, 'My dear, you've got to get away from your mother.'

I said that to force him out into a place where I could see him clearly. I thought he would get angry and argue with me, and try to persuade me what a wonderful woman she would be to live with. But he said, after a very short pause, 'Yes. I must.'

I looked at him to see if he was beginning to fight at last. His tone told me nothing. But he was just melancholy. He went on, 'I shall go to the guru tomorrow and ask him to receive me back into my religion. Will you come with me and be a Sikh?'

I wanted him to kiss me, but God was important too. I didn't know God at all. No one had ever suggested that He was an

Anglo-Indian. He must have been a Jew actually, though the padre didn't often say so out loud. It was rather like no one except Sir Meredith Sullivan actually getting up in public and saying, 'I am an Anglo-Indian.' They'd made him a Sir for that. I didn't really believe one word of what the padres said about God. The Virgin Mary made me wonder, every time I thought of her: Who was it, *really*? If I didn't believe the padre, why shouldn't I not believe the guru the same way, and all the time believe what I really believed?

I said, 'I'll become a Sikh – if you'll promise to kiss me the day before, and promise to leave your mother's house the day after.'

'Where shall I go?' he asked.

I said, 'Find a house where we can live. We're being married on July the first, aren't we?' He hadn't answered about the kiss, so I added, 'If you kiss me.'

I wondered if I meant 'kiss'. It was awful to force myself on to him like this. I'd never done it before. I told myself that I had to find out whether he loved me, not just admired me. That was why I was forcing myself on him. I was being honest, that's all.

It was true, but also I had listened to too much English gossip, read too many romantic stories of love in the East. Would he sit opposite me, his knees crossed, and draw me to him? Would he shine in jewels taken from some family vault, and would his body be pale golden and glistening with sweet-smelling ointments? It was a tale of the Arabian nights that I saw in my mind, of a man strong and beautiful and determined to have me. Then all would be well, and there would be no more curtains – if he was like that.

But – I found myself frowning fondly on him. As so often, I wanted to pat his head and tell him to cheer up. A couple of sentences I remembered from my first school reader fitted the feeling perfectly: DO NOT SOB, BOB. BE A MAN, BOB.

I am not sure how the rest of the morning and the early part of the afternoon passed. I only remember that it was peaceful inside the Sirdarni's house, and very still outside, and I couldn't find the quarrelsome courage to go on any more just then about K. P. Roy. People never move about much on a hot-weather afternoon, but this was something different – eventually the stillness became an uneasiness that crept inside the quiet room where I was playing dominoes with Ranjit. The Sirdarni had been out when we got back from the river, and she did not come in until shortly before four. We ate at five, and at six I went home. I wanted to go alone, but the Sirdarni said that Ranjit would – must – go with me.

We saw no one on the way except a fat woman running, waddling like a duck, down a side alley. 'You were right,' Ranjit said. 'Something is brewing.'

I said, 'And your mother knows about it. That's why she made you come with me.'

Then on the Pike we met an old farmer with his wife and his two grown sons, all on a bullock cart, all heading toward the city. The farmer stopped us and asked whether what he had heard was true.

'What have you heard?' Ranjit asked.

He cried, 'What! *You* haven't heard? And you live in the city?'

'I've heard nothing,' Ranjit said.

The old man said, 'There is no rioting, then? The soldiers are not out? I will be able to sell my vegetables to Kurrum Chand? The girl was not killed?'

'There's no rioting,' Ranjit said, and then the old farmer told us what he had heard. The Moslems had risen and raped and murdered a little Hindu girl who had innocently thrown a cowpat at the mullah. He had all the details except exactly when it had happened – some time this morning was all he knew. 'I don't know why we tolerate those Moslems,' he said, wagging his beard. 'They are few, they live here on our sufferance, and now look what they've done! I hear they fell on a procession of our Hindus the other day and slaughtered twenty. And then the Gurkhas came and killed twenty of them in revenge. Because the Gurkhas are Hindus. That was good. Did you see that?'

'Nothing like that happened,' Ranjit said wearily. 'I don't know about a girl being killed today, but there's no rioting. You can go into the city.'

The old man's old wife turned to examine me more closely in the sunless evening light as the bullocks leaned into the yoke. We got on to our bicycles, and Ranjit muttered, 'Rumour, hate, fear. When will it end?'

'When we've stopped trying to shield Ghanshyam, who is not K. P. Roy's brother, but K. P. Roy himself,' I said suddenly.

But Ranjit answered, 'I can't send my mother to jail,' and my obsession of guilt, of going in a wrong direction, swelled a little larger in the bottom of my throat.

25

RANJIT left me at the edge of the Old Lines, and I went on alone to the house. Mater said supper was ready. I told her I'd eaten already. She did not complain that she had not been told; she was interested only in what I had eaten at that Indian-style meal. She asked me a score of questions about it and afterward sighed and shuffled off to wash.

Almost at once I heard Patrick's motor bike and went quickly to my room. I didn't want to see him then. As soon as the front door opened Rose Mary shouted, 'Mater! Where are the bandages?' I got up quickly, went into the hall, and asked what was the matter. Mater came out of her room in bedroom slippers and a dirty slip, her face and hands dripping water.

Patrick stood under the light in the hall, glaring at me, his chest rising and falling. A thin trickle of blood flowed down his forehead, down the left side of his nose, and into his mouth. His left eye was full of blood. There was a small jagged place on his forehead, high up near his hair. I felt a little sick and suddenly angry with everybody. I ran through Mater's room and found the iodine and the bandages where they were always kept, on a high wooden shelf in the bathroom. Rose Mary knew that perfectly well, but she could do nothing but stand there, shaking and yelling, while Patrick's hurt needed seeing to.

I hurried back into the hall and said, 'Come into the parlour and sit down under the light, Patrick.'

Patrick put out his hand and pushed me away. He said, 'I don't want your hands on me. Rose Mary, you do it.'

Rose Mary took the bandages from me. I returned to my room. Now they had forgotten a basin of water and a sponge to wash the wound. I filled my own basin, took it through to the parlour, and held it while Rose Mary washed Patrick's face.

'What's happened?' I asked again.

'Your friends in the city threw a stone at me, that's all,' Patrick said. 'Hit me on the forehead. It might have gone in my eye, but a bloody lot you would have cared.'

'Go away,' Rose Mary cried shrilly. 'Can't you see Patrick doesn't want to talk to you? You have no shame, or you would be so ashamed of yourself you would cut your throat.'

But Patrick didn't really want me to go. A rough bandage was round his head by then, and the blood no more than a dirty stain across his face. He wanted me to stay while he worked off against me his feeling of helplessness. I wanted to stay because he needed looking after and because I knew that nothing had changed, whatever he was doing with Rose Mary, or however desperate it made him to see me wearing a sari and going out with Ranjit.

He shouted, 'Yes, you should cut your throat! They are meeting there in the city, your Wog friends, and throwing stones. You would have thrown one yourself if you had been there, I bet. They are getting ready to catch another of us and cut him open and castrate him. Do you know they did that to poor Mr Macaulay? What had he done to them, the dirty cowards? They are filthy, dirty savages, all of them – nothing else but savages!'

The basin shook in my hands. I wanted to tell him it was not *the* Indians who had mutilated Macaulay, it was only *one* Indian, a bad man called Roy. But Roy had arranged everything too well, and now another set of people in Bhowani were hot inside and clamouring for revenge. And Macaulay, whom everyone had disliked – especially Patrick – had become a martyr just because he wasn't an Indian.

Patrick said, 'And I bet Kasel, the lazy rotter – I bet he was there!'

I carried the basin out. The telephone rang in the hall, and I answered it. Colonel Savage was on the other end. He said, 'Is Taylor there? I want to speak to him. When I've finished with him, I want to speak to you.'

I stood beside the telephone while Patrick spoke. When he put it down he turned to me with triumph glowing in his face. He looked like a victorious soldier in a war painting. He said, 'At

212

last! The A.F.I. is called out! Now we will show your Wog friends what's what.'

Then I took the telephone and listened and watched Patrick hurry out. He was a lieutenant in the Auxiliary Force, India, and the senior officer of the force in Bhowani. Now he'd go running around knocking on doors and routing out all the Anglo-Indian guards and drivers and telegraph operators and clerks who formed the A.F.I., and shouting to them to meet as soon as they could outside the rifle kote at the station.

Savage was saying, 'Mrs Dickson is arriving on Two-Ninety Up Passenger from Delhi. It's supposed to get in at nineteen forty. She's coming earlier than we expected, and I've sent Henry Dickson down to Shahpur with about half the battalion on a scare. I want you to meet her and take her to her bungalow.'

I said, 'Very good, sir.'

He said, 'I'm sending a six-by-six down for you now, with a guard of four men, as the city looks like blowing up. I may be there myself, but don't count on it. Has Taylor gone to get his circus fallen in?'

I said, 'Yes, sir.'

He said, 'All right. The truck's on its way.'

I hung up. I thought of changing into a uniform sari but decided not to. Savage hadn't told me anything about the reason for the A.F.I. being called out, except that mention of the city blowing up. He hadn't told me anything about the scare that had made him send Dickson and all those men to Shahpur. Shahpur was at the southern limit of the district, fifty-four miles away.

The truck did not arrive for fifteen minutes. I waited outside for it, in the white sari with the blue border, which I had worn all day. It was dark then, and I saw men hurrying out of houses and along the lamplit roads toward the railway, or bicycling quickly in the direction of the Pike.

I knew those men in all their changes. I knew them as men in white shirts and khaki shorts who played an occasional game of tennis and drank beer in the bar, and trod on my toes at the dances. I knew them as railwaymen, when they were not so much people as symbolical figures, in white drill coats and trousers, a green flag and a red flag furled together in one hand, or in their driving clothes, or in the ordinary suits they wore to the offices.

And I knew them as they were now – all in khaki, with web belts, big boots, big topis, rifles – as men who, being white or claiming a drop of white blood, were members of the Delhi Deccan Railway Regiment, Auxiliary Force, India. The A.F.I. weren't often called out, because they all had their vital duties on the railway. When they were, it was always in this kind of situation. They were a second line of 'Europeans' who could in emergency support the regulars of the British infantry when the Indians rioted among themselves or against the British.

I saw the six-by-six coming and noticed that two others followed it. Those two turned off into the Institute compound. I wondered if the A.F.I. were going to use the old armoured car. It had been made in the Loco Sheds at least twenty years before. The floodlights were on over the tennis courts – sometimes we used to stretch a canvas floor over them and dance there in the hot weather – and as I passed by in the front seat of the six-by-six I saw the garage doors open and a group of fellows, working under Patrick's violent gesticulation, pushing out the armoured car.

When I reached the station I went to the Stationmaster's office to ask whether Molly Dickson's train would be on time. He told me it would be late, perhaps an hour late. It should be at Sona Peth now, but in fact it had just left Khusode. Khusode, Aslakheri, Malra, Dabgaon, Sithri, Sona Peth, Bargaon, Bhowani Junction – forty-eight miles, four furlongs. I went up to the Traffic Office to see what was happening in the city.

A junior clerk on duty there told me that Ranjit was expected to come in later. I went to the window and leaned out. There were the usual signs of trouble – no beggars, no tongas, no Sikh Buick – but there was no trouble. The streets were totally empty, and I heard no sound from the city, no band, no drum, no shout. The street lamps marched away in irregular line up the Street of Suttees. Someone was on the flat roof up there opposite the Blue Lane corner.

I heard the throb of a powerful motor engine. A backfire made me jump, and then the A.F.I. armoured car turned into the station yard. The two six-by-sixes followed it, stopped, and fifteen Gurkhas tumbled out. They stretched and began to light cigarettes. The armoured car stopped. It was fully battened down, its turret a smooth grey dome of steel and its machine-gun pointing up the Street of Suttees.

Savage arrived in his jeep and drew up alongside the armoured car. He shouted, 'Open up,' but the crew inside probably couldn't hear him. Nothing happened.

Savage grabbed Birkhe's kukri and gave the car a tremendous bang with the back of it. The turret top opened slowly, and Patrick's head came out.

'Why have you locked yourselves in there like a family of sardines, Mr Taylor?' Savage said in a distinct voice that carried up to my window.

Patrick saluted. A yard lamp showed every detail of his uniform from the waist up. The two brass stars winked on each shoulder, and his enormous pre-war-pattern topi was badly dented. He shouted down, 'It is the order, sir, to close down the car when we are in action.'

Savage said, 'Oh. Thank you for telling me.'

Patrick said, 'It is nothing, Colonel. I say, what –?'

Savage went on. 'But you're not in action, Mr Taylor. You are standing by. Now get everyone out of that thing, and draw your revolvers from the kote. Who did you give the key to? Good. After that, come back here – but just sit around. Relax. Have you been wounded already?' Patrick's topi was perched on top of the big white bandage.

Patrick said, 'I was hit by a stone in the city not long ago. The bloody Congress wallahs did it. But about leaving the armoured car, Colonel. We must be prepared at all times. I think we ought to stay here in it. It is my responsibility, you know.'

Savage said, 'No, it's not. I have given you an order, so the responsibility is now mine. What do you think the Gurkhas are here for except to give you warning and local protection? And for Christ's sake store those dung-basket hats in the station somewhere. You're unlikely to get sunstroke at this time of night, and with them in the car there's no room for you.'

'But Colonel –' Patrick began.

Savage said, 'Mr Taylor, what I gave you just now was an order, not a basis for negotiation.'

He turned his back and came into the station. He had been amazingly polite, for him. I suppose he recognized that Patrick

215

was doing his very best, as always. I watched while Patrick climbed out of the turret and sulkily ordered the other two men, Pelton and Ted Dunphy, to follow him.

Then Savage came into the room behind me. I turned to face him, and he said, 'If you started wearing those winding sheets in order to shake off Mr Taylor, you're a hell of a lot cleverer than you have a right to be, with your other armament.' He came to the window and stood moodily beside me for a minute, then pulled out a cheroot and moved away to the other window near Patrick's desk.

The station yard was like an empty black pool, the light shining here and there on it and dark shadows in the corners. The shape still crouched on the flat rooftop over there, waiting. People were waiting in all the houses, but nothing happened.

Savage suddenly told me a Hindu girl had been killed – no one knew how or when. So it was true after all. They'd found her body in a dry well in the city, with Arabic letters written in ink on her forehead that said: 'There is one God.'

I still wanted to ask him exactly why the A.F.I. had been called out, and why he had sent half his battalion to Shahpur, but I was sure he would snub me if I did, so I held my tongue. The last time I had been alone in there with an officer of the Gurkhas it was Macaulay, and he'd been leaning over me in this same window.

Two young men, Indians, came walking together down the middle of Suttees toward the station. They entered the area of light and walked less hastily and began to talk to each other as they came on. They were ordinary young men in their early twenties, clerks perhaps, come here to catch the train. They must have hurried nervously through the deserted city and now smiled and spoke to each other rather hilariously because they had reached safety.

Then they saw the armoured car and decided they'd like to go and have a look at it. They must have been over-excited with the sudden relief.

Patrick stepped forward into my view, his hand on the pistol in his webbing holster. The young men got nearer. Patrick shouted roughly in Hindustani, 'Keep off!'

The young men stayed where they were, near the right front wheel of the armoured car. One said insolently, 'Who are you to order me about? This is public taxpayers' property. We paid for it.'

He was wrong there, as a matter of fact. The railway had made it and given it to the A.F.I. without charge.

Patrick drew his revolver and shouted, 'You keep off, or I will shoot you!' The bandage shone white round his head, and he stood in a heroic posture, his legs braced and his revolver arm steady.

I shouted, 'Patrick, don't be a fool!'

Savage leaned out of his window to shout too, and the Collector's little Austin turned into the yard. Govindaswami had the habit of racing his engine before switching off. He drew up the other side of the armoured car and did not see Patrick behind it. Savage shouted, 'Taylor! Put that pistol away!' but the Austin engine was racing, and one of the young men put his hand on the heavy steel mudguard. Patrick fired.

The Indians jumped and began to run away across the yard, yelling. Patrick took aim at them, to fire again. Savage shouted, 'Jesus Christ!' grabbed the double inkwell off Patrick's desk, held the lid tight shut, and threw it down. The solid glass hit Patrick on the back of the head, and he stumbled slowly forward and fell flat on his face, red and blue ink blending to form a huge purple pool on him and all round him.

Savage shouted down to Dunphy, 'You – stand by that car but *do not shoot!* I'm coming down.' He turned and ran out of the room. A pair of Gurkhas stepped from deep shadow at the near end of Suttees and held up their rifles, the bayonets fixed. The running young Indians stopped, looked this way and that, gradually calmed down, and walked back toward the station arch. Govindaswami bent over Patrick, wetted his finger in the 'blood', lifted it to his nose, and sniffed, bewildered. Savage arrived, and Govindaswami stood up. The two stood talking in low tones, looking down on Patrick's motionless body.

At last Patrick stirred, and I felt my muscles go loose. My chest ached with anger at him and pity for him. He tried and tried, and only got hurt, whatever he did. I was going to run down and take him to the hospital – could anyone else have the patience to worry about him? How could I? – when I saw that Savage was kneeling down to look at him. At the same time I heard an engine whistle to the north.

I had to go. As I passed the booking office I caught a glimpse, through it, of Govindaswami and the two young Indians and Savage, all talking together, while Patrick leaned dizzily against the side of the armoured car with Dunphy supporting him.

The train came in. There were only two first-class compartments on it, and Molly Dickson was in one of them with the two dazed, whining children and a fat old ayah and all the paraphernalia that Europeans travel with in India – bedding rolls, ice boxes, chilumchis, thermos flasks, suitcases, servants' tin boxes, Kia Ora bottles, two bull terriers on one leash, soda-water bottles, hurricane lanterns, pressure lamps in wooden cases, and half a hundred shapeless bundles rolled in grey dhurries and tied with frayed rope.

Molly Dickson stepped down quickly to the platform as soon as the train stopped, and was at once surrounded by shouting coolies. I forced through them to her side and said, 'Mrs Dickson, I'm Victoria Jones. Your husband couldn't come, so Colonel Savage –'

Molly's blonde hair stood out untidily all round her head. Her face was sharp-featured, with a pointed nose. Her lips were thin, but she daubed them with lipstick so that they looked larger. Her skin was dry and marked by tiny lines; her blue eyes were big, restless, and beginning to fade. She stared at me and cried, 'Victoria Jones – Vic*toria*!' She flung her arms round my neck, kissed me, and stepped back. She said, 'But why on *earth* are you wearing –?'

I interrupted her quickly. 'We'd better hurry up, Molly. The city is disturbed. Colonel Savage has sent a truck for you.'

The Gurkhas were walking out of the station beside the coolies. Everyone had gone except Ayah and the children. Janet, the elder child, tugged at the skirt of my sari and said, 'Auntie Vicky, are you an ayah now?'

'Shhh, Janet,' Molly said. 'Now run along with Ayah. Is Rodney here, Victoria? What's he done with my poor Henry now? I bet he's sent him as far away as he can so that he – Oooh, Rodney!' She stood on tiptoe, shrieked, and waved her hand.

Savage came up to us and saluted her with a short smile. She flung her arms round his neck and said, 'I've just been telling Victoria you must have sent Henry away so that you could tuck me into bed yourself.'

218

He said, 'You flatter yourself, Molly.' He disentangled himself and looked her up and down. He said, 'Not too bad, considering you're a bit of an old koi hai now. I didn't know you knew Miss Jones.'

'Oh, *yes*,' Molly cried. 'I've had lots of lovely gossip sessions in Delhi with Victoria. You know, all about our female insides, and men, and –'

He said, 'My dear girl, you needn't tell me. I know you. Come on.'

We walked out of the station and stood a moment between the jeep and the six-by-six. The armoured car was on our left, and suddenly Molly Dickson saw the purple pool in the road. She stepped back and shrieked, 'Ber-lood! Rodney, have you shot someone?'

He said, 'No, but I'll shoot you if you yell like that again. The city's jumpy, and female shrieks in the night don't help. How's Mr Taylor – what is your name, Corporal?'

Ted said, 'Corporal Dunphy, sir. Patrick's a bit groggy, but he'll be all right. The Collector took him off to the Railway Hospital.' Ted chuckled. 'That was a very good shot of yours, sir. I bet you play cricket.'

Savage laughed and said, 'First slip. You're in command here now, then? Got another man for the crew?' He began to explain the orders for the night.

When he'd finished he slipped into the driving seat of the jeep and told me to follow with Mrs Dickson in the six-by-six. He revved up his engine, and the jeep began to move. Birkhe was sitting upright alone in the back seat. Molly and I scrambled into the front of the six-by-six alongside the driver. The body of the truck was full of Gurkhas, dogs, luggage, children, and Ayah.

Molly watched the jeep moving slowly along in front of us and said, 'Is that man in love with you?'

'Colonel Savage?' I said, very surprised. 'Good heavens, no. The opposite, rather, from the way he behaves.'

Molly said, 'That doesn't mean a thing. Rodney has complexes where other people have manners. Don't you think he's got *it*, though? Not that he's ever shown it to me.' She laughed abstractedly. Molly always talked like that, and usually about that.

A stone smashed into the windscreen directly in front of our driver. He swerved sharply and pressed his horn button, and Ayah screamed in the back. Savage swung round in the jeep and must have seen the scarred glass. The street was bare and the houses on both sides bolted and barred. Savage slowed and shouted back, 'Any damage?' I answered, 'No, sir.' He raised his hand and increased speed.

Molly said crossly, 'He takes it very calmly. We might have had our eyes put out. What d'you call him "sir" for? You're out of the WAC (I) now, aren't you? What *are* you doing here, anyway?'

Watching the jeep ahead, and thinking of answers for Molly, I saw Birkhe's head jerk sideways; then he clapped his hands over his eyes and rolled forward in the seat. The jeep stopped with a jerk. We were on the Pike then, where there were bare patches and scrubby small fields between the separate shacks and huts and hovels. The Sudder Savoy restaurant was just ahead on the left. Savage shouted an order, and the Gurkhas tumbled out of the back of our six-by-six. Little Birkhe rocked backward and forward, his head in his hands. Savage bent back to take a quick look at him.

Molly muttered, 'My God, what's happened *now*?'

Savage threw the jeep into gear and flung it across the shallow ditch to the left. The searching headlights jumped on to three Indian youths of about fifteen or sixteen hurrying along the line of a low wall. The jeep shot forward, and its lights pinned the boys like moths against the wall. They stopped running and stood, blinded, their faces suddenly vacant with terror. The Gurkhas ran forward, and by the time they arrived Savage was out of the jeep and walking slowly into the brilliant light. He stood in front of the boys and must have been speaking to them, though I could not hear. The Gurkhas stood around in a half-circle, the tommy-guns levelled and a bayonet point weaving from left to right.

When Savage turned his back and walked to the jeep, three of the Gurkhas put down their arms and advanced on the boys. The boys shrieked and yelled for mercy, but the Gurkhas knocked them down and began to kick them with their big boots, and leaned down and punched them in the face. I heard their boots thudding for a moment or two, and then Savage started up the jeep, and the lights swung away, leaving the boys and the Gurkhas in darkness, as Savage slowly brought the jeep back on to the Pike.

He came over to us and said, 'Are you all right?' His voice was stiff and harsh.

Molly said, 'Yes, after a fashion. What have you been doing to those poor boys, Rodney? You are a bully, really.'

He said, 'Shut up, you stupid bitch,' and got back into the jeep. He was always murderously angry and profane when a Gurkha had been hurt or insulted or even misunderstood. By our lights I saw him put his arms quickly round Birkhe in a sort of hugging pat, and one of the other Gurkhas got in to hold Birkhe up in the seat; then we drove on.

Molly said, 'He hasn't got any right to speak to me like that. If it wasn't for what Henry would do to me, I'd report him, and then he'd be in trouble.' She fumbled for a handkerchief in her bag and blew her nose.

Major Dickson wasn't there, of course, when we reached the bungalow, but the bearer had food and baths and drinks ready, and, looking at Molly's white face and her eyes that were always anxious, I did not want to stay and be talked with. I made excuses and drove away in the six-by-six as soon as it was empty. I found Savage waiting in the road outside the offices. Birkhe had gone.

He said, 'Four-thirty, here, Miss Jones.'

I thought I had not heard him properly. I said, 'Four-thirty in the morning, sir?'

He said, 'Yes, for Christ's sake. With your shoes laced up and a notebook and pencil and –'

'I'm sorry, sir,' I said quickly. I was really sorry for him, and asked, 'How badly is Birkhe hurt?'

He said, 'He got a bottle or a stone on the side of his head. Like Surabhai. It came within a quarter of an inch of putting his eye out. I'm going to the hospital now. I think he'll be all right, as a matter of fact.' He glanced at me and said shortly, 'It's sensible of you to ask. Look, I'm going to apologize to Taylor for what happened this evening as soon as I get a chance. I suppose you think I'm gloating because I've made him look a bloody fool again. Well, I'm not. Taylor's a better man than his luck lets him show. It wasn't anybody's fault tonight. With Taylor it never is. And I'm going to apologize to Molly for calling her a bitch. And

221

to you for –' He stared at me, and said, very low, 'No, not to you.'

He smiled, and I saw he was absolutely exhausted. He said, 'Yes, four-thirty. You know, I nearly killed those boys, and what good would that have done Birkhe?'

26

It was a lonely time of day, a few minutes before half past four next morning, as I bicycled to the battalion offices, and not only because the Pike was dark and empty, and the houses silent. It was lonely even when I passed the long column of trucks and jeeps, their lights out, but full of men, drawn up on the approach road and on the hard grass outside the offices. Major Dickson must have returned with the detachment that he had taken to Shahpur. There were no lights in the Kutcherry as I passed, but I thought the police bus was there, and I thought it too was full of men.

Savage was waiting in his jeep, and radio and escort jeeps were drawn up behind. As soon as I parked my bicycle he called me, and I got in beside him, and we drove to the Collector's bungalow.

The sweeping lights showed two tongas standing in front of the main steps, and Lanson's Chevrolet and the Collector's Austin. In that still hotness the smell of the tonga ponies' dung was rich and strong, and it was mixed with petrol fumes and flowers and the watered lawn and the laid dust to make an Indian hot-weather night. In the distance I heard motor engines humming and knew that the convoy of Gurkha trucks was on the move, going south toward the city.

The curtains were drawn in Govindaswami's study, and the lights seemed harsh to me, coming in out of the soft night. Mr Surabhai was there with his two pleader friends, and the Sirdarni-sahiba, and Ranjit, and a Moslem gentleman, and Mr Lanson, and the Collector.

The Collector was writing at his desk. The others sat in silence, waiting. Savage said. 'Good morning, Collector. We're on the move.'

Govindaswami got up, nodded, and turned round. He sat

down on the edge of his desk, his feet on the seat of the swivel chair, and his shiny black hands locked below one gleaming white knee. He said, 'Good. I have asked you all to come here because in one way or another you are the leading citizens, official and non-official, of Bhowani. As you know, we have been trying for some time now to find K. P. Roy and a lot of explosives and ammunition that he stole. We have not received the co-operation we ought to get. So today we are searching the city. All the Gurkhas and all the police will be engaged. The A.F.I. will keep order in the streets. But before we cause a lot of trouble to everybody, I want to ask you all, for the last time, if you can give me any information. Mr Surabhai?'

Mr Surabhai's eyes popped, and he said, 'Your fellows are commencing already to turn our city upside down, hugger mugger, enter every dwelling-house, affrighten one and all, the lady in her seclusion and the old man in his hour of rest, and all without hint of authorization or precept?'

'I have authority, Mr Surabhai,' Govindaswami said.

Mr Surabhai cried, 'Merely the authorization of this so-called pseudo-government. What balderdash! At all events I shall not lift one little finger to help in the location of Mr K. P. Roy. He is nothing but a patriot of the first water. He has proved it by the acid test: he has been to jail.'

The Collector said, 'Mr Surabhai, K. P. Roy's group threw the stones that started your trouble with the Moslems the other day. K. P. Roy murdered the Hindu girl. K. P. Roy derailed the troop train and killed two Indian firemen and an Indian driver. K. P. Roy probably murdered a British officer here and certainly hung a sign round his neck which implied that Congress had been responsible. K. P. Roy set fire to Maslan and ruined twenty poor people. And you want to help him? You think that is true patriotism?'

Mr Surabhai's eyes had grown bigger and bigger during the Collector's recital. Now he fidgeted unhappily on the edge of his chair and said, '*You* indicate that Mr K. P. Roy has committed these offences. How do I know you are not merely hoodwinking me? Give me proof, mister.'

Govindaswami said, 'I can't. We just know he's done them all – he and his group.'

Mr Surabhai shrugged violently and said, 'Then why should I

223

help you? Hearsay is no jolly damned good at all. Besides, I have not seen or heard rumours of Mr Roy.'

The Collector sighed and turned to the other two, at Surabhai's right and left. They knew nothing. The Moslem gentleman knew nothing. Then he asked the Sirdarni-sahiba.

She said in Hindustani, 'I don't understand English.'

The Collector replied sharply, 'That is a lie, Sirdarni-sahiba. Where is K. P. Roy? When did you last see him?'

She said, 'I don't understand English.'

Savage said, 'This is the lady who was urging the Congress men to charge my fellows in the Street of Suttees that day. The one who wanted to cause another Jallianwala Bagh.'

The Jallianwala Bagh is the name of a place in Amritsar where there was a terrible massacre in 1919. Some people said General Dyer's soldiers had meant to kill all the civilians; others said the massacre happened because there was a panic.

'I was at the Jallianwala Bagh,' the Sirdarni said unexpectedly in English.

'Were you responsible for that too, Beji?' Savage asked in Hindustani.

The Sirdarni shot him a hard look, said, 'I don't understand English,' and pressed her lips together.

Savage laughed cheerfully, bowed, and said, '*Touché.*'

The Collector waited patiently, his head bent, while this exchange went on. Then he turned to Ranjit. 'And you? Have you heard anything since I last saw you?'

'No,' Ranjit muttered.

'Miss Jones?' he asked me.

I pretended not to hear so that I could have a second or two in which to think. It might come out all right. They'd get K. P. Roy if they were going to. If they weren't, they wouldn't. They thought he had killed Macaulay, so, unless they caught him, they'd go on thinking it. The Collector was giving me a long time. He must know. Then why did he say that Roy had killed Macaulay? Anyway –

'Miss Jones?' he repeated.

'I've heard nothing, sir,' I said.

He said, 'Very well. That is all. The search will begin at once. A head constable is waiting outside to escort you to your homes.'

Colonel Savage made no move to go out with the group of Indians, so I waited. I tried to catch Ranjit's eye as he passed me, but he wouldn't look at me.

When they were gone Lanson and Govindaswami talked briefly in a corner. Savage turned to me and said, 'Now, your job. I'm setting up my headquarters in the station yard – in the lorries. You'll find the maps for this operation in the office lorry. The whole battalion's here, but if a trainman notices that there are no guards on the various bridges, tell him there are, that they're just out of sight.'

I wrote in my notebook. He must have got his company down from Lalkot and perhaps even borrowed back the other, the one he'd left in Cawnpore. Henry Dickson's move to Shahpur was a blind. The tents would probably still be standing down there in some secluded place, with a sentry or two left to keep anyone from finding out that the soldiers in them had gone away.

I could hardly write, the feeling of guilty despair was growing so strong in me. Ranjit's mother was lying. Every moment that I held my tongue tied me more closely to lawlessness and violence. Any action I took or word that I spoke to break free would cut me off from the new India that I was so close to finding.

Savage said, 'The search is beginning in the western segment of the city, nearest the railway line, and working east and south. Stay at headquarters. The field mess is open there now. You may be wanted at any time for interpreting, or to help us get into zenana apartments. That's all.'

When I looked up I saw that Lanson had gone. Govindaswami said suddenly, 'When are you going to be initiated into the Sikh religion, Miss Jones?'

The question nearly brought my panic into the open, for it burst like a searchlight on the other part of my position – my way ahead. The talk of derailments and murders and K. P. Roy had focused my despair on the problems of becoming an Indian in these circumstances. The Collector's question gave bright outlines and black, black shadows to the goal itself. *Could* I become an Indian? What was the Sikh religion, which I was so lightly proposing to enter as a kind of haven where Savage and Patrick couldn't get at me?

Slowly I answered the Collector's question. I said, 'Monday next.'

The Collector smiled and patted my shoulder. He said, 'Don't sound so worried. I'm sure you are doing the right thing. Ranjit's one of the nicest young men there are, but he needs his religion. It ought to be a tie between you, and between the two of you and the things in India that are older and better than this.' He waved his hand, perhaps at the sound of motor engines in the distance, perhaps at the atmosphere of squabbling and mistrust hanging about in the room, perhaps at the portrait of Queen Victoria over his desk. But I *was* worried all the same, and, with the other things, more than worried.

Govindaswami asked me when the marriage was to be. I told him, 'July the first.' He hoped that Colonel Savage was giving me plenty of leave for it. Savage said, 'She'll be out of the Army before then. I've written to G.H.Q. Unless you want to keep me hanging around any more, Collector, I've got some work to do.'

Govindaswami glanced at him, but his calm black face and his steady voice showed no anger or remonstrance at Savage's sharp tone. He said, 'No, Savage. You'd better be off.'

Savage strode off. In the doorway he turned, hesitated, and said, 'You may rely on me.'

Govindaswami's face broke into a smile and he rose and clasped Savage's hand. Their old joke again. 'The scoundrels must be made to suffer for the wrongs they have inflicted, Savage. Society demands it,' he said.

'No – society must be protected,' Savage said. He went out, got into his jeep, and waited, frowning to himself, while I adjusted my sari and climbed in after him.

When we reached the station yard he left me there and drove away. I climbed up into the office three-tonner, looked at the maps, and tried to work out when the search would reach the Sirdarni's house – late in the afternoon, probably.

Light came, the sun rose, and a Gurkha brought me tea, bread, and bacon and eggs. The A.F.I. armoured car came back from a patrol, and I saw that the crew had been changed. Men in the A.F.I. did their railway duties, then hurried to this, then went off again. Obviously they couldn't keep it up for long. I understood then why they had been called out. The trouble last night hadn't

226

really been bad. Govindaswami had used it as a heaven-sent excuse to call out the A.F.I. so that all the Gurkhas and police would be free for the house-to-house search of the city.

Twice we got messages on the walkie-talkies that sent me to houses where Moslem ladies, their men away, were entrenched in the zenanas and refusing to admit the Gurkhas. I found the Gurkhas were working in groups of about six or a dozen, each group accompanied by a single constable. The Moslem ladies were delighted when I came. They whispered to ask me how much of the secret Hindu store of ammunition had been found. As for themselves, of course they hadn't got any. They adjusted their veils and cheerfully showed me and the grinning Gurkhas all over their houses.

Then Patrick came into the yard on his motor bicycle to resume command of the armoured car. He had put on clean uniform, his head was professionally bandaged, and his big military topi sat on top of it.

I walked over to him, but he turned his back on me. I said, 'Patrick,' but he did not answer.

I said, 'Patrick, are you all right?'

No answer.

I said, 'Patrick, Colonel Savage didn't *want* to hurt you. He had to. He did it to save you from getting into awful trouble. I saw it all.'

Patrick wheeled round on me, his pale eyes blazing and his face red. He said, 'He was trying to make a fool of me, like all of them are trying to make fools of all of us now. You are a – a traitor!' He turned his back again.

Perhaps he was waiting for me to put my arms round him and beg for forgiveness. But I couldn't do that. I could only try to find words to make him understand that I knew how he felt. Anything I said would have to flick the really sore place, the ridicule that was the heart of the matter, the ludicrous wound under the splendid bandage.

I climbed slowly up the stairs to the Traffic Office. Ranjit was working there alone, as I had hoped. I said, 'Ranjit, do you think any of that explosive is hidden in your mother's house?'

He put down his pen and looked at me sadly. He was always sad. I would have to stop him from thinking of these things all the time. He ought to smile when he saw me. There was always something that might be love in his face, but it was always blended with melancholy, so I could not be sure.

He said, 'I don't know.' He changed the subject. 'I'm seeing the guru every day now. He wants you to go to him tomorrow.'

I said, 'Saturday? What for?'

He said, 'To talk to you. He wants to give you time before Monday to think over what you are doing.'

'I won't change my mind,' I said bravely and quickly, not daring to face the truth. Of course I had thought of changing my mind – a hundred times – but where was I to go? Back to the sneers of Rose Mary?

Gently Ranjit took my hand. He said, 'You are so good, Victoria. When we are married we will get a house and then – oh, it will be truly wonderful.'

'You must get a house for us before we are married,' I said sharply.

'I'm trying,' he muttered. 'It is very difficult. There are not many houses, and those are expensive.'

I said, 'I don't care, you've got to get one, Ranjit.' He looked so miserable that I put my hand on his cheek and stroked it gently. I said, 'I'm sorry, but *please* cheer up, Ranjit. You make me feel we are going to be executed instead of married.' The gauze curtain was there, and so was my old impatience with it, my desire to tear it down. I slid my hand round and rested it on the back of his neck. I whispered, 'Kiss me. You promised.'

I felt the muscles in his neck stiffen, and he was trying to move his head back, but I held him and put my parted lips close under his. He said, 'Oh, Victoria, I can't, I mustn't! Look, they can see from across the yard.'

With a strong effort he jerked away from me. His eyes were wild and his chest heaving. He said, 'I must not. I want to, Victoria, but I must not. When we are married everything will be all right, I promise you. I adore you so much, Victoria. I will do anything for you.'

I said, 'Except leave your mother's house. Or kiss me.'

He said, 'I can't.'

I turned away from him to dab my eyes. I didn't feel insulted, only hurt and sad. The Sirdarni was holding him. Perhaps he had told her all about my wanting to be kissed, and asked what he should do. After we were married he wouldn't be breaking over any barrier when he kissed me. Then he wouldn't be choosing between his mother's authority and my love. But now, if he kissed me, he would have done something important, and so would I.

I wondered if any woman had ever hung so much importance on a single kiss. But of course it would have ended beyond kissing. Not there in the office, but somewhere, that night, I would have brought him to me. Then I would have known whether I really loved him, and whether his mother's hold on him was too strong for me to break.

So far, I had failed. Ranjit wouldn't even kiss me. I would have to go farther along the course that I had set myself. I said, 'I'll go and see the guru. What time?'

He said, 'In the evening. Don't go now, Victoria. I like to look at you.'

I smiled at him and put my handkerchief away. I said, 'I've got to go. I'll see you tomorrow.'

He said, 'Victoria – do you know, are you allowed to tell me when the Gurkhas will reach our house?'

I said, 'I know and I'll tell you, whether I'm supposed to or not. About five o'clock. Not before. Why?'

He said, 'I think I ought to be there. I am afraid my mother will do something that will get her into trouble.'

I couldn't resist saying, 'Could you stop her, Ranjit, if she had made up her mind?'

'I don't know,' he answered seriously, 'but I would try.' I came as close to the point of loving him then as I ever had.

When I got out into the yard I found the Collector and Savage and Second Lieutenant George Howland gathered round a six-by-six inside which were an old man and woman, roped together under guard, and half a dozen oblong boxes.

Howland was a burly young man with a loud and hearty voice and a sort of beefy slyness that got on most people's nerves very quickly. He was telling Govindaswami how he had found the explosives. 'Buried under the woodpile at the back, it was,' he said triumphantly. 'But I made 'em show me.'

'They knew it was there?' the Collector asked sharply.

'Not 'arf they didn't!' Howland said. His cockney was meant

229

to be funny, but also he spoke like that to hide the fact that he had a real, but slight, cockney accent.

Savage said quietly, 'What do you mean? Tell me what you said to them.'

Howland said, 'Well, sir, when we found it under the woodpile I showed 'em the bayonet and said, "You knew it was there, didn't you?" and they gave in and said they did. I mean, they nodded.'

The old man quavered in Hindustani, 'What is the young sahib saying now? We cannot understand him. How should I know what evil men hid these boxes under my woodpile?' He was nodding his head all the time as he spoke.

Savage said, 'You're a bloody fool, Howland, as well as a born bully. Get that truck unloaded and get back to work.' Howland saluted sulkily and turned away.

Govindaswami undid the old couple's ropes and spoke quietly with them. Then he patted their shoulders and told them they could go home. Savage said, 'I'll take them. Who are they?'

Govindaswami said, 'Darby and Joan. He's a wheelwright – he was, rather. He retired years ago. Someone dumped this stuff on them.'

Savage nodded and turned to help the trembling old woman into his jeep. When she hung back he bent and said something into her ear. She started and then burst out in a high delighted cackle. The old husband grasped Savage's arm, and, all laughing, they drove away.

Govindaswami watched them go. When he noticed me there near him he said, 'Our Colonel Savage is five parts genius and five parts fool. Or five parts angel and five parts devil. He is divided in both planes.'

Suddenly I got the strangest feeling of being sorry for Colonel Savage. He did have complexes, just as Molly Dickson said. I knew about inferiority complexes – good heavens, I ought to – but it made me shiver to think how Colonel Savage kept hating himself because he did things well and was lucky.

During the afternoon ammunition and explosives continued to pile up, until by a quarter to five only four hundred pounds of PEK and a few oddments, including fuse, were still missing. Several men had been questioned and released. One woman was in jail for further questioning. Govindaswami did not think any of them, except perhaps the woman in jail, knew anything about the explosives that had been found on their property – down dried wells, under the woodpiles, under the eaves, under bhoosa stacked in cattle sheds, among sacks of grain in the stores.

At ten to five Ranjit came down from his office and bicycled quickly away up the Street of Suttees.

A minute later it suddenly struck me to wonder why a curfew had not been imposed, why movements of trucks and cars and bullock carts had not been stopped. I asked Chris Glass. He looked surprised and said, 'Didn't the Sahib tell you? He's borrowed a couple of companies from the Thirtieth Raj Rif in Gondwara, and old Sammy's borrowed police from all over the shop. There's an outer cordon two miles out on every road and track. The whole of this searching business here is to frighten the stuff – and Roy – out of Bhowani. If we catch something in a cart, the carter's *got* to know where it came from and where it's going, hasn't he?'

At a quarter past five Savage returned from a visit somewhere, presumably to the outer cordon, and ordered me into the jeep. He didn't say where we were going, but I knew.

He stopped the jeep a hundred yards short of the Kasel house, got out, lit a cheroot, and stood for a few minutes watching the slow progress of his men down the street. They were doing ten or a dozen houses at a time, five or six on each side of the street, and other parties were working other streets in the quarter at the same time. I noticed that there was no guard at the end of the street, and thought again of the outer cordon.

A group consisting of a havildar, a naik, eight riflemen, and a foot-constable came out of a house near us and walked forward. Mr Lanson's Chevrolet drove up. Lanson, a sub-inspector of police, a head constable, and the Subadar-Major got out. Together they all advanced on the Sirdarni's house. Mr Govindaswami's Austin buzzed up. Savage and I saluted him, and then the three of us fell in at the back of the procession.

The outer door at the foot of the long stair was locked. The police sub-inspector banged on it and shouted, several times, 'Open, in the name of the law,' but the door did not open.

The sub-inspector, a tall and handsome old Moslem, turned to

231

the D.S.P. with a question. Lanson nodded. The police tried to barge the door open with their backs, but it would not budge. Subadar-Major Manbir watched them and pulled restlessly at his drooping moustaches. After the third attempt had failed he spoke to the Gurkha havildar, who had a crowbar. Grinning cheerfully, and grunting with the force of his blows, the havildar broke down the door. We began to climb the gloomy stairs.

'Halt or I fire!'

It was Mr Surabhai's high voice, ringing and booming in the stairwell. We all stopped. Lanson called out, 'Put that gun down! Have you got a licence for it!'

Mr Surabhai shouted, 'A licence, now? Since what illegal ordinance or by-law must a gentleman be in possession of a licence for his ancestral bow and arrow, Mr Lanson?'

Lanson muttered something unintelligible.

Mr Surabhai cried, 'You are breaking and entering, and making burglarious entry, I warn you.' A brilliant flash of light made me blink. Lanson ducked, and his hand dropped on to the butt of the pistol in his holster. Savage turned slowly to look at him, his eyebrows raised.

Mr Surabhai cried, 'There, now I have the photographic record. There will be more, mister. *I* know you have a search warrant. *I* say it is illegal claptrap. Every single thing which you do in this house shall be emblazoned across the headlines of the world, mister. Your brutal actions will jolly well show up in *The Times* and *The New York Times* and *La Prensa* and *La Vie Parisienne*. Come up now. Please be careful of yourselves, gentlemen, there is an unfortunate rut in the fourth step – here.'

He turned, and we followed him silently up the stairs. Savage's face had hardened, and I knew him well enough to realize that he was shaking with laughter. Lanson was flushed and furious at having mistaken a flash-bulb for a pistol shot.

The search began. The Sirdarni sat motionless in her chair, with Ranjit standing behind her, and did not speak. Mr Surabhai and a small dark man followed the searchers everywhere. The small dark man's name was Chandrabhan. He used to make a living by photographing British soldiers against a Taj Mahal backdrop in a shack outside the Sudder Savoy, and now he ran a studio near the station. His flash-bulbs popped regularly.

232

Govindaswami, Savage, Lanson, and I stayed in the big room but didn't speak at all.

At last the sub-inspector came in to tell Lanson they had found nothing and nobody on this floor or the floor above.

'What about the floor below?' Lanson asked.

'There is no floor below, sahib,' the sub-inspector said, puzzled.

Lanson said, 'Of course there is, Inspector-sahib. We came upstairs from the street, didn't we?' Lanson was still hot under the collar and would not meet Savage's eyes. 'There was a padlocked door on the left near the foot of the stairs,' he said. 'That must lead into a lower story.'

'There is a place, Mr Lanson. It belongs to my mother,' Ranjit said suddenly. 'It is a yard, and there is a room off it where empty sacks used to be stored. But my mother lets it to a merchant. It is quite empty now.'

'No, it is not empty, dash it,' Mr Surabhai said. He was wearing green socks and violet suspenders that day, and he was not carrying his umbrella. His hands were full with the ancient bow, and the quiver was slung across his back so that three or four moth-eaten arrows stuck up above his shoulder. He went on, 'There is a sick lady resting there. She is a close friend to me. She can by no account be disturbed. Here the primary evidence thereof – this had been photographed.' He fished out a slip of paper and handed it triumphantly to Lanson.

Lanson said, 'This is signed by Datt, Collector. You know – Datt.' Datt was a doctor who specialized in youth pills for men and so on, and he was a well-known Congress Left-winger in Bhowani.

Govindaswami said, 'I know.'

Lanson read the note and said, 'He says that the woman, Lakshmi, spinster, is seriously ill and may not on any account be moved or disturbed. Why is the lady here, Mr Surabhai? She must have been moved to get here.'

'I moved her here in order to ensure perfect peace and quiet, that's why,' Mr Surabhai said. '*Then* Doctor Datt, L.R.C.P., Calcutta, gave me the attached notification. Not before! But you will search the place, nevertheless, eh?' He sounded suddenly anxious.

'We shall search it, Mr Surabhai,' Govindaswami said. 'I won't deprive you of any evidence of our brutality.' Mr Surabhai looked relieved.

Govindaswami told me to come along, and I followed them down the stairs. Mr Surabhai refused to produce the key for the padlock, so the havildar took his crowbar and broke that door down too, to the accompaniment of popping flash-bulbs and the click of Chandrabhan's large, old-fashioned press camera.

The yard was small, square, and empty. The house had been built over it. Light filtered in above a high wall on the north side, and there was a room under the south side, with a grimy window and a door, Mr Surabhai took station in front of the door, his arms outspread. When Chandrabhan had photographed him defending the door against us, he stood aside.

Govindaswami was about to open the door when Chandrabhan said, 'Excuse me, please, Collector-sahib. One moment.' He changed places, opened the door, and slipped inside. As he went in I got a glimpse of a thinly-clothed woman lying on a string charpoy. Govindaswami saw her too and raised his eyebrows at Mr Surabhai. Mr Surabhai said, 'The poor unfortunate female is sick of the palsy. She is utterly respectable spinster, mind you, but Doctor Datt, L.R.C.P., Calcutta, has prescribed fresh wholesome air and no supernumerary weight of clothings, you see?'

'I see,' Govindaswami said, and walked in.

The woman started up on the charpoy, put her hands to her face, and let out a piercing scream. The flash-bulb exploded.

Govindaswami walked over to the bed. Chandrabhan murmured apologetically, 'Collector-sahib, please have the goodness to go back to the door. The shutter did not trip. It is unfortunately a very old camera.'

The Collector walked back. The woman screamed again. That time the shutter tripped, and Chandrabhan thanked Govindaswami profusely. Savage was so pale with looking cold and stern that I thought he was going to faint. I knew enough of Indian politics and Indian-language newspapers, and of Mr Surabhai, to realize that all this was, for him, the core of the search. There might be explosives hidden in the house, there might be murderous revolutionaries in hiding nearby – but all that mattered was that he should get evidence of British brutality. He was of the old school of Indian politicians, who had developed this into a kind

234

of game, which the British were kind enough to play with them. So, while my mind was obsessed with the real dangers, the visions of the diseased 'rat i' the arras', poor dear Mr Surabhai led confidently to his set-piece – British officials and their Indian stooges viciously disturbing a sick woman in her seclusion.

'Search the room,' Lanson said angrily and muttered under his breath, 'Damned farce!' But he was wrong. The woman was a respectable member of the Congress group. She really was ill – Mr Surabhai wouldn't be a party to any subterfuge. The screams were acting, but she was really in pain and was suffering, in mind and body, for the sake of India. It wasn't farce. It was tragedy.

But Mr Surabhai thought it was drama. He cried, 'Farce, you say? You will not find it any farce, no, nor drawing-room comedy high or low, when the photographs of *this* outrage are shown in all their infamous detail, I can tell you. Then you will say, "*Blast!*" nothing less.'

Govindaswami said to the woman, 'I'm sorry you should lend yourself to this.' She only stared at him, her lips tight and scornful.

Govindaswami said, 'Look under the bed. Then you'd better get the doctor to see her again, Surabhai. You may have done her real harm by moving her here.'

The sub-inspector got under the bed. Mr Surabhai stood tongue-tied in the middle of the very hot and overcrowded room, his eyes growing larger and larger until they were ready to pop out of his head, but no words came to relieve the pressure.

The handsome and distinguished-looking sub-inspector crawled out from under the charpoy with a lump of iron in his hand. He was very embarrassed from having a respectable lady just over him, and only on a string charpoy. To Lanson he said, 'This, sahib, nothing else.'

Lanson turned the broken piece of fishplate over, then quickly fumbled in his pocket, got out a handkerchief, and wrapped one end of the fishplate in it. He held it under Mr Surabhai's nose and said, 'Did you put this there?'

Mr Surabhai stared at the black rusted blood, and the blond hairs sticking to it along one of the fishplate's sharp edges. He whispered, 'That is – blood?'

Savage said, 'Macaulay's blood? Macaulay's hair?'

Lanson shot him a quick, angry look. Mr Surabhai stammered, 'M-murder! This is the same blunt instrument that committed murder?'

Of course it was. K. P. Roy hadn't cleaned and buried the fish-plate as he had said. He'd kept it, waiting to find the best opportunity to use it.

There was not enough air in there for me to breathe. I was beginning to suffocate. I wanted to scream that there was no need to get excited, because I had killed Macaulay and I had had good cause. It was necessary that I say something, because Mr Surabhai would have a stroke if I didn't. Lanson was moving forward on him. But when I opened my mouth the hot, scented air rushed in and filled my whole head and my ears and nose, and blotted out the grimy light and the crowd, and the woman's body swung slowly round with the bed, and up and up ...

27

RANJIT was beside me again as I bowed before the holy book, as Ranjit's had been the first face I saw when I recovered from fainting in that terribly smelly room below stairs in his mother's house. His face had been above me, the fuzz of new beard growing like a halo round it, the cold metal of the new bangle on his wrist touching my neck. I had thought, He does love me, he's left his mother upstairs and come running to me. I must have shrieked aloud.

In this bare square temple, the Sikh gurdwara, the book, the Guru Granth Sahib, rested on a white cloth below a canopy. The guru stood behind it, gently waving a fly-flicker back and forth over it.

Ranjit straightened his back, his hands folded, his head bent. He murmured, '*Wahiguruji ka Khalsa, wahiguruji ki Fatteh!*' I murmured the phrase in my turn. My mind ran over the things that as a Sikh I must do and have. Had I done them, had I got them? A plain iron bangle hung round my right wrist. I had not cut my hair since seeing the guru. I wore no lipstick or powder. I was a woman, so I did not have to carry the dagger. There was a comb in my hair. I was wearing pants; they were not anywhere near knee length, but surely no one would look to make sure? I was unveiled.

I stood on the threshold of a new life. It felt more like the edge of a cliff.

There were about twenty men and women there. The five Loved Ones who would perform the baptism stood a little in front of the others. Kartar Singh, the labour leader, was one of the Loved Ones, and his wife another. There was an iron pot on a pedestal close in front of me. Ranjit stood at my right hand. The Sirdarni was not there. Earlier, the guru had refused to let her come because she cut her hair, wore no bangle, and refused to believe in the divine precepts of the Ten Gurus. Also, she had no intention of admitting her faults before a court of five. It hadn't mattered in the end, because she was in jail.

The guru stood before the holy Guru Granth Sahib, bowed, and opened the book at random. She said a short prayer in a firm voice and then read a passage where he had opened the book. The people stood with folded hands. There were no seats or benches.

Had Pater stopped crying yet?

I was afraid, but there was nothing strange or barbaric about this. Substitute a word or two, make a mental reservation, and it could be a Christian service. But nobody really wanted me to be there, except Ranjit, and the solemnity weighed me down. Ranjit was here because this was a stronghold for him. If these people would let him in, he'd be able to stop worrying and fretting.

The Sirdarni was in jail because she wouldn't say anything about the fishplate. Mr Surabhai and the merchant who rented the little room had also been taken to jail, but after questioning them Lanson had let them go.

I knew why. Govindaswami had said, 'First, there's no doubt that K. P. Roy put the fishplate there. Second, he put it there as a follow-up to the "Quit India" which he put on Macaulay's body—to confirm the impression that Congress was responsible, and that Surabhai knows more than he is telling about the murder. But I absolutely refuse to believe Surabhai knows anything about it. If Roy wants Surabhai behind bars for some reason – and I can think of several – let's put someone else in instead. The

Sirdarni-sahiba. Good heavens, with that fishplate in the house we're justified in jailing Ranjit if we want to.'

Lanson had argued, but the Collector was firm. So the Sirdarni-sahiba was in, and the others out. Surabhai had protested. Ranjit had protested. Even the Moslem League had protested, but the Collector wouldn't budge.

In the gurdwara, Ranjit left my side, and I began to follow him, but Kartar Singh's wife motioned me to stay where I was. Ranjit went and stood meekly before the senior Loved One. The old man had a long white beard, and the muscles of his neck couldn't support his heavy head, he was so old. Ranjit said in a firm low voice, 'I have broken the Raht. I beg forgiveness. I beg to be received back into the true faith.'

The old man nodded his head slowly. He said, 'Your fault has been great. For many years you have stayed outside our communion, the only true communion. But there is forgiveness and love in the Guru Panth.'

'*Sat Sri Akkal!*' all the congregation shouted with one voice, and I started nervously.

He said, 'But you were led astray by one who should know better, one from whom you had the right to expect wisdom and sound advice. Therefore your punishment shall be light.' '*Sat Sri Akkal!*' 'Take this cloth and this water. Go on your knees and wash the feet of each true Sikh in this room. And remember, my son, that this punishment is but a touch from the guiding hand of those who love you, in God. Hold no bitterness in your heart.'

Ranjit stepped back, knelt, and began to wash the feet of an old Sikh coolie near him. Next to the coolie stood the Buick driver. I had seen his two-tone shoes in the courtyard, and now Ranjit was stooping over his bare feet, washing and drying.

The old man cried, 'Let us all beg forgiveness for our sins, in our hearts, even as this our brother has begged forgiveness.'

'*Sat Sri Akkal!*'

Ranjit did not wipe my feet. I was not yet a Sikh. He passed by behind me, moving slowly on his knees. I heard a low sound and knew he was sobbing gently as he did his penance. He came back to my side, and I turned to look at him. He was proud and exalted.

The old man stepped closer to us and looked us in the eyes, first

Ranjit, then me. He began to speak in a quavering voice that strengthened as he went on:

'*Hear me. This is the faith of the Guru Panth.*
There is one God.
In the love of God is the only hope of salvation.
We believe in Guru Govind Singh and we say every day five
*   prayers, as he taught us.*
We believe in the five Ks. The kes – the unshorn hair, which is a
*   sign of devotion. The kachh ...*'

I knew this part by heart. I began to think of K. P. Roy. That hurt – but nothing else could stop me from thinking of the cliff-edge gaping before my feet.

'... do you hear? Will you obey?'

Ranjit raised his head and shouted, '*Wahiguruji ka Khalsa, wahiguruji ki Fatteh!*' – Glory to the Khalsa, which is ever victorious! The congregation shouted it after him.

For a second I thought I would not be able to get out the words. They stumbled together in my throat, but the second time I managed to say them, softly and clearly: '*Wahiguruji ka Khalsa, wahiguruji ki Fatteh!*'

The other four Loved Ones approached and stood in a circle with the old man round the iron pot.

'This is the water of immortality in God,' murmured one, and poured water into the pot.

'This is the sweetness of God's love,' murmured another, and shook a handful of sugar candies called patashas into the pot.

The five squatted down in the 'heroic attitude' round the pot, left knee up, right knee on the ground. Ranjit did the same, and slowly I followed.

Kartar Singh drew from his belt a twelve-inch double-bladed dagger and held it out in his hand. He began to stir the patashas into the water, reciting as he stirred:

'*The One, Aum,*
*   The true word,*
*   The creative spirit,*
*   Free of fear and hate,*
*   Timeless, birthless, self-existent ...*'

239

His voice went on and did not become a drone. All the congregation knelt around. But their kneeling was not humble. This 'heroic attitude' was the position from which a warrior could best spring up to thrust his spear into the stomach of an enemy attacking him.

This was not like the padre's Christianity, after all. There was nothing formal here, nothing taken for granted, nothing half-believed, nothing polite. Ranjit had changed so that I did not know him any more.

Kartar Singh finished the *Japji* and handed the dagger to the old man. The old man began to recite as he stirred the pot. The other four held the rim of the pot with both hands.

> '*The One, Aum,*
> *By the Grace of the Guru –*
> *Thou the formless, colourless, markless,*
> *Thou the casteless, power beyond measure,*
> *Thou the light that knows no wavering …*'

I had read it all in a little book they'd given me a week before. Reading it by myself in Number 4 Collett Road had not been like this.

> '*Thou beyond all action,*
> *Thou beyond all desire,*
> *Thou beyond all enjoyment,*
> *Thou beyond all protection,*
> *Obeisance to Thee!*'

The words beat down like big steady hammers, merciless, emphatic. I used to ignore the padre's drone. Even K. P. Roy wasn't any good to me now. Another Loved One took the dagger, stirred, and began on the *Swayyas*:

> '*Some worship stones and place them on their heads.*
> *Others suspend the lingam round their necks.*
> *Some see God in the south, others bow to the west.*
> *Some fools worship idols,*
> *And others worship the dead.*
> *In false ceremonial the whole world is enwrapped.*
> *They cannot find the secret of God.*'

Suddenly it was over. Ranjit made a cup of his hands, the right above the left. I did the same. In turn each Loved One poured the amrit into our hands. Five times we drank. Five times the amrit was touched to our eyes and hair. Five times we cried, '*Wahiguruji ka Khalsa, wahiguruji ki Fatteh!*' Everything that was left in the pot we drank, sipping in turn.

The Loved Ones stood up, and all together shouted, '*By the Grace of the One Supreme Being, of the True Name, of the Breath, devoid of fear and enmity, immortal, unborn, self-existent – the Enlightener!*'

Five times they shouted it. They were holy, and I was not holy. They were leaning over me, threatening. But I knew why Ranjit had to come back to this.

The old man boomed, 'And these are the four chief sins – the cutting of your hair, the eating of halal meat, the committing of adultery, the use of tobacco. Do you swear to forgo these sins, now and for ever?'

Ranjit shouted, '*Wahiguruji ka Khalsa, wahiguruji ki Fatteh!*'

But I didn't love Ranjit. I liked him, I respected him, I wanted to look after him and rescue him, but I didn't love him. I whispered, '*Wahiguruji ka Khalsa, wahiguruji ki Fatteh!*'

'*Sat Sri Akkal!*' hissed the congregation like a hundred snakes.

The old man stepped aside, the perspiration pouring down his face. The guru behind the canopy opened the holy book and looked at the top left-hand corner. He cried, 'The first letter of the first word is K – a good omen! What name shall we of the Guru Panth give this our new sister?'

The Buick taxi-man said, 'Kalwant.'

Katar Singh's wife said, 'Kirat!'

But my name was Victoria. Victoria Jones. I was a cheechee engine driver's daughter.

My name was Victoria.

I stumbled to my feet and ran out of the gurdwara. The congregation fell suddenly silent behind me. I grabbed my bag, left my sandals, ran across the little square by the pool, turned, and ran down the street. Pieces of the service thundered round like chariots in my head:

Conquering various countries of the world,
With the beat of drums and kettledrums and tambourines ...

241

If Ranjit came after me I might even now stop and go back with him and submit my neck to the two-edged sword, my spirit to the iron faith. But it was terribly important that I should not stop for him or go back of my own accord. He must break away from them for my sake, and come running after me, whatever the congregation thought, whatever the Loved Ones said.

> *Having first remembered God the almighty,*
> *Think of Guru Nanak.*
> *Then of Arjun Guru and Amar Dass and Ram Dass ...*

It was awful of me to run away and leave him. But he didn't *need* me, however much he loved me – and I thought he did love me, in his fashion. He didn't need me; he did need the Guru Panth.

> *Remember the five beloved ones, the Master's four sons, the forty saved ones, all the righteous ...*

I slowed a little and looked over my shoulder. The people in the street were staring at me, but Ranjit was not coming. None of the Sikhs had left the gurdwara.

> *O joy! My mother, I have found my lord and guide!*

I saw the station in front of me, and black smoke drifting away at the north end. It must be a goods train, but 98 Up was due in any minute now – the train Pater would take from Bhowani on to Gondwara. No, today he was going only as far as Timrai Junction – another driver ill, some changes in the rosters. I broke into a run.

> *The blest! they attach themselves to the Enlightener,*
> *Who rings unbeaten bars of music on their souls!*

I reached the station yard as 98 Up whistled for the Farriers crossing. That was not music for the soul; it was one of our people, his hand on the whistle cord, sending the shrill voice of the engine out over the roofs of the city, over the plains, reminding them of steel and people and wheels grinding on the rail.

I ran on to the platform and stood on the edge, breathing in great gasps, my sari billowing about me.

Ninety-Eight Up came snaking in under the north gantry, under the high tower of the North Box, past the mud wall behind the Parcel Shed. Farther back there was a gold mohur tree in

242

bloom, its branches leaning out over the carriage roofs. The line of dark red carriages, swaying and grinding slowly, followed behind the engine. Each jerked to the left, to the right, as the bogies caught the points. The driver sat there on his jump seat, leaning out over the red-hot iron wall of the cab, his eyes screwed up in the glare. The engine ground to a stop in front of the Up Starter.

Pater came out of the Stationmaster's office, his red bandanna on his head and the tin box with food and a thermos flask in his hand. I ran to him and threw my arms round his neck.

28

PATER put down the box and patted my shoulder awkwardly. He stood a bit away from me and said sadly, 'You are still glad to see me? That is good, anyhow. What is your name now?'

I wiped the tears from my eyes with the back of my hand and answered, 'Victoria Jones. Oh, Pater, I was frightened.'

Pater's eyes grew and grew and became blurred and watery. He put out both hands, caught mine, and pressed them, but could not speak. The driver from the train came and stood beside us. Pater turned to him, and they talked. The other man handed over a small box and a book and walked away.

I said, 'Pater, I must get away from here. I'll go and stay with the Roviras in Gondwara for a few days. Let me come with you. In the cab.'

He said, 'In the cab, girl? Oh, I wish you could, but I would lose my job. This is Ninety-Eight Up, man, not a night slow goods on the branch!'

I knew it was useless to argue, although at that moment I wanted nothing in the world as much as I wanted to be on the engine with Pater, rushing noisily away from Bhowani and the Sikh congregation and the new name beginning with K, which had bright new iron chains hanging from it.

Savage came up to us. He said, 'Good afternoon, Mr Jones. I'm coming down to Gondwara on this train. I'm coming in the cab as far as Shahpur – military duty' – he winked – 'a personal reconnaissance of the rail, from the engine driver's point of view.'

'In the cab?' Pater said. 'On military duty? Why, *that* is the answer! My girl here has just been asking to come in the cab with me, and I had to say no. But if you *order* her, on military duty, no one can say no, eh? She is going to Gondwara. And – oh, Colonel, I must tell you. She is out of this damned nonsense about becoming a Sikh. I am so pleased, and I bet you are too.'

Savage said to me, 'You're going to Gondwara?' I waited for him to ask nastily who gave me leave to go anywhere, but he didn't. He said, 'Consider yourself so ordered. And you didn't have time to change into uniform.'

Pater pulled out the big railway watch from his trouser pocket. 'We must get a move on. You will dirty that nice uniform, sir. You ought to wear old clothes for this job.'

'It's an old set,' Savage said. 'After you.' He followed Pater and me up into the cab. Pater picked a piece of dasootie out of a box and began to rub his fingers through it. From then on he did that all the time. He settled himself on the jump seat, put on a single glove, and told the fireman to hose down the footplate.

A pea-whistle shrilled down the platform. I saw Mr Glover, the conductor-guard, his white uniform glittering like a jewel as he stepped out into the sun from under the shade of the platform canopy. He waved a green flag. The Stationmaster passed on the signal to Pater.

Pater said, 'We are quite a crowd in here, aren't we? But I have had more than this, when half a dozen of those damned inspecting officers want to see why the drivers are using so much coal.' He laughed delightedly, grabbed the whistle-cord, which stretched in a tight loop over his head, and tugged sharply. 'Show me the key, Mothi,' he said.

The first fireman reached down the bamboo hoop with its slotted steel ball from its place. Pater began to explain to Colonel Savage what it was for.

'You only have to use these on a single line?' Savage asked, handing the key back. It was good to hear him asking silly questions. I didn't understand how any grown-up, educated person would not know at least that much.

Pater said, 'All ready now?'

He slapped the younger fireman on his bare brown shoulder. They were both burly fellows, Hindus, bare to the waist, below that wearing blue dungarees cut off at the knee into long shorts. Each wore a filthy white turban on the back of his head. Mothi was about thirty-five, Tamoo about twenty-five.

Mothi opened the firebox door. The furnace was a deep roaring bed of violet flames. Tamoo shovelled in coal. The safety valve on the firebox crown, a little in front of the cab, burst into a drumming buzz, and steam shot up forty feet into the air.

Pater tugged the whistle-cord again and opened the regulator which is a long lever. *Whooof!* the platform began to slide back. The safety valve shut down with a click as the steam went into the cylinders. *Whooof!* I saw the Stationmaster writing in a notebook; *whoof* – a man could still walk beside the train; *whoof* – he'd have to run; *whoof* – run fast; *whoof, whoof, whoof, whoof!*

Pater twirled a small wheel under his hand to shorten his cut-off. The exhaust settled down to a steady tramp, two beats a second – *whoof-whoof-whoof-whoof-whoof.* I could see a section of the boiler through the little forward window. The boiler was long and black and had three stainless steel bands round it between the front of the firebox and the back of the smokebox. The engine had a short thick funnel. The smoke and steam jerked up in exact time with the trampling beat. The boiler, the bands like steel girths, searched like a huge animal for its way among the maze of rails. Out in front of us the rails stretched like a hundred tangled snakes between the yards and the Loco Sheds, but we found our own path under the gantries. The sun had put out all the green and red eyes, so that the signals were like a page of semaphore for us to read, their drunken arms giving us the message. It was a book I had learned to read without being taught, the way I had learned English and Hindustani. I muttered the messages of the signals to myself, hugging myself with pleasure to be here, even in a sari, and not there in the gurdwara: Branch Line Crossover, clear. Up Yard Approach, clear – that was interlocked with the next one – Up Loco Shed, clear. Up Repair Shop Junction, clear. Up Yard Exit Junction, clear. In banks and rows and separate stands the arms fell back.

Number 4 Collett Road passed by. Our little house sat quietly there in its semi-detached compound behind the straggly hedge. Then there was nothing but the tramp, tramp, tramp of the engine, then a level-crossing, and tongas waiting, and lorries waiting behind the gates, and fifty men and women waiting.

Pater opened the regulator a little wider and spun the small wheel. The engine beat changed from a tramp to a hurried, less forceful breathing. My own breathing eased with the engine's. I felt that my nerves and muscles were slowly relaxing and settling back into old, well-worn places, and it was the jerk and heave of the footplate under my feet that was doing it.

Mothi opened the firebox door. Tamoo stood braced against the violet, near-white glare and threw in his first shovel loads to the full extent of the six-foot handle – two at the far back of the fire, one right, one left. Then with a short overarm twist of his wrist he let the coal fall off the shovel just inside the opening.

We passed Minoli Up Home signal. It was clear. As soon as he had seen it Mothi had nodded across to Pater. Hunched in his corner, Pater had nodded back.

In Minoli station we threw out the key for the section from Bhowani to Minoli, and picked up the one from Minoli to Babrotha. It was all done at speed, a projecting arm on the engine side whipping the new key off a post beside the line.

Minoli, Babrotha, Bijai. The sun beat down on the cab roof, and my head began to ache.

Khajaura, and Pater turned his little wheel, and the beat shortened and quickened as the train flung down the bank to the Karode bridge. Then we slowed heavily and rode out on to the bridge. All the time the engine hunted like a dog, swinging its nose from side to side as it rushed forward. This was the bridge someone had tried to blow up, or pretended to try to blow up, the night the ammunition train was looted. K. P. Roy. The wheels of the train made a long clamour, sometimes almost a tune, under the arched steel girders. The river was very low and small in its wide bed.

Mothi opened the firebox door. I shielded my eyes with my hand.

Karode. Pater heaved up the regulator again and lengthened his cut-off, and the exhaust dropped back into the same deep thunderous tramp as when we had started from Bhowani. The sides of the cutting rose in slabs of reddish jagged rock. Yellow grass clung in the crevices, and there were jackal holes level with

246

the cab, so that I could see into them a little way, and some bright small yellow flowers there on the thorn bushes.

The engine had taken me away from the five Loved Ones, but now it was beginning to punish me. The hollow thunder and the ceaseless pound and heave began to pull me apart. I had never been on an express, never been more than ten miles in the cab of any engine. I should not have come here for this test, so over-wrought and frightened and tired. I began to be sure that some great catastrophe was coming to meet us, or lying in wait for us, some point of explosion that would bury the five Loved Ones and the sari and my weeks of nervous effort. It would be appalling, but it would have to come, as a sort of expiation.

Pater yelled, 'Now we have up grades, but easier than this, all the way to Mayni. Twenty-three miles.' Gradually but definitely our speed increased until we were going steadily uphill at about thirty-five or forty miles an hour.

Pater settled back and lit his pipe. He sat like a sack on the jump seat, jolting heedlessly with the engine.

Pipalkhera Up Distant – on! Pater put up his hand, and the whistle screamed. Half a mile ahead the notched yellow arm of the signal nodded down. The firebox glared open.

My mouth dropped open. My head throbbed. I waited for the explosion, the derailment, the catastrophe. We ran shrieking through Pipalkhera. The Stationmaster stood on the platform with a flag, and there was a coolie asleep under a small tree, two dogs fighting on glaring yellow sand, the shadowed bars of the water tower across the tracks, our wheels hitting the points with a quick stammering thud-thud, and a cow in a field on the right – and out. Pipalkhera Up Starter, and we ran away into the reeling plain.

Lidhganj.

I looked ahead. The line ran straight, like an arrow, racing forward from under the boiler down the centre of the right of way. Now low jungle lay grey in the heat on either side. Pater passed round tea. We emptied the thermos, and Mothi made more. Colonel Savage lit a cheroot. I watched the line ahead. There would be a break in the shining ribbon. I would have a second after I saw it to gather myself for what was going to happen.

Taklana.

The line tilted more steeply up, winding to the left, round to the

247

right, round to the left. On the banked rails the engine leaned over the bushes and groaned and clanked, and the pipes drummed, and all the faces of the dials were steady, and the water gauges were steady. The steel plate that covers the join between the engine and tender slid backward and forward, right and left, under my feet. Mothi opened the firebox door, and I covered my eyes. I saw nothing, but I heard, and by then I knew it by heart – the long throws, the scoop and heave of coal from the forward part of the tender, the rustle under the roar as the coal fell, a short heave, and again, and the long shovel scraping on the footplate with a ringing note like a bell. The firebox door slammed and shut out the suck and roar of the fire. I heard the heavy gurgle of the water swaying in the tender behind me – four thousand gallons. I heard the hiss of the small hose, and, 'Pardon, miss-sahiba,' I moved my feet, and Tamoo hosed down the footplate and squirted the coal in the tender. Shiny black chips lay in the shallow water. Steam rose, but in a minute the footplate was again dry and dusty. My feet were burning. J had left my shoes outside the gurdwara. Tamoo scrambled up on to the tender and shovelled coal down from the back to the front. Then he ran down the slope of coal and grabbed up the long-handled firing shovel. Mothi lifted his arm, and the firebox door clanged open.

Savage was shouting something across to me. Unwillingly I opened my eyes to the searing-white, heaving furnace. Savage shouted, 'I said it would be worth being derailed for this.'

We ran through Mayni. A goods train standing on the passing line made a long clattering blur as we hurried by. Now we had two lines – one up, one down – all the way through Mayni Tunnel and into Shahpur. Pater pointed forward with the stem of his pipe. 'Mayni Tunnel. One and a half miles, and climbing all the way. It will be hot.'

Savage stood up and stretched unsteadily. He said, 'Hot? What do you call it now? It must be a hundred and thirty in this cab.' Pater chuckled and nodded. The sun was low now on the right, but it had been a burning afternoon, and always the furnace flaming thirstily there by our feet.

The sides of the Mayni cutting climbed higher, became more red, more rocky. They climbed above the sun, and there was shade down on the line, but the heat did not get any less. Pater

248

held down the whistle-cord for a long five-second blast. The mouth of the Mayni Tunnel gaped wide and black and suddenly swallowed us.

At once it was dark, and our world and our train vanished in the shouting of the exhaust, though I knew the headlight was on. But I could not breathe. I could not breathe. The air was too hot to breathe. The firebox door clanged, and I held my eyes open and for a fraction of a second saw blue shorts, a bare and hairy leg, the brown face and the perspiration pouring down and the drips sizzling on the steel plate. Then the heaving white fire swallowed it all. The air hurt my nostrils, bored into my eyes, burned in the back of my throat. I opened my mouth wide. Suffocating, I jumped to my feet. Savage's blue eyes hung in front of me; his face was dead white in the fierce glare, and his mouth was open. His hand fell on my arm, his fingers dug into the flesh above my my elbow. His eyes were amazed, then I saw angry fear, then plain anger, and with a huge effort he sucked in a breath. As though we had only one brain between us, I breathed with him. The fierce light dulled, the long shovel clanked and flew over the face of the fire. Gritty smoke beat back in heavy violent pulses from the tunnel roof, and the smoke was red hot. I closed my eyes again and sat still, breathing the air slowly and painfully, shutting my ears against the terrible, enlarged clanging of the engine. This was the catastrophe that I had been waiting for. My mind was gone, surrendered to the heat. The will that kept me here and made me breathe was not my own. Savage's hand pressed on my bare arm, telling me when to breathe. Without it, I would have jumped over the side.

But I was safe. I opened my eyes and made myself breathe. Savage relaxed his grip, but his hand still lay, weightless, in the crook of my elbow.

We climbed up through the yelling darkness. As a test I made myself pick out, from all the clanging and grinding and shrieking of steel, the slow *whoof, whoof, whoof* of the blast. Each beat threw a pattern of light on to the roof of the tunnel.

The boiler burst out into daylight, and the air was ice cold. I stood up, trembling, to let it play over me. I was soaked in perspiration, and the clammy sari was clinging to my body. Savage went slowly back to his own side.

Pater ran one finger across his forehead and down each cheek, dashing a river of perspiration to the footplate. He said, 'It is always hot coming up, Colonel – because of the cut-off being high and the regulator open. One hundred and sixty-seven degrees; a fellow took the temperature once in there in his cab. But that was three o'clock in the afternoon, with a coal train. Now we are over the top, and there is Shahpur.'

The fish-tailed distant signal was on. Pater closed the regulator with a heave. The steam pressure rose quickly. The safety valve lifted with a pop, and steam hissed out and blew back in a thick cloud over the cab roof. Pater opened his vacuum brake ejector slightly and closed it again. The engine heaved, the brakes sighed, the wheels sang a slower tune.

I saw the platform: Up Home, clear; Up Starter, on. Pater eased the brakes on. All down the train the wheels sang louder and slower. The platform swung out to meet our buffer beam, missed, and slid by. The wheels set up a low, quiet scream. That died, and with a last heave the footplate was still. The steam rose in a tall straight column from the safety valve; the smoke gathered in a grey pall above the boiler.

29

I TURNED my head slowly because my neck hurt. I heard the bustle and murmur of people, sounds which grew louder as my mind focused on them. There *were* other people in the world then, and there was my Pater standing on the platform beside the engine, a long-nosed oilcan in his hand. I saw him bend over the connecting-rod and touch the back of his other hand to the ends of the axles. The water tower, white-painted, stood high over the station buildings on its steel stilts. I read the name painted in huge black letters on it: SHAHPUR. Colonel Savage had gone.

I climbed carefully down to the platform. The engine had beaten me all over my body with rubber and steel rods. I went to my father and asked, 'Where is Colonel Savage?' I ought to ask Savage for leave. He had been nice not to make a fuss in Bhowani in front of Pater.

Pater looked up, a drip from the oilcan falling on his trousers. He said, 'Didn't you see? You must have been in a daze, girl. He went back to his compartment. He said he'd see you in Bhowani.' He looked at me with concern, his eyes screwed up. I understood so well now the reason for that habitual tightening round the eyes. My own eyes were half closed, and I did not want ever to open them wide again. There was too much light if you did. 'Are you all right, girl?' Pater asked anxiously. 'Was it too much for you, then?'

I said, 'No, Pater. I'm all right. It was hot in the tunnel though, wasn't it?'

He said, 'It is always hot in the Mayni Tunnel on up trains. Look, you had better be going. Tell Jimmy Rovira I am sorry not to see them. It has been a long time. You have got a compartment? The train is full.'

I said, 'Yes. Thanks for letting me come on the footplate. It was wonderful.'

He said, 'Don't thank me, Victoria. It was the colonel's doing. He is a fine gentleman. We would make a good driver out of him if he ever wants to leave the military department. You tell him that. Yes, you tell him that!' He chuckled delightedly. Then he said, 'And, Victoria, I can't tell you how pleased I am about the other thing. It would have been all wrong. But there, you found that out for yourself.' He bent over the piston-rod and ran his eye along the heavy grease-shining steel of the guide bars.

I walked down the platform, threading slowly through the crowd. Dogs searched under the train for scraps. One had only three legs. There were always plenty of those – dogs that had not learned while they were puppies when to move out from under the wheels. I had not had time to reserve a place in the train, and I wondered why I had told Pater otherwise. I walked down the train, looking in at all the windows. The third-class passengers, jammed into their long, uncompartmented carriages, stared back at me without curiosity. Showers of peanut shells flew out of the windows, and occasional sharp jets of betel juice added to the spattered red stains on the stone. All the second-class compartments were full of prosperous Indians or British warrant officers. As an Army officer I could travel first class for second-class fare, but I didn't have the proper forms.

I found an Anglo-Indian family of three in a second-class four-berth compartment. I did not know them. I hesitated in front of the compartment because I had been up and down, and except for this the train was full up. The husband stood in the doorway and said, 'Don't come in here. Our little girl has the whooping cough. You will never get a wink of sleep.' He spoke in Hindustani with no attempt at sympathy or politeness. His little girl looked very well. There were black stains on my sari, and my feet were dirty and sore.

Absolute exhaustion hung very close over me. I had to sit down soon, or I would fall down. I started to walk back up the train.

A voice said close to my ear, 'Did you run away in such a hurry that you forgot to book a place?'

Colonel Savage was sitting in a cane chair by the open window of a first-class coupé. Beyond him I saw Birkhe putting out a hairbrush and a comb and a bottle of whisky on the little table. The top berth was folded up and the bathroom door open. A round plaster covered part of Birkhe's forehead near his eye. Savage had taken off his boots and socks and opened his bush shirt. A Penguin book lay open in his lap. His face was clean and newly washed. Beads of fresh perspiration were forming to run down the clean face, and his hands and fingernails were clean.

I said shortly, 'Yes, sir.'

He said, 'Come in here.'

I shifted my weight from one foot to the other. I muttered, 'I can't do that, sir.' The weaving footplate was under my feet. I saw the breathing fire and heard the bell-clang of the long-handled shovel and felt myself rolling where I stood.

'Don't be a fool,' he said. 'Come in. You can hardly stand.'

My palms were slippery wet. I could find Mr Glover, the conductor, and ask him to get me into the train somewhere. But that meant more walking about, more searching. I wanted just to stand there and cry. Mr Glover's pea-whistle blew peremptorily from somewhere miles away. The hubbub on the platform rose to a continuous, unfrightened shriek.

Savage put down his book, came to the door, opened it, and stepped down. He took my arm and helped me up into the compartment and pulled the door shut behind him. The engine whistle blew. Mr Glover's whistle blew. I stood in the narrow space between the lower berth and the wall, looking down at the brilliant blue-spangled border of my sari. Why had I ever put that on? How long ago had they given me sugar and water to drink and stirred up my insides with a two-bladed dagger?

The platform noise rose sharply, and the train jerked and began to move. I sat down suddenly, my knees turned to milk. A man clasping a hot chupatti, throwing it from one hand to the other, ran furiously alongside the train, shouting, 'Open the door, brother.' He disappeared. Birkhe had disappeared. Savage had disappeared.

I heard the tinkle of running water, and Savage came out of the tiny bathroom. He stood over me, holding with one hand to the edge of the upturned upper berth, swaying to the lilt of the train as it picked up speed. He said, 'Get in there and have a shower now. I've left all my things. The towel's a bit wet. Here.'

He gave me his hand, pulled me up, and pushed me into the bathroom. I locked the door carefully, testing it twice, and began to undress.

I took off my sari and looked down unbelievingly at myself in panties, girdle, and brassière. What had I put a girdle on for? As a last line of defiance, to prove to my skin that I was not really a Sikh? It had left ribbed lines on my behind, and it was soaked with perspiration. I washed out my pants and then leaned over the basin and closed my eyes, pressing my forehead against the cold mirror in futile exasperation, because I had remembered that I had no others. The day was not ended even yet. I had no place to sleep until I got to the Roviras', God knew when. I opened the window and hung the pants out to dry in the wind, jamming them under the glass, then turned to the shower.

Afterward I wanted to clean my teeth. I ground them together, and the grit grated like sand between them. I sniffed Colonel Savage's toothbrush. It was supposed to be a terrible thing to do, but I needed it. He had used it, so he would not notice if I did. He might hear through the door. No, the train was making too much noise. He couldn't kill me even if he did smell toothpaste on my breath. I took the toothbrush, put on a lot of paste, and began to scrub and rinse.

When I came out of the bathroom I felt clean except for the stiffness in the sari. Being clean changed the sort of tiredness I had. Before, I'd had a nervous headache, a kind of restless exhaustion. Now my legs and eyelids were heavy and my body was calm and my mind turning over very slowly. I sat down carefully on the lower berth.

Savage said, 'You still look as if you'd been under a steamroller – but you're clean, at any rate.'

He put down his book, got up, and poured a lot of whisky into each of two tumblers. He rummaged under the berth and dragged out a tin box half filled by a single huge block of ice. Three bottles of Murree beer and half a dozen bottles of soda water lay on the ice. They had melted forms for themselves, like hares, and the dirty water was sloshing about in the bottom of the box with the labels floating in it. Savage jerked open the cap of a soda bottle on the metal opener built into the bathroom door, and began to pour. 'Say when,' he said.

I said, 'When, sir.'

He took his own glass, slumped back in the chair at the bottom of the berth, and put his bare feet up on the wall opposite. He said, 'When are you going to stop playing hare and hounds with your WAC (I) commission?'

I drank, and answered automatically, 'I don't know what you mean, sir.'

He said, 'For Christ's sake stop calling me "sir" for a few minutes and answer a question honestly.'

I knew why he was being abusive to me. He wanted me to get so angry I would say more than I meant to. But I was too tired.

He said, 'I suppose I can't call you a traitor to your king and country, because you'll flourish your beautiful new sari at me and say that George is not your king and this is not his country.'

It was a short strong whisky he'd given me. I expected it to burn my throat, but it didn't. Perhaps I didn't have the energy to react, certainly not enough to argue. He was still trying to make me angry. But he didn't know that I was glad to be with him because he wasn't a Sikh, because I understood everything he said, even the abuse. I looked at my empty glass, and he refilled it. I began to say, I haven't been a traitor, but it seemed a waste of time. The dust whirled away in a long plume, light against the twilight, past the green-tinted windows. It had seemed pitch dark in there at first, but not now. I saw with surprise that the electric lights were on.

I said, 'I didn't know what to do. I wanted to be an Indian. Everything went wrong.'

'Murder is wrong,' he said.

He said it quite gently. I said, 'It wasn't murder, it –'

He interrupted me. 'They died. Someone killed them.'

I said, 'Who died? What do you mean?'

He said, 'Those B.O.R.s in the smash at Pathoda. You saw some of them die, didn't you? That's why I made you go up there with me.'

My heart was bumping and the glass slowly shaking in my hand.

He said, 'I know you are lying about K. P. Roy. I've always known. You know something about him.'

I sighed, put down the glass, and slowly wrung my fingers together. Now was the time for me to get free, while the wheels beat *clickety-clack*, *clickety-clack*, and the dust hung in a pale motionless blur on the darkness, and the electric lights shone reflected in the windows. When I had spoken I would have no place to go at all – in the cantonments, or the city, or the Railway Lines.

I gathered myself and said, 'But I killed Lieutenant Macaulay.'

Savage carefully put down his glass and said, 'Tell me.'

I said dreamily, 'I killed Lieutenant Macaulay. In the yards. There was a goods train passing.' I told him about it. There had been a goods train while Ranjit stood beside me staring down on the body. It had passed by on the other side of the rows of wagons, easing up opposite us so that the chains clanked and the buffers struck together, *clang-clang-clang* all down the train. The brake van would have stopped just the other side of where we crouched in the black grit, but the signal must have gone off and the light blinked to green, and even now I can hear the strain on the chains and the heave of the train and the slow whoofing from the engine as the driver opened her up to go on north through Bhowani Junction.

I said, 'He was trying to rape me. He put his hands on me.'

Savage's face was cold then, and his eyes brilliant. He seemed short of breath. He said, 'But you'd led him on.'

I knotted up inside, and my skin began to shiver of its own accord. I said, 'I didn't!'

He said, 'Christ, I *saw* you. The day the battalion arrived you backed your luscious arse into him. In the yards – near where you killed him.'

I jumped up and stood over him where he sat tensely in the chair. I screamed down at him, 'In the yards he put his hands on me that day, and I wouldn't stand it. But I didn't want to get him into trouble with you, that first time. That is what happened! Then in the Traffic Office it was worse. Ranjit saved me, and I wanted to complain. Patrick complained for me, but you pretended you thought it was Ranjit he was complaining about! You knew all the time who it was. You thought I ought to do what he wanted because I am only a bloody cheechee. I killed him with that fishplate. I found it under my hand when he threw me down!'

I shouted out the whole story. I told him about Ranjit and Ghanshyam. I told him how my fear and shame had changed to pride when the Sirdarni talked to me. I got it all out.

Then I fell back on the berth, picked up my whisky, and drank it.

The train ground to a stop. 'Timrai Junction,' Savage said, not looking out. 'Your father leaves us here today.'

I muttered, 'Yes.'

Mr Glover knocked on the door and came in to look at our tickets. I sat on the berth, thinking miserably of what a mess I was in, while Colonel Savage bought a ticket for me. Mr Glover gave me a curious look as he went out; he knew my family quite well. Birkhe came in with more bottles of soda and a plate of chicken sandwiches. He put them down on the table and asked whether the colonel-sahib wanted anything more for the moment. Savage shook his head. I saw Pater walking down the platform beside the train. He had put his coat on now and taken off the red bandanna. He looked old, tired, and very dirty under the glaring lamps. He saw me in the compartment and made to come forward, but then he saw Colonel Savage and stopped, smiling. He waved his hand and went away.

Birkhe said, 'Salaam, sahib. Salaam, miss-sahiba,' and got out, closing the door behind him. The train jerked forward.

When Savage spoke again his voice was quite different. It became conversational, but the kind of conversation people make when a bigger thing is in their minds and they are bottling it up until it is ready.

He said, 'Macaulay had it coming to him. And then a couple of days later you appeared in a sari. It was pretty obvious, you know.'

I said, 'Oh, was it really?'

'Govindaswami was sure you'd done it. I *knew* you'd done it. Another of our yard sentries saw you crossing the railway and skulking along Limit Road when you were supposed to be in the Institute.'

Munching a sandwich, I asked why the Collector didn't have me arrested.

Savage told me: Because he thought I'd find out, sooner or later, that K. P. Roy and the Sirdarni weren't the best friends Ranjit could have, and then I'd be able to help him – Govindaswami – a lot.

Savage found a tin of cigarettes in his parachute bag and gave me one. 'Better smoke this to exorcise the presence of the One, Aum,' he said.

I saw him in clear focus, but a little larger than life. I heard his voice that had so often sounded cold and nasal, now as clear as a tenor bell. The narrow little compartment magnified him, and I could also see his face reflected in the glass of the window. An electric light bulb glittered above his head. I lifted my wrist to look at my watch. My hand moved slowly, and I noticed that the skin of my wrist was flawless. The watch hung steady, all by itself, a thing apart from me and apart from everything else. To test the sharpness of the separation I looked at other things in turn, and listened to other sounds beyond the tick of the watch. It was true. Each object that I concentrated on separated out and became wholly important, obvious, all-absorbing. I looked at Colonel Savage's forehead. Three beads of perspiration hung there above his left eyebrow. I thought of my own forehead. It was cool and smooth. I thought of my ears. I knew the shape of them, and perspiration was forming behind them. Later it would run slowly down the side of my neck.

I said, 'It was awful, trying to be an Indian. No one understood me.'

The inane words hovered there, quite clear and full and round above me, and stayed in my ears as echoes. Unhurriedly I tried to bring them back to change them. There was plenty of time before they left me for good and set out on their journey to Rodney

Savage in the chair. I said, 'Pater and Patrick don't understand what is going to happen. Ranjit doesn't understand what is happening. You don't understand what has happened. But I found I couldn't change myself.'

He said, 'I know.'

I said thickly, 'You knew? You've been so beastly to me.' If I spoke clearly and was honest with him, he would see what it was really like. Then he would be able to help me. He was strong enough. I said, 'May I have another drink, sir?'

I smiled at him to tell him I didn't really mean the 'sir'. He said, 'You're half drunk already. Are you sure you want another?'

I said, 'Yes, please. And another cigarette.'

I sank back on the berth, rested my head on the parachute bag, and lit the cigarette. It took a long time, but Colonel Savage did not get up to help me. I blew out the smoke in a long thin stream. I said, 'Even a cigarette tastes better now.'

He said, 'Do you think I've never been afraid?'

I closed my eyes. It was wonderful. I'd told him, and now I didn't have to worry any more. He'd tell me what to do. The cigarette tasted lovely, and the whisky was warm and wonderful in my stomach. It was not hot, but just lovely and warm in the carriage. There was a warm, almost forgotten thing, like a thin silk blanket, wrapped round me. Slowly I recognized it. It was security, it was protection, it was happiness.

My God, it was him.

He was moving slowly in the compartment. I heard his chair creak, then his bare feet on the floor. He knew, a fraction of a second before I did.

His lips came slowly down on mine, and his fingers slid slowly back in my hair. For a breath I held my lips closed against him, then all the sensations separated out as before, and there was only one. I parted my lips and hung for a long time on his mouth. The lights clicked off. His hands moved, and my ache was gone. The train rocked him closer against me, and a million miles away the whistle shrilled.

The train ran through a station. Lights flashed in at the windows, each light like a blinking, vanishing thought on the surface of a deep waiting. I think I'd always been waiting for this.

258

The station flung back under a long stammering of the wheels across a score of sets of points. I opened my eyes to see his dim face, so tense and hard and close, and put my arms round his neck.

Later I heard my voice crying, 'Yes,' and, 'Yes,' and long, long afterwards I sat up, took my whisky, and looked through the glass of the window at the racing darkness and the black shadow-trees. He lay there – I knew him all of a sudden, the man with the complexes – hating himself for being so passionate and expert.

I bent over him, kissed his forehead, and whispered, 'Why didn't you –?'

'Do this sooner?' he finished for me.

I nodded and kissed him again. I said, 'I didn't know, but I think you always have.' I remembered what Molly Dickson had said – 'Is that man in love with you?' Rodney must be quite an easy person to understand as long as you weren't involved with him.

He lay back, his hands joined behind his head. He said, 'I believe in ordeal by fire – that night at the Institute when they wouldn't dance with you, for instance. Other times. I wanted to see what you were made of. Perhaps I felt too serious about you, too. I did think you were angling for Macaulay though, at first. I couldn't stand it. Then I knew that it had to be you. It had to be you, like this, without a word spoken, without any begging or asking or refusing or petting or ogling or hand-stroking.'

He hummed the tune: 'It had to be you, it had to be you, it had to be you.'

I had been drunk. But that had all gone and left no hangover. I didn't remember ever feeling better, ever in my life being so warmly wrapped up in certainty. I swayed against him on purpose, as the train swayed, so that my breast would press against him. He kissed my breast, and on his lips something slipped through the warmth and security, and I said, 'I don't want to fall in love with you.'

He raised his head, frowned at me, and said, 'Don't you? I rather hope I do fall in love with you. Perhaps I have. I'm not sure.'

'Why do you hope?' I closed my eyes lazily. I wanted to kiss his feet and wash them so that he would be cool. But already, again, I saw his eyes.

'Oh, Rodney,' I said, 'be careful. I'm afraid I am going to love you.' For a minute more I was able to think and hold on to a little fear, even under his mouth. Then I gave up my power of thinking, gave it to him with everything else that he wanted. Over and over in my mind, before I slept, ran the tune and the silly words – 'It had to be you.'

BOOK THREE

Rodney Savage

male, thirty-four, English, unmarried;
lieutenant-colonel commanding 1st Battalion
13th Gurkha Rifles, Indian Army

30

I WOKE up with a start and a bright light in my eyes. The silence was as loud as it is after a concentration of 155s had just hit you. The wheels had stopped, the windows weren't rattling or the berths creaking or the carriage frame murmuring. Someone's body moved across the light outside, and I saw a face at the window six inches from my head. The man was cupping his hands to hold out the light so that he could see in. His nose was flattened against the glass. I could have moved or pulled up the shutter, but I wanted to see Victoria, naked, getting up. She sprang up and knelt on the berth by my head. She and the face stared at each other for a second. She looked as beautiful as – a naked woman kneeling by a naked man's head. Then she jerked up the shutter and gasped. 'Rodney, Patrick's at the window!'

I rolled out and flipped down the catch on the door. We were off. I knew that it must have been Patrick. As soon as I get something good and wonderful and kind, like Victoria, I start to lose it.

I stood up, yawned, and pulled down the blind on the door. The door shook and rattled. Taylor hammered on it with his fists and shouted, 'Come out! I saw you! Oah, you dirtee little slut!' He had a strong, Anglo-Indian accent. Victoria's was only noticeable when she got excited.

She stood there, trembling, like a big smooth doe, between the berth and the wall. I examined her carefully, to remember. God knew when this would ever happen again. I put one hand round her neck and tickled her with the other. She tried to push me away, but I held her and kissed her hard while the door shook and groaned. Then I said, 'You'd better take your clothes and get dressed. In there.' I nodded to the bathroom and stooped to pick up my trousers.

'But – what about Patrick?' she said. She stood in the tiny bathroom, the door open, struggling into her brassière and girdle.

'What about him?' I said. I began to brush my hair. She couldn't find her pants – in Punjabi, her *kachh*, signifying self-restraint. The door-handle rattled. Taylor's mouthing was almost unintelligible. 'Oah, come out! Oah, you slut! Oah, you –!'

She whispered, 'Do I look all right?'

I switched on the bathroom light and looked at her, and said, 'Okay.' I smiled and tried to make out that I was quite relaxed. I pulled a cheroot from my case and told her to put some lipstick on. Otherwise, she'd never looked better. Sex suited her.

She had to smile when I told her that, and she gave me a quick kiss before she picked up her lipstick. Patrick hammered and hammered. Another voice joined in outside there, and I recognized it as Bill Heatherington's. Bill said, 'Please be quiet, my good man. Do you know if this is Colonel Savage's compartment?'

Taylor yelled, 'I don't know! Why the hell should I know? Of course it is his. I saw him with –'

Bill said, 'There's no need to shout.'

'There,' Victoria whispered breathlessly, 'I'm ready.' She smoothed out the folds of her sari and stood quivering like a violin string. It was the kind of situation people tell me they dream about and wake up sweating with embarrassment. I stood there, puffing steadily, and all the lights were blazing in the compartment. I told her, 'You look like a recruit on his first quarter guard.'

She said, 'Oh, *Rodney*! What are we going to do?' She was entangled in God knows how many sets of values that didn't mean a damned thing to me, or that I'd grown away from – but I wasn't going to give her up. I made up my mind at that instant that I would fight – that I must fight – for her with everything I'd got.

So I opened the door. Taylor stumbled on the top step and burst in like a bomb. I put out my arm to steady him and said, 'Careful, Taylor. You'll be hurting yourself.'

He stood there, pressed back against the wall, with his chest heaving. He was like a big, brave, clumsy buffalo, even to the pale blue-green eyes. He didn't seem to notice me, though my hand was resting on his sleeve, but glared directly at Victoria. Bill Heatherington stood behind him, outside the door. Bill is plump and fortyish, with a small fair moustache and blue eyes. Behind Bill was Birkhe, his eyes dancing and his face as unreadable as a Bath bun. Indian passengers hurried past in the light streaming out of the station buildings. The vendors and hawkers chanted their wares up and down the platform. A clock face directly above Birkhe's head said 10.16 p.m. This was Gondwara.

Taylor shook his left fist under Victoria's nose. In his right hand he brandished her pants. They were pink briefs with a thin edging of lace round the legs. Taylor bawled, 'I saw you lying naked on thee bed, like a tart! Naked on thee bed, I saw you. Oah, you are a –! Oah, you –!' He lashed out at her with his fist. I tightened my grip on his arm and pulled him back with a jerk, so that his fist hit the wall, not very hard. Bill Heatherington was laughing silently.

Taylor turned on me and bawled, 'And you, you stuck-up rotter! Just because you are a colonel in thee military department you think you can play fast and loose with my girl. You tried to get me out of thee way by killing me with an ink bottle, didn't you?'

I was sorry I'd never had a chance to apologize to him about that. Now wasn't the time. I said, 'Please talk softer, Taylor. I have a pierced eardrum. And stop insulting Miss Jones. I don't know whether she is your girl, but I do know that she is my Intelligence Officer. She was not naked, nor was I.'

'I saw you!' he screamed, pounding the berth with his hand.

Heatherington broke in with, 'Want any help, Rodney?' and climbed on to the upper step of the door.

I said, 'No thanks, Bill. Mr Taylor's rather excitable, but he is not dangerous.' I don't know why I had to be so unpleasant. Well, I do. Plain, common jealousy, available at all Woolworths.

Taylor went quite pale and said slowly, 'I will shoot you, Mister Colonel bloody Savage, I will shoot you.'

I said, 'I think defenceless Indian clerks are more your mark, Taylor.' It wasn't fair, but I don't play fair. I play to win.

Taylor stared at me and said with a kind of shocked wonder, 'You are a cad, Colonel Savage. You know I was onlee doing my duty to protect the armoured car.' He was a most admirable man, really.

I said, 'I understand, Taylor. Now – get out.'

But he stood there still, in his dirty white shirt and his old St Thomasian's tie and his down-at-heel black shoes, between us two colonels of infantry. Then he said, pleading with Victoria,

'Vickee, you _were_ on the berth, weren't you? I saw you. I am not drunk.'

She waited for me to answer. She wanted me to speak, and then it wouldn't be her own hands that destroyed him. But I am not a cricketer. I am only a good first slip. I said nothing. At last she said, 'No, I wasn't. Please go away, Patrick. I don't want to speak to you.'

Taylor's big hands opened and closed, but there was no one he could strangle there; they groped round for something to hold on to, but Victoria had moved out of his reach. He turned and stumbled out – with her pants.

Victoria's knees were shaking, and she sat down suddenly on the edge of the berth. Bill cleared his throat twice, obviously wondering whether he should say anything about what he had just seen. He kept his eyes away from Victoria. Someone blew a whistle, and I said, 'We'd better get off the train.' I told Birkhe to bring out our kit.

It was cooler on the platform. I had begun to develop quite an eye for the beauty of the railway, and I don't mean Victoria. The train made a good curve on the curved platform, and was finished off by a curve in another plane, the engine's boiler and the stainless steel bands round it. The signal up there flicked to green, and the highlights on the boiler and on the steel bands changed from ruby to emerald.

I wondered why Bill had come down to meet me. I told him I could have found my way out to his camp. Then I said, 'You haven't met Subaltern Jones, have you? Victoria, Bill Heatherington. He commands the Thirtieth Raj Rif.'

'I've seen your name often,' she said, holding out her hand. Bill murmured, 'How do you do, Miss Jones.'

The train pulled out, southbound, and the empty rails were left there shining under the lights. I had to put Bill straight. I said, 'Victoria is a WAC (I). She's been doing Battalion Intelligence Officer as well as Railway Liaison Officer for me.' I paused a long time and then added softly, speaking directly at Heatherington and looking at him and smiling, 'And, she's a very nice girl.'

Heatherington grinned cheerfully at her then, she smiled back, and all the awkwardness had gone. It's as easy as winking, if you're born a son of a bitch, in the happy American phrase. The trouble is that the only people I like are people who can't do it, like Birkhe – and all Gurkhas, for that matter – and Taylor. Now Heatherington's inquisitiveness was satisfied, and Victoria's reputation was at least partly refurbished. Heatherington was still smiling, as though saying to himself, Well, you lucky bastard. Or perhaps he was smiling because Victoria was so beautiful and in love, and a very nice girl. Anyway, his look was just that – very nice, nothing more.

Heatherington clicked his tongue, stopped, and fumbled in his pocket. He handed me a signal form and said, 'Here, Rodney. This came for you an hour ago. I've just remembered that I came to the station to give it to you.'

I took it, read it, and handed it to Victoria. This is it: SECRET. TO 30 RAJ RIF FROM 1/13 GR. FOR LIEUTENANT-COLONEL SAVAGE PERSONAL FROM COLLECTOR BHOWANI BEGINS TAYLOR HAS AUTHORIZED SEVERAL AFI MEN KEEP ARMS WITH THEM AS PERSONAL PROTECTION AGAINST ANTI-EUROPEAN ACTIVITIES HE CLAIMS TO HAVE RECEIVED YOUR PRIOR AUTHORITY RESULTING SITUATION INFLAMMABLE PLEASE RETURN BHOWANI EARLIEST TO DISCUSS WITH ME REGARDS GOVINDASWAMI ENDS

She handed it back to me and said slowly, 'Patrick has a pistol on him. I saw it in his pocket.'

I hadn't noticed that.

I worked out that Taylor must have come down there to talk to the lieutenant of the Gondwara A.F.I. platoon. He'd find himself in front of a firing squad for fomenting a mutiny if he wasn't careful. I wondered where he'd got to. I told Birkhe to ask the Stationmaster where he was, and bring him to us if he could.

'*Jee-lo, huzoor,*' Burke said.

It didn't matter a damn where Taylor was, except that I wanted him back in Bhowani after I'd talked to Govindaswami. I said, 'Victoria, your leave is cancelled.'

She smiled at me, her lips parted and the big warm bedroom eyes shining. She said, 'It doesn't matter, sir. I hadn't even warned the Roviras that I was coming.'

It was lucky in one way that this affair came up at that moment. Otherwise she might have been thinking more of Patrick the wronged lover, instead of Taylor the angry buffalo.

I said, 'And now, when does the next bloody train on the Delhi bloody Deccan bloody Rail-bloody-way bloody well leave for Bho-bloody-wani?'

They laughed, and I took Victoria's arm and said, 'Let's go and get something to eat.'

'The next train back is Number One Down Mail, depart Gondwara twenty-three thirty-three, arrive Bhowani Junction oh-five forty-seven,' she said happily. She knew the time table by heart.

Heatherington said, 'My God, the girl's a walking Bradshaw.'

I said, 'She's a railway girl, from Bhowani. She's been wearing a sari to find out whether she prefers it that way.'

Bill glanced at her in the light streaming from the door of the European refreshment-room. He seemed to notice for the first time that she was an Anglo-Indian. He shook his head and said, 'It must be damned difficult.'

She smiled at him for that and said quickly, 'It is.'

Bill pushed open the door of the refreshment room, and I said, 'Not in there, Bill, for God's sake. I've had enough racing murghi and stewed prunes to last me until I'm ninety-five.' I led them a couple of doors along, into the non-vegetarian Hindu restaurant.

They followed me, and as we stood inside I caught Victoria looking at me with wonder and surprise in her face. By God, I knew why. I was young again, no more than twenty-five. There hadn't been any war, and I hadn't ordered a hundred attacks, and I hadn't got any M.C.s. She'd done it, simply by lying naked to take me, and answering me with love and gladness.

She laughed aloud with happiness, and Bill said, 'Miss Jones, when you smile you really are the most beautiful thing I've ever seen.'

So I had done the same to her.

She laughed again and said to Bill, 'You've been in India too long, sir, or you wouldn't say that to me.' She smiled, and looked at me to acknowledge how wonderful it was that she, an Anglo-Indian, could say a thing like that. Whatever happened afterwards, I knew she was rid of that fear for good. (George, you may give me another medal.)

The manager popped out of the back of the restaurant like a weevil out of a biscuit. 'Sahib!' he cried. 'You have come to *wrong* place! This is restaurant, Hindu, non-vegetarian.'

'I know,' I said, holding up my hand. 'But we are Hindus, non-vegetarian.' The place was empty, no trains were due in, and I asked him whether it would be all right. He beamed and said, 'Yes, yes, sah, quite all right, sah!'

'Then speak Hindustani to me, brother. You're not a Bombay bearer, and I'm not a gora,' I said in Hindustani, and his smile widened. This pidgin English was one of the worst things the wartime invasions of India had done, and I couldn't stand it any more than I could stand soldiers saying, 'Very good, sir.' I told the manager, 'As a matter of fact, we are on our way to attend a Congress meeting in Delhi as guests of the Mahatma and the Pandit. We are hungry. We also want some whisky to drink to the early departure of the English. Oh, yes, there'll be one more of us coming.'

He cried, 'Yes sah, yes sah. *Jee-han, sahib, jee-han, jee-han! Congress wale!*' He hurried out, shaking with laughter.

We leaned across the table and talked. Victoria laughed and talked with us. Bill and I disposed of the shop which I'd originally come down there to discuss with him, and she knew what we were talking about and made notes in my notebook for me. Birkhe came in and sat down with us. No one knew where Taylor was. Every now and then Birkhe and I would talk in Gurkhali while Victoria joked with Heatherington. The food came; we ate properly with our fingers and talked of Delhi and Bhowani, Calcutta and Bombay and Manali, Peshawar, Rawalpindi, and Poona, Razmak and Quetta. Victoria didn't really belong to that world, but for the moment she could believe she did. The people she'd worked with in Delhi wouldn't know Razmak from Friday, but she had heard enough to recognize the right cries, so she drank more whisky and got as high as a kite, but without getting frisky. The engine and I had given her such a going over that her body had become separated from her mind. Her body sat quietly in the chair, recuperating, while her mind sang and rejoiced round that room like a nightingale.

I saw her once look down at her sari. She giggled to herself, and we three men smiled at her because she was a lovely woman, and laughing. She didn't tell us why she was giggling, and we didn't ask. It was all natural and wonderful for her. She had to do nothing – not think or worry or wonder – just sit back and smile and

269

be a beautiful woman, her love visible and obvious in her eyes and in her smooth skin and flat belly and long-stretched embracing legs. By the time we got out of there I was in love.

Number 1 Down Mail rode slowly into the station, and Victoria stood talking to Bill while I got the conductor-guard to unlock a locked coupé. It was nearly midnight, but she didn't care a damn by then about getting into a compartment with me. She stepped up ahead of me and leaned out of the window to say good-bye to Heatherington. Late passengers hurried by, and station coolies struggled past with boxes on their heads. After the usual bouts of whistling the train began to move. She waved at Bill for an unconscionable time, but when she couldn't see him any more she turned and closed all the windows.

I said, 'Patrick's on the train.'

She said, 'Oh?' She was fiddling with her back hair in front of the mirror, turning her head this way and that. The pupils of her eyes were big and soft, and there were small dark rings under the lower lids. Her skin was the colour of dark ivory or pale milky coffee, and quite matt, unwrinkled, and calm. She said, 'I'll lock the doors.' She bent down to each door in turn and then pulled all the blinds.

She stood in the narrow space over me, and I saw her eyes begin to glisten. I used to see them as bedroom eyes, and they were, but they had all Victoria in them, so there was a lot of guts and kindness there as well as bed. She said, 'Rodney, I'm afraid. I love you.'

I said, 'I know.' It was impossible to imagine that this was all there could be for us. I undressed her carefully, with the love flowing out of my fingertips. She stood upright, proud as Diana, her legs braced apart against the rocking of the train.

We lay on the lower berth, struggling and sleeping and then struggling again. Jesus Christ, I thought again, it's impossible that all this flood of affection, and the shelter I've given her against fear, should come from just nothing but sex. She fell finally asleep at last, but I lay awake with my arm round her, listening to the night rushing by like a torrent, and listening to the wheels hammering, and thinking of her, and India, and the fellow up there, one of her people, as awake as I, who was taking us on behind the searching light of Number 1 Down Mail.

31

At Bhowani it was good to see Victoria getting out of a compartment down the train. I'd woken her up at Shahpur and put her there from some damned silly idea of protecting her good name. It was too late for that by then, and I know that secretly she would have preferred to stay with me – not to flaunt me, but simply because she wanted to be near me.

I was standing on the platform talking to the Collector. Govindaswami looked very black in that clear morning. His complexion was as unshiny as if he'd powdered it, and there was no sun to pick out the highlights on his cheekbones and jaw and frontal bones. I thought, Perhaps he does use powder. I wondered what shade would produce that strange strong-grained surface, which was almost purple in this placid lighting.

During the night Victoria had told me that K. P. Roy, in the guise of one Ghanshyam, had been hiding in the Sirdarni-sahiba's house. Ought I to tell Govindaswami this? I decided not to, because Sammy had always been sure of it anyway, and because Roy wasn't there now – we'd searched the place.

I beckoned to Victoria. When she came up I said to Govindaswami, 'Victoria ran away from the Khalsa, Sammy. But she's feeling better now. She burned her feet.'

Govindaswami looked at her keenly. He missed nothing. He was disappointed about what had happened to her, but I think he understood. He'd been through the same thing himself. He said to her, 'You tried, anyway. You'll both come and breakfast with me?'

Victoria began to say she really ought to be going, et cetera, but I said, 'Come along. We're going to talk shop, and I'm sure the Collector can lend you a notebook and pencil.' She made a gesture with her hands. She wanted to put on a skirt and a shirt, both clean, and get a pair of shoes on her feet, but she wouldn't leave me for that.

They'd sent down my station wagon, one of those ugly steel boxes sitting two feet above the axles, and it was waiting in the yard with Howland at the wheel and Tula, the driver, in the back.

Govindaswami murmured his thanks to me for my thoughtfulness in sending the wagon to pick him up on its way to the station – the Austin was always tricky to start first thing, he said.

I jerked my head, and Howland let go of the wheel unwillingly and moved back. I drove; Govindaswami sat beside me; Victoria sat with Howland in the second row of seats, and Birkhe with Tula in the third. As we left the yard I glanced over my shoulder and saw Patrick Taylor standing under the station arch, staring after us. Victoria saw him too.

Govindaswami and I talked in the front seat, but not about the A.F.I. situation. I did my best to keep up my end of the conversation and at the same time listen to Howland and Victoria behind me. I heard Master Albert say, 'Bee-yootiful plates a' meat you got, sis.' The little sod was eyeing her bare feet, and I thought, If I'm getting jealous over Howland, of all the impossible people in the world, I'm in for trouble.

Then Howland muttered, 'Don't be so snooty, Vicky. We'll be seeing lots of each other.' She said politely, 'I'm afraid not, Albert. I'll be released any day now.' Then I had to answer some question of Govindaswami's, and the next thing I heard was Howland saying, 'I'm walking aht wiv yer big sis, if you want to know. We go to the pitchers and 'old 'ands. She's a nice piece of homework, if you ask me.'

I was a fool not to see then and there how the situation was taking shape. I noted that Howland was trying to go to bed with Rose Mary. I noted that Rose Mary was a good deal smarter than Master Albert, so he'd probably finish up by getting married to her. I noted that Patrick had now been deserted by Rose Mary, in whom he obviously used to find a safety valve when Victoria left him. What I did not see, like the clever swine I am, was that the troubles were beginning to pile up too thickly on Patrick, and troubles were his trumps.

We got out at the Collector's bungalow. Behind Govindaswami we filed into the dining-room. Howland took the station wagon back to the lines with Birkhe and my small kit. After breakfast we moved to the study and sat down in the familiar, comfortable chairs. Sammy's authentic Oxford chamber-pot stood on its table in the window, full of flowers. The sun came up behind the trees along the railway line.

I put my hands behind my head and settled back. I caught Victoria looking fondly at me before she dropped her eyes to her notebook. Then we began. I said, 'I take it this A.F.I. business is just an excuse, Sammy. What's really happened? Has Surabhai laid an information against you for selling pardons after hours?'

Sammy didn't laugh. He said seriously, 'No, it's the A.F.I. A nice two-way hate. First, as you know, there's been a good deal of anti-European feeling in the city. Some of it is peaceful, and some of it, stirred up by Roy's people, is vicious. There has been no incident reported to me of an actual assault on or by a European.' He glanced at me and paused. I stared blandly back. I had never reported the bottle-throwing and the beating-up of the youths the night Molly Dickson came, but Sammy obviously knew. He went on, 'The Europeans, however, live up here in cantonments with a few hundred Gurkhas round the corner, and they seldom go into the city. The bad feeling has found a vulnerable target in the Anglo-Indians – stone-throwing, minor assaults, pushing and shoving in the street, abuse, and so on. Well, Taylor came to see me and claimed they weren't getting proper protection from the police. It's true enough, because we just don't have enough police.

'And the second factor is that Sir Meredith Sullivan has died, and Wallingford, the chairman of the Education Trust down in Bombay, has taken the opportunity to announce that he intends to proceed with the sale of St Thomas's.'

At that point a faint unidentifiable glimmering of real understanding must have come to me, because I remember thinking, It's really piling up on Taylor – and being sorry for him, and admiring him for fighting.

I asked Sammy what sort of man Wallingford was, besides being a Bombay box wallah, and Sammy said, 'He gets a lakh a month. He is an elderly white gentleman, very white, and a pillar of the Yacht Club.'

I said, 'I see,' and I did.

Sammy went on, 'The Anglo-Indians are extremely resentful. The community is in a worse temper than I ever remember knowing it. And it is leaderless, not only here but all over India, with Sullivan dead. And then Taylor went off – this was the day before yesterday, in the morning – and the next I heard was when Lanson told me he saw Tupper, the telegraphist, in the bazaar, brandishing a revolver at a shopkeeper who'd given him some back-chat.'

'Was Tupper in uniform?' I asked quickly.

Sammy said, 'Yes.'

I told him he couldn't stop a soldier in uniform from carrying arms if his officer ordered him to.

He said, 'I know. But it's obviously just a ruse. The point is that some of the Anglo-Indians – not all – now carry arms when they are not in proper military formation or under proper military command. Sooner or later there will be a thoroughly un-pleasant incident. Someone will be shot – an innocent bystander, if Taylor is involved – and someone will be lynched.'

'And K. P. Roy will be very happy,' I said.

He said, 'Yes. *Did* you give Taylor any such authority?'

I thought. Taylor had wanted to keep a guard over the armoured car while things were tense. He had talked about the difficulties of opening the rifle kote at odd hours, and the distance between the kote at the station and the armoured car in the Old Lines. I had suggested keeping the car in front of my quarter guard, and he was very insulted. So I told him his guards could keep their arms by them at night – chained to their bodies, the same as we do on the Frontier – until some fixed time every morn-ing when the kote must be opened and the arms properly checked and returned. I told this to Sammy.

Sammy said, 'H'm. He put a pretty wide interpretation on that.'

I said, 'Why can't people mind their own bloody business?'

Sammy said, 'Running the trains? While you and I run the country? How you can smoke those cheroots at this time of the morning, I don't know. I want to get those arms back into the kote, and I don't want our A.F.I. here – or even Taylor – to get into bad odour with the Army or the railway. They're on the dirty end of the stick – in the dirty middle, as a matter of fact. What do you think's the best thing to do?'

The Collector's pencils were soft BBs. They blunted in no time and smeared under Victoria's hand as she wrote. She grimaced in the pause of our talk and stole another look at me. I'd have liked to know what she was thinking about. She may have been remem-bering I'd seduced her by filling her with whisky. I bet half a hundred old hags down there in the Old Lines had warned her of the vileness of such a trick. (Unladylike behaviour will always get you into trouble, my dear. Fail to extend the little finger of the right hand when drinking a cup of tea, my dear, and you might just as well reserve your bed in the maternity ward.) Or she may have been thinking of Patrick's new trouble.

'I did discuss this with Dickson yesterday,' Sammy said.

I said, 'And he was willing to obey orders? He's a good chap, though, Collector.'

'A better fellow never stepped,' Sammy said, the smile suddenly and startlingly splitting his black face in two.

I said, 'Yes, but this needs the services of a four-letter man, and I know just the one.'

'What are you proposing to do?' he asked.

I said, 'My God, haven't you got the decency to pretend you don't know who I mean? I propose to talk to them.'

He said, 'Do you think that'll work? Taylor is not an admirer of yours.'

He was wrong there. Taylor did admire me, for the wrong reasons. I said, thinking quickly, 'I'd like you to write an urgent message to Taylor, telling him you fear there may be a big riot in the city today. Tell him to have all his A.F.I. fallen in, armed, at' – I glanced at my watch – 'ten o'clock. I'll go down then.'

Sammy said, 'My dear Rodney, you must tell me more than that. I am on the receiving end of a too efficient telephone connexion to an efficient governor and his officious chief secretary.'

I said, 'I'm going to tell them to put their arms back where they belong, and I'm going to explain that brickbats are a sign of affection in the Land of the Robin.'

'The Land of the Robin?' Sammy said.

I said, 'You see, you don't know everything about this country in spite of your correct coloration. The Indian robin carries his red breast on his bottom, Collector.'

He laughed and said, 'Are you going alone?'

I said, 'Yes. This is a melodrama, isn't it?'

Then he said, suddenly quite harsh, 'Very well. Don't make a mess of it.'

I stood up. I'd heard the jeep come. I sent Victoria home in it and, after fixing a few things with Sammy, I walked over to the offices. I told Henry to get the battalion fallen in at ten for Internal Security action, placards and all. Then I went to my bungalow, bathed and shaved, and told my bearer to iron the uniform I was wearing.

A few minutes before ten I got out of the jeep, on the Pike, and began to walk down the long road toward the Railway Institute. I could see the A.F.I. fallen in on the tennis courts with the armoured car on their right flank and Patrick wandering up and down in front.

I also saw Victoria standing in the shade of the Institute veranda. She had changed into a skirt. I thought she had come to see me deal with a ticklish situation.

I heard someone shout, 'Thee colonel is coming!' That was Dunphy from the turret of the armoured car. I walked on, alone, down the middle of the road toward them, the sun in my face. Patrick tried to keep up a nonchalant flow of chatter with the men standing easy in the ranks, but they were watching me. I was the man who'd come to give them a chance to have a good crack at the Indians in the city. The silence grew until Patrick had to swing round and, like them, watch me. He was chewing his lip continually. He was working out in his mind what to say to the man he had seen naked in bed with his girl.

I reached their makeshift parade ground and stopped, my hands behind me. The jumbled houses of the city squatted on the rise of land across the line there, the roofs pulled down over their heads so that they seemed to be asleep under a sheet of dust. There was a smell of coal from an engine in the yards, and a drift of smoke tinged the wavering air above the railway lines.

I stood still, looking at Taylor. He came to his senses with a start, turned clumsily round on his heel, nearly overbalancing, and shouted, 'Platoon, 'shun!'

He swung round again, saluted, and yelled, 'Number Three Platoon, Third Battalion, the Delhi Deccan Railway Regiment, present and correct, sir!'

'What is your parade state, Mr Taylor?' I asked him, speaking very quietly.

He said, 'Oh, the parade state. Mr Donoghue, what is the parade state?'

The sergeant said, 'One officer, three sergeants, twenty-one rank and file, sir.'

Patrick said, 'That's it, sir. Oh, yes, and one armoured car.'

I said, 'Stand easy, please.'

He swung round, remembered he had not saluted, swung round, saluted, swung round. He shouted, 'Platoon, stand at ease! Stand – easy!' Once more he swung round, then stood at ease, stood easy. Someone in the ranks tittered. The essence of my business was to transfer the hopes of the Anglo-Indians from Patrick to myself. He was certainly helping me.

I strolled forward, smiling genially. I said, 'We'll have to get Mr Taylor a job on the turntable, won't we?'

Patrick flushed furiously, and I got a glimpse of Victoria's white face. *Quem Deus vult perdere, prius dementat.* I thought she was trying to tell me that Patrick had a loaded pistol in his holster. Perhaps she thought she was. But the men were already much more relaxed. A voice from the rear rank said, 'Some of those traffic graphs look as if that's where he made them anyway, sir – on the turntable.'

I smiled and stopped. The tittering and talking stopped. I said, 'Gentlemen, I've come here, first, to thank you for your work in the emergency last week. I haven't had a chance to see you since then. I'm speaking for myself and all ranks of my battalion. Thank you. Now I will read you a telegram which has just arrived. It is from His Excellency the Governor. It says: "Please convey to Lieutenant Taylor and all ranks of Number Three Platoon, Third Battalion, the Delhi Deccan Railway Regiment, A.F.I., my appreciation of their steadiness in the recent emergency, and my thanks for the invaluable help they gave to the cause of law and order on that occasion." Here, you'd better frame this in the drill-room.' I folded up the telegram and gave it to Taylor. From the corners of my eyes I saw Victoria knotting and unknotting her fingers. The telegram had been sent less than half an hour ago, at my urgent request. Actually, the Governor had not been at all pleased with Number 3 Platoon, 3rd Battalion, the Delhi Deccan Railway Regiment, A.F.I., especially not with Patrick. His Excellency had heard about the shooting and the inkwell. I was the fellow he was pleased with.

I said, 'So far, so good. But I think you will all realize that there are people, some of them not a thousand miles from here, who are *not* pleased with that telegram or the things it says. These people I am talking about do not like the A.F.I., and would welcome any chance to discredit it.' I paused a long time, then added, 'Although they don't mind using it when they need it.'

I paused again. The men muttered to one another in the ranks. It was obvious that my hint could mean only Govindaswami. Patrick stood with his hands clasped behind his back, staring at my shoulder a couple of feet from him, and the sweat was pouring down his face.

'One of the handles these people are trying to use against the A.F.I.,' I went on, 'is this business of arms being carried off parade. I authorized that.' I suddenly turned my head a fraction and looked hard at Patrick. Again he flushed. I went on, 'But when I did that, I hadn't thought the matter out carefully enough. Nor did I realize how very anxious some people are to get the A.F.I. totally done away with. They do not like either the A.F.I. or the community which supports it. Such people will use any incidents in which members of the community are involved to harden their attitude. For instance, they will be able to use one single incident to finish off St Thomas's for good.'

Taylor said loudly, 'St Thomas's is done for already. Sir Meredith Sullivan is dead, and the Trust are going to sell the school.' A lot of men cried out in agreement with him.

Carefully I played my highest card. I said, 'No, St Thomas's is not done for – yet. There is still hope. I will be happy to write to Mr Wallingford, backing you up, and trying to make him realize what an injustice it would be to sell the school – if one of you will go down in person and explain how strong your feelings are. You need a new leader. *But*,' I went on quickly, 'for your sakes, and for the sake of St Thomas's, I am going to rescind the authorization I gave last week. All A.F.I. weapons will be kept in the kote. They will not be drawn out except by men who are going on a regular parade with an officer. Mr Taylor!'

Patrick started and said, 'Sir?'

I said, 'Some arms and ammunition are in the possession of men not now on parade. You will see that they are handed in to the kote by two p.m. today. Bring the kote corporal and his book up to my office at that time.'

Patrick stared straight in front of him but did not answer.

A man in the ranks spoke up uncertainly. 'But sir –' He stopped.

I said, 'Yes?'

He said, 'The Wogs are throwing stones at our womenfolk, sir. They're doing dirty things in front of them and shouting filthy remarks. A lady isn't safe outside her house here, and we're not getting any protection from the authorities.'

A strong murmur rose from the ranks, Patrick shifted his position convulsively. His right hand kept straying to his pistol butt as though he needed reassurance that the weapon was still there in its holster. He had half closed his eyes. Like that he could probably imagine me naked on the berth with Victoria, instead of armed with a star and crown on each shoulder.

'I know what's been happening,' I said, 'and I'm going to put a platoon of my regiment in the Old Lines here, as from tonight.' I spoke quickly and a little louder than before, and didn't give them a chance to speak again until I had finished. I said, 'I'm going to have that platoon down here by tea-time – if it costs me my commission.'

Again I paused. Only one person in Bhowani could complain if a platoon of Gurkhas was used to give specific protection to the Anglo-Indian community. That person was good old black Sammy.

I said, 'Now you all know what Gurkhas are, and I know how generous you are. But please, for heaven's sake, don't give them any rum, and damned little beer. That includes you, Tench.'

Tench was pure English, a gang supervisor. I'd met him at the Institute a couple of times. He'd been a regular private of British infantry, Ortheris-type, and gone to the railway with twenty-one years behind him and sixteen pages of red ink in his conduct sheet – all drunkenness. He joined in the laughter. I went on. 'Now let's get these arms back in the kote before Mr – well, someone – sends an alarmist telegram and has the Black Watch parachuting down to take them away from us.'

An old driver spoke, a man who looked ludicrously out of place in his lance corporal's uniform. 'Will we be able to get at the arms if we need them, sir?'

I said, 'Of course. I told you. For any parade under an officer.'

I wondered for a second how I was able to stand there arguing with soldiers in the ranks. But I'm a hell of a clever fellow.

Private Tench spoke up. 'Sir, is this the emergency what we were fell in for, then, sir?'

I grinned and said, 'Yes.'

Tench said in a loud aside to the man next to him – hell, it's no use trying to record what he said because no one except a soldier will understand that he was paying me a wry compliment.

'Tench, there is a lady present,' I said.

Tench shouted, 'Sorry, Vicky. But 'e's a proper one, ain't 'e? Worse nor my old Sar'n't-Major Sparrow in the Brummagems.'

I told them to be quiet. Then I said, 'Let me see if the A.F.I. can act like real soldiers for a change. I know your jobs are much more difficult, much more valuable, and much more important than being a poor bloody infantryman like me, but –' I hardened my voice, so obviously that it was like a semi-joke, a challenge. It would do them good to think of me as a proper red-necked colonel of infantry. I roared, 'Let me see if you can pretend for five minutes to be soldiers. Mr Taylor, carry on!'

I turned away. I heard Patrick's boots crunch on the crushed rubble of the tennis court. I, and every man on parade, and Victoria on the veranda, heard his mouthed, mutilated abuse. 'You rotter, I'll show you, I'll ... man to man.'

Victoria shrieked, 'Rodney, look out!'

I turned slowly round, very slowly. I saw Tench, the old soldier, with the reflexes of seven thousand nights in edgy barrack rooms behind him, step forward and raise his rifle and aim at the middle of Taylor's back. I heard the rapid click of his bolt, and his shout – 'Look out, sir!'

Taylor's face was white in the shadow of his huge topi, and his lips were moving. His fingers jerked on the butt of the pistol, and his whole hand trembled. He had the muzzle unsteadily aimed at the pit of my stomach, and only five feet away. Tench kept up a steady soft blasphemy.

I looked Patrick in the eye. If I did the right thing, he'd fire. As he was aiming at my stomach he'd probably hit my arm, or miss altogether. In another of those illuminating flashes, I felt that I ought to let him wound me, preferably quite badly. But my brain and the animal will to win were still too strong, and I was beginning to feel angry with this oaf who kept coming between me and Victoria. I wanted to finish him for good.

After a long wait I stretched out my hand and said, 'I'll take your pistol now, Mr Taylor.' I stepped forward and took hold of the muzzle. For ten seconds both of us held the pistol – Patrick the butt, me the muzzle, which was pointing at my stomach.

I didn't pull, but suddenly I felt the weight of the pistol in my hand, and Taylor was stumbling off the parade ground, and there was a long sibilant *ssspheew* of men breathing. I said, 'Sergeant Donoghue, carry on with fifteen minutes of close-order drill, please.'

Donoghue quavered, 'Yes, sir.' I saw Victoria slump down in a chair and cover her face with her hands.

I went after Taylor and caught up with him as he was wandering about in the middle of Limit Road like a man with sunstroke. I hadn't finished with him yet. There were a couple more inches of the knife to get in under his liver.

I went up to him and said, 'Taylor.'

He stopped, looked at me, and mumbled, 'Can't you leave me alone?'

I gave him the pistol and said, 'It's still loaded. You are an officer, and you may keep it. But I want your promise that you will not fire it at *anyone* – except me.' He looked at the pistol and at me, and gave up trying to understand. He said, 'I will shoot myself.'

I said, 'No, you won't. Only me. If you had an ounce of guts you'd go down to Bombay and see Mr Wallingford.'

He shouted, 'I have got the guts! I am not a coward! But I would only make things worse. You don't understand.'

I understood only too well. Whatever he did went wrong. That was the last two inches of knife. I said, 'How do you expect anyone to stand up for you if you won't stand up for yourselves?'

He said, 'I cannot get leave from the railway in time.'

I said, 'Of course you can. Or go without leave.'

He said, 'By God, I *will* go, Mister Colonel Savage! I'll show you! You watch me!'

I went with him then and there into the Institute, wrote a letter to Wallingford, and gave it to him.

Don't forget I loved Victoria. Don't forget I wasn't ninety-six

281

and as wise as Bernard Shaw. I was just a man who didn't realize that if you don't temper the wind to the shorn lamb a hell of a lot of nice people are going to want to take the lamb right under their overcoats.

32

AT four o'clock that afternoon Victoria came through to my office with some damned piece of bumf or other, and found me smoking a cheroot with my feet up on the desk. My heart did a climbing turn when I saw her again – about an hour since I'd seen her last in there – and I said, 'Is this all you can find to do?'

She stood by the desk, smiling at me. I swung my feet down, picked up my hat, and told Chris I was going back to my bungalow. I told Victoria to come along.

She said, 'I told Mater I would be home early.'

I said, 'Come on,' and held the door open for her. She ducked under my arm and got into the jeep ahead of me. Her skirt looked very tight and full of Victoria, after the saris. I remembered that Taylor had a pair of her pants. I wondered if he'd thrown them away or was keeping them in his pocket. Probably keeping them.

As we drove off I could feel her relax. I had taken charge, and for the moment that probably meant more than anything else to her. There comes a point when anyone says, I've had enough of deciding. The road swept smoothly past, riflemen jumped to attention and saluted me, the quarter-guard sentries presented arms. She tucked up her back hair as the wind tugged it out from under her cap.

I felt her glancing at me. My God, it was written on my face plainly enough that I was going to take her straight to bed as soon as we reached the bungalow. She huddled closer to herself on the bouncing seat. She was glad that I had taken charge, but still –! She was deciding to jump up as soon as the jeep stopped, and cry, 'No, darling! You have to make me want to, first. It says so in Marie Stopes.' But I could make her want to, without moving a muscle or even looking at her. That was what Taylor had been up against in the morning – certainty against uncertainty. When he pulled out his pistol he was really asking me whether it was right for him to shoot a man who insulted him, knocked him out with an inkwell, and went to bed with his girl. As I have explained, I damned nearly told him it was.

I stopped the jeep, and Victoria's skirt was shivering on her thighs. Her face was hot, and her eyes big and uncertain. I touched her elbow and walked slowly beside her to the bedroom. I closed the door gently, turned to her, and took her hands in mine.

I didn't say anything, because I'm not built to ask favours. But I was asking her, all the same. I could feel my face slackening, and cursed and swore at myself for being so weak. She ran into my arms and overwhelmed me with kisses. Then she undressed quickly, and it was me who shivered and she who whispered, 'There, there!'

When we had made love I slowly recovered my wits. I told her to have a bath. The tub was full of cold water.

The sheets were soaked with our sweat, and she got up quickly. Lying back on the bed, I said, 'The towels are in the bathroom. Victoria, what are you going to do if it does have to be me?'

She said, 'I don't know. I've never felt like this before.' But I think she had. She was all female and never counted and never remembered.

She went into the bathroom, and I heard her splashing about. Then she began to sing. 'It had to be you, it had to be you, it *had* to be yooooy!' She could not sing well.

I went in quietly. The cold water had brought out goose-pimples all over that satin skin. I said, 'Don't we know any more words to that damned song?'

She looked up and laughed, and her breasts wiggled, shaking off drops of water. I said, 'Move up. Get your great bottom over,' and climbed into the zinc tub with her. Those things are only four feet long, if that. She shrieked, 'Look out! There's no room. It's going to tip *over*! Oah, *Rodney*!'

We lay on the stone floor while the bathwater sloshed over us and soaked the towels. I splashed her and began to scrub her back with a hard brush. She yelled, 'No, no, it hurts! You are a baby, really.'

'Oah, I am a babee, am I?' I said. I teased her, and her eyes

283

went soft, and I knew she would die for me then, because it was I who had given her the power to laugh about that accent. She got herself under control and said, very ladylike, 'Please stop scrubbing me with that brush, Colonel Savage. You are making me bleed.'

I held down my hand and hauled her upright. The sex was over for the moment, and I worshipped her, and warnings of being without her were going like butterflies in my stomach. I suddenly stepped in and took her as tightly in my arms as I could. She was cold and wet and fresh against me, and I was cold and wet and fresh against her, and all our nerve ends tingled, and our faces shone, and cold water ran down our foreheads and into our mouths as we kissed.

I went out and left her to finish drying by herself. She was so happy she could not even sing. She found me in the living-room.

Ramsaran, my bearer, came in with the tea tray and went out again. I motioned to Victoria to pour. I said, 'Tell me about the sari.'

She said slowly, 'It was going to be like a magic carpet. It was going to take me away from all the squabbling, and the topis that have to have waterproof covers on, and the betel-nut stains that mater tries to hide.'

(And was my bed going to be a better magic carpet, my totem pole a better magic lamp? The answer was yes.)

She said sadly, 'It worked. The sari carried me away all right. But the place it took me to turned out to be foreign and frightening, and full of strangers.'

(If a girl who is half Indian and half English proves to herself that she is not at all Indian, may it not logically be argued that she must therefore be entirely English? It can indeed so be argued.)

I said, 'They've opened the Club to non-Europeans.'

She said, 'They – who?'

I said, 'The Club committee.' I sipped my tea. It was hot as hell.

She said, 'But they can't do that.'

I said, 'What do you mean, they can't? Do you think it's against the law?'

She said, 'No, but –'

I knew what she meant. In practice, clubs were for Europeans

284

only, or for Indians only, or for Anglo-Indians only. There were exceptions – the Willingdon in Bombay, for instance – but generally that was the custom. No one had the power to abolish a custom.

I said, 'Well, they've done it here. Tonight the Collector, lord and master of Bhowani, is going to be allowed to enter the Bhowani Club as a member. Unless he's blackballed or doesn't pay his dues, anyone will be allowed in. Only Indians are going to be allowed to blackball other Indians, once it has got started.'

She said, 'Our people would have been blackballed if we'd ever tried to join. We didn't, though. Some of the girls have been taken there as guests, during the war. Even the girls never used to go before the war. Is it true that the young officers would get into trouble if they took one of us to the Club?'

I told her that they'd be invited to transfer to the R.I.A.S.C., which is trouble enough, I suppose. I said, 'Anyway, there's a dance tonight, and I will drink myself insensible if you don't come with me. Will you?'

She put down her teacup. Already the candour and carelessness of the bath were a long way back for both of us. Why couldn't we spend our lives in beds and baths and trains? They were all closed compartments, the rest of the world shut out. She said, 'Must we go?'

I said, 'You mean you'd rather keep me in my proper place – bed?'

She said, 'No, Rodney. I just think it will be awkward for you and for me. I've been so unhappy, I don't want to –'

I said, 'Victoria, bed is wonderful, but don't you feel that there ought to be something behind it or beyond it?'

She said, 'There is! I admire you so much, darling.'

I told her to commit intimacy with her admiration. She winced and begged me with her eyes not to go sticking knives into her, because she would have to love me whatever I did. But I do keep one rule and that is, no deception. I always want to win, but I discovered long ago, at Wellington, that it's not good winning on false pretences. I don't win just to win, but to have. I'd massacre Taylor to the best of my ability, but if Victoria married me she must know *me*, and know she was marrying Rodney Savage, not a dear sweet kind polite cuddly little teddy bear. She had a bad

285

influence on me. Ever since I saw her I'd kept wanting to be polite and kind to her. It took a large physical effort to be myself – well, shall we say the kind of myself I had long ago made up my mind to see in my mirror: cold, cruel, efficient, ice-blue eyes, all steel and sex. Ha!

I said, 'Don't you think we ought to find out more about each other? How we live, how we think, what we are? I know your geography pretty well now, all your hills and valleys. Hadn't we better study each other's sociology and anthropology?'

'There'll be history too,' she said sadly.

I sat back. That was the wisest thing she'd ever said. I said, 'Please come. Long dress. Ten o'clock. I'll fetch you.'

She asked if I'd be in evening dress, with a true female's desire to see her man looking unnaturally distinguished. I said, 'The Auk stopped all that frivolity at the beginning of the war. Please don't think I despise Patrick.' I made her wrench her mind on to it, but she saw at once that I had not really changed the subject.

She said, 'No, I don't think that. You were marvellous with him.'

I said, 'I was a c-a-d, and you know it, but I didn't have much choice this time.'

Everyone had run true to form – the uncertain Anglo-Indians, looking for a leader; Govindaswami the wise and black, shouldering the abuse; myself; Victoria.

I felt a powerful longing to ask her the usual insane questions that people in love do ask each other. 'When did you first think you' – sigh – 'liked me, darling?' 'I loved you the first moment I saw you, I think, darling – but I suppose I pretended to myself' – sigh – 'that I hated you, darling. I was afraid of being hurt, darling.'

I took the letter out of my pocket and handed it across to her and said, 'I think you ought to know why I was in such a hurry to get you into bed this afternoon.'

She read it and asked slowly, 'When did this come?'

I told her, 'This morning.'

The letter was from G.H.Q. It terminated her duty with my battalion w.e.f. June the twelfth. It announced that on the same date she was to begin again on her three months' leave pending release from the service. Today was June the twelfth.

286

I said, 'But I'll be willing to *pay* when you're a civilian. Quote a rate. Piecework, or time and overtime.'

She said absently, 'Don't be nasty, dear,' and I felt as unstable as a plate of jelly.

She stirred her tea. I could see her mind slowly ticking over. She thought she ought to get out while she could. She thought it was foolish to hope that anything would come of this beyond what had already come – peace and sexual ecstasy. And confidence. She didn't think I had any intention of marrying her. She wondered what she would feel like when it ended. But she said, 'I'll stay with the battalion until the three months are up, Rodney – if you want me to.'

'You'll get no pay,' I told her.

She said, 'I get full pay while I'm on leave pending.'

I said, 'Okay. I'm sure I can fix Nigel. Of course I want you to. Never in my wildest dreams did I think I'd have an I.O. who could fill out an intelligence report *and* a brassière. Just for that, I've put you in for the M.B.E.' I went over to her and ran my fingers up under her hair. I pressed and released the loose skin of her scalp, and she sat back, moving her neck comfortably and purring.

I could still feel her head under my fingers when I reached her house a few minutes before ten o'clock that evening. I ran up the walk and knocked. Through the door I heard her mother say, 'Don't keep the colonel waiting, Victoria.' I heard her snap, 'Why not?' and grinned to myself. She was a woman with no parts missing.

I heard mumbling inside. Mrs Jones's voice said, 'That is a very noisy little car he has. What is it? Will he give you one?'

Victoria muttered, 'Shhh! Mumble, mumble … oh, Mater, why *should* he mumble mumble? Good night.' The door opened, and they came out. The hall light glinted on the grease in Mrs Jones's stringy hair. Her stockings were hanging in wrinkles on her legs, and she was wearing felt bedroom slippers. She told me that Rose Mary would also be at the Bhowani European Club.

On the way to the club I asked Victoria what was the latest on Rose Mary. She said, 'She's having dinner with Howland – at the Sudder Savoy, I believe. Afterward they're coming to the dance at the Club.' She sat glumly beside me, worrying about it. She asked suddenly, 'Is it true that Howland owns a big trading concern in England?'

He had told me that often enough, but I didn't believe him. I didn't know whether to be sorrier for Howland or Rose Mary in that set-up.

As we neared the club I made up my mind that I intended to marry Victoria. She was learning who I was. She must now be given a fair chance to see what I was, in the terms of my society, and decide whether she wanted to try and fit in there. There must be no deception, positively no mirrors.

She had never been inside the Club. As we went in she braced herself as though she expected to face a battery of insolent monocles, but in the hall the only starers were the glass eyes of a pair of buffalo heads. I waited there for her until she came out of the Ladies' and then told her we were meeting the Dicksons in the murghi-khana.

She laughed cheerfully. It seemed a fine joke to her to call the lounge the henhouse. I looked at her curiously, and she stopped laughing. It was a very old joke, but how was she to know? In the Institute people were ladies and gentlemen.

Molly Dickson greeted us with a shriek. 'Vic*toria*! You look *beau*tiful, *Rod*ney, *dar*ling! Do you like my dress?' She was wearing a black sheath with no shoulder-straps and no back. Her back was not good; the spine and shoulder-blades showed clearly. I could never understand how such a fool could know so easily when I was acting and when I wasn't.

Victoria sank back in a chair and looked round. Henry Dickson stared at her, his brow furrowed. He was trying to think of something to say. She decided she had to help him. She said, 'Those are lovely pictures,' and pointed at the wall.

Henry turned his head slowly and looked at them. He said in surprise, 'The "Midnight Steeplechase"? Well, personally I rather like them, but Rodney says he's collecting a fund to be awarded to the first mess or club that hasn't got them.'

Molly overheard and shrieked, 'Do you mean to say you've never seen *those* horrible things before? Wherever have you been? Oh dear, that was silly of me, wasn't it? Don't mind me, Victoria. I've got a brain like a sparrow.'

'Like a hen sparrow in April,' I said, but I'm damned sure she

288

said it on purpose, to underline some of Victoria's difficulties for her. I could see she liked Victoria a damned sight better than she liked me.

The brigadier wandered in, a glass of *crème de menthe* wavering like a green tulip bud on the ends of his slender fingers. Henry and I got up. I said, 'Good evening, Nigel. I didn't know you were here.'

He said, 'Good evening to you, Rodney. Good evening. I'm on my way back to Kishanpur from another of those eternal conferences at Agra. You don't have any problems, do you? Good, good.'

I wilted; even Henry tried to act decadent; and Victoria cheered up as she listened. I assured the brig that all was well, although life was quite too wearing and coarse-making. He hoped I wouldn't be rude to Reginald again. Reginald had come to him almost in tears, he said. Reginald was a very clever young man, but shy and sensitive. And of course he wasn't a soldier, thank heaven, so he didn't understand. Absently People-Psmythe let his hand fall on Victoria's knee. Later he gave her the yellow carnation from his button-hole. He was not in uniform. She pinned it in her hair. He drifted off.

I said, 'One day I'm going to put a grenade in People-Psmythe's thunderbox, and I hope to God Reginald's on it with him at the time.'

Govindaswami was there in a mixed British and Indian party. Later he asked Victoria to dance with him. I wondered what I would do if he started making trouble for her about the Macaulay business. He was a damned good chap, and I hoped I wouldn't have to double-cross him.

Our group in the murghi-khana kept changing. People talked about India a bit, but mainly it was the war, or England, or their future plans – cottages in Devonshire, future meetings at the Berkeley Buttery, prospects for the Grand Military at Sandown. The younger fellows talked to Victoria, and they were a little too young to know how not to be patronizing. Others did it deliberately. She was obviously a blackie-white and obviously in tow of me. There were plenty of people who didn't like me, and I saw at once that they were taking this perfect opportunity to get at me through her. She saw it too. My armour was too good for them as

289

a rule – I mean the gongs and the rank and my war record and other things; the right ties, the right cries – but to them Victoria seemed a big hole in it, right under my heart. Right under my fighting arm, anyway.

Howland and Rose Mary were dancing cheek to cheek. Howland waved violently to Victoria across the floor while she was dancing with me, and shouted, 'Wotcher, Vicky!'

But on the whole it was no worse than I had expected. There were the nice ones, like the Dicksons and young Chris Glass; and the neutral ones, like Turnbull and Clewiston and Lanson; and the spiteful ones, like Mrs Lanson. She sat a long time with us, talking about England, and every time Molly tried to turn the conversation into some channel where Victoria could join in, Mrs Lanson switched it back to England. She was working on a deliberate plan, because finally she did turn to Victoria and say in acid mock-apology, 'All this talk of Home must be awfully boring for you, Miss –?'

'Jones,' I said.

'Oh, yes, Miss Jones. But you see, this club was supposed to be a place where we could get together and never seen an Indian face – except the servants, of course – and remember our homes so far away.'

'Miss Jones is half Indian,' I said, 'but wholly a lady.' I stared straight into Mrs Lanson's eyes, daring her to answer back. I had to show her, and others like her, that I could fight even if I was in love with a cheechee. Also I was so angry when I saw Victoria's face that I wanted to use a saw-bayonet on the woman. She flushed and stuttered, 'Why, she – why, you –' But she just didn't have the nerve to say out loud that Victoria was my mistress and therefore a tart.

Lanson said, 'Come on, 'Tricia. Let's dance,' and took her away.

Victoria sat with her head up, meeting no one's eyes, until Molly muttered, 'Oh, for God's sake let's have some bubbly to get *that* taste out of our mouths.'

Then Victoria asked me how I thought Patrick would get on in Bombay. He'd left on the mail at three o'clock.

She couldn't stop thinking of him. The more trouble he got into, the more she'd feel that she was the only person who could

look after him. Hearing her ask that was like hearing the
referee on his way to counting you out – *four*! Well, there was
time yet, and I had begun, faintly, to realize where the danger
lay.

33

THE next time I had her in my bungalow was late Friday afternoon, two days after the dance. She'd been to tea with Molly
and came along to me afterward. It was almost dark when the
bearer showed her in, but a full moon was rising. It was quite
dark when we'd got over the immediate urgency, and the moon
was shining in at my drawing-room windows.

She was subdued, and I asked her whether Molly had been telling her too many obstetrical horrors. She shook her head and
said, 'No. She was asking whether you and I are serious.'

I said, 'I trust you told her what she could do with it?'

She said, 'No, Rodney. We talked a bit. She's very kindhearted,
and she was nice to me in Delhi when she didn't have to be. I
mean, you weren't there with Henry Dickson as your second-in-
command.'

That was a nasty dig. I gave her a drink, sat down, and said,
'Tell me. Come and sit here.' She sat next to me on the big sofa,
curled her feet up under her in the way women can, and leaned
against me inside my arm. She kissed my ear suddenly and then
settled back.

She said, 'As I turned into the Dicksons' drive I was thinking
about the Club the other night, and not looking where I was going. You know I went there directly from the office. I collided
with a Chinese box wallah who was coming out. It was funny,
really. The Chinaman keeled over slowly, holding on to his
handlebars all the time, until he crashed; then the huge box on his
carrier burst open, and green and purple and silver silks and satins
poured out in the dust under that gold mohur tree. I wasn't hurt,
which made me all the more frightened, and I yelled at him and
called him names and asked why he didn't look where he was
going, and told him he might have broken my leg.'

It was an interesting game to work out – since I knew Victoria's worries quite well – what this was leading to.

Then she said, 'Well, Molly was standing on the veranda when I got to the bungalow, and she'd heard the crash and me shouting at the Chinaman. When we got inside she said, "You know, while you were ticking him off down there I thought for one awful minute it was your sister. I thought, Oh God, Rose Mary is coming to pay a social call." I asked her why Rose Mary should call on her. She said, "Because she is going to marry Master George Albert Howland or die in the attempt." I didn't say anything because, you know, it does look as if she's right, doesn't it?'

I said, 'It does.'

She went on, 'Then Molly said, rather carefully for her, "It would be an awful pity, I think, don't you?" and then she started to ask questions about us – I mean, were we serious – was I, and –'

I said, 'You poor girl. You must never get into a talk like that again without some reserve ammunition – which you must not fire off except in the last resort. Here.' I got down and knelt on the floor beside her. I said, 'Victoria, my intentions are to reach your heart by the shortest and least heavily defended route, which God has provided for the purpose, and then to ask you to marry me.' I got back on the sofa, but she knew I wasn't joking. She put her head against mine and kept it there and didn't speak or move for a long time.

She said, 'Molly intended to find out, I *did* want to tell her to mind her own business. I thought, We'll never find out what's good and what's no good under this continuous pressure – will we?'

I bit her ear to save myself from saying that perhaps the pressure was part of our problem. Without it, the problem would be altered. It wouldn't be the one we faced, so any answer we came to might be the wrong answer.

Victoria said, 'But even her inquisitiveness was helpful, really, because it made me think. I had to ask myself how important this is. I had to think about it all, and I decided that sometimes I was carried away by love, so it must be love. But at other times, when I'm not with you, I know I've been calculating what it would mean.'

'For you?' I said.

She said, 'Yes. I don't know what it would mean for you. How can I? You would work that out for yourself, wouldn't you? You hadn't asked me to marry you, and –'

'I *haven't*,' I said.

She went on as though I hadn't spoken. 'And I don't know whether you will. You never make a mistake, do you?'

I was going to say something to make her jump, but, goddam it, I found myself purring complacently. I said in a pompous way, 'Oh, I make mistakes. Was Molly hinting that people can be lonely in marriage if they don't belong to the same clubs? Even if their bed does work overtime?'

Victoria said, 'Yes, she pointed that out. But then she said'– and she imitated Molly – ' "My God, I think sometimes I'd be happier with a Hottentot than with Henry – with *any*one who just *once* a year, *some*how, made me want to stand on my head and wiggle my toes in the air." And then she said, "I'm telling you all this just to muddle you." But she was really trying to warn me that everything isn't wonderful for Anglo-Indians in England, not in the upper classes. Then she was reminding me that if we had children one might be as white as you and the other very dark, darker than Mater.'

I said, 'Mrs Mendel-bloody-Dickson wants a good –' and Victoria said, 'Now, Rodney, it was you who called me Miss Starkie.' She was quite right. So was I, that first time. The fate of Miss Starkie was one of our hurdles. I thought of two kids in England – brothers at Wellington, say – one white, one dark. People would blink when they saw them. They'd force themselves to treat the dark one the same as the other, and he'd be bound to feel it. Jesus, if a dark one was born to us, people would go round saying Victoria had got into bed with a Negro at the docks for money. They'd say anything if they thought she and her children were a danger to their own lily-white sons and daughters.

Victoria said, 'But what Molly didn't say, which would be very important, I think, is that you would be thinking you had to look after me and protect me all the time. Like you did in the club.'

She began to talk about Molly's kids. They were nice-looking kids, both of them, both fair-haired and white-skinned and blue-eyed. And of course she hadn't changed the subject.

That gave me an idea. I could make a mistake, and go on

making mistakes until we got results. I mean, I could make sure Victoria got pregnant by me. Then she wouldn't have to think any more, because in her society mistakes of that kind are not rare. There is a well-organized way of dealing with them – an unhysterical marriage. There would also be a fine astringent irony, for me, in the resulting situation, when my numerous ill-wishers would joyfully conclude that I'd been trapped at last, and by a cheechee girl. If the child happened to be a little brown-skinned, they'd decide with still more pleasure that it wasn't my doing at all, but some other Anglo-Indian's – probably Patrick's – or an Indian's.

As I've said before, I was beginning to realize how many trumps Patrick Taylor held. A child would give me the ace, though. And yet – in spite of her willowy figure and full brassière and bedroom eyes – Victoria was a wise woman. She'd be capable of taking the baby to the man she really wanted to marry and saying, I love this baby and I have loved the man who fathered it on me. But I want to marry *you*.

I said, 'I'll take you home.'

She said, 'But I thought you –' and I said, 'Yes. We'll walk. I'll push your ruddy bike.'

Some of my subalterns, particularly Master Albert Howland, had been mishandling the battalion vehicles when they'd taken them out for private purposes. So I'd just cancelled my general permission for officers to use them. Of course I could have taken my jeep just the same. A C.O. doesn't have to obey his own orders; often he can't. But I'm a wary sod, and I keep honest on the principle that every peccadillo and minor carelessness gives someone a hold over me.

We set out at once but didn't hurry. We walked through cantonments, holding hands in a most unmilitary way. A lot of men saw us, and one or two smiled as they saluted, but they weren't being superior. For some reason the Gurks like me as much as I like them, and as they are also believers in the religious merit of copulation I thought some of the little blighters were going to throw garlands or flowers at us, they looked so pleased and congratulatory. I thought suddenly, How much longer am I going to be surrounded by people like this? I wanted to leave Victoria and go off and play cards in the N.C.O.s' club.

We strolled on down the Pike. The moon was full, and the city shone brilliantly clear on our left front. On the right the day's dust over the fields and the mist above the river were full of moon-light. My thoughts couldn't have been farther from Burma and the late unpleasantness, but listening and noticing had become a habit, so I heard the pi-dogs barking crazily on the edge of the city about three hundred yards away across the Pike. I stopped and listened to see if I could hear anything more, but I couldn't. Victoria waited patiently, and then we went on again, but I was uneasy.

As we passed the Collector's garden a tonga trotted up the Pike from the city toward our lines, with seven Gurks jammed in it. I recognized Mandhoj's voice; he was a little devil in B Company who would always find any mischief there was going. He had put a frog in my boots once, in recruits' camp. They recognized me, of course, in that light, and all tried to salute, sitting three deep in one another's laps. The clip-clop of the pony's hoofs got fainter up the Pike, and we went on down.

About a hundred men and women swept silently out from be-tween the houses on the left of the Pike. I saw them before they saw me, and thought of running – but there was nowhere to run to. Victoria stiffened beside me, gasped, 'Rodney, look at –' and then they were all round us. I saw that each man carried a stave – a big balk of wood, rather – and noticed a couple of men with steel crowbars. They didn't touch us, but they were all round us and saying nothing. I didn't have my carbine with me.

Mr Surabhai forced his way through, peered into our faces, and hissed, 'Sssst! or you are a dead man – and a dead lady, of course. Good evenings, Miss Jones and Colonel Savage, it is indeed a pleasure to meet you here.' He shook us by the hand in turn. Then he glanced conspiratorially up and down the moonlit Pike and whispered, 'On, on! We must take this lady and gentleman with us, as they are of the opposition party and will be otherwise in duty bound to give intimation of our progress to the authorities. Please to come with me. Keep close at hand, and do not make one effort to escape!'

We crossed the Pike with them, and I saw the Kutcherry ahead and knew what they were going to do. We hurried across a patch of fallow land and stopped at the side of the Kutcherry, behind the offices.

Mr Surabhai waved his umbrella – he was not carrying a club – and said, 'We have had enough high-handed behaviour on your parts. It is scandalous that the Sirdarni-sahiba should be held in prison without bail. We are going to release her from vile durance.'

I said, 'Good show,' and edged closer to Victoria. I looked around carelessly, trying to sum up the faces. This was an operation anyone could be proud of. The people must have left their houses at different times and gone by different paths to a rendez-vous outside the city. Then they had moved across country, using the full moon, and here they were, unsuspected, on the blind flank of the Kutcherry. Surabhai was the leader, but he hadn't arranged this. There was a pale intense-looking young fellow near him, who, I thought, was Roy's hand in this particular job. I did not think the crowd would hurt Victoria or me, but the police sentry at the jail had a rifle, and once he fired, God knew what would happen.

The intense young man whispered to Surabhai, 'Comrade, hold the woman and walk with her in front of you to the jail. Tell the sentry she will be hurt if he fires or does anything to call for help.'

He had a quick mind, that fellow. Obviously meeting us couldn't have been in the original plan. Surabhai said, 'But my dear fellow, we couldn't do that. That would not be chivalrous.'

The young man swore, but he realized at once that he wouldn't shift Surabhai, so he said, 'Hold the man then.'

Doubtfully Surabhai said to me, 'Would you mind that, Colonel?' and I said, 'Not a bit. A pleasure.' The young fellow grabbed my arms and twisted them behind me, and we and Surabhai and a few others walked round toward the main gate. I told Victoria to stay back, but she wouldn't.

The police sentry was not placed to prevent people from getting into the jail from outside, but to prevent the prisoners from get-ting out. The jail is merely a row of cells leading off a veranda. That is one side of the Kutcherry, and the Treasury and offices occupy two other sides. The fourth side is open, but bounded by a fence of high iron railings. The big double gate in the fence is the only way to get into the Kutcherry.

We reached the gate, and Surabhai called the sentry. He wan-dered over, trailing his rifle butt on the ground behind him, and said, 'What's the matter, brother?' He was a stolid bullock of a U.P. Moslem.

Surabhai said, his voice breaking with excitement, 'Open, comrade, in the name of freedom.'

The constable said, 'What's that, what did you say? What's the hurry?' The lights were kept burning all night along the jail veranda, and I saw the Sirdarni's face at the bars of her cell, the one farthest from the gate.

The young fellow said, 'Open, you swine, or we will batter these English people's heads in.'

The sentry was beginning to get annoyed. He said, 'I can't open for you. There is no order. Who are you, anyway? It's Mr Surabhai, isn't it?'

Surabhai screamed, 'Yes, yes, open, comrade! We have come to rescue –' and the young man whistled between his teeth, and the rest of the crowd ran forward with the staves and crowbars. Surabhai at last succeeded in making the constable understand that we would be hurt if he took any action, so he stood still and glared angrily at Surabhai. His blood was up by then. The crowd began to push and batter at the gates, all together. The young fellow saw me moving over to get close to Victoria again and shouted, 'Stand still, or I'll kill you,' and Surabhai wailed, 'Oh, no, don't do that, dear fellow, not on any account!'

From her cell the Sirdarni shouted, 'Climb over the wall, you fools!'

Several men ran round the side and began to climb the back wall of the offices. The constable stood pinned, looking at me for a sign, and the young fellow stood behind me with his club raised.

Two pairs of car headlights jumped on behind us and lit the whole iron fence and us and the backs of the offices and the people trying to climb the wall there. Govindaswami's voice said, 'What is the meaning of this?'

Surabhai swung round and gasped, 'The police! Oh botheration!' He ran forward, doubtless to give Govindaswami a piece of his mind. I saw a row of perhaps fifteen police, with lathis, ranged alongside the police bus and the Austin, and three or four more at the flank, with rifles.

The young fellow behind me screamed, 'Charge them! Kill them!' and took a swing at my head. I collapsed backward into

297

his knees, and as he stumbled forward I got him hard under the chin with the top of my head. He went down, but I had no time to kill him because I saw Victoria being bowled over in the swirl of the mob. Also I remembered that the killing season was over for a few years, and I would do better to use my other talents. But it was too late to try and calm the people down. The damage was done, and they were surging forward at the police, and stones were flying. The police counter-charged, swinging their lathis, and the two mobs met round the bus and the Austin.

'Break them into small groups,' Govindaswami shouted. Everyone was yelling. The police riflemen didn't take part in the battle, but ran over and pointed their rifles at the men trying to climb the wall. The men scrambled down quickly because they were fully exposed and must have felt very naked.

Good old discipline began to tell, and soon the little knot of police was clearly winning. I picked up a stick and fell on the back of the mob. The intense young fellow had recovered and was in the thick of the fight. He had plenty of guts.

Suddenly Victoria screamed, 'There's K. P. Roy!' But no one heard her except me.

I shouted, 'Where?' She came up beside me and pointed and began to say something. Looking where she pointed, I saw a fellow in the *melée* swing a police lathi up and round. Then I was unsighted, and I could not swear whether he or another man did it, but the lathi caught Surabhai a real smash on the side of the head. Surabhai fell, the people milled about, and again I saw the lathi swing up – and down. There were no police within fifteen feet of Surabhai. I didn't have to ask which was Roy then, but I couldn't see him any more. I dived into the ruck, but someone shouted, 'Flee! Run!' and everyone took it up, including Govindaswami, and in ten seconds the moonlight was speckled with the shadows of people running like mad in all directions. In ten more seconds they'd vanished among the scattered houses and hedges.

I ran to Govindaswami and told him Victoria had recognized Roy in the crowd. Sammy said, 'Not much use, but we'll try.' He turned on the panting police and rattled off orders that sent them running every which way. Some climbed into the bus, and that lumbered off down the Pike. The sentry opened the gate. Sammy ran into his office and began telephoning the police barracks. Soon more constables were hurrying out on bicycles and on foot to patrol the level-crossings and road junctions and river fords within a mile of the Kutcherry.

Victoria was sitting there in his office with us, pale but contained. We gave her a drink of water and a cigarette. She hadn't been hurt physically.

At last the excitement was over and everything had been done that could be done. Then we relaxed, and I asked Sammy how he had managed to put on such a fine Campbells-are-coming act. He said sourly, 'Private information.'

We talked some more, and then I asked if he'd drive Victoria and me down to the Old Lines and bring me back with him. He nodded, and we went out to get into his Austin.

Partly it was the moonlight making everything white round there, partly it was the excitement and each one of us having had other things to think about – me of Victoria, Victoria perhaps of me, Govindaswami of his job and Roy – but we'd none of us noticed the body lying on its face near the off front wheel of the Austin, the body in a white dhoti and scarlet suspenders, yellow socks, and co-respondent shoes, with a little blood round the head and a Gandhi cap lying stained with blood beside a police lathi five feet off.

Victoria stopped and swayed like a tree in a high wind, but she wasn't going to faint. She whispered to herself as I put out my arm to hold her. She knelt down. Neither Sammy nor I did, because we knew – partly by the way the body lay, partly by the broken hole in the skull, partly because it was so inevitable.

The darling lifted up his head in her arms and tried to wipe away the blood. She wasn't disgusted by mere violence any more, as she used to be, just because the results were messy. She saw a man badly hurt. That was no time to think about the real mess violence causes and is caused by, which is not so easily visible. She was full of compassion. She laid his head down at last and said, 'He's dead, isn't he?'

Sammy said bitterly, 'Yes, they murdered him all right. They even managed to get a policeman to do it for them.'

I said, 'No. It wasn't a policeman.'

Victoria said, 'I saw too. I'm almost sure it was Roy.'

Sammy asked me if I was sure. When I told him yes, he looked hard at me and said, 'Did anyone else see?'

I didn't think so. Sammy said, 'It doesn't matter. Here's the lathi. We'll never be able to make anyone believe it, whatever we say, however much we exonerate the police in an inquiry.' I thought of suggesting we burn the lathi, but I know the right cries well enough, and I kept my mouth shut. Anyway, the sentry would have seen us.

Victoria said angrily, 'Are you going to leave him lying here while you work out who is to blame?'

Sammy took her arm and said gently, 'No, Miss Jones. But if we don't consider now what is the right thing to do, there will be more blood shed here, and elsewhere in India, because of this.'

She thought a minute and said suddenly, 'Please take me in your car to get Mrs Surabhai and Ranjit.'

'Ranjit?' Sammy said, surprised. But she knew what she was doing, and all at once I did. That was the hell of a woman, and becoming bigger every hour.

As they were leaving I said, 'Do you want me to carry him in?'

Sammy said, 'Please. And will you get your doctor? The civil surgeon's gone to Kishanpu with Lanson. And do you know what for?'

'No,' I said, obviously.

Sammy said, 'Because Brigadier ffoulkes-Jones thinks his Alsatian chef is trying to poison him. The *foie gras* tasted funny last night, he reported.'

They drove off. Surabhai certainly had a knack for wringing good honest comedy out of the most unlikely situations. I carried him in, and by the time Sammy and Victoria came back Chaney had examined him and pronounced him dead of a fractured skull. We had also washed his face, closed his eyes, arranged his clothes, and laid him out on Lanson's table with a handkerchief over his face.

Victoria supported Mrs Surabhai as she came in. She was a battle-axe of a woman, and Sammy had told me she used to give Surabhai hell because he wasn't a mixture of Rockefeller and Bismarck. Perhaps she loved him. You couldn't tell, because by custom she had to start keening and yelling and tearing her clothes to pieces. I wished to God that Manbir's old wife were there to help

Victoria look after her. Finally some friends arrived in a tonga, and Govindaswami gave them permission to take the body away.

Then we were left – Victoria, Sammy, Ranjit, and I. Victoria had taken charge, and Sammy waited quietly. She held Ranjit's hand for a minute and made him sit down. The rest of us stood. She said gently, 'Ranjit, dear, you are a secret Congress man, aren't you?'

He nodded. He seemed a lot tougher than he used to be – not chest-beating tough or gangster-tough, but as if a lot of willow had been taken out of him and steel put in instead. I was not surprised. The Sikh religion is strong meat to take on an empty stomach.

Victoria said, 'And you don't really like working on the railway, do you?'

He shook his head. He was looking at her and weighing her to see where she was going next, what she was trying to make him do. A week ago she could have twisted him round her little finger, I knew, but not now. He didn't dislike her – if anything, he loved her more than he ever had – and I knew he'd been in love with her from the same moment I was, perhaps earlier.

She said, 'Both Colonel Savage and I saw this lathi' – it was in the corner, complete with blood and hair – 'kill Mr Surabhai. But it was not a policeman who did it.'

'Who was it?' he said.

'K. P. Roy,' I said.

'No,' she corrected me. 'We didn't actually see Roy do it. This is what we saw.' She explained clearly and finished up, 'So it was either Roy or another man in the crowd. Roy was the nearest. It was not a policeman. And the rescue only turned into a riot when first your mother told them to climb the wall and after that the young fellow – the one with a pale face –'

'Mehta,' Ranjit said.

She said, 'When Mehta told the people to charge the police. I am almost certain K. P. Roy wasn't with them when they crossed the Pike and caught us, because I was looking for him. He must have been hanging about on the outskirts, waiting for his opportunity.'

'His opportunity to do what?' Ranjit said quietly. As I say, he wasn't antagonistic. This new Ranjit, you had to show him.

'To start on his campaign to break India from within,' Sammy said. 'What's holding you politicians together now except hatred of the British? Who will succeed Surabhai as local chairman here?'

'Mehta could,' Ranjit said. 'Mehta was getting ready to take over when we were all sure you were going to keep Surabhai in jail – after the fishplate was found.'

I'd always wondered why Roy put the fishplate there. Now I knew.

Victoria said, 'Mehta could succeed – but so could you, if you left the railway service and came into the open.'

Ranjit sat there a long time, quite still. Finally he looked at me and said, 'Do you give me your word that it was not a policeman who killed V. K.?'

I said, 'Yes.'

He got up then and said, 'Very well. I will think it over. I could out-vote Mehta if I tried. I have never thought of trying before.'

'Even if you win, you will have a hard fight to get the actual control out of the hands of Mehta and his friends,' Sammy said. 'They'll try to make you into a figurehead.' He was a cunning bastard, and, of course, an Indian.

Ranjit said, 'I do not think I will be afraid of that. But you must not imagine that the local Congress, under my leadership, will be any less hostile to you and what you stand for. Or that the struggle for a free, united India will be allowed to die or weaken in Bhowani.'

Sammy said, 'And I don't want you to imagine that anything you care to do now will give you the smallest privilege against the law.'

'I will tell you in a day or two,' Ranjit said. He turned to Victoria and said, in front of us, 'You were right to leave the gurdwara, and me, when you did, Victoria. Thank you.' He took her hand and kissed it gently in a very European gesture – perhaps his last.

Sammy said, 'Do you want to see your mother for a minute?'

Ranjit thought and said, 'Yes, please. Alone, please.'

I borrowed Sammy's Austin and took Victoria home. It was about midnight, and I was thinking of Surabhai and wishing he could have been killed more gloriously – say with Probyn's at

302

Meiktila. I was betting myself a thousand to one in pounds that even then his last words would have been something as immortally incongruous as 'Oh botheration!' when Patrick passed us on his Norton, doing about seventy. He must have come back on 599 Down, the slow train from Bombay to Delhi, which reaches Bhowani Junction at 23.29.

34

THE following Sunday we were at the Collector's again. It was about half past eleven in the morning, and Sammy was signing papers at his desk. A coppersmith bird donged with maddening persistence among the bushes in the garden. I went over to the windows and peered out between the horizontal slats of the venetian blind. The garden was shimmering with dry heat.

Victoria sat quietly with her hands in her lap and watched me. She had a steady look that finally began to disconcert me, so I said, 'Do you mind if I go out and shoot that bloody bird, Collector? Or do you keep it as a pet?'

Perhaps Victoria was estimating me as a father. Perhaps she thought I'd eat my young if they whimpered out of whimpering hours.

The tenor bell started ringing in the cantonment church. The coppersmith resented the competition and doubled his rate of donging.

Sammy said, 'Please don't shoot it, Savage. It will certainly be sacred to someone, somewhere, in this godforsaken country. Don't you ever go to church?' The bell tolled, and an ashtray on Sammy's desk buzzed in its reverberations.

I said, 'No. I am a decent chap, and my memorial shall be a thousand lost golf balls. Except that I don't play golf.'

Victoria was fairly well educated and very intelligent, and she had educated herself a lot more since she left school – but as far as general background of culture went, she was a lightweight. Sammy was a light-heavy, and I am a smart welter. My chance remark caused a small look of vacancy to pass across Victoria's expressive eyes. She rearranged her hands and waited for us to get on to some subject she could understand. Meanwhile she probably mulled over things, such as the qualities of fatherhood, which she was quietly satisfied that I couldn't understand.

I looked at the thermometer hanging in the shade of the veranda outside. I said, 'A hundred and nine, and it's what? Half past eleven? This can't go on much longer.'

'A week, more or less,' Sammy said. He scribbled his long signature on another document, blotted it, and turned round. 'Now –'

I sat down, brought out a handkerchief, and tied it loosely, as a neckerchief, round my neck. Sammy's white suit was immaculate, but his collar hung in wet folds. He ran his finger round it and said, 'My third today. I expect to get through five or six more before bedtime. I put on the second in honour of an early visitor.'

He waited. He liked his little touches of drama.

I said, 'All *right*!' I put the tips of my fingers together and said, 'I confess that I am baffled, Govindaswami, as to the identity of your early visitor.'

'Ranjit,' he said.

'I am unbaffled,' I said.

He said, 'He came here to tell me what he knows about K. P. Roy. It isn't much more than we know already. Roy got a tooth or two knocked out on Friday night. Otherwise he's in good trim and working hard.'

I asked if Ranjit had seen him (Roy) since the fight at the jail.

Sammy said, 'He says not. Mehta told him the news – before *he* told Mehta that he was a candidate for the local Congress chairmanship.'

'He's doing it, then?' I said. 'Leaving the railway and all?'

Sammy nodded, and I said, 'We ought to give Victoria a medal or something.'

Victoria said, 'Not me. The Guru Panth.'

Sammy nodded and went on. 'Well, Ranjit thinks he will be elected at a meeting tomorrow. He is already out of the railway. His mother wouldn't tell him anything about Roy, but from what Mehta let slip Ranjit thinks that Roy is still hiding in Bhowani.' I asked Sammy what, if anything, he wanted me to do about it.

He said, 'Nothing, I hope. The police are at work. This evening

304

I will get some plain-clothes men from Agra and Cawnpore. I have good hopes of catching Roy this time.'

'It will be the hell of a trial if you do,' I said sourly. 'Worse than that I.N.A. farce at the Red Fort. Think, is your trial really necessary?'

Sammy said, 'A trial will be better in the long run than a mysteriously dead Roy. I am a servant of the Government of India, not of Mr Djugashvili or of the late Mr Schicklgruber.' He stood up, delicately mopping his brow with a huge white linen handkerchief. He said, 'All I want you to do is stand by at an hour's notice. But remember, please, if I am forced to employ you – no mysterious deaths.'

'You and your bloody Old Cheltonian tie,' I said. I stood up and started slowly for the door. He was a strong man, Sammy, and one of the few who really don't prefer to use their strength against other people. I asked him what they used to call him at Cheltenham.

He said, 'Nigger, at first. Later, Sammy.'

I asked him if he'd enjoyed it there.

He said, 'Yes. God knows why. I got my Fifteen cap as scrum half. The other sides used to complain that they couldn't see me on muddy days.'

I laughed and held the door open for Victoria. The jeep was waiting under the shade of the trees, with Birkhe curled up comfortably in the back seat. We braced ourselves for the hot dry shampoo of air. Victoria put on her dark glasses. Sammy said, 'We must end the run of Roy's melodrama with all speed. There's a famine starting in parts of Madras.'

We spent the day together, in the mess and at my bungalow. A good deal happened, both what was obvious and what could not be seen. When she left me she bent down and kissed the inside of my wrist. Her lips were cool and wet, and the queer forlorn passion of her movement leaped up my arm so that I could not take my hand away. It wouldn't move, and my knees went weak from love. The tonga driver watched interestedly from below. When she loosed my hand she stumbled down the steps and climbed into the tonga and jolted away. I stood on the veranda till she had gone, and long after that.

She didn't get the chance to tell me until some time later what happened then, but as her story is complete and mine only joined it half-way through, it is her story that I will tell here.

She found Number 4 Collett Road empty, airless, and like an oven. It smelled different to her – stranger even than when she first came back from the Army. It smelled of meals eaten long ago, of the tang of betel nut from her mother's secret vice, of Rose Mary's powerful scent and her father's pipe.

She wandered about, opening windows to let in the air. The sun was down, and she saw blue wood-smoke and grey coal-smoke dimming the horizons, and heard the squeak of a bullock cart.

With luck, she thought, her family would stay out until she could get into bed and pretend to be asleep. She sat down in her father's chair in the parlour, kicked off her sandals, and closed her eyes. She meant to rest for only a minute before going to bed. She wanted to think about herself and me – just as I, up in cantonments, wanted to. But I couldn't. I was worrying about Roy then, and wondering what I could do to help Sammy.

Victoria decided that during the day she had been near something final and right – but when, exactly? When was it that she had heard the whisper of a knowledge beyond her own knowledge?

(The circumstances in which she told me of this time were such that she wanted to explain all her thoughts to me. It was another day, another climate, and we will come to it.)

Was it when we had talked, in the mess, of Ledru-Rollin, and she didn't know what we were talking about? When we played Bartók and told her it was Korngold? When I took her to the cemetery to see the grave of my great-grandmother? When she had agreed to come out and spend a week-end in camp in the jungle with me? When Patrick came to tell us that he had failed in Bombay, and we both realized that he had come at that time hoping to find us in bed, to hear us perhaps, and so suffer the last pains of love? In my bitter politeness to Rose Mary, when she and Howland came to the bungalow to get permission to take out a truck – which I refused?

She reached no conclusion, sitting there in her father's parlour except that she was wildly happy and steadily unhappy. She could place the happiness with great exactitude – it lived in, or grew from, the wide and slippery gulfs of my bed. The unhappiness she could not isolate. The last thing she heard before falling asleep in the chair was an engine whistling for the level-crossing a mile up the line.

She awoke slowly to hear someone saying, 'Wake up, please, Miss Jones.' The voice was small, polite, and flat.

She opened her eyes. A man in a coolie's loincloth was standing over her. His hand rested on her arm, the fingers pressing gently just above her elbow. There was some light, a creeping-in of visibility through the open windows. The man's face was neutral, and he was K. P. Roy. He held a big Army revolver loosely in his right hand. His arm hung straight down as though the revolver was too heavy for it.

The slow freeze began at the back of her head, spread forward across her scalp, down her face, into her neck. Suddenly it caught at all her muscles together so that she jerked in a convulsive spasm and sat back where she had been in the chair, but lower.

'Do not make any noise, Miss Jones,' Roy said. He talked oddly, like Winston Churchill, because of his missing teeth.

She waited. They were always supposed to say, I don't want to hurt you, but – and push the pistol forward and bare their teeth and narrow their eyes. But she thought that K. P. Roy didn't mind whether he hurt her or not. The depth of his indifference was not to be calculated. He said, 'Can you tell me anything about the Collector's plans for capturing me? I would like to know where the military and police posts outside the city are. I thought you would know.'

She whispered, 'No. I don't know.' She moved her eyes to the clock. The hands were very dim on its blurred white face. Twenty past nine, or a minute afterward, about. Roy's eyes flickered and came back to her. She spoke quickly. 'They didn't tell me anything.'

He said, 'You weren't discussing the plan with Colonel Savage in his bungalow all this afternoon?'

She said, 'No.'

He said, 'What were you doing?'

She said, 'We were making love. That's all I went there for.' The revolver was big and shiny blue, and it took away her pride.

Roy said, 'I see. When do you expect your father, mother, or sister back?'

She said, 'I don't know.'

He stepped to the window and glanced out. It was the street light that shone dimly in. Her hands had joined together and were wringing, one in the other, slippery with wetness. Roy's body gleamed as he moved about.

Roy came back to her. He said, 'The situation is this, Miss Jones. All the roads and trails leading out of the city are blocked. There will certainly be military patrols in the fields, since Colonel Savage is an efficient officer, but I do not know exactly where they are.'

He was wrong there, by a few minutes. It was 21.18 when I persuaded Sammy to let me help, and the first of my patrols didn't get into position until 21.45.

Roy said, 'I cannot expect for a second time to have such luck as I had in escaping from the affair at the jail. Mr Govindaswami was better informed than I expected. You were not hurt at that time?'

Victoria said, 'No.'

He said, 'You were lucky. The railway lines also are blocked, and an armed policeman is in the cab of every engine leaving Bhowani. But I think that with your help I can surmount these obstacles. Mr Dunphy is backing out of the yards now with the Down Goods for the Bhanas Branch. It departs every night at about this time, as you know. In a few minutes Mr Dunphy will return through the station and start out. I want you to come with me now and stand by the line and wave some suitable object to induce Mr Dunphy to stop his train. When he does so, you should speak up to him in the cab and keep him busy for a minute or two. You should ask him something, or tell him something, which will seem to him of sufficient importance to warrant your having stopped the train. Remember it is only a goods. What do you suggest?'

She wrung and unwrung her hands. Ted Dunphy was in love with her. He might be able to see from her face that she was in terror. But she would have to control herself, or Roy would shoot her and the policeman, take over the train, and ride his luck.

She said, 'I could invite Ted to a dance.'

Roy shook his head. 'Today is Sunday. There is no dance occurring sufficiently soon to give your request the necessary urgency.'

She could think of nothing except that she could think of nothing. Roy spoke more sharply. 'Very well. You shall tell Mr Dunphy that Mr Taylor has threatened to kill you, and you are therefore afraid. You shall ask Mr Dunphy if he knows where Mr Taylor is so that you may hide from him. Yes.' He nodded. 'That will do very well, because it will also account for your obvious state of agitation. Kindly put on your shoes now.'

She fumbled with her sandals and at last got them on. Roy squatted on the floor and watched her. The clock ticked. All the noises of the night passed round the little house but never came in. The people next door tuned up their wireless. They must have just come back from somewhere, she thought. The Institute. A visit. The wireless was giving a talk, and the speaker sounded pompous, as though he had a hot potato in his mouth, his voice and the words mashed together to form a meaningless boom like frogs in a pond.

Roy stood up quickly and said, 'Out!' and jerked up the pistol so that the big black snout touched her breast. He had seen something outside. She sprang up from the chair, and his arm held her upright against the drag of her knees. They hurried into the passage, turned left, passed out of the back door. He closed the door carefully. She heard her mother's voice, quite loud and clear. 'No one told me why it is wrong to –' It shut off. She wondered, What is wrong? Chewing betel nut? Trumping her partner's ace? The lecturer thundered and boomed.

They passed behind the servants' quarters, slipped through the bushes, and stood a moment on the other side. She saw no one up or down the line. Looking to the left along the straight, she saw the lights of the station and among them the white eye of an engine's searchlight. It was dark there at the edge of the bushes, darker than in the parlour, because the street lamps did not shine there, and the yard lamps were only a glow in the sky.

They crossed the main line and moved, one behind the other, Victoria in front, into the triangle of wasteland. On the other side of it the Bhanas branch runs in a steep left-handed curve, turning from south to east. They crouched down beside the single stretched wire that leads from Bhowani South Box to the branch line's Up Distant signal. The houses were close and dark opposite.

She heard the shimmer of sound in the rails as soon as he did. Straining her ears, she could hear the slow beat of the engine's exhaust. Ted Dunphy was coming out. The headlight shone on the main line behind them, then on the wasteland as the engine took the points for the branch, then on the branch line. The wheels' flanges ground against the inside of the rail. Roy said, 'Stand up now.'

She stood up. She had to wave something, he had said. She had nothing to wave. If she lifted her hand Ted might just wave back at her and not stop.

Roy said, 'Here, Miss Jones.' He pushed something soft into her hand. She recognized it as the little bolero jacket of the dress she'd been wearing all day. Roy said reassuringly, 'I will be right behind you, but concealed.' She heard the clank of the coupling rods and the roar of the blast. The light blinded her, and she began to wave the jacket. The focus of the light narrowed to a single glare in her eyes, then faded, passed by, and spread out. She heard the grinding of brake shoes, and the buffers went *bang-bang-bang* all down the train.

The cab stopped directly above her. Dunphy stuck his head out and said, 'Victoria. I thought it was you. What is the matter?' Behind him the constable lowered the rifle he had held aimed at her while the train slowed.

She glanced wildly round with an idea that that would tell him something was wrong. But she realized at once that it would seem perfectly natural – as soon as she had said her piece. She tried with her eyes to make the constable understand that he was not to look at her but to jump out and run back down the train. That is a hell of a message to pass with the eyes. She saw Roy crouched under the overhang of the tender.

She said, 'It's Patrick.'

'Patrick?' Dunphy said foolishly.

She caught a movement under the tender. They were on the right of the train, so the guard, looking out from his brake van, would see nothing on this sharp left-hand curve. She thought that it wouldn't be long now before Roy was on the train, and then she would be free.

She said, 'Patrick's talking about killing me. Where is he? I want to hide from him. I'm frightened.' She felt worse about telling that lie than anything else.

Dunphy was worried for her, but he had the train to take to Bhanas. He said, 'I don't know where he is. Isn't your father at home?'

She said, 'No,' and Dunphy licked his lips uncertainly. Up there in the cab his face and the policeman's were red and shadowless in the glare of the firebox. At last Dunphy told her to go to his house, where Mary would have to help her until her father came in. He was troubled, in spite of knowing about me, because he couldn't leave the train and help her himself.

She said, 'All right. I'll be all right. Thank you,' and stepped back.

Dunphy couldn't do any more. He opened the regulator, and the wheels began to turn. The tender ground past her. She looked for Roy and could not see him. The first wagon passed, and the second. They kept on passing. She began to breathe more easily. She was beginning to feel weak from relief, but when she got her lungs filled she was going to scream. The brake van would come, and the guard would hear. She decided Roy was a fool.

Her mouth was open, ready to scream, when the voice spoke behind her, again urgent and now as hard as – as mine, she said. It said, 'Up!'

The train had picked up to walking speed. All goods wagons have a long handbrake bar, which is held in position, either on or off, by metal pins. The brake bar lies horizontally just outside one of the projecting axle-boxes. Roy seized the back of the waist of her dress, and a bunch of skin inside it, and forced her forward against the wheel of the coal wagon. She had only one escape from being pushed into and under the wheel. She caught the hand-grip above the brake bar and jumped up. Her dress fluttered out and hung against the greasy axle-box. She was furious, even in her fright, because it was a white dress and would get filthy. She scrambled on up, one foot on the brake bar, then got her hands over the side of the wagon. She tried to scream but had no breath. Roy's hand rammed up under her behind, and she fell over into the wagon. A second later Roy followed her.

She lay beside him on top of the piled coal. Her chest hurt

where he had forced her over the side, and she wanted to cry, but she managed to hold it down. Roy worked quickly, heaving coal to one side. The wagon rattled and groaned and swayed and rushed on. Roy said, 'Help, please. This is now urgent.' He had tucked the revolver into his loincloth.

She knelt on the coal and pulled it aside as he was doing, until her fingers hurt. Soon Roy said, 'Lie down there.'

She lay down in the hollow, and he pushed the coal back over her with his foot. The lumps slid down until they covered all but a tiny piece of her face. Her dress wasn't white any more. The big lumps lay three and four deep, hard on her chest, and harder underneath where they pressed up into her spine. Roy bent over her and said, 'If the train is searched, do not move or make any kind of sound. But, should I say, "Get up," then get up quickly. Do you understand?'

She said, 'Yes,' and told him she couldn't breathe.

He said, 'I think you can. I shall be close by, Miss Jones.'

She watched the stars that hung steadily in the sky above. The moon was coming out from behind cloud. Sometimes branches of trees whipped over and flung back. Roy had a form ready in the coal, but he did not get into it. He sat up near her, his head just poking over the side of the wagon.

The train's speed increased to about twenty-five miles an hour. She thought that a long time passed. Then the rattling and grinding began to slow, and she heard the engine labouring and the exhaust blasts separating out as Dunphy lengthened his cut-off for the Sindhya bank. Devra station is a mile up the bank. After that the line climbs all the way, through Bharru, Pathoda, and Adhirasta to Sindhya Tunnel summit – which meant that the train wouldn't be doing more than ten or twelve miles an hour. The jungle begins just beyond Devra.

A signal passed by, and she saw it was green. They stammered over a set of points. There were electric lights to the side and a load gauge sweeping directly overhead. A load gauge is a metal bar, curved to conform to the shape of the top of a wagon or carriage roof, which is hung on chains above the line in certain places to show how high open wagons can be loaded – with machinery, for instance – on that particular stretch of line.

That was Devra. She heard the engine whistle and a Hindi

phrase from a man beside the line, and more points. Roy sunk his head as the lights passed.

A little later the vacuum brakes ground on all down the train. On that upgrade it came to a stop quickly and stood, the metal creaking for a time until each piece settled under the new stresses. She understood at once, and remembered. A kachha road crossed the line about there. There were empty fields on both sides and no cover, except for a patch of scrub on the right a little farther back. She decided I must have put a search post here to cover the railway, the kachha road, and the main Bhowani–Kishanpur road, which was a hundred yards off to the left. She remembered that the line curved there, and noted that her wagon was tilted to the left on the banked rails.

Roy said, 'Now be very still.' He lay down in the trough he had scratched for himself and pulled down coal until it covered him. Something shoved noisily through under the coal near her face and pressed against her ear. It was cold, round, and hard.

She heard a faint crunching on the gravelled lineside path. It was coming from the front of the train. Listening hard, and holding her breath so that the coal would not creak and drown the sounds, she tried to interpret what she heard. It was nailed boots on the gravel. The boots were coming regularly closer in a smooth rhythm of movement: *crunch-crunch*, for ten or a dozen paces – the clang and scrape of steel on steel – a pause – another clang – a thud – *crunch-crunch*. On both sides of the train.

She worked out that Gurkhas were coming down the train, climbing up to look into each open wagon or inspect the door seals of the closed wagons, then jumping down again.

The muzzle of the revolver seemed big enough to engulf her head. She prayed, Oh God, make them not see us because I don't know what he'll do. She swears she thought of me and told herself that if only I was there in person all would be well. She closed her eyes.

She heard the clang against the side of their wagon. Another pair of boots was moving about, stamping, on the gravel below. She heard the heave and the small gasp of effort as the Gurk scrambled up. A light flashed against her eyelids. He *must* see. She opened her eyes, peering up through the interstices of the coal and hoping the light would reflect back from her eyes. But the light

313

wandered away. It clicked off. The Gurk (he was Baliram, a nice kid but no ball of fire) jumped back to the ground with a thump. Coal-dust tickled her nostrils. She breathed in deep, wrinkling her nose, trying not to sneeze. The boots crunched along to the next wagon, which was a high closed one. She heard the metal seals rattle on both sides, and the heavy bolts shake. The pistol pressed a little harder against her ear. She swallowed the sneeze. The engine blew off steam with a drumming roar that seemed close, although she knew they were much nearer the back of the train than the front.

Soon the steam pressure dropped and the engine fell silent. In the silence she heard car engines and saw lights sweeping across the sky above her. Roy struggled out from under the coal and knelt up to peer over the side. She moved her head to watch him, and the coal grated against her cheek.

Faintly from the back of the train someone shouted, '*Sab thik chha*' – the Gurkhali for 'Everything okay.' From the front someone else acknowledged the message. The brakes clicked off, the engine exhaust gave out a loud whoof, the wagon rolled back a few inches, then jerked forward. The train began to move.

35

THAT was where I came in.

When she left my bungalow I tried for a time to think dispassionately about us. The effort failed, (*a*) because I am not dispassionate, and (*b*) because I thought Sammy was making a mistake in not using my battalion more in this attempt to catch Roy. I worked out a plan whereby we could help, warned Chris, and after some argy-bargy got Sammy to agree. Soon my jeeps and six-by-sixes were moving out to cordon the roads and railways and form flying patrols in a few of the more likely jungle areas.

I went myself to Taylor's house in the Old Lines, knocked on the door, and walked straight in. It was a chummery he shared with another bachelor. It was what I had expected – dark furniture, antimacassars and gimcrackery, a mixture between Victorian respectability and the special ramshackleness that only a bachelor in India can achieve. Except for one thing – the trophies. Taylor stood up slowly when I came in, but I wasn't looking at him. At some time or other he had shot a good buffalo, a black buck, two bears, a leopard, the usual things. As decorations for a house they were terrible; as a sidelight on Taylor, they were unexpected. He had been very clumsy that night we searched the villages round Malra.

Taylor stood up, his face settling obstinately. He was like a bull waiting for more goading.

I said, 'Taylor, we're out after K. P. Roy. Would you like to come with me? Let's see if we can't share the honour of catching the bugger.'

After a while he said, 'I'm not lucky, Colonel. If I go with you, you won't catch him.' That room was as lonely as an asylum, in spite of the congress of dead animals peering glassily at us. I was surprised at Taylor's reaction to me. I had expected abuse, refusal, perhaps even a fight. Something had beaten him down a few sizes. But for purely selfish reasons, I didn't want him to be so perpetually up against it. So I said, 'But *I'm* lucky. Here.' I held out my hand. 'I'm in love with her, goddamn it.'

He took my hand slowly, and I thought he was going to cry. In some ways he had a hide like a rhinoceros, in others he was worse than the princess with the pea. He pressed my hand and said, 'I know you are. I have just realized it. I hope you will be very happy.' I've never seen a fellow look more miserable. He said, 'I didn't tell you this afternoon. I threatened Mr Wallingford with the revolver when he refused to stop the sale of St Thomas's. I was mad. I lost my temper. It was only Mr Stevenage who persuaded Mr Wallingford not to send me to jail.'

I waited. There would be more.

He said, 'On the way back I threw the revolver into the Nerbudda so that I wouldn't be able to do anything silly with it again. Now I have a telegram from the Deputy Chief Traffic Superintendent asking me to explain why I was absent without leave.'

I counted in my mind: a charge of intimidation, and probably assault as well; a court-martial for losing an Army revolver and six rounds of ammunition; dismissal from the railway; sale of St

Thomas's. What a man. The miracle was that he was still here, subdued but basically unchanged.

I said, 'Forget it. We'll see what we can do later. Meantime, bring a rifle and come along.'

He didn't talk any more but got out a rifle and came with me. In ten minutes he was quite cheerful again. He had extraordinary resilience. I drove straight back to my battalion headquarters and found Chris Glass in a state about a report that had just come in from Ranjit, via Govindaswami, on the telephone. Ranjit said he had reason to believe that Roy was trying to escape from Bhowani on a train. That had been about twenty minutes ago. The cordon was in position by then, but I thought I would go out and take a look for myself. I asked Taylor if there was any train regularly scheduled at this time. He looked at his watch and said, 'Yes. A mixed goods to Allahabad, via Bhanas.'

The phone rang. It was Sammy. He said, 'Kartar Singh has just come in to tell me that the night goods to Allahabad stopped on the branch line for a minute, and he saw a woman in white talking to the driver – fifteen minutes ago. Kartar lives near –'

I am alive to wear my M.C.s because in certain matters my brain goes off like a bomb. I said to Taylor, 'Who's the driver of that goods? Quick!' He thought and said, 'Dunphy, probably.' I dropped the telephone and ran for the door. Taylor just managed to get in over the side as I got the jeep moving. Birkhe dived head first into the back seat.

I don't know what a jeep's maximum speed is, but we did it, all the way.

The goods train had been searched when we reached the cordon, and was just starting off again. I blared on the horn and flicked my lights on and off and yelled, 'Stop!' Dunphy saw me and stopped his train. I couldn't afford to waste time wondering. I had to act as though I knew Roy and Victoria were on the train, not just thought they might be.

Lilparsad came running, and I told him to get his two vehicles out in the fields, one on each side of the train, with their headlights on. Their lights went on, Victoria said later, just in time to stop Roy from breaking for it. He was on the point of going over the side when he saw my jeep arrive.

The Gurks spread out, and I got a couple of Bren guns down

beside the vehicles where the gunners could see along the lights. The guard of the train left his brake van and started to walk forward to see what was happening.

That was Roy's chance, and he saw it much quicker than I did. I went slowly on with the line of Gurkhas, keeping level with the men, who were now breaking into every locked wagon and examining every open wagon inside and out, top and bottom. We were well past the middle of the train when Lilparsad, on the other side of it, shouted, '*Hinnu lagyo, sahib! Terain hinnu lagyo!*'

By God it was, or rather five wagons and the brake van were. Taylor was beside me, and I shouted, 'Patrick, the back of the train's rolling. Stop it!' Then I realized the guard was nearly up with us, and nobody could stop it. Simultaneously I realized it was no accident. Thank God my jeep was up beside me, with Birkhe at the wheel. The runaway wagons were perhaps fifty or a hundred yards away and gathering speed downhill and disappearing beyond the reach of my headlights.

Someone fired a shot, and I saw the guard roll over. He'd been nearest to the runaway part and must have run back, but Roy had got him while he was trying to unpin a brake lever and hold down the handbrake on the wagon nearest us. I saw Roy and Victoria scrambling toward the brake van.

By then Taylor and I and Birkhe and two others were bounding over the field in the jeep. Birkhe ran the jeep alongside the runaway, which wasn't going more than ten or fifteen miles an hour, and we hurled ourselves at the end wagon. Roy began to fire at us from the brake van up front. Ranbahadur '92 got hit in the arm and fell off. Birkhe was in the jeep, and so three of us were in that back wagon – Taylor, Rifleman Bishansing, and me.

Victoria had lost a sandal here. Roy must have been here under the coal with her. Obviously he must have been in this wagon to get down, seal and disconnect the vacuum pipe between it and the next one ahead, uncouple, give the disconnected part of the train a push-off down the slope, and jump in.

The wagon immediately ahead of us in the runaway section was a high closed one. We couldn't see a damned thing unless we got on top of it. Taylor was wild with excitement. He charged across the gap and went up like a gorilla. Immediately a bullet whanged against it on the other end. Taylor dropped on his stomach as we followed him up. We crawled to the forward edge. From there we could see. Ahead of us, in order, were a wagon full of sacks, one full of wood, one that looked empty, and the brake van. Roy leaned out of the brake van's right window and fired twice at us. I fired quickly with the carbine but missed. We were doing over twenty then, and the lights of Devra station were close in front.

I gathered myself to jump down into the well of the wagon in front. Roy couldn't kill two of us if Bishansing stayed up there and kept his head down with the Sten whenever he tried to poke it out to fire.

Just as I jumped I saw Victoria's head and shoulders appear in the moonlight, and an arm with a revolver right beside her ear. Taylor had bunched to jump with me, but he saw Victoria too, and instead of jumping forward his reflexes sent him leaping up, shouting, 'No! Stop, we –' and then a shadow like an eagle's wings flashed over my head, and Patrick disappeared with a clatter and an extraordinary *whoomph*. We were running through Devra station, and the lights blinked flash-flash-flash on us, faster every second. I looked back and saw Patrick hanging on to the load gauge, his legs dangling and his body draped like a scarecrow's across it. The *whoomph* was the air being driven out of his lungs, and the clatter was his rifle falling on to the wagon top and thence to the ground.

He had jumped up to warn me not to go on, because of Victoria, and the load gauge had swept him off.

He might have been killed, his ribs crushed in against the steel bar of the gauge. He might have fallen down unconscious fifteen feet and some inches and broken his back. But he wasn't, and he hadn't. He was hanging up there like a clown in a circus, with his legs kicking. The Devra platform staff might be rushing with ladders to get him down. But they wouldn't be. They would be hiding, thinking that he was K. P. Roy, while he groaned and swore and shouted for someone to come and get him down. I couldn't do anything about getting to Victoria, and I didn't think Roy would hurt her without cause – if only because it would waste time and ammunition – so I knelt on the sacks and called Patrick every name I could think of.

I hadn't had time to give Lilparsad any further orders but, as I'd once pointed out to Victoria, I wasn't running a kindergarten.

The two six-by-sixes were tearing down the road, which ran parallel with the line there about a hundred yards over, and gaining fast, their headlights and the moon churning the dust into gigantic luminous galloping wraiths.

The map of the country spread out in my head. Where was there cover? Roy had the vacuum brake lever in his van and could stop us any time he chose. I remembered a patch of rocky scrub jungle that faltered off into water channels, ditches, hedges, and two straggly villages – an impossible place in which to catch a single and singularly skilful man.

It was a sweet taste, like honey and whisky, to see one of Lilu's trucks jerk off the road and head across the fields at forty miles an hour to get behind that area of dirty country. What the hell did I want another wife for?

But Lilu ought to have had my crown and pip while I took his three stripes – only three were more than I deserved. For not until then did I realize what an utter fool I'd been. I jumped up, leaned over the forward edge of the wagon, and shot a hole in the vacuum brake coupling. The brakes jammed hard on, sheets of flame streamed out, the steel screamed under the torture, and I all but went over on to the rail. While I struggled to save my balance the brake-van door opened with a crack like an eighteen-pounder, and Roy stepped off. He hit the right of way, folded, and rolled forward like a ball in a cloud of dust. I got in one shot before he found his feet, then he was running like a hare among the stones and scrub. We had stopped on the very edge of the bad country. Two seconds earlier, and he'd have had thirty yards of open ground to cross; I would have found my balance, and I couldn't have missed. Bishansing sprayed the trees with his Sten gun, but it was no good. I jumped to the ground and ran after Roy for a minute, but when Lilu's men arrived I handed over to them and went back to the little line of wagons.

She was lying on the floor of the brake van, and I got very cold inside. I knelt down, preparing myself to say good-bye to her. I put out my hand, and she stirred and muttered, 'Are you hurt – hurt – badly hurt, oh, Patrick, 'rick?' She'd got a bang on the head when the brake van stopped so suddenly. She spoke in a thick muddled way and didn't know what she was saying, but she was going to be all right.

319

Because I had tightened up to say good-bye for ever, what she did say was not terrible. The welling-up of love and relief in me could have absorbed worse than that without a wince. But still I wouldn't give in.

I had a hard job keeping my voice steady when she came to properly and asked whether I was all right, and held on to my hand, and then – much later – asked after Patrick.

Patrick arrived on a bicycle. He was in some pain, but I had decided that the only part I could play was the part of R. Savage, and let the audience file out in good order when they've had enough. I said, 'A hell of a time you choose to practise pull-ups. Take your coat off.'

He took off his coat and shirt, and I had a look at him. He was badly bruised, but I didn't think any bones were broken. Chaney would see to him when we got back. But something else had happened to him. I won't say he actually grinned at my crack, or that he actually answered back, but he somehow shrugged the whole thing off. The bend of his back, in his pain, said, Better luck next time, and showed much more of his true character than he was capable of putting across in words. The eerie thing was that this new 'feel' in him had been put there by nobody else but R. Savage. On the way back to Bhowani I gave him another couple of verbal jabs, just to make sure. All he did was nearly pulverize my hand when we left him at his bungalow and say, 'By God, I wouldn't have missed that for anything, Colonel. And you saved Victoria. She would have been a goner without you.'

Then I drove Victoria to her bungalow, and kissed her before I took her in, but gently, and she thought I was the most beautiful tiger she'd ever come across in her walk, as a woman, through the jungle.

36

THE next Thursday I went into her office and asked her if she'd finished. She nodded, and I said, 'Let's do something indecent, then. Let's go over to the Club and have a drink.'

She looked at her watch. She said, 'But it's only half past four. We can't have a drink yet.'

I said, 'That's what I meant. I want to prove to one and all that I've lost my moral fibre.' I picked up her handbag and held it out for her.

She sighed and smiled and came round the desk toward me. I said, 'Fourteen days' C.L. for looking fond.' She was very happy with me, and she loved me, and it was exactly like waking up in the holidays from school – say on September the first, when the sea in the early morning has begun to take on the Chinese-print mistiness that warns of the end of days.

But this camp in the jungle wasn't going to be a misty ending. I would make it instead into a pearly beginning. I would, I would, I *would*.

While we were walking along the grass beside the road I said, 'Thinking of tomorrow?' Tomorrow we were going off into the jungle. I hadn't been thinking of anything else.

She gathered herself and said, 'Rodney, I can't come.' She went on quickly. 'Really, I can't. I haven't cared for myself, and I don't now, but this is going to hurt Pater. He's bound to know. We can't hide a thing like that. You're not even going to try, are you?'

'No,' I said, 'I wasn't.'

We walked slowly, the sun at our left. Barracks and a line of big trees hid the river. It was another hot still afternoon, and few people were about. I found myself thinking of Ranjit. He'd lost her, but he'd gained something in the process so that now he was calm, contented, and grown-up. I wondered if that would happen to me.

In the deserted club, with my drink in my hand, I must have looked so troubled that she weakened. She suggested I ask the Dicksons to come too. She thought they wouldn't mind if she and I shared a tent. But I had it fixed in my mind how it was going to be in the jungle. It was going to be an idyll of exploration. Victoria and I would explore the jungle, the wild birds, the animals, and each other. Birkhe and old man Manbir were going to be there because I saw them in the idyll – but certainly not Molly Dickson, or even Henry. I wanted to isolate Victoria from pressure and show her another world which was a part of me. But it had to be all or nothing.

Finally I said, 'If you feel like this about hurting your father, we'll have to go and speak to him.'

321

She said, 'Rodney, you mustn't!' and put down her glass quickly.

I said, 'Not me alone, Victoria – we!' I would have preferred not to bring her father into this yet. So far, it was our own damned business and nobody's else's. But I thought that it would probably be all right to see him. I didn't think he would be as hurt or as outraged as Victoria expected.

She said, 'I won't do any such thing, Rodney. How can you expect me to go to my own father and tell him I'm going out there alone with you, and ask him if he minds?'

I said, 'We're not going to ask him if he minds. We're going to ask him if he approves. I don't want to hurt him any more than you do. Where will he be now?'

She said, 'At home. Just getting up. He usually sleeps all Thursday afternoons. But –'

I said, 'Good. Finish that drink, and we'll get a tonga and go down.' I called for a khitmatgar and told him to fetch a tonga.

When we clambered into the tonga our combined weights nearly lifted the miserable pony off the ground. To counterbalance us the driver crept out along the near shaft. He cracked his whip and shouted, 'Hey! Hey, huh!'

I said, 'This is the way the world begins, not with a whimper but a –' I waited, my hand raised. The pony scrabbled for foothold, touched down, and farted thunderously. I said, '*Bang!*' The pony trotted down the club drive.

The tonga was a very suitable vehicle for us on that errand. The tonga abolishes all distinctions of caste, colour, and class. Nothing more undignified could have been thought up if people had spent a thousand years trying. Pater would feel very superior when he saw us.

As we passed the Silver Guru's tree she said, 'What are you going to *say*, darling? What do you want me to say?'

I said, 'I don't know. This is your father, you know. You like him, don't you?'

She said, 'Yes.'

I said, 'You're not frightened of him?'

She said, 'No.'

I said, 'Well, I like him too.'

Then we were there, and I saw Pater peering at us with astonishment through the parlour window. I paid off the driver while Victoria waited for me. She didn't want to face the walk alone. Pater met us at the front door. He had bedroom slippers on his feet, rimless reading spectacles on the end of his nose, and a crumpled *Civil and Military* in his hand. He said, 'Hullo, Colonel. This is a nice surprise.'

I listened carefully but could hear no other sounds in the house. Mater and Rose Mary were probably out. Pater said, 'Have a bottle of beer, Colonel?'

I refused with thanks. Victoria led into the parlour, and Pater and I followed her. Pater sat down in his big chair, and she balanced on the arm of it. I remained standing, by the window. I said, 'I've come to see you about Victoria, Mr Jones.'

Pater got up slowly. 'Victoria?' he said. For a moment it looked as though he did not believe his ears, then the smile spread across his face, showing all his bad teeth, and he fumbled for his spectacles, took them off, and seemed to be on the point of crying. He said, 'Victoria. My little girl. You want to talk to me about her?'

I said, and found my voice going harsh, 'Yes. I am in love with her. I want to take her out into the jungle for the week-end. I want your approval.'

Pater sat down. His hand trembled as he put the glasses back on his nose. He said, 'Oh. I see. For the week-end.' 'Week-end' is a wicked word. 'Three days' sounds much more virtuous.

He was looking up at me, into the light. I towered over him, though I am not tall, because he was all shrunk up in the big chair. I didn't want to bully him – and I knew it wouldn't pay, either – so I moved round and sat in a chair on his other side, so that then the hard light was in my eyes and behind his head.

'Oh,' he said again. 'Shooting. What do you hope to get, sir?'

I said, 'Leopard. Perhaps a jungle fowl or two.'

He said, 'Oh,' and then was silent. He moved his head a little from side to side. Like me, he was listening to know whether Mater and Rose Mary had somehow crept back into the house and could hear what we said.

He lifted his head and met my eyes. He said falteringly, 'I am sorry, I must ask – are your intentions honourable, sir?'

I said, 'Mine are. I'm not so sure about Victoria's.' Victoria

323

looked at me, thinking I had made a bad joke, but I wasn't joking. I went on. 'I'm in love. But marriage lasts a long time. It's supposed to be important. You know that there will be difficulties enough, made by other people, if Victoria does marry me, without our making difficulties for ourselves. I think if we can get away together for a few days it may help us to think straighter and reach the right answer.' I didn't mention Patrick, and I didn't say in so many words that I wanted a chance to build up the kind of relationship with her which Patrick had grown into as he grew into his men's clothes.

'Oh,' Pater said. He picked up the newspaper, smoothed the rumpled sheets, folded it, and put it down again. He said, 'You haven't said anything, girl. Do you want to go with the colonel? Do you love him?'

Victoria said, 'Yes.'

I could read her father's mind as easily as I could reads hers – My girl's reputation means a lot to me. But the colonel is an Englishman and a real gentleman. But even if he is, he ought not to seduce my girl. But she was going out with that Indian fellow, and how wonderful it would be if she could get an Englishman instead – an English colonel. He might marry her, after all. If anything happens by mistake, he will, because he is a gentleman. It is too good to be true, really. But he ought not to seduce her. Why does he ask me, why doesn't he just take her away and bring her back? He knows I will have to pretend to know nothing about it even if I know everything.

Pater said, 'It is like the companionate marriage that you have in mind, then, like they have in America?'

I said, 'Sort of. A week-end's not enough for that, I suppose – but I've worked with Victoria a lot. We know each other pretty well.'

Pater picked up his pipe, tapped the bowl on the floor beside him, and put it down again. He said, 'I love my daughter, Colonel. I love both of them. I would be very happy if you are the right man for her. I am an old fogey. We were not so honest in my day. *We*' – he glanced at Victoria, his face damp and a blurred wink in his eye – 'had to take out the girls *sub rosa* – under the rose, you know. But our intention was the same, I should say. It didn't always work out properly. We made mistakes then. Women are very good at deceiving you, Colonel.'

'Some are,' I said.

He said, 'Don't let this little minx take you in.' He reached out his arm, caught her round the waist, and squeezed. His eyes were brimming over with sentimental tears.

He got up with sudden animation, nodding his head as he digested and understood what was happening there. His feelings came slowly to him, but they were true. He had realized the size of my love for Victoria. 'Yes,' he said. 'Yes, that will be a great thing for you, Victoria. Mind you do not deceive the colonel. If you do not really love him, if you cannot make him a good wife, you must say so.' He paused in his pacing up and down the little floor, and said anxiously, 'What about your mother? Shall we tell her? And Rose Mary? Are you going to keep it secret from the other officers, Colonel?'

I said, 'I'm not going to tell anyone what I'm doing. I never do. My second-in-command has to know where to find me.'

Pater said gloomily, 'Her mother will not ask any questions. Nor will Rose Mary. Because they will both know in no time.' He cheered up. 'But that can't be helped. The important thing is to make sure you two do not make a mistake, eh? Oh, it is wonderful to be so young and in love, and a colonel too! Man, you are a lucky girl!' He hugged her again and shook my hand and said, 'Go on, Colonel. Kiss her. I won't mind.' I lifted her chin – only a little, she was so tall – and kissed her gently on the lips while Pater crowed with happiness beside us. Then Pater wouldn't be satisfied until I had a bottle of beer with him, and over the beer we talked sentimentally for an hour.

At last I said I must go, and Pater made me kiss her again behind the front door. Then we left Victoria inside, and Pater walked with me up Collett Road – to help me find a tonga, he said. I felt Victoria watching us from the parlour window. I could almost hear her saying to herself, Men are extraordinary.

Pater wouldn't go direct for a tonga, but forced me into the Institute and made me drink another couple of bottles of beer. He talked as though Victoria was already a bride. His mind was dancing rosily among nuptial delights and the spring of love. To him I had become not a seducer but the giver of those delights to his little girl. He never referred to her except as 'little', and she was a big healthy girl. He began to tell me what a 'pretty little girl' she had been as a child. He showed me a snapshot of her in a goddamned pinafore and a topi, complete with waterproof cover. He sighed as he thought of love and young women and beds – and, Jesus Christ, so did I, and I put my hand on his arm and told him several good stories for no other reason than that I felt drunk with pleasure. Men are indeed extraordinary.

37

THE next day Victoria arrived at my bungalow in a tonga at about 05.15. She was wearing khaki slacks and her WAC (I) bush shirt and carrying a small suitcase. The day was coming and the night going, and the streamers of both met high above us while the east was green and the west indigo. It was not cool, it was not hot. It was not light, it was not dark.

I'd hired a bazaar lorry, and it was standing outside the bunga-low with its sidelights burning. Birkhe had hung a hurricane lan-tern from the roof inside, and under its yellow gleam you could make out a satisfactory holiday-going litter of tents, cooking pots, bedding rolls, and sacks. The driver and cleaner were fiddling with the engine, their heads together under the raised side of the bonnet. I helped Victoria down from the tonga and kissed her hard. To let go at all I had to do it suddenly. She nearly fell. I turned away from her and asked the driver if we were ready to go yet.

He said, 'Nearly ready, sahib. One minute.'

We sat on the veranda steps, smoking and talking, while the light strengthened, for twenty minutes. Then I walked over to the lorry and said, 'How many more seconds in this minute?'

The driver grinned deprecatingly and said, 'It is an old lorry, sahib. Twelve years.'

'Twenty,' I said. It was an old Chevrolet chassis, visibly bent out of true, on which the usual wooden body had been roughly fitted. A latter-day Cubist had painted it in blue below and yellow above, and had also put in the Taj Mahal and a cow with a Mona Lisa smile. The top was piled high with sacks and boxes which the driver was taking out to Pathoda and Devra for other people.

After twenty more minutes the sun was thinking of coming up. Victoria had smoked half a dozen cigarettes, and I a couple of cheroots, and our mouths were hot and dry.

I got out another cheroot. But I hated the cheroot and I hated the world. This trip wasn't just a rutting expedition. It was my heart and bowels that wanted Victoria the most. All women are properly constructed for rutting, whether plain or fancy. There is a military proverb: Bad beginnings make good endings. I never believed it. And it was all her damned sister Rose Mary's fault. I said that aloud.

She said, 'Rose Mary? What has she –'

I said, 'Rose Mary and Master George Albert Howland. Don't you remember last Sunday?' That was when Howland and Rose Mary had come to get permission to use a battalion vehicle and I had refused them. If it hadn't been for them I'd have used one of the battalion trucks instead of hiring this wreck.

Finally I relaxed and was able to laugh. If Victoria decided not to marry me on the ground that I couldn't organize a shooting expedition properly we would both do better to confine our thoughts to fornication. I said, 'What the hell, boys, what the hell, she had her boots on when she fell. Let's have a drink.'

'Now?' She was really horrified. 'Rodney, you're not drinking too much, are you?'

I said, 'No, darling. I'm just living continental. Haven't you ever seen those French workmen knocking back brioches, coffee, and anise at seven o'clock in the morning? Damn it, of course you haven't.' I kissed her cheek quickly. 'But you will. Christ, I have the right to disobey my own orders. I don't know why I don't get a six-by-six from the lines – but I'm not going to.'

'Ready now, sahib,' the driver said.

Old Manbir Pun, the S.-M., appeared from the back of the bungalow, saluted, and climbed carefully into what was normally a second-class seat, the bench behind the driver. Birkhe wheeled up a G.S. bicycle, and he and the cleaner got it roped down, with a good deal of trouble, on top of the sacks on the roof. I started automatically to get into the front seat with Victoria, but changed my mind, and we pushed in alongside Manbir and Birkhe. Manbir was not pleased. He always had a liver first thing in the morning. The cleaner whirled the crank handle round and round. The engine spluttered, fired, hummed. The driver engaged gear, the cleaner darted round and hopped in beside him, and the lorry began to move.

We swept noisily out of the drive. Soon we turned off the Pike on to the Kishanpur Road. The driver tucked his left foot under him on the seat, and the cleaner pressed down the clutch for him when he wanted to change gear. As we bumped across the railway line at the level-crossing I said, 'Is it safe to say "We're off" yet?' which was a bloody silly question to ask, considering the number of years I'd been in India. But Victoria nodded and smiled and got out her cigarette case. Birkhe stood up at once, swaying with the lorry, lit a match, and held it cupped in his hands till long after the cigarette was drawing.

Birkhe was one of the nicest people I'd ever known. He didn't have a mean thought in him. He was shy and intelligent, and he pulled my leg when he felt like it.

Old Subadar-Major Manbir sat on the far end of the row, his eyes half closed, smoking a pipe. The dust-cloud rose behind us and was sucked forward in our wake so that soon we were sitting in a thin gritty fog. Manbir hated the dust. He coughed and hawked and spat over the side and glowered at the road ahead, but there was nothing he could do about it – except one thing; he could take it out on someone else. In one sense we were the C.O., the S.-M., and a rifleman of the 1/13th. Not in another sense, but in another plane of the same sense, we were father, son, and grandson.

Birkhe was saying something, and Manbir interrupted him by leaning across him to tap Victoria on the knee. He said, 'Miss-sahiba, you must marry the colonel.'

Victoria was completely nonplussed. Hell, she was only a woman. She looked wildly at me for help and stammered, 'Why, Subadar-Major-sahib, I don't know, I don't think –'

I was enjoying myself. This was something Victoria ought to know about. I didn't say a word, and Manbir took no notice of me at all.

'You must,' Manbir repeated. He tapped her on the knee again. He said, 'You make his heart big. With you he will not spend so much time wondering what people think of him. Besides, you will have many children.'

Birkhe sat sandwiched between them. He knew better than to open *his* mouth.

The old man was wearing grey flannel trousers, a brilliant green shirt, and his small round black mufti cap. Victoria mumbled something. Manbir said, 'I did not think it would be good for you to marry him at first. Most of your people are like jackals, who follow the tiger but are always yelping, always frightened. But *you* are different. You must marry him.' He fell into a fit of angry coughing, spat over the side, and said, 'This dust! Stop the lorry, sahib. I want to blow my nose.'

I told the driver, and we squealed slowly to a halt. Manbir got out, blew his nose on his fingers for a couple of minutes, patted dust out of his clothes, and got back in. He said, 'All right now.'

I told the driver to start up and said, 'Off we go again!' I was feeling as cheerful as a cricket. Manbir's liver always made me laugh.

The lorry would not start.

We sat there for five minutes, all squeezed together in the heat. I began to feel less cheerful. Manbir said, 'This is foolish. I'm going to send Birkhe back to get one of our six-by-sixes.'

I said, 'No!' I jumped down and stared up and down the empty road. I recognized the place. There was a field on the right, and beyond the field the railway – the Bhanas branch – and beyond that the jungle and rough grass where K. P. Roy had escaped from the brake van. I could just make out the houses of Devra about two miles ahead at the foot of the rising brown hills. Behind, between us and Bhowani, a column of black smoke hung in the air. It must be a goods train.

I said, 'Father, you're responsible for this because you couldn't blow your nose out of the window like any ordinary human being. Get all the kit over to the railway there, and stop that train. The miss-sahiba and I will go on the bicycle.'

Manbir paused as he hoisted a tent on to his shoulders. He said, 'Both of you? In this heat?'

I said, 'Why not? When everything goes wrong, make it worse. We'll see you at the camp.'

The old man muttered, 'This is not sensible,' and staggered off across the field. The train was appreciably nearer. Birkhe was already half-way to the line, and the driver and cleaner were staggering along with more kit. Victoria and I stood a minute, watching them; then I picked up the bicycle.

I felt good again. Everything had become very funny and exactly right. I said, 'Hop on. You're well padded.'

She looked doubtfully at the heavy green bicycle and said, 'Where? On the carrier?' I said, 'In the Army we call it the arse.' I was really feeling like that. I told her that sitting side-saddle across the bar was best. She heaved herself up. My arms were on each side of her, and she said she felt quite comfortable for the moment. We wobbled off.

She gasped, 'Be careful, Rodney!'

I said, 'I'm being careful. Keep still, woman.'

I managed to look back once or twice, but soon a grove of trees hid the broken-down lorry and the little group waiting by the line. Farther on, we heard the engine's outraged whistling. I described Manbir, complete with his liver, standing foursquare in the middle of the line, his hand raised, and the cowcatcher stopping a foot from him, and the heads stuck out of the cab windows, and the shouting and swearing. She began to giggle.

'Two miles of level, and then about ten miles uphill,' I said. 'What the hell are you laughing at?' My mouth was close to her ear, and I wanted to nibble at it, and I did. I said, 'Lean back on me. It's more comfortable. It'll keep us warm, too.'

She snuggled back against me. Devra passed behind, and the road left the fields and rolled slowly into scattered trees, into heavy jungle. The sun poured through the trees to make burning red and yellow pools of light in the road, their edges indistinct among blue-green shadows. There weren't many travellers about. A little naked girl in charge of a flock of goats stared at us from a clearing and ran off to hide herself when we came so close that she could see it really was a new kind of monster that climbed puffing up to her.

On the climb I leaned rhythmically from side to side to increase my weight on the pedals, and breathed heavily in her ear. She said, 'Don't strain yourself, darling.'

I gasped. 'I – won't – I – like – this.'

She said, 'You are a babee,' and I could hardly make the bike go for the ecstasy of loving her. I began to sing, gasping breathlessly, in time with my slow heaves on the pedals. I sang: ' "In tropical climes there are certain times of day," ' but all I could remember after that was 'out in the midday sun', about twenty times over. Away to the right the goods train passed us, labouring out of sight in the jungle. My girl leaned back more comfortably and sang with me.

'Bharru,' I said after some time and stopped pedalling. She slid off, eased her legs, and smoothed out the seat of her trousers.

'Sore?' I asked.

'A little,' she said.

I said, 'Let's get a drink.' I wheeled the bicycle toward an old man sitting outside his house at the edge of the village. He brought us milk in an earthenware jar. Victoria drank dubiously. It had not been boiled, and I bet she'd been told a thousand times never to drink milk that had not been boiled. Quite right too. I told the old man about the leopard we were going to shoot, and when he refused payment for the milk I gave him a couple of Trichinopolies. Then Victoria and I sat down under a tree and played scissors-paper-stone for an hour, and afterward dozed off with our backs against the tree for another hour.

When we set off again the hill seemed steeper. I tried to sing but soon gave up for lack of breath. I said, 'Oh, why didn't I fall for a petite little piece, instead of a great healthy lump of female?' and she made the bike wobble from side to side, and it was like that all the way up.

Near Pathoda the road and railway came together again. The road curved down to cross a stream which the railway jumped over on a small girder bridge. There had been a derailment there just before I arrived in Bhowani. During the week Manbir and I had come out here and reconnoitred the place for this camp. It had seemed to me then that this valley would be good ground on which to fight my last battle against Patrick Taylor. The gong kept striking – was it seven or eight it had got to? – and I knew this would be the last battle.

It was not in my mind to use the camp to show Victoria what a fine open-air type I was, and by feats of prowess against our dumb chums invite comparisons between myself and the clumsy Patrick. My hopes were deeper and, I think, truer. I wanted to delete every frame of reference, both hers and mine, so that we could examine each other by nothing but what was in us. This valley was to be our Eden. In the jungle there is neither white nor brown, black nor khaki. In the jungle the history of men doesn't count; the quality of one man does. I prayed that I had that quality for her.

I had not thought Patrick was deep enough for her. Now that we had reached the jungle, I was not so sure. The mere fact that he shot animals meant nothing – but those heads were good. To get heads like that you have to spend many hours, many weeks, alone. It might have been the pot-hunter's lust that drove him – but he had never mentioned his trophies. It might have been in-credible good luck – but the words 'Patrick Taylor' and 'good luck' were not in the same dictionary. If he'd got those heads, with his clumsiness and his unserendipity, he'd got them by will-power, determination, and nothing else.

However, I too had a will and some determination. We both loved her. These thoughts about Patrick came to me only once the whole time – when we were approaching the railway bridge and the stream near Pathoda. For the rest, Victoria and I were alone together.

Beside the stream a footpath led into the woods to the north. I turned the bicycle on to the path, and Victoria covered her face with both hands against the whipping branches and tried to shield me as well. The path ran down with the water, sometimes close to the bank, sometimes winding and climbing a hundred yards off. After a mile the path dropped steeply down. I let go of the brake, took my feet off the pedals, and yelled, 'Yippee!'

The bike gathered speed, and Victoria stiffened. There was a clearing below on the bank of the stream; one tent was up, and Birkhe and Manbir were putting up the other. We crashed on faster and faster, and she screamed, '*Rodney!* Don't be a fool!' We shot, bouncing, across the clearing, and I headed the bike to-ward a thick bush. Then I let go of the handlebars, and we both put up our hands and crashed down among the bending twigs and the rushing leaves.

I helped her up and dusted her seat officiously, while she grumbled at me. Birkhe called out, 'The sahib has come.' Manbir said, 'I can see that, O one-pubic-hair! Make tea.' We smelled wood-smoke and saw a little fire burning between four big stones near their tent. I called out, 'Where's the shikari?'

Kulloo came forward. He'd been squatting at the edge of the

trees, but I hadn't noticed him. He was a small wiry man. He said, 'I am here.'

I said, 'Any news? Have you tied the bait out?'

'There is news.' Kulloo was a man who spoke in measured tones and would not be hurried. He said, 'The leopard killed two days ago, up the river, the other side of the railway.' He pointed upstream. I could just see a corner of the railway bridge among the distant tree-tops.

'He is a young male,' Kulloo continued. 'He killed a small chital. I found its remains the same evening. He will be hungry again now. I have bought a kid in the village and tied it out. You are late, sahib.'

I said, 'I know. I'm sorry. Is it a good noisy kid?'

'It is well spoken,' he said.

'We'd better get a move on,' I said.

Birkhe brought tea, and we sipped it slowly. Then he delved in a yakdan and brought out some food I'd had cooked and wrapped in Bhowani. Manbir filled the thermos. He was in a good temper again. I blew on my tea and told Victoria we really ought to have been in the machan earlier than this. She said, 'But then we wouldn't have bicycled up the hill, would we?' and smiled at me. Birkhe handed me my shooting coat, and I began to load up – rifle, ammunition, nightsight, torch and attachment, matches, hurricane lantern, all sorts of odds and ends. 'Okay,' I said at last. 'Now get your coat, and we'll start.'

A few minutes before, Victoria had looked tired, but that was all gone. She walked behind Kulloo along the path, and I behind her. We followed the stream north for half a mile while the jungle thickened up on both sides, until we came to another small clearing very like the one in which the camp stood. A group of tall trees across the stream dominated both banks. On the near side a single big tree stood at the edge of the clearing. The machan was wedged in its lower branches where the tree forked, about fourteen feet up. A white kid, tied by a short rope to a stake in the centre of the clearing, watched us, its ears twitching. A little boy was sitting at the foot of the tree with a tin-can in one hand and a stick in the other. Kulloo said, 'You have not seen or heard anything?'

'No, Father,' the boy said.

The kid bleated loudly and tried to come up to us, but its rope was too short.

Kulloo said, 'Good. You had better get up now, sahib.'

A rope hung down from the tree. Victoria looked unhappily at it, so I went up first, and between me and Kulloo and the little boy we soon had her scrambling over the edge of the machan. It swayed as she came on, and she sat down quickly. I let down the rope again, Kulloo tied the rifle to it, and I hauled up. One by one, everything came up. Victoria sat forward nervously and peered over the edge. The little boy threw up half a dozen stones, and I caught them and put them in a safe place. The kid shook its ears and watched us, silently now.

Kulloo turned up his face and asked, 'All well, sahib?'

I said, 'All well. Don't come before sunrise unless I give the usual signal.'

He said, 'All right, sahib.'

We watched the thin little man and his son walk off, one behind the other. In a minute the trees hid them. The white kid looked after them, opened its mouth to bleat, then glanced up at Victoria and me on the machan and decided there was no need to feel lonely. It wandered two or three times round its post, tucked its feet under it, and sat down.

'That kid's too intelligent for its station in life,' I muttered.

'I do feel sorry for it,' she whispered back. It was a pretty little animal with a pink nose and a short twitchy tail.

'So do I,' I said. I picked up the rifle, took a thin cord from my pocket, tied one end round the small of the grip, and the other end, fairly short, to a branch of the tree beside me. Then I fixed the torch and the nightsight, loaded the rifle, slipped on the safety catch, and leaned back against the tree trunk. From there I took aim at the kid and at a few other points round the clearing and then laid the rifle down.

I felt Victoria fumbling in the pocket of her bush shirt for a cigarette. I put out my hand to stop her, and kept it over hers. After a few minutes I whispered, 'Relax.' She was all tense. The first time an old peacock screamed she was going to go up like a jack-in-the-box. I thought we were quite likely to see some peafowl soon. There were a few bijasal trees across the stream into which they might come to roost.

334

The jungle quietened as the day faded. Slowly the edges of leaf and tree blurred, the water ran slowly, and the sound of its tinkling grew louder. She sat unmoving beside me, her hand under mine. Something passed between our hands so that she was no longer taut, while I was keyed up to see, as though for the first time, miracles that I had seen a thousand times. The evening came, and after that the dark, and I held her hand so that she should remark the mystery of those changes. She did not stir when the first peacock crashed in with a heavy beat of wings and a scream and a thud as it landed in the branches opposite. The kid began to bleat. For half an hour the peafowl flew in and settled noisily on their roosts. In the darkness the screaming, high in the trees over there, was eerie but yet so obviously familiar that she moved her hand under mine and pressed a little closer against me. I moved carefully to let her settle back against the tree. I put my left arm loosely over her shoulders, and she went to sleep. She was a drowsy peahen, and I a wakeful cock, and we were alone.

About one o'clock I heard something moving below us. The sound was little more than an exhalation in the dry leaves at the foot of our tree. The moon was just rising. I pressed Victoria gently under her left ear. She reached down as though to pull up a sheet, remembered, and pulled her hand back quickly. I squeezed a little harder and took my arm away. My hand brushed over her hair, and then I brought the rifle up.

There were two sounds – the small, determined, restless stamping of the kid, and the other. The kid was a white blur, the other, nothing. The moonlight had not reached down there yet. Only the tops of the trees were silvered a long way off on the hillside.

I snapped on the torch, and the shaft of light sprang out. I felt Victoria holding her breath as she waited for the bang. A yellow, hang-tailed pariah bitch stood there, blinking in the light, on the other side of the kid. I switched off the torch.

She squeezed my arm sympathetically. I lowered the rifle across my knees and reached out for the thermos. She uncorked it for me, and we drank slowly, carefully not to let the tea gurgle in the neck of the flask. Mosquitoes whined about us, and there were lumps on my face and wrists. The pariah ran away noisily. I wondered why it had taken so long to go.

When the tea was put away we watched the moon riding up

among cumulus clouds. It was a hot, close night. An aeroplane passed over, below the cloud base, its lights weaving like fireflies among the terraced branches. She took my hand again, and we both wanted to be up there with the pilot, to look down with him through the slanted windows on this jungle and ourselves. There was thunder in the south-west. When the plane had gone the thunder soared and grumbled round the jungle. She would find it strange to live in England, where the monsoon never came. Silent lightning hovered impatiently among the trees guarding the southern horizon.

The mosquitoes came back. I had learned to take them, but Victoria had a skin like a baby's bottom, and she twisted and turned and couldn't get comfortable, anyhow. I think she longed for the end of the night, and certainly she sighed with relief when the leaves began to take on a silvery bleach. The stream quietened, and a dim mist drew on across the grass, a mist as insubstantial as a bridal veil. Soon we could see the post the white kid was tied to, and Victoria fell asleep.

Then next time I nudged her she was on the edge of wakefulness, anyway. She had stirred, half awake and half asleep, as the peafowl woke up and crashed out of their trees and flew away. She sat up with a luxurious sigh and turned her head to smile at me. She stretched back her arms and yawned. In one second she was going to say, 'I bet I look awful.'

I jabbed the point of my elbow into her ribs, and she swallowed the yawn and looked up. The kid was there, circling round its post, facing outward its head bravely down. The pariah bitch circled round outside the kid, her teeth bared, trying to work up the courage to attack this thing which she knew had no teeth and no horns and yet stood so fiercely at bay.

Still Victoria hadn't seen.

The bitch darted in a pace, lost her nerve, and fell back. She was thin, and swaybacked with the weight of the milk in her dugs.

I murmured, 'Look right.'

Victoria turned her head. Behind a tuft of grass not much higher or thicker than a woven waste-paper basket there was a leopard. The leopard crept forward upon the bitch, its stomach pressed close to the ground and its elbows high. When the bitch was facing in its direction, the leopard froze. When the bitch circled, the leopard crawled forward. The light was good and strong now. The mist hung in the jungle to the sides, and over the river, but not in the clearing.

The pariah darted in and caught the kid by the leg. The leopard bunched together, all four feet close set under the middle of its belly. Its tail rose slowly, like a bar. I fired.

The leopard's tail sank down. The pariah let go of the kid and burst out in a frenzy of yelping. Victoria sat up with a gasp of excitement. I sat back and roared with laughter. The bitch streaked off, yelling, along the path toward the camp and village.

I said, 'She thought it was the kid who made that bang. That'll teach her to bully poor defenceless animals. Now, do you think you can throw a stone as far as that leopard, while I cover it, or are you really all woman?'

She took the stone and threw it out awkwardly, while I held my rifle aimed at the leopard. I suppose there's some good anatomical reasons why women always look as if they're trying to throw their hands away when they throw a stone. The stone fell far short, and Victoria said, 'It's not fair. How can I throw sitting down?'

I lowered the rifle and said, 'All woman. It's just as well, usually. Now you can admire another of my masculine skills.' I took a second stone, tossed it out with my left hand, and got the rifle up into my shoulder before the stone fell. It landed by the leopard's nose, but the leopard did not stir.

'Fluke,' Victoria grumbled.

I said, 'How much will you bet?' and threw another. That hit the leopard in the flank, and Victoria said, 'Oh, darling, it's really dead.'

I fired twice into the air with a ten-second interval. Victoria kissed me.

I said, 'Let's finish the food while we're waiting. Tea, girl! I'm thirsty.' And soon the shikari Kulloo came with his son and Birkhe and Manbir, and we walked back to the camp with the leopard slung on a pole among us and the kid bleating contentedly at our heels.

At the camp Kulloo wanted to know whether he should begin to skin the leopard immediately. I said, 'No, it'll keep till dusk. Let's have a skinning party then. Bring along anyone who wants to come. Bring Bhansi Lall the Stationmaster-babu. Can you get five or six gallons of toddy?'

Kulloo's taciturn face creased. He said, 'I can get it. I'll hang the leopard in the tree there until evening. I'll want some oil to keep the ants off.'

I nodded, and Kulloo and Birkhe and the little boy hung the leopard from a low branch and isolated the branch from the ground by banding the bark with kerosene.

When we had washed and eaten another breakfast we both felt sleepy. We went into the tent and loosened our clothes. The tent flies were up and the flap open so that the breeze could flow through. Victoria was ready first and lay quiet on the bedding. It was soft underneath and smelled of cut grass and leaves. I lay down beside her and closed my eyes. I don't suppose she had ever slept in a tent and it was a while before she could absorb the special drowsiness of a sunny morning in the jungle. I heard Manbir grunt something to Birkhe, and Birkhe answer, '*Hawas*.' A minute later the old man passed across the front of the tent with my shotgun on his shoulder. He did not look at us as we lay there, and soon the trees hid him.

In the end Victoria slept before I did. In sleep her face was calm and unmoved by the even breathing that lifted her chest. There was none of the sulkiness which used to be in her expression when I first met her. A dawning of worry touched her mouth and round her eyelids, and I reached out my hand to stroke her. But I didn't know what was the thought that had flitted into her sleep, or whether the touch of my hand would soothe or alarm her. Soon the buzzing of the flies turned to a rhythmic drone, and Birkhe's small movements ebbed about the camp, and a train made a distant musical resonance in the jungle as it passed over the iron girder bridge, and I fell asleep.

We awoke together. I looked at her and put out my hand to her face. I said, 'Get your bathing suit and come and have a swim.'

When she rubbed her forehead the sweaty dirt fell off in little black rolls, and she made a grimace of disgust at herself. She got what she wanted out of her suitcase and followed me to the stream. We worked up barefooted against the current, our trousers rolled above our knees. Half-way to the railway bridge we came to a pool. It was ten or twelve feet across and no more

338

than waist deep at best, but the water fell into it down a low fall and made white bubbles, and then swirled round in broad cool green streaks. It was late in the afternoon – I didn't know or care exactly what time. Saturday afternoon. Victoria looked at the pool and round at the trees and said hesitantly, 'Here?'

I said, 'Yes, why not? It's a good place.'

The path we had bicycled along ran somewhere up the hill there to the left. Victoria turned and began at once to walk toward some thick bushes quite a way off. Now, how did she know they were there before she turned round? I said, 'Hey, I want to have a look at your nakedness. I'm not sophisticated like some of your friends.' She turned back and began to blush furiously. She just said, 'I forgot,' and started to undress near me. In a minute she was standing there with all her clothes off, and whatever it was that had made her blush just now, it wasn't prudery. It was a memory – and not of me.

A woman lying naked on a bed is one thing, a woman undressing by a pool of running water with sunlight and shadow on her flat belly, and her face turning to you, shy and proud, is another thing. Her eyes met mine, and she stood quite still. Slowly the little smile faded from her face.

She wanted me to step across the grass and put my arms round her. I wouldn't go, because I knew the exact shape of her lust and every intimation of it in her voice and face and body, and this wasn't it.

She said, 'Rodney, please,' and lifted her arms a little.

I said, 'Here?' There were stones and spear-grass about, but I wasn't thinking of them. Spear-grass doesn't stick into the naked skin, and there was plenty of soft turf between the stones.

She said, 'Yes, here, Rodney.' So the memory was here.

But even if she had been Rose Mary, there is a limit to the amount of pleading, even special pleading, I can withstand from dumb female eloquence. Furthermore, I was in the hell of a rage that this had to be so. I went for her like a tiger, and we made unrelenting animals out of each other for ten or fifteen minutes. Perhaps that's what she wanted, but whether it proved anything I don't know, because she didn't tell me.

In the evening we ate chupattis, rice, dal, and goat (not the kid). I'd thought of taking some champagne and cold ham out to the camp, but champagne has unfortunate connotations for me, of chorus girls and Brighton, so I didn't. I don't think Victoria would have minded.

After dinner Birkhe started a new bonfire near the edge of the stream, and the villagers and Stationmaster Bhansi Lall walked down from Pathoda to join us. Some of them cut wood for the fire; some exclaimed over the leopard and lifted it carefully down under Manbir's orders; some dragged dry stones from the river bed and set them as chairs round the fire for us, and then Birkhe spread blankets over the stones. We sipped sweet, hot Camp coffee and watched the villagers whet their knives. When they were ready, Kulloo, the shikari, came up to me and said, 'How are you going to mount the leopard, sahib? It will make a difference to the way we skin it.'

I asked Victoria how she wanted it.

She began to ask whether I was really going to give it to her, but that was Rose Mary's kind of coyness, so she answered, 'I'd like the whole skin, flat, you know, so that it can be a rug.'

I told Kulloo that. In case he had not understood, Bhansi Lall, who was in tremendous form, told him again. Kulloo walked away and gave a shout. The six or seven villagers round the carcass gave an answering shout and bent over, all together, to begin the skinning. Soon one of them began to sing. It was in dialect, and I did not understand. It was a hot night, but the fire and the song and the leopard made us forget that.

Victoria said, 'Darling, why don't you keep the skin yourself?'

I met her eyes and said, 'I don't want a damned moth-eaten spotted carpet on the floor or a pair of glass eyes on the wall. It is very proper, though, that you should have a skinned leopard beside your bed. You can warm your feet on him in the morning.'

I lit a cheroot. The song of the villagers dropped to a low chant. A jug of toddy stood beside them, and they passed it round from hand to hand as they sliced and sang. I listened and thought from a few words I caught that they were singing about a battle. I asked Bhansi Lall.

He said, 'They are singing of Moslem times, Colonel-sahib. There was one terrible battle-fighting in those times.'

The leopard's carcass, white and bright light-red, lay out on the grass among the dark brown men. The bloody pelt hung loose, held to the body at a couple of places only. Several of the villagers were drunk. When the work was finished they began to caper about the grass, waving their knives and long-handled axes, their faces bright and their black hair streaming behind them. They looked like savages, but they weren't.

This was my India, not because of the capering or the drunkenness but because these people had no desire to become like me, nor I like them. There had been a place for me round such fires as this for three hundred years. The Ranjits and Surabhais, who were trying to change themselves, didn't light bonfires and dance round them. They read Paine and Burke and spoke in English because the ideas they were trying to express did not exist in their own language. If I and my sort had an idea, it was to make Indian wood into better wood, not change it into bakelite. In general, though, our great virtue was *not* having an idea.

It was a bad feeling to realize, as the villagers beat on drums and Manbir and I and Birkhe kept time with them, that Victoria must have an idea. Otherwise, why had she got herself mixed up with Ranjit? It wasn't love for him, not on her part. It wasn't lust. She had an idea.

I gave her another drink from our whisky bottle. The bonfire roared, the villagers sang, and the sound of the cool water was drowned.

'That was an old song,' Kulloo the shikari announced. He stood before us, bowing slightly, swaying lightly. He carried a small jug of toddy in his hand and waved it rhythmically. He intoned, 'Now we will sing another song, about what our fathers saw in the Black Year.' He bowed again and staggered back to join the rest.

Bhansi Lall said importantly, 'Black Year is meaning year of horrible Indian Mutiny, Miss Jones. That was incident when all peoples behaved most jolly indecently. One thousand, eight hundred and fifty-seven, Anno Domini.'

I clapped my hands as the villagers sang. I felt as wild as a coot and more than somewhat drunk. The gravestone in the Bhowani cemetery said:

Here lies
JOANNA
beloved wife of
Captain Rodney Savage
13th Rifles, B.N.I.
May 10, 1857

I'd been here before, but I didn't live here. I only came here to work and fight and build, to dance and drink and fornicate.

In the beginning, the villagers' song exulted, and Bhansi Lall muttered, 'These words are relating story of battle-fighting, shootings, and bloodstains.' The song hushed, the capering stopped, and Bhansi Lall muttered, 'Now they are mentioning that dead bodies of English ladies and gentlemen were found in bush, or down well of drinking water. These jungle people are most insanitary and wild, really.' The song rose. 'Further battle-fightings. They are recounting punishment of sepoys' treasonable outlook.' The song fell; the singers stood in a rough circle, and an old man recited. Bhansi Lall muttered, 'Now words are in honour of Her Majesty Queen Empress Victoria, lately lamented. Words are implying that Queen Victoria was daughter of many gods and devils. They say good queen possessed eyes of purple hue and was standing nine cubits in stature – which is bloody lie, by God. They are *most* insanitary peoples.'

Victoria muttered, 'My head's swimming!' The music shrieked harshly, the bamboo flutes wailed, the little drums throbbed. When the villagers sat down to drink, only the drumming was kept up.

My Birkhe beat cheerfully on a madal, which is a deep and narrow Gurkha drum. Manbir had another. We'd brought three out from H.Q. Company store. Manbir gave me one and said, 'Beat, son.' His face was flushed dull purple, and his green shirt glittered metallically in the firelight.

He stood upright and said thickly in his horrible Hindustani, 'Listen, villagers. That was a good song of yours, though I did not understand a word of it. Now I will sing you a better one, about our Gurkha war with the Chinese – oh, hundreds of years ago.'

I jumped up and grabbed his arm and shouted, 'No, Father,

don't sing that. Let's sing and dance the Pilgrimage of the Lord Buddha to Gaya.'

He held on to my arm to keep himself from falling. He said, 'All right, son. That's a good idea. Birkhe, you come here with that madal. No, stand over there. Miss-sahiba, you sit *here*. Drink more whisky. My son and my grandson here can't really dance at all, but they're younger than I am. Now!'

He stepped out into the centre of the clearing. The madals were hung on string round our necks so that we had our hands free to beat them at both ends. Victoria wrapped her arms round her knees and watched us.

By God, we were good. At first all three of us stumbled occasionally, and twice Manbir tore a strip off Birkhe for beating the wrong rhythm, but we settled down quickly. It's a long dance and a slow dance. The villagers and Kulloo and Bhansi Lall squatted round the edges of the clearing and clapped the time with their hands and never took their eyes off us. We three had been drunk and funny to begin with, and perhaps out of place because we came from mountains and seas unbelievably far from that jungle valley. But as the tale unwound, the place made room for us, as it had done for many like us before. The fire behind us didn't die; the villagers fed it. Our madals throbbed, and soon Kulloo picked up the main theme that we sang and quavered it on his flute, and the trees soughed under a night breeze.

The dance ended. Victoria sat expectantly, waiting for a crash, a pose, a last attitude and a rumble of drums – but of course it just died away, and when Manbir and I went toward her I think she still wasn't sure whether that was part of the dance. Then Manbir put one arm round me and the other round Birkhe, and I said, 'You taught me well, Father, didn't you?' and Manbir answered, 'I taught you well. Back in Manali, when you were a recruit.'

The villagers took their leave, some uproarious, some suddenly shy. Bhansi Lall shook our hands with great formality and waddled away, singing in a nasal tenor, for he too was drunk. He'd asked me a couple of times during the evening whether the rapscallion K. P. Roy, Esquire, had been laid by the heels. He hated K. P. Roy as only a babu can who's had his precious regulations trampled on.

Manbir and I sat beside Victoria for a while, all staring at the fire, then he and Birkhe went to their tent, and Victoria and I sat alone while the fire sank lower and lower and made no sound. Once or twice she glanced over her shoulder, and I said, without looking round, 'I hope a tigress is watching. With her cubs. Will you come down to the river?'

She walked slowly with me across the grass, holding my hand and twining her fingers in mine. There were marks on the grass, picked out by the dull fire and the thin glow of the hurricane lantern in the door of our tent – marks of blood and dancing feet and spilled toddy, and yellow hairs, and a sharp smell of meat and wood-smoke.

I stopped on the top of the low bank above the stream, where the light met the dark. The water was black and the trees pale. She put up her other hand, turning to me, and gently stroked my face and laid her cheek alongside my cheek.

I turned her so that the light from the fire, unseen itself but reflected down from the woven ceiling of leaves, touched her face. I put her there so that her eyes and the corners of her mouth would help me to understand the changeable, deceptive, compulsive twining of her fingers. Then I broke all physical touch between us and stood back from her.

Certainty was very near for both of us, but it wasn't with us.

I took her wrist and did what she had done to me once before. I turned it over and kissed the inside, holding my lips quietly there. She bent over my head, and her hair moved softly across mine.

38

AFTERWARD I never could remember how the Sunday morning passed. I had a little surprise brewing for her, and I know we had to hang round until the time came. I think we all sat about in the camp for a while and then went out with the two shotguns. Birkhe and Manbir came too – in fact, surely, it had been their morning? I gave them the guns and myself trailed along behind with Victoria, throwing stones into bushes for them and picking up and carrying the game they killed. Oh, yes, I remember now.

There wasn't any game. There was a cocky-olly bird and a green pigeon. Old Manbir and young Birkhe stalked a bird that sat preening itself on a tree. They approached from opposite sides, took careful aim, and doubly blew the bird to pieces, and afterward whispered to each other in excited grunts. And Manbir let off both barrels at a fish in the pool under the railway bridge and drenched himself from head to foot; but he got the fish.

The other part of the day, the magic and decisive hours, began after lunch. I glanced at my watch and asked her if she'd like to come for a stroll up toward the road. It would be a shame to spend this last afternoon pounding our charpoys, I said. I told her to bring her jacket. Obediently she stubbed out her cigarette and went along with me.

I talked busily, pointing out the birds and naming the trees along the path, the same we had come bumping down on the G.S. bicycle, and I don't think she suspected anything, not even when we saw the shine of chromium and glass through the trees near the end of the path. She said, 'Look, Rodney, a car. Do you think – oh dear, do you think something's happened, and it's come to take you back?'

I didn't answer. When we stepped out on the road she saw that it was a Rolls-Royce station wagon. Mole was sitting in the driver's seat. He's slender, quite dark, and about my age. He was wearing a tan palm-beach suit and a panama hat. His chauffeur, in the Kishanpur yellow drill livery, was sitting beside him. The chauffeur whispered to Mole when he saw us, and Mole got out, not hurrying. He was standing by the bonnet and the huge glittering headlamps when we came up.

I touched my hands five or six times to my forehead and said, '*Salaam, Rawan-sahib, bahut bahut salaam!*'

He said, 'Hello, Rod. And this is your beautiful lady?'

I said, 'Yes. Victoria, curtsy nicely to His Highness Diprao Rawan, Rajah of Kishanpur.' She caught the sides of her slacks and curtsied, laughing up at him, and I was pleased with her. I said, 'He is called the Rawan, but you did that so prettily that you may call him Mole. He's an honorary brother of mine. Mole, this is Victoria, and you can damned well bow. "Where are your manners now, Master Dip?"' I spoke the last bit in a shrill, curt voice, and we both laughed. The old jokes are the best.

'She was a terror,' Mole said. He gave Victoria a bow, sweeping low his panama hat. 'Victoria what?'

'Victoria Jones,' she said.

He said, 'Good. Hop in.'

We three squeezed into the front seat, and the chauffeur sat splendidly alone in the back. 'Look a little more dignified and acknowledge the salutes for me,' Mole told him. The chauffeur grinned more widely and began to raise his hand to left and right to the peasants who salaamed as they saw the big car with the yellow flag on the radiator cap come racing down the road.

'You never told me about this, Rodney,' Victoria said reproachfully. 'I could have got myself a little better dressed than this. Where are we going?'

I told her, 'Kishanpur. It's only about thirty miles. Mole's going to introduce us to some princely luxury. He's going to show us how the idle rich live.'

Mole said, 'I'm not idle, and I'm not rich.' He swung the Rolls on to the dusty shoulder of the road to rush past a string of lumbering bullock carts. 'But I have to pretend to be, or the politicians would have nothing to rave about in the Monkey House. I'm richer than Rockefeller compared with these people, of course – but so are you, both of you.' He took one hand off the wheel and waved it at a family of four standing open-mouthed on the roadside.

'You won't be for long,' I said. 'I hear that Congress proposes to nationalize the princes. They're going to use you as travel agents in America, selling passages to India. Gandhi told me, last time I met him, that *your* post was going to be in Squedunk, Pa. – or is it La.?'

Mole said, 'Please, Rod, please let's not talk politics for the moment. Did you get your leopard?'

I said we had, and he asked me to tell him about it.

I said, 'Victoria, you tell him. My throat's dry.'

She told him, and the road flew back, and we came to the Kishan. It is a wide river, and we crossed on a ferry. To the right the heavy castle hangs on the far bank above smooth water. Mole said, 'That's where I live.'

She cried, 'Oh, it's beautiful, and so big!'

He said, 'It's in decay, but I have to live there. That's where I belong. Wait till you see it.'

The Rolls squeezed through the narrow turns into the entry port. We went into the courtyard and circled round the tinkling fountain. 'This is the only part we keep open,' Mole said. 'Those rooms up there. The rest – even the outside walls are falling down.'

We went in. It was cool in the long, high corridors, but I smelled at once the familiar mustiness, which hung everywhere, even under the lived-in smell of the rooms that Mole still used. Victoria sniffed surreptitiously, but Mole noticed and turned to her with his languid look and said, 'Can you smell it too? Decay. Change and decay. What do you want to do till dinner-time?'

I asked him if his wife was there.

'No, she's away,' Mole answered. His drawl was extra languid, so I knew that Sumitra was still busy in France with a Russian count. There was a lot we didn't have to explain to each other.

I told him we'd like to wander round. I wanted to show Victoria the tapestries and the dungeons.

He said, 'You know your way. I have to work.'

She walked with me round the castle. Afternoon passed into evening, and I found in the castle, as often before, mirrors for everything I was feeling. That day it was a place that agreed with me in wanting to fight, but sighed with me that it was no good fighting, and echoed my whispers – that it too loved her. My keenest memory is the sound of Victoria's shoes in the long stone passages.

'Why is he your brother?' she asked once.

I told her. 'Because his great-grandmother and my great-grandfather tried to kill each other in the Mutiny. *Her* son became *his* ward. We've kept it up, generation by generation, ever since.'

'What's going to happen now?' she asked.

I didn't answer her. That was a question. Instead, I stopped and knocked on a door and said, 'Mole forgot to tell you that he does keep one other room open – this one. It's his study. He's not in.' I pushed the heavy door open and stood aside. It was a light and luxurious apartment. An ormulu-encrusted table stood at the right of the room's three wide windows. Isfahan rugs covered the floor, and there was a large divan under the centre window. A man sitting at the desk would look out across the river into British territory.

I was looking out across the river, but I wasn't seeing anything, not even Victoria right in front of me. I must have had a queer expression on my face when I realized that Victoria was saying, 'What's the matter, darling? What's happened?'

I jerked my shoulders to shake off the invisible Old Man hanging on them. I said, 'History. That's the trouble with it. Come on.'

Dinner took us a big step to where we were going. I often wonder whether Mole knew exactly what he was doing to us that night. He has flashes of rare insight, but he doesn't always care to act by the light they give him.

We waited in the drawing-room for him, and then he swept in, shimmering in the full ceremonial dress of the Rawans, brilliant yellow with diamond necklaces and ruby rings and tight white trousers. I stood up and said, 'Oh no, Mole! What do you want to do this to us for? Look at our clothes.'

'Forget yourselves,' he said, ushering us forward. 'See only me and imagine you are mirrored in me.'

In the dining-room the table was dark, the flowers lightly banked round it. He had golden champagne and three attendants in yellow, and the atmosphere was Europe mated with Asia. That's what had made Victoria. But this was as strange and wonderful to her as – I was.

I didn't know when I'd see Mole again, so over the soufflé I asked him what his immediate plans were.

He had only to say, I'm going to stay here, or, I'm going to shoot myself, or whatever the hell he had in mind. He said, instead, 'I want to go away. I want to be out of here before Nehru sends a pair of earnest Calcutta B.A.s to tell me that I'm oppressing my people. I don't want to meet them. I could only reply that they are quite right. And I have no more chance than the man in the moon of making them understand what this means – this.'

He turned to the old fellow beside his chair and said, 'Old friend, your time has come. Go and jump off the battlements on to the hard ground.'

The old man's expression did not change. He said, 'For the honour of the Rawan! Is there time to make a prayer and say my good-byes?'

Mole said, 'There is time. This task that I give you is to be delayed until you see me break a promise. Then you are to jump, on top of me as I walk below, that I may die.'

348

The old man inclined his head slightly and said, 'For the honour of the Rawan!'

Mole said to us, 'Do not imagine that he won't do it. He will. There are not many left like him, of course. Doubt is spreading fast.' He turned to Victoria and said, 'You are shocked?'

She said, 'It was rather frightening. It seems so – out-of-date.' And Mole said, 'It is. But you realize that if the King Emperor told me to jump off the battlements, I would do it at once – and with pleasure.'

'Why?' I said, knowing the answer.

He might have answered, Personal loyalty, or tradition, or faith, or continuity – or, It's the simplest system. But he said the same thing in a way that applied more particularly to our problem. He said, 'Because these are my people. Because I belong here. That's why I'm staying.'

He had said enough, and the rest of the meal was quiet. Soon after we'd finished our brandy he asked us to excuse him. He had work to do until we were ready to go back to Bhowani.

I took Victoria's hand and led her along vault-like passages and up stair after stair until we came out on the flat roof of the castle. The heat of the earth and the smell of the water were mingled up there in the high still night. She leaned over the parapet at my side. Again the lightning flickered round the western horizon. The waste of trees stretched away there to the west, rising and falling in breakers of darkness and lesser darkness. I lit a cheroot and turned my head to watch the smoke drift north against the bright stars.

Music stretched round us in the sky and hung in the cliffs of darkness by the outer walls, weaving a silk web about the fortress. It was Mole's gramophone. He wasn't working. He was feeling. I whispered, 'The *Missa Solemnis*. Poor Mole.'

Poor me. Poor little darling boy Roddy, because he can't get everything he wants in the world. And he's such a brilliant boy too. I threw the cigar over the edge and caught her, and she twined round me and sucked my tongue despairingly into her wide wet mouth.

When we got back to Bhowani it was late. I sat in my drawing-room for quite a while and then wrote William Stevenage a telegram. William was a member of the Board of the Presidency Education Trust. He was the man who'd saved Patrick from jail when Patrick threatened Wallingford on that trip to Bombay. William was a box wallah too, but I had known him at school – I was a squealer in the same dormitory when he was one of the Upper Ten – and I always did want to be a bloody Boy Scout.

39

STEVE ELLINGTON was due to come through Bhowani at 16.44 on Friday – that was on Number 98 Up. Steve had commanded a British battalion next to us for a good spell of Burma, and though I do not like the majority of British Service types, I liked Ellington and his battalion. Now he was on his way back to England with three or four officers and a lot of B.O.R.s, who'd all fallen due for Python at the same time. We'd arranged to give them a reception in the thirteen minutes 98 Up spent at Bhowani Junction.

These railway-station parties used to be quite common before the war. The cause of them was always the same – someone going home to England. We'd sing up and down the platform and drink a lot in the refreshment room and make a great nuisance of ourselves. The Indian passengers enjoyed the show as much as we did. The Anglo-Indian station and train staffs were much glummer. No one could or would arrest us in those days. It was all very lordly and magnificent. I suppose the railway people felt about our antics much as we felt about their A.F.I. – that they were ludicrous and rather shameful, but you couldn't do anything about them.

The monsoon had broken, and it was raining like hell when we got to the station, Victoria and I and all my officers in a large group. The part of the platform sheltered by the canopy was crowded with would-be passengers. We were early, and then we found that Number 98 was going to be twenty minutes late. In a mob we forced into the European refreshment room and shouted for whiskies and sodas. We left the mess orderlies on the platform, guarding a tin trunk full of ice and champagne bottles. The orderlies kept a clear space round themselves by waving their hands and shouting 'shoo!' at everybody, as to goats. The jemadar-adjutant was there with a few N.C.O.s and a few crates of beer. The rain beat steadily down on the edge of the platform and ran off in a stream down the gutter between the rails.

There is nothing depressing about the first month of monsoon rain. It takes at least that long to get over the delight of seeing it and feeling it. But I suddenly decided I couldn't stand the noise and wet capes over the backs of the chairs and the damned jollity in the refreshment room. I said, 'Here, I've had enough of this. Let's get out on the platform.' I drank my whisky and got up. Victoria came with me.

We struggled out through the crowd. Rose Mary was there with Howland. Howland raised his glass as I passed him, and shouted, 'Wotcher, chief! Have one on me, Colonel. I'll be on this train in a month.' A momentary anxiety crossed Rose Mary's face, a quick calculation. She would have to make sure within that month that she would be on the same train. Any sensitive girl would think twice before doing anything that Rose Mary was doing.

I stopped by Howland and said, 'Thank you, no. And I've told you before that in this regiment subalterns address field officers as "Sir", not "Major", or "Colonel", or even "Chief". You are not in the Royal Army Pay Corps, unfortunately.'

Howland edged back from me. His beefy face, already flushed, settled into hurt resentfulness. Victoria followed me out, and as she passed them I heard Rose Mary mutter, not too loudly, 'Your boy friend's got a liver this afternoon, hasn't he?'

Outside, I didn't wait for Victoria to speak, though I don't suppose she was going to. As we pushed through the mob I said, 'If you're about to ask me to be nice to Howland, don't. I've always been the same, and he's always been the same. He's convinced that I don't see his good qualities because I'm a narrow-minded regular. I'm convinced that he's one of the most naturally talented blighters I've ever come across. He will go far in civilian life. And he and Rose Mary will make a fine pair.'

There was no doubt that Rose Mary had hooked him. He'd asked to see me early that morning, as man to man. It was an interview which would have driven me to a yammering incoherence of fury at the best of times. He asked me to give him my considered opinion on the wisdom of marrying an Anglo-Indian. Did I think it would work out all right? 'You're so wise, Colonel. I know you don't like me, Colonel, but I do admire you, Colonel' – three bags full, etc., etc. Oh, Master Howland needed to have his name written on the soles of his boots so that when he disappeared up my arse the adjutant would know where to find him. He had the salesman's aggressive ability to spot any spark of generosity – which he would call a weakness – and with it he had the salesman's sense of self-preservation. He didn't actually mention Victoria, but because of her he thought he could force me to get matey and swop confidences, measurements, and performance details with him. The fat sod.

We stopped near the station entrance, and I glowered at the people struggling in with their boxes and rolls and bundles. Victoria saw Govindaswami farther down and drew my attention to him. I peered over the heads of the crowd. He was talking to Ranjit – and the Sirdarni-sahiba. It looked as if she was catching the train. He'd never pressed any charge against her, so she'd been out of jail for more than a week.

We waited, pressed close by the crowd. Patrick passed by, pushing and shoving as usual. But, looking round, I saw Indians shoving and Gurkhas shoving, and we had been shoving, and no one seemed to mind. Perhaps there was a different atmosphere in Bhowani since Surabhai had died for democracy.

Patrick didn't see us before he turned up the stairs to the district offices and disappeared. When he had gone Victoria said, 'Has he seen Mr Stevenage yet?'

I said, 'How the hell do I know? I'm not his keeper, though God knows he needs one.' William Stevenage had arrived the day before on his way to visit the cement orchard or glue mine or whatever it was his firm owned at Cholaghat. But of course my telegram had also had something to do with his arrival. He was staying with Sammy for a couple of days before continuing his journey into the mofussil. I'd had a talk with him about things in general. He hadn't come to the station for this party.

Sammy came up to us and tipped his panama nicely to Victoria. He said blandly, 'Can you tell me why the arrival of a train is so exciting? Even when one is grown-up and presumed to have become blasé?'

I said, 'A steam engine is a libidinous symbol representing lusts that you absorbed into your subconscious at the age of one month while you lay asleep in a cot in your parents' bedroom. In and out and round and round. Don't try to fob me off with dirty notions at this time of the afternoon. Where's the Sirdarni-sahiba going? Visiting friends?'

Sammy sighed, removed his panama, and mopped his brow. He answered, 'You could call it that. The friends live in Warsaw, whence there is a good train service, I believe, to the east.'

I said, 'She's going to Russia? Are you people letting her?'

He said, 'We can't stop her. It's a world conference of some kind. She will be back. But not for a year or two. Not till after you've followed *your* friend away, on this train, and gone back whence you came.'

I said, 'And Ranjit?'

He said, 'He made her go – by becoming a Sikh. It's been a great triumph of love and determination for him. She was trying to be two things at once – and to make him the same – a Communist and an Indian. It can't be done. So they're parting here at Bhowani Junction, he to become an Indian, and she to become a Communist.'

I drew on my cheroot and looked carefully over Sammy's calm bony face. I took the cigar from my mouth and said, 'You know, Govindaswami, you are a dashed good fellow, for a native. Allow me the privilege of putting you up for my club next time you are in Town.'

Sammy's face became solemn. He said, 'You are extraordinarily kind yourself, Savage. In fact, you are a white man. I presume that some of your best friends are natives?'

I said, 'Indeed that is so, Govindaswami.'

He said, 'It is such men as you who help me to forget my unfortunate pigmentation. But tell me, Savage, do you not fear that Clutterbuck will whiteball me?'

I said, 'All right, all right, here's the train.' Sammy turned and led the way through the shrieking people on the platform. Patrick came down the stairs just before we got to them, and stood with his hands in his pockets. Sammy passed close to him and said, 'Good afternoon, Mr Taylor.' Patrick ignored him but said, 'Good afternoon,' to Victoria and me and tried to smile.

As we went on Sammy said, 'He's having a bad time. You have heard that he is under a month's notice of dismissal from the railway?'

Victoria stopped dead among the seething crowds, as if he'd punched her over the heart. The engine of 98 passed by, clanking and hissing. Her father would be along soon if he wasn't here already. Above everything else I heard the shrill foxhunting yells from the end of the platform, and the shouts, and Molly Dickson's shriek – 'Oh, come down and *kiss* me, Steve, you gorgeous beast!'

I saw Steve in the door of his carriage and thought, There he is, on his way out. Soon I would go. We'd all go. It wasn't desertion, for us, was it? It was the British people deserting their responsibility, wasn't it? Then why didn't I stay? Because I didn't belong here, not as a stone or a stream belongs. Or a cheechee engine driver's little girl, in a big topi with a waterproof cover, playing in the dust beside the red-hot rails.

We went down to the crowd. Everyone was out on the platform, jabbering like monkeys beside the train. The rain hissed on the carriage roofs and drummed on the canopy and ran whispering down the window panes. Birkhe had three champagne glasses insecurely held in his hands and an anxious look on his face. A cork popped, and Molly shrieked, 'Goody! Simkin!' I managed to get hold of Steve Ellington.

Steve's eyes flickered when I took Victoria's hand and said, 'This is *it*, Steve.' But he was well trained, and the flicker went, and his smile widened, and he said, 'You poor girl! It looks as though you haven't lost your luck, Rodney,' and the damned fool meant it. He didn't care about her colour any more than I did. In the beginning he'd come out from England with his head full of the usual British Service notions about 'native troops' and 'the babu mentality' – I'd had the same notions – but, unlike Winston Churchill, Steve had had the chance to grow out of them. When his boys took the Kyaukpadaung Ridge they didn't have to dirty their boots in the mud. They could tread on the Gurkhas and Dogras who lay there already, thick as autumnal leaves that strew et cetera. He was never very white after that, except as a joke.

No, it was the fact that she was a half-caste that made his eyes flicker. Anglo-Indians weren't brave, or even despicable. They were never in situations where they could be either. They were only comical. They tried to marry British soldiers. They spoke like Welshmen. They wore topis at midnight.

We started drinking toasts. Farther down, the B.O.R.s leaned out of the windows, knocked off the tops of the beer bottles against the side of their carriage, and shouted cheerfully in pidgin Hindustani to the Gurkhas. Old Manbir had now arrived down there to join the jemadar-adjutant's group.

Victoria was looking strange. The champagne seemed to have gone straight to her eyes. She was turning her head from side to side and examining us as though we were a lot of strangers. As though she were saying to herself, Where do I belong in this? Among the frenetic passengers waving from the upper decks, or among the ordinary people who were contorting their faces into smiles but would stay behind? I knew the answer damned well, just as I knew I'd been a traveller for too many generations to change.

Victoria's father passed by on the outskirts of our crowd. She waved desperately to him to come to her, but he grinned and held up his lunchbox and thermos and train orders. He had to go. He looked foolishly happy with his red bandanna and hunched shoulders and bad teeth. Both his daughters were here among the officers, and they were both drinking champagne. Champagne didn't mean Brighton to him. I saw him stop a little farther up and look back at us all: Rose Mary, her glass in her hand, shrilling with laughter; Victoria, her flank touching the flank of a lieutenant-colonel.

A little later the conductor-guard blew his whistle imperiously. The engine whistled. None of us took any notice, except Victoria, who said, 'The train is due to go now.' Five minutes later the conductor-guard came up, brushing specks off his starched white drill, and touched my arm. He said, and he had a terrific cheechee singsong, 'Thee express is late now, sir. Please ask thee officers too board thee train.'

'Oh, keep the damned train here,' I said. 'Give it a drink. Have a drink yourself. Birkhe, give the conductor-sahib a drink.'

'Mr Glover can't drink on duty, sir,' Victoria said. This Glover knew all about that night we'd had in this train. He'd been the conductor that night too. He didn't like me because of it. He was smiling now, but sweating and angry under the white drill, and

355

afraid to show it. Why didn't he show it, damn him? He said, 'Please ask them too board thee train now, sir. It is me who will get into trouble, sir.'

I said sourly, 'That would be terrible,' but Steve and his people climbed back into their compartments. Glover blew his whistle and waved his green flag. Four B.O.R.s dashed out of the refreshment room with three bottles of beer in each hand and scrambled into their carriage. The rest cheered raucously.

The engine whistle shrieked, and the train began to move. Ellington was standing in the open doorway of his compartment, well back, to be out of the rain. His other officers had filled their toothmugs with champagne and were shouting toasts – 'Piccadilly!' 'Roll on!' 'Three cheers for General Twist!' '*Up* General Twist!' We were not behaving at all like Old Wykehamists, probably because none of us were.

Patrick pushed past behind us. I suppose he had a message for Glover, or perhaps he was just going that way and shoving because his name was Patrick Taylor. He wasn't being obstreperous about it, just clumsily determined.

Birkhe was there, squeezed on to the rainy edge of the platform with a lot of empty champagne glasses in his hands. He was smiling at the B.O.R.s as they passed so close to him. A lance-corporal leaned out and tried to grab his hat as a souvenir. I began to smile, but Birkhe jerked his head and slipped – and he could have saved himself, but champagne glasses are beautiful and expensive, and Patrick's big arm jumped out at him, and the back of the carriage came, and Birkhe fell between it and the guard's van. Victoria's glass tinkled on to the stone behind me. I thought I heard it tinkling for five minutes. I heard myself whisper among the tinkling, 'Oh, Birkhe.' If there was a sound from under the wheels the rumble of the train and the cheering and the yelling hid it. Only a few people had seen.

I jerked forward. Some of the B.O.R.s had seen; their faces were frozen; one leaned out, trying to look down under the train. Glover heard my shout. He was standing in the open door of his van; perhaps he had seen Birkhe's legs falling away. His face was dirty white and blown up and full of pop eyes and a shrilling whistle. He disappeared inside his van, and the train jerked to a ferocious stop.

I ran to the back and stopped a minute, looking down on the line. He was cut neatly in half and not quite dead in the rain. I jumped down and took him – the top half of him – in my arms. I took his top-knot and pulled gently and whispered, 'God is taking you up, son. Good-bye, good-bye, good-bye.' And God knows whether the little bugger heard me, because he died.

I got back to Patrick in a jump and a couple of strides, and took his shoulder and pulled him round. He had been looking vacantly down into the space between the platform and the van. His face was silly, wet, floppy. I heard Victoria saying over and over again beside me, 'Rodney, no, no!'

I said, 'You pushed him under.' I was beside myself, boiling, trembling.

His face slowly began to steady into shape. His pale eyes enlarged, and his big hands went down to his sides. He said, 'Yes, I pushed him under.'

Everyone was suddenly quiet, and my trousers were drenched in blood and my shirt in rain.

It was no use going on any more. Everything went flop inside me, and my eyes stung. I muttered, 'Nine, ten, out. Don't be a fool. You were trying to help him. Otherwise he'd be alive.' I turned to Manbir and ordered him to tell me when the burning was going to be. I ordered Henry to go and tell Mr Jones and Glover and the lance corporal that the accident was not their fault.

Sammy came up, and Patrick said to him, 'I pushed Colonel Savage's orderly under the train.'

Sammy said, 'On purpose?' I looked round the circle of sickly eyes. Ellington was there. The champagne flush had turned mottled red and white and ugly on all their faces. Taylor said in answer to Sammy's question, 'On purpose? I don't know.'

Ranjit was there. He said, 'Mr Taylor didn't do it on purpose, Collector. He was trying to save the soldier.'

Patrick turned on him and shouted, 'I don't want your help!'

I said, 'In the name of Jesus — Christ, will you all get away from here. Taylor did not do it on purpose.'

I thought I was alone on the platform for a time. Molly Dickson tried to speak to me, but I shook her off. I turned and went out.

357

A woman was there with me, though, running along beside me, trying to keep up, her short skirt too tight for her, with a look on her face I'd seen once before. Victoria.

She came to my bungalow with me, and we sat down and drank in silence. She was there, but I'd lost her. Later I put on the gramophone. I wouldn't change or wash, but kept all the blood on myself. I thought of finishing the whisky bottle, but I wasn't a civilian to reward a dead son and a lost lover by getting stinking drunk to forget them. I stopped drinking and asked Victoria why she wasn't with Patrick. 'He needs you more than I do,' I said.

She said, 'Not tonight, Rodney. But I love him.'

That was my woman, to give me the knife when I needed it most. I said, 'Lift up your skirt.' I didn't think for a second that she'd do it. But she did. Her thighs were as fat and round as they'd ever been. I started for her.

She said calmly, 'Go and bathe and take off your clothes.'

That resistance, a moment sooner, and I'd have gone out of there and hated her and carried the whole day like an ulcer under my tongue, to my grave. A moment later, and I'd have had her, and hated her as much as I was hating myself. But she was all woman.

I looked down at myself and nodded, and went out to the bathroom. Afterward she came quietly to the bed and lay down – not a mother, not a lover, just a woman – and took me into her arms. I don't think there was anything in the world but that, from her, which could have helped me then. I didn't forget Birkhe. I told her about pulling his top-knot, which Gurkhas keep because they believe that God will pull them up to heaven by it when they die. I talked a lot about Birkhe, and then the war, and the regiment, and Manbir, and my father.

Then she talked, peacefully, endlessly. It was at this time that she told me about the night Roy came for her, and the escape in the goods train. She lay beside me, smoking cigarettes and talking and getting water for us to drink.

I might have felt sad because this was surely the last time. I might have decided that I could always have her as long as I was in Bhowani. It wasn't like that. This was Bhowani Junction.

I might have asked in what way she loved Patrick. It wouldn't have hurt me then, whatever she answered. But I knew. Patrick

358

had drawn her back to him a little more quickly by his bad luck, but the twin roots of the matter were that she was an Anglo-Indian and that she had always loved him – and even those two were really one. She couldn't desert her people, and he was one of them. Even his luck was Anglo-Indian. She had wanted to go, first with Ranjit and then with me. But she physically could not. She had always loved Patrick. They'd grown up for each other. Then the great changes swept across India and the world, and she had searched, not by deliberate plan but because the wind of change blew through her too, for ways of escape from a life that had come to seem small and doomed. Patrick was a part of that life. He had become petty, helpless, and hopeless. She'd tried becoming an Indian – but she wasn't an Indian. She'd tried becoming English – but she wasn't English. An idea of the future, of herself as a dweller in India, had sent her to Ranjit. Sexual passion, the knowledge of herself as a woman, had sent her to me. But this was Bhowani Junction.

She was a big girl. She hadn't come out of all this like a Hollywood film star, with her hair metallically immaculate and her face untouched by thought or pain. We talked about the future of her people. When we English left India they could look beyond the telegraph lines and the railway lines. There would be nothing they could not achieve then, depending only upon themselves. From Bhowani Junction the lines spread out to every Indian horizon for them.

And she had learned that sex is a good thing in its place, and she wasn't going to hurry Patrick or be hurried, but she was quite sure it would be all right. The angry mating she'd forced on me beside the stream – what was behind that? Patrick, of course. He'd taken her once to the place, and not even the animal perfection of the fusion between her and me had been able to wipe him out of her mind, as she had hoped it would. That was the point at which she stopped drifting. Then Mole gave her a push, and Patrick brought her to shore. Patrick and Birkhe.

So there we were, at one o'clock in the morning, arrived at last at Bhowani Junction. All change at Bhowani Junction! Tigers over the footbridge for Number 2 Up Mail, people to Number 3 Platform for the slow train for the Bhanas branch!

BOOK FOUR

Patrick Taylor

male, thirty-six, unmarried;
under notice of dismissal from the service of the
Delhi Deccan Railway

40

AFTER the terrible thing happened I stood for a long time where I was, because I was not able to move. I had tried to help the colonel's Gurkha orderly, and now he was under the train. At least, I could have sworn I meant to help him, but standing there on the platform it was like going mad because I thought, How *can* these things happen so often unless I *do* mean them? There was a book I read once by a German fellow about how everything that we do is caused by our mothers, or if it isn't our mothers it is because we really want to do them. Like when we forget to pay a bill we do not really forget, but are saying to ourselves, I'm damned if I will pay that bill.

So when the colonel pulled me round I had to tell him, yes, I'd pushed the orderly under the train. It would have been wrong to try and get out of trouble. I wanted the colonel to kill me then, because I deserved it and there was nothing I was good for, and the Indians were going to be the bosses in India, and I was sacked.

He looked as if he would kill me. He looked more terrible than anyone I have ever seen, with the blood drenching his trousers and the bottom of his bush shirt, and the rain splashes all over him, and the tears in his eyes. For me, the tears were by far the worst. I didn't understand what happened after that, why he said, 'Nine, ten, out,' why he said I hadn't done it on purpose. But he is a gentleman, and I suppose he didn't want to get me into more trouble than I was in already. I don't remember anything really that happened there on the platform except Kasel trying to butt in.

I know Victoria came to me and took my hand and spoke to me. But the colonel loved her, and she was the only person who could stop him from killing himself or somebody else; and I didn't feel angry any more about losing her, only sad, because I had lost her to a better man and one who could give her a hundred times more than I could, so I told her to go away and look after him. Govindaswami took some notes too, I think, and then I wanted to go home and be alone in my bungalow.

As I turned to go I remembered I had an appointment with Mr Stevenage in the Collector's bungalow at six o'clock, to talk about St Thomas's. It was too much. I said, 'Oh, damn, oh god-damn!' I noticed Kasel was beside me then, and he said, 'Let me take you to your home in a tonga, Mr Taylor.'

I had been making up my mind I couldn't go just then to see Mr Stevenage. He would understand. Govindaswami would surely have the decency to explain to him what had happened at the station. But when Kasel said he would take me home in a tonga I knew I must go to see Mr Stevenage, however badly I felt. So I said to Kasel, 'I'm not going home. I have an appointment with Mr Stevenage. It is about St Thomas's.' I had to explain to Kasel that it was about St Thomas's so that he would not think it was just a party I was going to after the awful thing I'd done, murdering that little Gurkha.

Kasel said, 'I would like to come with you, Mr Taylor.'

I said, 'This is nothing to do with you. It is about St Thomas's. I told you.'

Kasel said, 'Please let me come. I am interested in St Thomas's too. Perhaps I can help you with Mr Stevenage.'

I thought, as clearly as I could at that time. Kasel was out of the railway service and had become the local Congress bigwig. *I* always knew he was a secret Congress wallah. Whether I liked it or not, he would soon be a big man in Bhowani. My God, he might even be the mayor or whatever they would have instead of collectors. I didn't like him, but for the sake of St Thomas's I would have to agree, if he really did mean to help us.

So we went along to the Collector's bungalow. Mr Stevenage was a young man – not forty then, I should think – and I liked him much better than I had liked Mr Wallingford. The first thing they did was give me a very big glass of Scotch whisky. Then we began to talk, Mr Stevenage, me, Govindaswami, and Kasel, and we talked for a long time. It was hard for me to argue with them because I had no official title; I wasn't president or chairman or leader of anything; I only knew how our people felt and how important this was to us about St Thomas's. Mr Stevenage was nice, as he had been while he was listening when I spoke to Mr Wallingford in Bombay, but I do not think he could have done much for us unless Kasel had spoken.

364

I couldn't understand at first what Kasel's game was at all. He didn't say that he thought we Anglo-Indians ought to have a better education than Indians. He could hardly say that, I suppose, as he was an Indian himself. He said that he thought it was education that would be the thing India wanted most in the future, and so he said the principle was wrong to take any school that was going, and teaching properly, and sell it to make a factory or offices out of it. India needed factories, but she needed schools more, he said. He said he couldn't promise what a Congress government in Delhi or in the provinces would do later, but we weren't talking about that. He thought that the school should be left going, so that such a Congress government could be free to make it fit into their plans, perhaps by enlarging it instead of abolishing it. I didn't like that idea much, about Indian boys being able to go to St Thomas's too, but after all it would be better than no one going. If the school was sold, Kasel said, Mr Stevenage and the Trust would be disposing of an Indian asset, which they had no right to do. He had a jolly nerve to say that, but Mr Stevenage only laughed and said, 'That's one way of looking at it.'

Then we talked some more, but it was clear that Mr Stevenage was really thinking about what Kasel had said, and after a time he said, 'I have always been against selling the school once the Anglo-Indian community made it plain that they wanted to keep it. Our duty was only to make sure that the community realized the economic facts. But what I and people who agree with me have lacked is a talking point to persuade the more orthodox members of the Trust board. Ranjit Singh's point – his veiled threat, we might say – is exactly what we need.'

Then Mr Stevenage said he couldn't promise anything but he thought he would be able to persuade the board to cancel their negotiations for the sale when he got back to Bombay. The board was already nearly evenly divided, he said, and this ought to settle the thing.

Then they gave me another whisky, and after some chat Mr Stevenage said to me, 'Would you care to consider transferring out of the Delhi Deccan and working for my firm as manager of our cement-works railway over in Cholaghat?'

It was a temptation, but I had to say, 'I cannot transfer, sir. I have been sacked for inefficiency.' The letter actually said it was for being absent without leave, but really it was for inefficiency. I was never very good, and I was making a lot of little mistakes over being so worried about Victoria.

Mr Stevenage said, 'Oh, I didn't know that. Well, efficiency is something you can't exactly measure, and I've heard differently about you. Would you like the job?'

Of course I knew all about his firm's little railway. It was forty miles long, single line, with a few passing places, running from the cement works at Cholaghat to the Bhanas branch at Sihor, which is ninety-four and a half miles from Bhowani Junction. They had a few little engines, and all the traffic was cement and machinery. It would be quite a come-down after the D.D.R., but I am a railwayman, and there is nothing else that I can do. Being offered this job was so like a miracle, when it happened on that day of all days, that I couldn't believe it. I said to Kasel, 'You haven't been getting this job for me have you?' If he had, I wasn't going to touch it; but he said, 'No, Mr Taylor.'

Then I said to Mr Stevenage, 'Who recommended me for this, sir?' Now that I was suspicious I saw that he must have known I was in trouble with the railway, and had been trying to let me hide it. He glanced at Govindaswami, who nodded at him, and then said, 'It was Colonel Savage. He is not a railwayman, but I have known him a long time and I have a very high regard for his ability in the judgement of character.'

If it was Colonel Savage I would be happy to take it. We had been misunderstanding each other at first because of Victoria, but that is what women always do to men, and now it was over. He had shaken my hand and never said anything about me trying to shoot him that day, and now he was in trouble.

I told Mr Stevenage I would be glad to work for his firm, and we settled some details. I was to go there as soon as my relief had come to Bhowani. Cholaghat is in the middle of big jungles in the northern part of Bandeklkhand, and the shooting is good. It is lonely there, but that would be good, and at any rate I wouldn't see many people to hurt them – or to have them hurt me.

Before I left, Govindaswami asked me if the railway was still keeping a good watch on the line in the district. That was not really my business, but I knew we were, so I told him. I supposed he was worried about three trains full of British troops, which were going through. He said, 'Oh, there are three troops trains tonight, are there? To Bombay, I suppose. When do they go through?' I told him the first one was due to pass Bhowani Junction at 02.30, and the other two at twenty-minute intervals after that. Then I thanked Mr Stevenage and said good night.

When I got outside with Kasel I had to shake hands with him. I didn't like him any more, mind, but he had helped us, and it was no use going on hating him. We would have to get along somehow, especially now that the English people were on their way Home. I said, 'What has made you so different, Kasel?'

He said, 'Partly K. P. Roy. You're not exactly the same yourself, Mr Taylor.' And that was true, but it was losing Victoria that had upset me.

I went to bed early and lay awake, thinking of Victoria and listening to the rain on the roof. I was happy for her that she had fallen in love with such a fine man, but I was sad for myself too, because I would always love her. I would have to go out with other girls sometimes until I got too old to care, I supposed, but I wouldn't love any of them any more than I had loved Rose Mary. Rose Mary was misbehaving with the fat officer Howland, and she was determined to make him marry her so that he would take her Home. She didn't love him at all, so really she was just running away from us. Victoria wasn't running away, because she did love the colonel. Also she wasn't misbehaving with him. Of course I used to think she was, but that was me being jealous. I couldn't help it, although I knew really that Victoria was not that sort of girl and the colonel was too much of a gentleman to do it with her until they were married. I'm positive that Colonel Savage wasn't even on the berth that night at Gondwara when I made a fool of myself and took her pants – I still had them hidden in a drawer – and Victoria had a sheet over her and was dozing. I can see it now. They must have been working.

It was sad to think about her, though, because of what we might have done at Cholaghat. The railway manager there has a big bungalow at the edge of the jungle. We could have had children who might become officers of the Indian Army just like Colonel Savage. Remembering something that Kasel had said at the meeting just now made me realize that that could happen. It was beginning to happen already, after all. One of our people was a captain in the Rajputana Rifles at Gondwara, with several Indians too. But when the English went there wouldn't be any officers except us and Indians.

I lay there dreaming of the railway and the jungle that would be there in Cholaghat for me, and thinking that Victoria would enjoy them too, because the colonel had just taken her out to teach her to shoot, so she knew something about the jungle now; and I saw my children doing anything they wanted to do in the world – air pilots, rich men, prime ministers, they were – when I turned over in bed and groaned, because Victoria would not be in the Cholaghat jungle with me but with the cows and the green fields in England, shooting pheasants in a tweed skirt like the pictures in the shiny English papers. Of course Colonel Savage had not been teaching her to shoot so that *I* could benefit.

The telephone rang, and I looked at my watch and saw it was three minutes past one in the morning. It was the Assistant Stationmaster, who is a fool of a babu, like Bhansi Lall. He asked me if I knew where Kasel was. I did not know, and I was ready to bawl at the A.S.M. for asking me at that time in the morning, when I thought, Damn it, Kasel helped me, perhaps I can help him; so I asked the A.S.M. what was the matter.

He said, 'It is Pipalkhera, sir. A lady has lost her gold bangle, and the Stationmaster is trying to get it back to her, but he cannot locate the lady.'

I asked him what on earth he thought he was talking about.

He said, 'Sir, following is gist of message shortly received from Stationmaster Pipalkhera. A party of three Moslem purdah ladies purchased tickets from there to Chakraj Nawada shortly before departure of Two-Ninety Up Passenger from Pipalkhera station. One man, probably servant, purchased tickets for them. These facts are remembered because printed tickets Pipalkhera–Chakraj Nawada and vice versa are not available, so clerk had to write out those long names many times, also in book. Also tickets were in second-class, denoting that Moslem ladies were not nobodies. The party was furthermore only just in time to catch train, and the manservant was compelled to hurry them up, with good force, into second-class coupé before train started from that station – e.g., Pipalkhera. The servant then departed.'

I said, 'Yes, yes. What has all this to do with Kasel, let alone with me?'

The A.S.M. said, 'You asked for situation, Mr Taylor, and I am giving it. If you are not wishing to know situation I am fully capable of waiting until tomorrow and inquiring further from Mr Ranjit Singh Kasel at that time.'

I said, 'Oh, go on then. But hurry up.' I was beginning to get sleepy.

He went on. 'Just recently, Stationmaster Pipalkhera noticed one gold bangle for lady's foot, broken through, lying neat platform at site where purdah ladies had boarded Two-Ninety Passenger. He is honest man, sir, so he telegraphed at once to warn Chakraj Nawada to meet incoming train, which is due there at midnight, and inform purdah ladies that bangle is in safe custody with Stationmaster Pipalkhera, who may be trusted to keep it in great secrecy until claimed. Reward would be in good order for such service, I think. But Chakraj Nawada has telegraphed that no such ladies were on train. So that is heart of matter.'

I said, 'Well, they got off somewhere to rest and have a meal and go on in a later train. Or they decided to spend the night at Shahpur. They do things like that. The ticket allows them to.'

The A.S.M. said, 'Those possibilities had not eluded me, Mr Taylor. But Stationmaster Pipalkhera in meantime examined bangle and found inscribed on it, as mark of ownership in just such eventuality as this, the name Kasel. We were thinking perhaps Mr Ranjit Singh Kasel might be knowing information that would help us to locate owner of bangle. Most probable owner is Sirdarni-sahiba his mother, but that lady left for foreign trip on Ninety-Eight Up Express. So here is further small element of mystery in affair.'

I thought about it, but I shall be damned if I could see what there was I could do, or even what there was that needed doing by anyone. So I told the A.S.M. to get hold of Ranjit Singh Kasel in the morning. In the meantime, my God, I was not a lost-property office.

I went back to bed and tried to go to sleep, but as soon as I lay down to sleep the sleep ran away and I was thinking of Victoria – as a baby, as a little girl, as a woman, the thousand things we had done together.

Then I got to thinking other thoughts about her, so to stop myself thinking about Victoria I began to think about the bangle. What could be the solution? I have read millions of jolly good detective stories, and this was like the same thing. This story about the bangle would be like a clue, and the detective from Scotland Yard (me) would have to work out where the lady was, because she would be the murdered man's first wife. Of course, the purdah ladies might have got off at any station, and there was no reason why anyone should report it. But suppose they hadn't? Suppose it wasn't the murdered man's first wife, but the master criminal in disguise. Then he'd have to get off between stations. But he couldn't, because it would be terribly risky, except in the Mayni Tunnel.

I nearly fell out of bed as the thought struck me. Suppose the purdah ladies were bolshevist women! The Indian women are the worst; Congress had some really terrible ones – like demons, they looked in their pictures, and their speeches made your blood run cold. Suppose three of them had dynamite hidden under their burqas. Both ends of the Mayni Tunnel were guarded by watchmen, but a bolshie could get in by buying a ticket on an up-train and stepping out when it was going very slowly up the bank in the tunnel in all the smoke and darkness. That was why they had travelled second-class, my God, because the upper-class compartments are nearly always empty except on mails and expresses.

I lay back and lit a cigarette. It was really a silly story. I daren't wake up Colonel Savage with a story like that, not after what I had done to him today of all times. The thought of getting all the Gurkhas up at one o'clock and driving fifty miles and then finding nothing, and the purdah ladies arriving at Chakraj Nawada on the next train, was like being surprised in the lavatory by a lady; it made me blush and shiver. Actually it would not be as bad as that, because the colonel wouldn't send anyone out. He would just tear into me and be sarcastic, and I would deserve it.

I sat up again. The troop trains were going through tonight. I got out of bed and walked up and down. I went twice to the telephone. Each time I walked away again. I cursed and swore and groaned. Then I fairly ran to the telephone, grabbed it up, and shouted at the operator and got Colonel Savage's number. Whatever they did to me, I had my duty to do.

The colonel sounded quite wide awake when he came on the

line. I said, 'This is Taylor here, sir.' Then I stopped. I couldn't go on with this balderdash.

I thought he would be in a terrible temper – as, my God, he could be – but when he spoke again he spoke very nicely and gently. He said, 'What's the matter?' and he called me Patrick.

I began to explain the whole thing to him, but the moment I said that the three women had not reached Chakraj Nawada, he said, 'The Mayni Tunnel. Tell me the rest later. Bring your rifle and get to the Collector's bungalow as fast as you can.' He rang off.

I threw on my clothes and was up at the Collector's very quickly. When I got there I found Ranjit there with Govinda-swami. I suppose Mr Stevenage had gone to bed. Govinda-swami said, 'Miss Jones has given me the outline of the story. Tell us the rest. The troops won't be ready for a few minutes yet. Ranjit came back to dinner here. Here's been here ever since. We had a lot to talk about.'

So I explained about the bangle and everything, and Ranjit first looked sad and then he looked grim, and he said, 'My mother *must* have gone to Bombay. I can't think of anything that would be more important to her than that. But the bangle. It sounds –' He stopped and thought and said, 'But I think she must have given that bangle to K. P. Roy to help him disguise himself for this.'

'It might have been only to help him raise money,' Govinda-swami said – to save Kasel from thinking that his mother was in such a murderous plot, I suppose. But Kasel said, 'I don't think so. The bangle probably got weakened and broken by being on a man's ankle instead of a woman's.'

Then Colonel Savage hurried in with Victoria. He said, 'Five minutes, Collector.' He turned to me and said, 'Why don't we stop all rail traffic until we've searched the line?'

I said, 'We could, sir, but I don't think we are really sure enough, are we? If you stop the trains now, with all the troop specials and the grain specials going down to the famine area, it would really be worse than wrecking a single train.'

Govindaswami thought for a time. He said at last, 'All right. Especially as I think we can be in time. There is nothing due through now before the troop specials?'

I said, 'There is an up goods. Roy won't touch that though, will he?'

Govindaswami went out to telephone. Inside the study I waited a minute or two with the others, and Victoria had a carbine just like the colonel's, and I couldn't hold my tongue any longer, but said respectfully, 'I don't think this is the proper kind of affair which Miss Jones ought to attend, Colonel.'

He looked at her, and then he said, 'Nothing women do is quite proper. But she's coming, to see you catch Roy.' That was rather a cruel thing to say, when he knew I would probably shoot one of his Gurkhas by mistake, but he couldn't help being cruel, and Victoria said, 'Yes, I'm coming, Patrick,' so I shut up.

Then Lieutenant Glass, the officer who had been adjutant of the Gurkhas since Lieutenant Macaulay was murdered, hurried in and said everything was ready. I squeezed into the back seat of the jeep beside Victoria. Colonel Savage sat in front, driving, with a Gurkha I didn't know beside him. He was an older man than Birkhe, and Colonel Savage called him Mandhoj and seemed to be just as pally with him as he had been with Birkhe. It was rather shocking, really, to think how quickly they forget people in the Army. *I* wouldn't have had another orderly for a long time.

The Austin followed us with Govindaswami and Kasel and two armed constables. After that there was a jeep with a wireless set and another with several Gurkhas; then a lot of the Dodge lorries and then another jeep. The rain had stopped for the moment, but the night was dark and gusty, and big pools of water lay in the road and on the Collector's grass.

We started off down the Pike, and the colonel said over his shoulder, 'Victoria, tell him the plan. And try not to do another Absalom this time, Patrick.'

Absalom was a fellow in the Bible who caught his hair in a tree. My hair is quite short, and it couldn't possibly get caught in a tree. Anyway, the branches were twelve or fifteen feet above our heads, so Colonel Savage had no need to warn me about that.

Victoria explained the plan. When we got near the Mayni Tunnel the Gurkhas would split up into four parties. One would go to the north portal, which was nearest us, and block any escape that way. One would do the same at the south portal. A third party would go up the hill, to the outlet of the ventilation shaft, which takes off from a stores chamber about half-way through the tunnel. The fourth party, which we were going with, would sweep the tunnel from south to north. There were other bits in the plan too. Lieutenant Glass was going to Shahpur station, and there were going to be walkie-talkies and other wireless sets and field-telephone lines, and more soldiers in reserve on the road and hiding everywhere in the jungle.

While Victoria was telling me all this the colonel must have been listening, because he said, 'Masterly. If you'd let me iron out those hillocks under your shirt I'm sure you could stay on with us for ever. Nigel wouldn't notice.'

She said, 'I'm not sure that the brigadier wouldn't prefer it, sir.' They both laughed. They were in awfully good temper, but somehow they included me in it, so I didn't feel bad.

The lights of the Austin threw our shadows in front of us and glittered in the water and mud that splashed out from under our wheels. The Deccan Pike runs like in a tunnel itself there, only the top is not stone or earth but the trees, which meet and sometimes twine together. We passed many bullock carts grinding slowly through the darkness. We forded the Cheetah a mile below the Karode railway bridge. The water was up to our axles, but it would soon go down, and the big ferryboats were still hauled up on the bank. The river does not stay deep enough for them until nearly the middle of July.

We had been going fast for a long time when the colonel slowed down and stopped. The convoy came up behind the little Austin and stopped. A lot of officers ran forward. The colonel held a quick conference and said, 'No lights from here on. Any questions?' Everyone knew what to do, and in less than five minutes we were on the move again.

The jeep hummed quietly. I would have said the night was pitch-black, but there must have been some light for Colonel Savage and the Gurkha drivers behind, because we went at a fast running pace. About there we came on a bullock cart going the same way as us, and passed it silently. The driver yelped with fright as we crept up on him out of the darkness and rolled silently by.

Again the jeep stopped. Victoria whispered, 'The party for the north portal is leaving its vehicles here.' I knew all that road very well of course, and the north portal was about half a mile away to the left. I was glad to notice that Victoria's voice trembled. I was not afraid myself at all at that time, except that I should do something wrong.

After a minute we started off again and five minutes later stopped again, for the party that was going to the ventilation shaft. Five minutes after that we stopped once more, and all got out. The Austin and the lorries closed up. The Gurkhas slid down, split into groups, and moved off the road. The jeep at the back of the convoy crawled past us and went on south, a Gurkha in the back throwing out cable from a drum as it went. Two Gurkhas passed close to me on foot, carrying another drum on a stick between them. The sky was a little lighter over us, and I saw the nodding rod aerials of the wireless sets. I expected to see the bayonets shining, but I remembered that this was a war battalion. The men's bayonets were black. They had been sandblasted years ago to give out no reflections. The colonel tapped me on the shoulder, and I got into a rough line with him and a lot of Gurkhas, and we started up the hill to the left of the road.

For a few minutes we hurried through scrub jungle and speargrass; then everyone stopped. Already I was soaked to the waist, and the trees kept dripping on our heads. We were on top of a steep bank, and at the bottom there were four faintly shining curves – two pairs of rails. We were just above the south portal of the Mayni Tunnel, on the down side. On our right there was the tall post of Shahpur Up Distant signal with its red light, and beyond that a dim glow in the clouds, reflected up from Shahpur station.

Everyone sat down on the top of the cutting. We were so wet it made no difference. I heard a rumble, and beside me Victoria looked at the sky, but I knew it was a train in the tunnel – the up goods. All the same it was a disturbing noise, just as if it had been thunder coming closer. Shahpur Up Distant flicked to green, and a second later we heard the clang of the falling signal. The rumbling grew louder. My God, I am a railwayman, but as I held my breath and listened that noise could have been coming from anywhere, and it was like being in another world to be sitting there among a lot of soldiers with a rifle across my knees. I stood up, and my shoes creaked, and a gust of wind blew a shower of raindrops on to me from the trees. The night smelled of the rain and the perspiration on the Gurkhas.

The rumble became very loud. Now it sounded like steel and

had a heavy rhythm, like a big steel drum. The earth shook, and I heard the rails singing. The curved rails began to shine, then the shadows got so strong you could see the shape of each stone of ballast and the edges of every fishplate and sleeper. The wind still blew in gusts, and now, in the headlight, the brown grass on the banks of the cutting seemed to run slowly about as the wind blew over it and the water hissed in it. The engine came out of the tunnel with a big *whoof*. Its searchlight showed up every blade of wet grass and made the lines curve off in front like snakes of light. The fireman opened his firebox door, and I sank down. Now it was a strong violet light shining back on the stone-faced arch of the tunnel portal, on the banks of the cutting, on us. Then it was gone, and thousands of red sparks drifted down on us in the wet wind.

The train passed at last. As soon as the brake van passed with its red light shining, and Shahpur Up Distant changed back to red, and the counterweight clanged down, and the driver up there shut off steam because he had come over Mayni Summit, we slithered down the sides of the cutting.

Some Gurkhas stayed outside the mouth of the tunnel, where we woke up a sleepy and frightened watchman. The rest of us moved in. A brick-lined drainage ditch runs down the centre between the two pairs of rails. We went in in five columns – one along each wall, one between each pair of rails, one along the ditch. No one made a sound except me, and I realized they must all be wearing their P.T. shoes. I took my shoes off as quickly as I could and went on in my socks. Savage was the third man in the middle column, in the ditch, with his new orderly, Mandhoj, just behind him. I was immediately behind Mandhoj, and Victoria behind me. Govindaswami was somewhere on the right with his policemen, and Kasel on the left.

One man at the head of each column had a torch. He kept it pointed down on the rails as he moved, switching it from rail to rail looking for explosive or wires. We went slowly. Behind the men with the lights it was black as the inside of a cow. I could just make out the inset refuges for the gangers, because they were even blacker. There is one of those every thirty yards on each side. Suddenly I got very frightened. This wasn't my job, and I wanted to know what I was doing there with these soldiers. They liked it.

I didn't. I would have gone back out except for Victoria and Colonel Savage being there.

Something fell on to my nose. I clapped my hand to my face and just stopped myself from yelling. Damn it, it was only water. I heard another train coming and looked about from side to side in the darkness. We must all get out of the way quickly. I listened and heard the engine's exhaust as clearly as anything. But, damn it, it was Victoria's breathing. And I am a railwayman.

From being frightened I became depressed because I remembered that all this was happening merely because the Station-master at Pipalkhera had found a gold bangle. The rest was my imagination. I was sure we'd go through the tunnel and find nothing; then I'd have to stand up to Colonel Savage. Anyway, I had a job.

The lights flickered on and on. My feet began to hurt, and I was wet and cold. We came to the chamber for permanent-way stores, which is set into the tunnel on the up side. No one was there. A Gurkha shone his torch up the ventilation shaft and spoke with the soldiers on top of the hill – it was not far up. No one was in the shaft. No one was on top of the hill – except the Gurkhas, of course. We went on.

We were a mile or more in and couldn't have had much more than a quarter of a mile to go to the north portal when the Gurkha on the left, which was the down line, stopped and said, 'Wires!' We all stopped. Three Gurkhas went farther on and lay down to protect us. The man who had found the wires flashed his torch, and Govindaswami, Kasel, Colonel Savage, and I gathered round it. Colonel Savage said, 'Well, I'm damned!' and then he spoke in Gurkhali, and the jemadar's wire-cutters went snip-snip.

Colonel Savage spoke to one of the signallers who'd been laying cable behind us, and the signaller gave him a field telephone. He spoke to Lieutenant Glass in Shahpur station and told him to stop all traffic until further orders. Then Govindaswami said, 'But where has K. P. Roy got to?'

Kasel said, 'There's no reason why any of them should be in the tunnel, is there? The last down train went through at twenty-two hundred – Five-Ninety-Nine Passenger.'

I said, 'No, there have been two down goods since then. If the last one was on time it came through about twenty minutes before we got here.'

Colonel Savage said, 'Then Roy could have got out before we blocked the portals.'

I said, 'Yes. But the troop trains are going to Bombay. Why has he put the charge under the *down* line? He is crazy, if you ask me.'

Of course Roy was not a railwayman, but he ought to know that trains keep to the left. The whole thing began to look crazy, because up trains cannot go fast in the Mayni Tunnel, so even if he'd got the charge on the proper line he wouldn't have done much damage, unless he'd blown the whole tunnel in.

But Govindaswami said, 'I don't think he's crazy,' and Colonel Savage said, 'Oh. I *see*. Who is?' and Govindaswami said, 'Wait and see.'

Then Colonel Savage said, 'We'd better get on. There may be another charge. Same formation as before.'

We started off. This time everyone must have been feeling that Roy and his men were very unlikely to be in the tunnel still, and we moved quite a bit faster. My feet hurt more too, because I was thinking more about them.

I don't know how long it took us, but we found no more charges and we were going along with the torches like fireflies in front when suddenly a light shone down from ahead and I saw the arch of the tunnel mouth, and there were three Gurkhas with revolvers. Someone from outside the tunnel shouted, 'Halt!' One of the Gurkhas shouted, 'Friend!' and at once a blast of machine-gun bullets ripped into the tunnel, and two of the Gurkhas with revolvers fell over, and some torches went out and other torches came on, and Colonel Savage swung round and dropped his carbine. The Bren guns outside hiccuped and roared hysterically, and orange flames streaked out everywhere in the darkness. I pushed Victoria down, jumped up, and shouted, 'Stop, it's us!'

For one second the firing stopped everywhere, and I saw the third Gurkha with the revolver running out into the rain. It was pouring again, and there were lightning and thunder. Savage ran forward, shouting, '*Don't* stop firing. Shoot that man!'

Some of the torches held steady; some waved wildly about, and I saw that Colonel Savage's right hand was bleeding and he hadn't got his carbine. Victoria was lying safe in the ditch behind me. My heart turned over when I thought that I had stopped them from getting Roy. Of course the Gurkhas outside had fired at once because they came from the war, and because the 'Gurkhas' with the revolvers weren't Gurkhas, and they'd said, 'Friend,' instead of giving the countersign.

I ran out after Colonel Savage into the rain. I was beside him in ten seconds. It was pitch-black whenever the lightning stopped. There were Gurkhas beside us, and I heard bushes shaking on the right. Savage shouted, 'First Thirteenth, stand fast! Shoot anything moving.' But the thunder drowned his voice.

In a thin streaky bit of lightning I saw a Gurkha walking across the hill about thirty yards up among the bushes. Savage said, 'There!' and flung up his arm. I shouted, 'He may not have heard your order, sir!' My God, I'd killed one Gurkha that day. But Savage yelled, 'Shoot, damn you!' and I took careful aim at the Gurkha, who wasn't hurrying, and shot him. He stopped, looked round, and waved his arm as though he was rather tired, and then fell face downward into the bushes.

When we got up to him he was dead, and he was K. P. Roy. He was dressed in jungle-green Indian Army uniform except for bare feet. You could buy those clothes anywhere, and a Gurkha hat is easy to hide under a burqa. I wiped the rain off my face – I was trembling like a jelly – and said, 'It was lucky he wasn't one of your men after all, Colonel.'

Colonel Savage said, 'I recognized him. That's how I saw him at the village near Malra, only it was moonlight instead of lightning.' Well, I'd seen what he'd seen, but, as I said, Colonel Savage was a man who *used* darkness, and I suppose he recognized something about the way the light moved as the man walked – but of course the real thing is that Colonel Savage would take any risks because his luck never let him down. He must have been thinking the same thing, because he said to me, 'Your luck's changed, Patrick. Congratulations.'

Govindaswami came out of the tunnel and told us the other two men were dead. Then Colonel Savage said to him, 'Well, Sammy, I think we can say that we've got the man who murdered Macaulay.' He waited quite a time before he added, 'Don't you?'

Victoria began to say something – she'd come up with Kasel – but Kasel said, 'As far as I'm concerned, I think so,' and Govindaswami said, 'In the circumstances, yes.'

378

Then Colonel Savage said, 'Good. Any objections if we resume traffic now?' Govindaswami answered, 'No,' and I agreed.

I was quite dazed and not even realizing how wet I was. Colonel Savage took the field telephone again and spoke to Lieutenant Glass. He said, 'C.O. here. All clear. Tell the Stationmaster, from Taylor, to resume normal working, and pass the message on ... Okay ... At the vehicles. About an hour and a half. We've got to go back through the tunnel.'

Govindaswami said, 'Yes. And I want to see the troop trains through.'

Victoria asked me whether I was all right, and I asked her whether she was. Her clothes were wet through, and her hair was soaked under her cap. Govindaswami was talking to someone on the telephone when I suddenly remembered the colonel's wound and went to ask him about it, but Victoria said, 'Don't bother him, Patrick. He got a bullet through the wrist. It's being bandaged now.'

Then we got into the tunnel, out of the rain, and the first troop train must have been waiting at Mayni, because it passed us almost at once. We got over on to the down line, and the driver was leaning out, looking at us as he went by. He was a fellow from Gondwara, Blair, and he looked surprised when he saw me with the soldiers.

The Gurkhas had cleared the charges away when we got that far, and they walked out to the north portal with boxes of the explosive on their shoulders, and the jemadar had the wires and the electrical gadget which would have set off the explosion. There was enough to blow half the hill down.

We came to the p.w. stores chamber and scrambled up into it. The floor of it is level with the floor of a flat, so that heavy stores can be pushed straight across without being lowered or raised. Savage looked up the ventilation shaft and said, 'The fourth man probably lowered the boxes of explosive down here. We'll find out one day.' Then the second troop train came. It passed so close, going slowly uphill on the up line, that I could have reached out my hand and touched the glass of the windows. The lights were on, but most of the troops were asleep. There were a few playing cards in their underwear and one man with a mouth-organ. It was a little past four o'clock in the morning then, but they were on their way Home, so I suppose they didn't want to sleep.

The last troop train only just got by before Number 1 Down Mail came into the tunnel from the other end. Govindaswami stood up, and we all stood up. I don't know what we were expecting. The searchlight of Number 1 Down Mail leaped into the tunnel, and she was already going fast. The beat of the exhaust was light and quick and getting quicker. The whole tunnel roared as the train wheels clattered faster and faster over the rail joints. The engine raced past on the down line. The driver leaned out and peered at us and waved his hand. He was Charlie Eastman of Bhowani. The carriages came. The first- and second-class compartments were dark, but there is always a light left on in the thirds, and Govindaswami said loudly and sharply, 'Look carefully now!'

The fifth third-class carriage was only half full. Everyone was sprawled all over, asleep in it, except for a little group at one end. We had all seen a thousand pictures of that grizzled, naked little man who was squatting on a bench there, his spectacles on the end of his nose, and his hands folded in his lap. There were three or four men and women round him, waving their arms, and he was talking, I think.

After the train had gone, no one moved or spoke for a long time. Then Colonel Savage said, 'And why is he awake at this hour?'

Govindaswami said, 'Because Lanson ordered him out of the train at Shahpur and wouldn't let him back in until you sent your message.'

Savage said, 'And what was the purpose of your cryptic conversation with Lanson back there?' I didn't know Lanson was in Shahpur station at all, but he must have been.

Govindaswami turned to Kasel and said, 'Lanson was arresting your mother. She got into that compartment with Gandhi at Gondwara – where she got out of Ninety-Eight Up. She had a loaded revolver on her.'

Kasel stood quite still and after a time said, 'The revolver was in case this failed? At the risk of her own life?'

Govindaswami said, 'Yes. To make sure. She does not lack courage, as you ought to know. This is the thing that *was* important enough to put off her trip to Moscow. But she'll set out again soon. We won't charge her with attempted murder, because Gandhi will only get her off if we do. She'll do a few weeks in jail for illegal possession of arms.'

Kasel said, 'When did you know the Mahatma would be on Number One Down?'

Govindaswami said, 'Long enough. His movements are not secret. I believed, and have been trying to make you believe, that K. P. Roy's people *had* to assassinate Gandhi. And as Roy was specializing in train-wrecking, I thought he'd probably attempt it by that method. But Wardha to Delhi is a long way, and the exact place and the particular journey Roy would choose were the problems. Both were solved by Mr Taylor.'

Colonel Savage said, 'Put *him* in for an M.B.E. too. For one thing, he's deserved it. For another, their gongs will rattle together like cymbals at the appropriate moments of joy.' Govindaswami looked quickly from the colonel to Victoria to me, trying to see if we understood what the colonel was talking about, I suppose; but Victoria was red in the face from so much excitement, and Colonel Savage often said the most extraordinary things which no one could understand.

At last we were out on the road. The Gurkhas had brought the bodies of Roy and the other two men there and laid them down beside the lorries. It was actually not raining. It was then about five o'clock.

Colonel Savage got slowly into his jeep and sat hunched in the back seat. Everyone was busy, and he was alone. He didn't look like he used to. His face was white and smooth, and – of course it must have been his wound, but if I hadn't known him so well I would have said he was lonely and miserable.

But it was silly even to think that *I* could help him, so I got to thinking how wonderful it would be if I really got an M.B.E., even for saving Gandhi's life, of all people, whom I would just as soon shoot really – when I saw a car coming very fast up the Pike from the direction of Bhowani and showering mud on everybody as it came. All the lights of the Gurkha lorries were on, and there were soldiers everywhere, smoking and talking and getting ready to go back. In the lights I saw that the car was a Brown Army station wagon. It stopped opposite us, and a tall thin old man poked his head out. He was wearing a pink shirt and he had a soldier driver, so he must have been an officer, I suppose, but he didn't look like one.

Colonel Savage seemed to wake up, shaking his head and putting his face back the way it really was. Then he held his wounded hand behind his back and strolled over to the strange man. He was quite pale, and his nostrils were tight and his eyes big and glittery blue. Victoria was there already.

The man in the car said, 'My dear fellow, what on earth are you all doing out in this terrible weather? You'll catch your deaths. Who *are* those people?' He looked at the corpses with the Gurkha hats over their faces.

Colonel Savage said, 'Oh, we're all playing soldiers, Nigel.'

The man said, 'Yes, yes, of course. I suppose you have to, to keep your wonderful little fellows happy. Do excuse me, Rodney. Paul has run away and sent me a telegram from Gondwara, of *all* places, that he's working in the club there. I'm going to persuade him to come back.'

'Paul's the chef, isn't he?' Colonel Savage said.

The peculiar man in the car said, 'Yes. We had a silly misunderstanding over some *foie gras*. How's Victoria?'

Victoria said, 'I'm very well thank you, Nigel,' and the old man said, 'Good. Keep beautiful, my dear. Nothing I can do for you, Rodney? No? Well, good-bye, good-bye.' Then he pulled his head in, and the car drove on.

Colonel Savage started to laugh – silently at first, but soon he was bellowing. Govindaswami and Ranjit began to laugh with him, and Victoria was absolutely shaking. I didn't really see anything to laugh at, but I couldn't stop myself from laughing with them, so there we all were, shrieking like lunatics, at five o'clock in the morning on the Deccan Pike a couple of miles outside Shahpur.

Victoria finally got herself under control and said, still giggling a little, 'Are you sure you don't want any morphia before we go back, sir?' and Colonel Savage bawled at the top of his voice, 'Will you bloody well leave me alone, woman? Go and do good works elsewhere. Buy a pair of shoes for the manager of the Cholaghat cement-works railway. How many men do you want to look after, anyway?'

She said, 'One,' and scrambled into the jeep beside me, and I began to curse and swear under my breath, because I'd left my shoes in the Mayni Tunnel.

MORE ABOUT PENGUINS

Penguinews, which appears every month, contains details of all the new books issued by Penguins as they are published. From time to time it is supplemented by *Penguins in Print*, which is a complete list of all books published by Penguins which are in print. (There are well over three thousand of these.)

A specimen copy of *Penguinews* will be sent to you free on request, and you can become a subscriber for the price of the postage. For a year's issues (including the complete lists) please send 30p if you live in the United Kingdom, or 60p if you live elsewhere. Just write to Dept EP, Penguin Books Ltd, Harmondsworth, Middlesex, enclosing a cheque or postal order, and your name will be added to the mailing list.

Note: *Penguinews* and *Penguins in Print*
are not available in the U.S.A. or Canada

JOHN MASTERS

'Mr Masters is a specialist who knows how to arrange his material. He has that intuitive sense of history that so many novelists of his type lack and yet, at his best, he can write as colloquially as Mr Joyce Cary' – John Raymond in the *New Statesman*

The following novels by John Masters are available in Penguins:

COROMANDEL

The 17th century beginnings of the Savage family in India.

FANDANGO ROCK

A wild, colourful, often terrifying drama set around an American air-base in Spain.

FAR, FAR THE MOUNTAIN PEAK

The ruthless career of Peter Savage, determined to reach the top 'at all costs'.

THE LOTUS AND THE WIND

The story of one of the most dangerous secret service missions in the history of British India.

NIGHTRUNNERS OF BENGAL

'The best historical novel about the Indian Mutiny that I have ever read' – New Statesman